The Cutting Horse

Born out of necessity long before sophisticated ranches made the job easier, cowboys often worked on the open prairies where there were no fences or cattle yards, and no chutes or crushes. They had to work as a team to cut a beast out from the herd for it to be branded or treated, while the cow naturally wanted to settle back in the safety of numbers.

It became a friendly contest among the ranch hands to see who had the best horse for the job. At the end of each day, only one cowboy earned the bragging rights.

The first official competition took place in Texas in 1889, but it wasn't until the sport became more popular, that a universal set of rules and regulations was implemented and in 1946, the National Cutting Horse Association was founded.

The competition involves a panel of judges, often two or three, a team of four turn back riders, who hold the mob together in the corners, and the rider, who has two and a half minutes to show their horse with a minimum of two cuts out of the herd. Once the cow is drawn away from the herd, the cowboy lowers his hand and rides with a free rein, only using his leg cues to direct the horse. A horse that has good cow sense will mirror image the cow, head to head, and each judge scores the rider based on their performance, with a top score of eighty and a bottom score of sixty, with seventy being a respectable result. A zero score is given when the rider gives up and leaves the pen early.

The quarter horse is bred as a cow horse and is suitable for cutting among other rodeo events. For a cutting horse trainer, it is a full time job. It can be tough work, though it is a lucrative industry that is driven by breeding, training fees, sponsorship and prize money, and supports other equine avenues such as saddleries, feed and supplements, farriers, vets, clothing, and much more.

Cutting horse trainers are no different to other professional athletes. They get paid to do what they love doing. Today, cutting is popular across all states of the U.S.A, Australia and Europe.

The Cutter

A novel by Linda Ellison

© Linda Ellison 2018

Linda Ellison asserts the moral right to be identified as the author of
'The Cutter'

Cover photo by Wild Fillies Photography

Design and typeset by Green Avenue Design

Published by Cilento Publishing, Sydney Australia

ISBN Paperback: 978-0-6483932-3-8

ISBN Australian Paperback: 978-0-6483932-2-1

ISBN Kindle: 978-0-6483932-5-2

This novel is entirely a work of fiction. Any resemblance to actual persons, living or dead, is entirely coincidental.

Instagram: lindaellison.author

For my cowboy x

Chapter One

It was back to business as usual at Double J Ranch.

While standing in the yards, the events of the previous week became merely a fragment of a thought. The rain had cleared and the sun was shining through in intervals, leaving a freshness in the air that was not reflective of his mood. But the work was a good distraction, and as the early morning rays filtered through the puffy white clouds and stirred up dust, the young cowboy kept the black steers moving up the loading chute and onto the back of the truck.

He climbed the fence and stood on the rail, leaning over, watching them make their way single file into the crate. The noise of their hooves on the metal floor drowned out their bellowing. Although it was a cool morning, he pushed his hat up and wiped the sweat from his face then pulled it back down again, leaving a dirty streak.

He didn't care. The last steer was loaded and the cowboy closed the tailgate, giving a sharp whistle to the driver. All clear. In return, the driver waved out the window and pulled away from the loading chute, changing gears up the long narrow driveway. The rumbling sounds of the truck became fainter as it neared the entrance at the top of the road.

The cowboy waved the next truck in as the driver carefully reversed up to the chute. As he signalled to the driver, the truck brakes screeched as they completed the stop. The driver killed the engine, climbed out of the cab, and walked to the back while fastening the strap on his leather glove, ready to unload.

"Hey Cutter. It's been a long time." There was a gentleness in his eyes and he spoke softly to the young cowboy like they were old friends.

"Hey Doug," Cutter replied, offering him no more.

There was an awkward silence between them before Doug felt the need to just come out and say it. "I was sorry to hear about Macca... Your father was one of the great cattle ranchers this side of Dallas. Not to mention he was damn handy on a horse."

"Yes sir, he was," Cutter agreed. "Taught me everything I know," he added, with a sense of pride in his Texan accent. Although he was not wanting to talk about the passing of his father, he was quietly thankful that Doug acknowledged him in that way. "Now, let's unload these girls and see what we got."

Doug had been delivering and picking up cattle from the Jones ranch for as long as Cutter could remember. From his streaky grey hair and creased skin, Cutter guessed that he was of the same age as Macca, though his mustache was full and overgrown, unlike his father who always had a clean face.

The cattle took their time and unloaded without a hitch. The dust hadn't even had time to settle from the last load before it was being stirred up again and they filled the yards, immediately finding the water in the troughs. Cutter's buddy, Johnny, was there to give him a hand and he started to move them out, knowing that Cutter desperately needed the help.

It was a monthly event. A systematic cycle that the ranch had been following for years. The fresh cattle would be used in the cutting pen for training the horses then turned out to get fat, and it worked well for Cutter who had the best training program available to him, while the ranch was well known and profited from producing the best cattle.

"If you don't mind, I'd like to stay for the service?" Doug asked hopefully, when the job was done.

"Macca would've wanted you there," Cutter replied as he was closing the gate. "Now, you gotta excuse me... I'm going in to get ready, before Marnie reminds me for the fifth time this morning."

They gave each other a nod and Cutter walked off towards the house. His stride was shorter than normal and his shoulders were sunken low, as if he'd been carrying the weight of the world. Though the reality was that he was tired and stressed, and was grieving in his own way.

He walked up the front steps of the double story homestead. It was simple and made mostly of timber with stone features, and matched the garage that was built towards the back of the yard. The large widespread porch wrapped around three of its sides, comfortably housing the weathered wicker furniture and an old timber swing that Macca had made many years ago for Cutter's mom. It was quite homely as well as inviting, and as Cutter leaned on the railing and looked out at the view, the smell of Marnie's delicious cooking spilled out onto the porch and filled the air.

He had seen it every day of his life, yet today was the first time in months that he had given the time to take it all in. As he stared at everything between the porch and the horizon, he found himself deeply drowned in his own thoughts.

Looking at the old timber barn, although it was in original condition, it was the first time he noticed that it was in the early stages of needing another paint, despite being as solid as the day it was built, long before he was born. It was where he'd spent every waking moment while he was growing up. Working, feeding and being on hand when a mare was foaling out. In the school holidays, it wasn't unusual for Marnie to have his lunch delivered there each day, and on occasions his supper too. Apart from the house, the barn was like his second home.

Cutter stood there in a daze. It had only been a few days since the passing of his father and he was torn between the relief of an exhausting three years taking care of him coming to an end, and his selfish need to wish him back. His head was unclear about all that had happened this past week and he rubbed the back of his neck, knowing there was nothing he could change and he would change all of it if he could.

He remembered back to the days when Macca showed him how to rope a calf, practicing on a bale of hay in the front yard. His mother would sit on her swing and watch, calling out encouragement every time he missed. A cute little boy with a big smile and a huge heart, with a dream of one day becoming a real cowboy, just like his dad.

These thoughts gave him some comfort, although he still couldn't manage a smile.

Beside the barn was an old timber structure with an iron roof that covered a small area of the sand yard. His thoughts drifted back to when he was fourteen. His dad had sent him to rodeo school in the holidays, for what he thought was a week long lesson on how to improve his skills in the rodeo arena. Roping, tying, wrestling and riding. He would learn more about cattle and horsemanship, fine tuning what he'd already experienced on the ranch. When he arrived home, it became obvious that his week away was just an excuse, as his parents had an enclosed working area built especially for him.

It was nothing flash or extravagant, but it was his. A place he could work and train the horses under in all conditions. It never occurred to him how it was paid for until later that spring when the house needed a few repairs and they just had to make do until the following year.

His life was flashing through his mind. From his most early recollections to the events of last week, and while he had the best in life on that ranch, it also held tragedies that crushed him.

He turned around and went to the front door, giving Cooper a pat on her head while she was lazing in her basket. He gave his boots a quick wipe on the mat and went inside. "I know I'm late, but it wasn't my fault. The trucks were held up," Cutter said to Marnie, in defense, as he went to wash his hands in a small basin to the side of the kitchen.

"I wasn't going to say that. But since you mentioned it..." She glanced over at the clock hanging on the wall. "You've got less than an hour to be there so you'd better get yourself moving."

Like Macca and Doug, Marnie was in her mid to late sixties. Cutter wasn't sure exactly and he'd never ask. Along with his mother, she practically raised Cutter and had lived and worked at the ranch for more than forty years.

She came down from South Dakota as a young woman looking for adventure and was employed by the Jones family as the housekeeper and cook. Her intentions were to stay a short while, earn some money then move on, wanting to work her way around the country one state at a time. What Marnie didn't count on, was the young and handsome ranch hand who swept her off her feet and romanced her into marriage.

During those early years, Double J Ranch went from a struggling one family operation that had been passed down through two generations to a modern and well equipped cattle ranch that flourished from the hard working and dedicated team that Macca and his father had put together. Much of the land was re-fenced and internal fencing was done to create smaller pastures so that cattle could be rotated. Wells were dug and dams were built, trees were planted and the land was cultivated. Over time the cattle numbers expanded with a new breeding system and were turned over more frequently, increasing the productivity and profits.

The house and kitchen ran like a dream with Marnie cooking and baking her way into the empty bellies of the workers, leaving them satisfied after three full meals a day. The more content the ranch hands, the more enriched their work life, and that was noticeable from the time she arrived.

As the years rolled on and the ranch grew, so did Marnie's need to start a family. She wanted a house of her own with a yard full of children, her own vegetable garden, a chicken coup and a milking cow, all to give her the freshest ingredients just outside her kitchen door to raise her family. Her husband had learned so much from tough old Charlie Jones and now he could turn his hand to just about anything on the land. Marnie believed they could make a good go of it together, breeding cattle and producing baked goods to sell to the local stores.

But after years of trying unsuccessfully, Marnie came to her own conclusion that she couldn't have children. The cracks began to show in her marriage and her world fell apart around her. Everything she loved and believed in was now the center of a deep bitterness from both sides. It affected her job in the kitchen which caused unrest between the workers, and eventually the dream of a husband and wife was shattered beyond repair. The divorce was ugly though quick and they both went their separate ways. Her husband was one of the better hands Charlie ever had work on the ranch, but he always said that a good housekeeper was harder to find than a good ranch hand, so Marnie stayed.

Cutter took his hat off so he could wash his face. He used the towel that was hanging within arm's reach, then he looked closely into the mirror that was above the basin. He was only twenty-eight, yet he could just start to see the fine lines around his eyes from spending days on end riding in the sun. Although he wore a hat everywhere he went, the elements were beginning to make their mark on his face and he studied those lines.

He'd never looked at himself like that before. Maybe it was because he hadn't taken the time lately to notice. Except that it wasn't the lines that fazed him the most. It was the sudden realization that he had the sole responsibility of the ranch now, with some fairly big-sized boots to fill. Whatever the reason, he stared into that mirror for a long time and the clean cut, blue eyed, fair haired cowboy stared right back at him.

"You ready to go?" Marnie asked, breaking his glare. She had walked back into the room dressed ready to go to the service, not noticing Cutter staring at himself. It startled him, since he didn't know how long he'd been looking at his reflection, and he decided that he was as ready to go as he was ever going to be.

He looked at Marnie. He'd only ever seen her dressed like that once before. Her black dress and small heels matched her bag. Her hair was let out, falling softly on her shoulders and with the little bit of makeup, it made her look ten years younger.

Cutter had no intention of getting changed or doing his hair. Instead, he put his hat back on and spun around. "I'll meet you there," he said, then he opened the side kitchen door and left.

The house was nestled among well established gardens and trees, strategically built there for protection as well as its broader view of the ranch. Water trickled down the shallow stream that ran behind the house, creating the sounds of a private haven only noticed by Cutter on a quiet night when he lay in bed. The stream was his mom's favorite place on the entire ranch. At least once a week, she would pack a picnic lunch and the three of them would go to the stream for family time. Spending time with her two favorite boys was important to her, and while they were sometimes too busy to care, Mary-Ann would insist on it. Later on, it became a treasured memory for Cutter as the years went by.

As he walked towards the barn, he looked down at his boots, with his hands hidden deep inside his pockets, not noticing the grass was overgrown and untidy with some parts of the fence strangled. There were fallen tree limbs stacked into piles that somehow missed the burn off during the winter, and the tractor sat alongside the fence where it had broken down only a month ago.

While the ranch held a natural beauty, general maintenance and upkeep had been neglected of late.

There were no cattle left in the yards and Johnny was nowhere to be seen. The only thing to take the quietness away, was the thoughts in Cutter's head and he knew that he had to get riding soon, if he was going to make his dad's funeral on time.

He walked into the barn and opened the gate of the filly he had in training and began to saddle her up. It was the way he liked to train his horses. Break them, train them, work them and ride them. Let them be horses and not just show ponies.

She was almost black with a narrow white blaze and two white feet. Her athletic build and early potential were promising characteristics from her sire, which Cutter had already trained. While he crouched down and was wrapping her legs for precaution, it made him think about the colt.

He was every trainer's dream horse. A one in a million champion. He would out perform and out score even the greatest of other horses every time, and for Cutter, the colt was his greatest achievement. From a foal in the barn to the breaking yard, Cutter knew there was something special about him. Although it wasn't until he put him in front of a cow that he realized just how special he was going to be.

But he would not dwell on the colt right now, and he finished wrapping the filly's legs and made some final adjustments to the saddle. He looked around the barn. It was empty. It didn't feel lonely to Cutter, since he'd spent hours there on his own while growing up, cleaning tack, mucking stalls and feeding horses. It was the one space he felt most comfortable, and he gave one last look around before he took a deep breath and put his boot into the stirrup, hoisting himself up.

Riding out of the barn past the yards of young horses that would soon need to be broken in, Cutter looked at Macca's horse standing in her yard. She was old now and her cutting years were long behind her. But she, like everything else on that ranch, was the connection to his father that he would need to keep going. He checked the time. It was time to get riding. He would ride to the far back corner of the ranch towards the resting place. He could have easily taken the truck and driven there by road, but he needed to be back in the saddle and the long ride was a good way to clear his head. The last time he visited the resting place was on his mother's birthday. He didn't like to visit there often and today was no exception.

As he rode out through the gate and up the first rolling hill, the barn began to look smaller. On the peak, he pulled the horse to a standstill and turned to look back at the house. Smoke was barely coming out of the chimney, the mist had now disappeared and the sun was striking the side of the barn. He scanned the landscape and soaked up the view. He loved this place. To Cutter, it was the only home he knew and it was everything to him.

Riding down the other side and through more open pastures, Cutter broke into a canter, feeling relaxed and free to be riding again. The land was in good shape and the cattle were picking up on the spring feed. Every fence line and tree, every dam and trough, was so familiar to him. There was not a place on the ranch that he did not cover by horse every day, as he always made it his business to know the daily progress of each herd.

He took the time to oversee everything briefly, keeping one eye on the time while the other was at work, until he reached another open yard where the wild flowers grew. Cutter pulled up and landed on the grass, holding the reins loosely and let the filly have a pick. He leaned down and pulled together a bunch of flowers. They didn't look like much, but it was the same flowers he'd always pick for his mom every birthday and Mothers' day since he could remember.

As he walked through the flowers, they reached his knees. It took him back to when he was a little boy. Macca would let him ride double, holding the horn on the saddle tightly with one hand and a bunch of colorful flowers in the other. As he grew older and could ride his own pony, they still went to the field of flowers together and as the years passed by, he'd ride there on his own. Even when he was a young man, his mother loved nothing more from her son than the beautiful hand-picked flowers. He adored her, and he was her world.

He followed the winding trail through the tree studded pasture where it opened up to a clearing near the roadside. Cars and work trucks had parked under the big old oak tree and a crowd had already gathered. All eyes were on Cutter and the silence was deafening to him. He rode over and tied the filly up to the fence and walked through the squeaky wrought iron gate into the yard of the resting place, where the Pastor was waiting on him to begin.

There were several graves within the yard, most of them with the name Jones. He walked past the weatherbeaten grave of old Charlie and before he could look at the freshly dug hole where Macca was going to rest, he stopped at his mother's headstone and crouched down, careful not to sit on his spurs. He read it, like he would do every time he visited. Mary-Ann Jones. Aged 46 years.

After all these years, he still found it hard to believe.

Cutter could feel the eyes staring into his back and he lay the flowers below his mother's headstone, then took the front seat next to Marnie. The Pastor was well known to Macca and the family, as well as the many locals who had gathered to pay their respects. He welcomed everyone and proceeded with the story of Macca's life. As for Cutter, he was miles away.

The Pastor's voice was drowned out by the stories in his own head, causing him to smile at probably the most inappropriate times.

He couldn't think of one particular time that he cherished more than any other, deciding that every day with his dad was a life shaping experience. In fact, if there was one comfort he held onto, it was the way his dad loved his mom. He put her first in every sense of the word and Cutter loved him for that.

"Bobby McKenzie Jones. Or Macca to his family and friends, is now going to rest with Mary-Ann. The love of his life. Only time separated them, and time has now closed and brought them back together again." The final words from the Pastor left Cutter's thoughts at peace and the resting place fell silent again.

It was over and done, and before he knew it, people began to leave. He looked at Marnie. She was dabbing her eyes dry and she stood up, still clutching her bag. Men in suits and ladies in dresses came up to him, giving their condolences and support, while Cutter in his jeans and boots hadn't even changed his shirt from the morning roundup. He shook the hand of the Pastor and thanked him, leaving Marnie to do the small talk as he couldn't wait to leave.

As he untied the filly, Johnny and Emma walked towards him. "Hey Cutter?" Johnny called out to get his attention. Ignoring him, Cutter got back in the saddle and rode away while Johnny stood there and watched, feeling helpless.

"He'll be alright," Emma said, and she slipped her hand into his. Although Johnny wasn't quite sure. He was there for Cutter when he lost his mom and he knew what the road ahead was going to be like.

Cutter was now on no time limit and he rode deeper into the heart of the ranch, looking for a distraction and wanting to be on his own. Checking fence lines and looking at the progress of the heifers, he wasted time unintentionally while his thoughts went back to his mom and Macca, this ranch that he loved and the horses he lived to train.

He also couldn't help but think of the financial stress that he had now inherited. The ranch had always provided well, with some years better than others, although it hadn't been an easy time since Macca's diagnosis as they struggled on with one hand down. From here on in, Cutter had to pick up the pieces and take all the responsibilities on by himself. Just the very thought of it was beginning to weigh him down.

As he rode on, he could feel the day warming up. Spring was in the air and he lost track of time while he enjoyed being back in the saddle. Covering every square inch of the ranch thoroughly, he was already making plans, starting with the filly returning to her training schedule and selecting the cattle that he would use up first.

On the return to the homestead, Cutter saw the barn in the distance. It was a sight that he would see at least once every day when he'd ride home. The heifers that arrived on the morning truck were now grazing in the corner of the closest pasture and Cutter saw this as an opportunity not to be missed. The filly was in her first year of training and had her first show in a few months' time. Cutter had always felt that she was ahead of schedule, until Macca needed him by his bedside constantly. Now, he was curious to see what she could do.

He switched from ranch to show mode and calmly made his way through the herd, gently moving them aside one at a time. He hadn't cut a cow in months, and it was from today that his training program would begin again.

The smell and the sounds of the cattle gave him a refreshing sense of normality. He was back and was eyeing each heifer, looking for a soft target. The filly was eager and her ears began to twitch, as he pressured one unwillingly away from the mob. He would ride by the rules of competition and he put the reins down, as he tightened his grip and got himself in position, ready for the heifer to make a run.

In a panic, the heifer ran tirelessly from left to right, fretting to get back to the herd while the filly kept her head low and blocked every move. Cutter let the filly show her ability. She had some big stops and executed every turn perfectly, tormenting the heifer and wearing it down. She was electric and had textbook moves that could never be taught easily, but came naturally from good bloodlines.

The cattle behind him were bellowing and keeping close together in the corner, while the heifer was desperately trying to get past. Only using his spurs to keep the filly in position when needed, she was in control of the heifer and was all over it.

His heart was racing as the rush he felt was something he'd not experienced for quite some time. He pulled the reins up, bringing her to a sudden stop. Although it was quick, it was also correct and it felt good. It put a smile on his face knowing the filly had what it takes. "We still got it," he said, impressed, as he rubbed her neck like he always did when a horse performed well, and he cantered back to the house with his spirits and shoulders lifted slightly.

When he tied the filly up at the front of the house and walked up the steps, Marnie opened the door to greet him. "Your last guests left fifteen minutes ago," she announced, trying to sound annoyed, though coming across mostly with compassion.

"Don't take this the wrong way, Marnie, but I really didn't wanna see anyone," he said, and he walked past her through the front door and into the office on the left side of the entry. His boots made a heavy thump sound while his spurs jingled as he walked. He slumped down in the big old leather chair behind the office desk and flicked the lamp on.

He sat there for a moment, wondering what to do first. He picked up a photo of his mom that Macca had framed on his desk. Her beauty was natural and you could see where Cutter got his looks from. Her hair was long and sandy blonde and her features were fine. Her smile was soothing for Cutter and it made him feel at ease.

"I've made you a cup of coffee and your favorite sandwich," Marnie said, as she walked through the office door holding a wooden tray.

"Mmm, beef," Cutter said warmly, as if he just realized that he was hungry from all that riding.

"Beef... Since when was that your favorite?" Marnie asked, and Cutter looked at her like she had lost her mind.

"It's been my favorite since before I can remember," he reminded her, then smiled at her when she put the tray in front of him with his 'Real Cowboys Sleep With Their Boots On' cup of coffee, and his favorite sandwich, with a slice of tomato.

She loved to play with him when the timing was right, and when it wasn't, she would be there to listen and give opinions only when he needed them. She cared deeply for him. Cutter never understood that to Marnie, he was the son she never had and to see him hurt, was hurting her more.

"You know that girl from Australia keeps calling the house, asking why you haven't been returning her calls," she said in a half suggestive way.

"What did you tell her?"

"That you would return her call today."

Cutter felt that Marnie's reply was more of an order than a request, without pushing the boundaries. "I'll think about it," he said, brushing it aside and not giving it too much more thought.

Marnie could see the stress in his face and she pulled up a chair, which was unusual for her to do, as the office was always a work space for Macca. She only dropped in tea or coffee and the occasional message then would leave. Cutter could feel a big talk coming on.

"Look, Marnie, I appreciate the concern here, but I really have to figure this out on my own," he said sternly.

She would be soft with him. "Let me give you something else to think about," she replied in her caring way, and Cutter let her continue. "Macca loved this place more than life itself. It was his first love, until he met your mom. He adored her and it made him realize that the ranch was only a means to making a comfortable life for you both. He'd have traded this place in a heartbeat to have your mom back."

"And I would too. But that's not gonna happen, is it? So now I need to make it work, or I'll be the one who loses it." His anger was not fierce and was directed more at himself than at Marnie. "If only I didn't sell the colt."

"You know you made the right decision," she said in support, trying to put a positive spin on it. "You know you had no other choice, especially when the bills kept coming in."

"I didn't sell him to pay the running costs here," he defended with a choked up voice. "I sold him to buy Macca some extra time."

"He never knew, did he?"

"No. I didn't tell him and he never asked. In the end he was too sick to go to the barn so he never realized he was gone."

Marnie pointed out the obvious. "That horse was a champion because you made him into one. You can do the same again. You've got some well bred foals down there," she said, referring to the barn and yards.

"I have," he agreed. "And the filly's coming along. But the colt was in a class of his own... I just hope that girl knows what she's doing with him."

"So return her call. Take up her offer and go find out for yourself," Marnie encouraged.

"I can't go to Australia for a month. I've got a horse in training, cattle work and a ranch to run."

"Cutter... She's paying for you to go. She's paying all your expenses and for your time. The ranch will be here when you get back. Johnny will help watch over things, and Lord only knows you need a vacation."

The vacation part was true. Cutter had taken care of Macca for three years while he was sick and the only time he'd left the ranch in the last twelve months was to go into town for supplies, or for his father's regular appointments at the hospital.

Marnie stood up as if to tell him the conversation had just come to an end. He started on his coffee. He was thankful that Marnie was there for him in more ways than one.

"So call her," she added before she turned around and walked out, pulling the door closed behind her.

Still feeling a tightness in his chest from his visit to the resting place, he spun around on his chair to look at the office wall. It was full of framed photos of the family, from years gone by to the most recent. As he sipped his coffee he stared at each photo, remembering the times they were taken.

They were reminders of his life. A little boy sitting on a pony with his mom on one side and his dad on the other, holding him close so he didn't fall. It must have been his fourth birthday he guessed. He glanced at the events he had won or placed at. Ribbons were tied around the horses' necks and he had a smile that was brighter than the sun. His childhood was great.

As they became more recent, it was noticeable how old he was when his mom was no longer in the photos and his smile had mellowed. Until the last photo on the wall, taken when he won the Futurity on the colt, held his attention. Macca stood with him on the arena floor at the presentation and his smile was back. Although it would be short lived, as Macca would soon learn of his illness and his battle would begin. It was the last photo taken of the man he held high as his role model and mentor. His father.

He spun the chair back around and stared at the phone on the desk, knowing that out of politeness he should return the call, despite having no intention of taking up the offer.

It's four a.m. in Australia, and in a dark room only lit by the remains of the fireplace, Raylee is sound asleep. Her phone is on the bedside table and lights up when Cutter calls. The ringtone wakes her instantly and she is annoyed. Then, sitting up on her elbow, she quickly reaches out blurry eyed to see who is calling her at this ridiculous time of night.

Her eyes take time to adjust, then she focuses on the name. The phone now has her full attention and she is wide awake, excited to answer it. She clears her throat and controls her enthusiasm. "Hello," she said, as if she has no idea who's calling.

"Hey. This is Cutter Jones," he introduces himself briefly, totally unaware of the time difference. "I'm just returning your call." He has no more to say and is handing over the control of the conversation.

"Cutter. Thank you for getting back to me. I'm sorry for all the phone calls but I needed to know if you had considered my offer?" She sounded very professional, even in the early hours of the morning.

"Yes ma'am, I have. And I appreciate your offer, but unfortunately I can't make it," he said, again leaving the phone chase up to Raylee.

She would not give up so easily. "I understand you're probably busy with your training, but I noticed that you haven't been competing for a while, so I thought you might have the time to come over and take a look at the colt?"

That was the bait. The colt was his weakness. He loved that horse more than any other he'd ever raised or trained, and was torn between the want to ride him again and knowing that he'd have to say goodbye to him for a second time. Although deep down, there was a burning of curiosity.

"How's he been going?" As the words spilled from his mouth, he immediately wished he could take back the question as he knew it was going to open up all his concerns.

"Well, he seemed to cope really well with the travel and he started off brilliantly. He won at every show he went to and had everyone talking about him. Then after a while and a few practice runs at home, he started to lose interest and became quite agitated."

Cutter could tell by Raylee's explanation that she was highly impressed with the colt, yet she was also concerned for him.

She continued on. "As the weeks went on, it got worse. To the point that he would just switch off and we don't know why... We've got some really good trainers here that I could send him to, but since he was your horse and you trained him, I'd like to think that you'd take a look at him first."

There it was. She pulled on the heartstrings. Cutter didn't want any other trainer looking at him or riding him. No one knew the colt the way he did and while he had no intention of going to Australia for any length of time, by the end of the phone call, she had him turned around.

"I'll be paying for your entire trip. Your ticket. Your time. We have a place you can stay here on the property and we have the best cook." Raylee seemed to be finalizing her selling points.

Cutter highly doubted the part about having the best cook, because no one could be better than Marnie in the kitchen. That wasn't the reason he'd be going. It wasn't what Raylee was saying, it was how she was saying it. She was concerned for the colt and was going to do everything she could for him.

At the end of the call after Cutter agreed to everything and they went through the arrangements, he hung up the phone and stared at it. "I can't believe she got me to agree to that," he said to himself out loud.

"So you're going then?" Marnie was standing in the doorway grinning at him. "I only came in to collect the dishes."

"Probably a decision I'll live to regret," he stated, with almost certainty.

"Now, when you get on that plane, you make sure you leave all those negative thoughts behind," she said with encouragement, as she picked up the tray.

"What, and have a good time?"

"Lord knows you deserve it." She turned around and walked to the door. "Now, do you want to go and pack, or help me with the dishes?" she asked playfully, balancing the tray while looking back over her shoulder.

"Where's my bag?" he asked, giving her one of those rare playful moments back and making her laugh before she left the room.

He looked back at the wall of photos and couldn't believe what had just happened. His focus had now shifted. His mind suddenly changed course and he sensed a lightness that he hadn't felt in months. A girl on the other side of the world who he'd never met, had just talked him into leaving the ranch for a whole month. Though he was looking forward to seeing the colt again, it did trouble him to understand what the issue was. He knew he couldn't figure it out from there and he went upstairs to pack.

Chapter Two

The last time Cutter had been to Dallas was with Macca to visit the specialist at the hospital. It didn't hold any good memories for him as they were sent home with a countdown of only three months. The treatment they had invested in had extended the time but when it eventually ran out, the clock seemed to tick faster. It all went downhill fast from then. Now he was back. This time he was on his way to the airport.

Dallas Fort Worth International Airport was as close to the city as he wanted to get. Trucks and taxis, buses and hire cars were all going at the one speed - fast. The sound of traffic, of car horns, brakes skidding and trucks changing gears was overwhelmingly loud and it totally annoyed him.

The old Ford truck stood out among the traffic. It was at least a decade older than anything else they had seen on the road, with dried mud splashed up the sides and dust covering the windscreen, except for where the wipers left a clear view. Cutter let Johnny do the driving so that he could be let out in the drop zone, as neither of them wanted to be there any longer than necessary.

They were life long friends and the same age, growing up on neighboring ranches. When Johnny's family moved in next door, the two boys started school together the following year and were inseparable. They shared their love of horses and of ranching, and while Johnny settled down and married his high school sweetheart, Cutter went cutting and had no time or need for a life of such restrictions.

They pulled in behind a lineup of other cars whose drivers were dropping, hugging and leaving. Cutter got out of the truck and went to the far back where he grabbed his bag, and he dropped it on the ground in front of him, leaning back in through the open window.

"Hey, have a good trip. And don't worry 'bout the ranch, I'll keep an eye on things while you're gone," Johnny said again to put his mind at ease.

"Thanks for dropping me off, bro," Cutter replied. "And don't forget the filly needs to be ridden at least three or four times a week. And you can put her out in the day yard each morning next to the barn... And she likes to..."

"Cutter," Johnny interrupted mid sentence. "Don't worry. It's all in good hands."

"Yeah, well everything had better be there when I get back," he said, making Johnny laugh even though he knew he was quite serious. There was not another person that Cutter would trust with the ranch and his horses, and he knew that Johnny would take just as much care as he would himself. As he stood up, he tapped the door where he had been leaning instead of saying goodbye.

"And don't come back with one of those Aussie sheilas!" Johnny shouted out as he pulled away from the curb. By the time Cutter had thrown his bag over his shoulder and turned around, the old truck was away, leaving him wondering what on earth a sheila was.

The check-in was easy enough, although the screening process took a bit of time. He was asked to remove his boots and hat so they could go through the x-ray scanner. Then he walked through the metal detection, setting the alarm bells ringing. The officer took one look at the big belt buckle he was wearing and she asked him to remove it.

She held the buckle in her hand, looking at the engraving of a cowboy riding a horse and she read the inscription. "Futurity Champion... You a real cowboy?" she asked. "Don't look much like one." She placed his buckle and belt alongside his hat and sent them through.

"Well they made me leave my horse out front," he said, trying to get a rise from her.

He walked back through the metal detection without raising any more alarms as she made her way to the other end of the x-ray machine. Being rather large and quite short, she waddled when she walked, yet she was cheerful. When Cutter met her on the other side, she picked up his buckle and gave it back to him.

"Too damn cute to be a cowboy if you ask me," she stated, and he just smiled at her from the compliment. "I take it these are your boots as well?"

"Sure are."

She leaned in close to him as if to give him a personal message and he leaned in to hear. "Next time, leave the cow shit back at the farm." They both looked at the other officer sweeping up the mess left from his boots on the x-ray belt.

"Yes ma'am. Sorry," he apologized, and he put his hat back on and finished re-dressing.

He didn't have to wait long for the announcement to come over the loud speaker, calling all passengers to Sydney, Australia. It was at that moment that he thought twice about boarding the plane. It was his need to see the colt again and the want to ride him that made him hand the ticket over and he didn't look back.

The plane was full and he settled into his seat by the window, sitting next to a couple who seemed too involved with each other to even notice they had a neighbor. That suited Cutter just fine. With the last three years catching up with him and a week he'd rather forget, it was his exhaustion that enabled him to sleep all the way to Sydney.

When Cutter arrived in Sydney, the immigration officer gave him an Aussie g'day welcome. They made small talk, mostly about the way he was dressed and where he was from, although it was his name that took some extra explaining. After a few routine questions, his passport was stamped and he was heading to the baggage claim area.

Once out in the arrivals where people were standing around anxiously waiting for their family and friends, Cutter sensed that feeling of being alone in a crowd.

He wasn't looking for a familiar face, he was looking for a driver that had been sent to pick him up. Only, he couldn't see his name on any of the signs that were being held up by the dozens of drivers that all looked the same.

He could hear people talking about him. Attention was drawn to him by what he was wearing and he was sure that these Sydney people had never seen a real cowboy before. As he stood there looking around, the interest in him was growing and he was beginning to feel self conscious, until a man in a suit approached him.

"You must be Mr Jones?" he questioned, although the man seemed sure he already knew the answer.

"Yes sir. But you can call me Cutter."

"Sure, Mr Jones. Welcome to Sydney. Miss Tremayne said that I would pick you out of a crowd," he said, and they walked together to the waiting car outside.

It was a crisp morning in Sydney, though not too cold. Cutter stepped out of the terminal taking in the first breath of fresh air since he left Dallas almost twenty hours ago. The sun was shining and the sky was clear, and he filled his lungs with a freshness that was unlike most other cities he'd ever been to. He always thought he could land anywhere in the world and be able to tell what season he was in. Autumn, was undoubtably his favorite.

The driver opened the trunk of the car and Cutter slung his bag off his shoulder into the back. "I got it," he said to the driver, as they both went to close it at the same time. They walked to the front of the car and got in. "You don't mind if I sit in front, do you?" he asked, prompting him to tell Cutter his name.

"It's Chris. And no, I don't mind," he answered. "Miss Tremayne always sits in the back when I pick her up. Spends the entire trip on her phone or works on her computer."

"I'll bet she does," Cutter mumbled under his breath, looking out the window.

Once they left the congestion of the city behind and drove out onto the highway, Cutter felt more at ease. He didn't like big cities as they are always over crowded. Tall buildings and traffic, cars fighting to change lanes or get a car park, and people bumping into you as you walk on the sidewalk. There seemed to be no common sense or courtesy and everyone is always in a hurry. Every city was the same to him and the least amount of time spent there, the better.

They drove for another hour, talking about nothing in particular but making the time pass more quickly. It was not much further up the highway that they turned off onto some winding country roads. Cutter looked out the window at the houses, taking in the way the countryside looked. The further they drove, the more open and spacious the landscape became and the more relaxed he was feeling.

"Welcome to The Hunter Valley," Chris announced, at the same time as they passed a sign which read the same. "You've just entered wine country."

"We nearly there?" Cutter asked, followed by a big yawn.

"Not too much further," Chris replied, noticing that his passenger looked tired. "You probably looking forward to a shower and breakfast?"

"Yes sir, you bet... After I meet the boss..." Cutter said, then added as he took a long look out the window. "...and see what she's done with my horse."

Cutter did admit that the vineyards and mountain ranges were quite spectacular. The sky was a perfect blue and he could tell that it was going to be a rather warm day, especially for autumn.

Chris began to slow down and put his indicator on as they drove past the black post and rail fence. There were horses grazing near the roadside, and further on near the entrance the smaller stallion yards, which Cutter looked at to see if the colt was there. He wasn't.

They turned into a driveway with a heavy stone entrance and high black gates that were closed. Chris put the window down then punched a code into the security pad and the gates slowly opened up. Driving steadily down the long tree lined driveway, there was a combination of vines and smaller horse yards on either side. It was a picture.

When the car pulled up in the parking area outside the stable complex, the two men got out. Cutter took a weary stretch, then looked around. There were cars and work trucks with Tremayne Family Wines splashed all over the sides, and horse floats with the Tremayne Cutting Horses emblem plastered from front to back. Everything was new and was in perfect order.

The inside of the stables was also a show piece. He looked into the oversized tack and feed rooms that were bursting with everything a cowboy would ever need in a lifetime. On the opposite side was the wash bay next to a padded crush and vet area. It was immaculately clean and organized, and Cutter knew that this operation took someone a lot of time and cost someone else a lot of money.

He walked through another door into a six box stallion alley, finding it empty. He looked around, anxious to find the colt and the girl who had convinced him to leave the ranch behind for an entire month. At the end of the breezeway was a short undercover walk to the working arena, and as he neared the end, one of the workers came through leading a horse back to its stall.

"Hey. I'm looking for Raylee Tremayne," Cutter said.

"Hey. You're Cutter Jones? Everyone's been expecting you." He nodded towards the arena where there seemed to be a hive of activity going on. "Straight through there."

As he neared, Cutter could hear the cattle in the arena, men's voices giving instructions and background music playing through the overhead speakers. He launched himself up onto the middle rail and was in awe. It was all impressive for a backyard, middle of nowhere, small country town operation. He'd been to some local events back home that weren't as impressive as this.

His eyes went straight to the rider and horse in the middle of the pen, and there he was... the colt.

He watched intently while his heart pumped fiercely in his chest. A young girl was riding his colt and he knew immediately that it was Raylee Tremayne. He'd never seen her before, only talked on the phone, and he was quite confident that the voice he'd only heard matched the look of this girl.

She led a few cows out from the mob and was having trouble separating them. The turn back riders were shouting out instructions, some of which she followed and others she chose to ignore. One by one she eliminated the cows and they made their run back to the mob. She was left with two, neither wanting to split. The turn back riders moved in and Raylee selected her cow. Her impatience spooked them both and they ran in opposite directions, leaving her with no option but to switch cows.

It was a complete mess and Cutter shook his head in disbelief. This amazing animal had so much talent he should have been able to cut the cow without a rider and instead, she made him look like an amateur.

The rest of the ride was just as bad and the end result was the colt switching off. It was right then that Cutter knew he'd made a big mistake. He just couldn't figure out which was worse. Having to sell the colt, or letting some rich girl with no professional experience buy him. Either way, he had to do the horse some justice and that was why he was there.

Raylee caught her first sight of Cutter leaning on the fence and she called for a break to the other riders. Riding over to where he was, she pulled up at the gate.

Her big smile became even bigger when she landed in the sand and walked closer to him. He opened the gate and she led the horse through.

Raylee Tremayne was all cowgirl. Her long blonde hair was half hidden under her black hat with her natural highlights complementing her skin perfectly. But there was something about her soft green eyes that drew him in immediately.

"Cutter... Thank you so much for coming. I'm Raylee," she said with a friendly smile, as she held out her hand very professionally.

"Nice to meet you," he replied, and he shook her hand. "And thanks for the invite."

Her handshake was unexpectedly firm and it surprised him. He took a moment to run his eye over her noticing that while she was dressed like a cowgirl, she was squeaky clean and highly polished. Her boots were new, her jeans were fresh and there was barely an ounce of dust on her jet black hat. Even her hair and makeup was perfect. It was as if she'd just stepped out of the dressing room, not out of the stables.

"Did you have a good trip?" Raylee asked.

"Yes ma'am, but it's a long way," Cutter stated, and he took the reins from her and ran his hand between the colt's eyes. The colt immediately began to respond, making noises and nodding his head as he started to move like he was anxious.

Raylee stepped back quickly. "What's he doing?" she asked in a worried voice.

"It's okay. He remembers me and he's just letting me know." Cutter rubbed him under his neck as he stood close by and the colt settled while he continued to talk and rub him all over.

"Wow, he really connects with you," Raylee said as if she were impressed, not jealous.

"I raised him from a foal and was with him every day," he explained. "This horse was my life for six years." He didn't take his eyes off the colt, not even to look at her.

"Well then, it sounds like you're the best one to figure out what's wrong with him." She took the reins from Cutter and walked the colt back to his stall. The turn back riders were making their way back into the stables also, heading for the tack room. Raylee began to tie the colt up and looked around for one of the boys. "Will you tend to the colt for me Jesse?" she called out, although Cutter thought it was more of a demand than a question. She put her boot up on the rail to take off her spurs.

"Sure thing, Raylee." Jesse was quick to agree and he started to walk over.

Cutter interrupted. "I can do it," he said, and he started to unbuckle the saddle.

It seemed that Raylee had other ideas for him. "Let Jesse do it. That's what they get paid to do, and besides, you've had a long day so I'll show you to your room so you can clean up and then I'll give you a tour."

Cutter wasn't sure if Raylee thought he needed to take a shower and change into new clean clothes, or whether she was just being polite, in a forcible way. Either way, he figured out early that she was the boss around here and what she said, goes.

He didn't want to leave the colt, but he knew he was there for a month and a shower did sound appealing. Following Raylee out of the stables and into the car park, she gestured for him to take the front seat of her car, noticing that his bag was already sitting in the back. It was a late model SUV, though as Cutter was unfamiliar with anything other than a Ford truck, it didn't mean much to him.

As they drove down the long, tree lined driveway, Raylee gave Cutter a rundown about the property. "We have a really good balance of horses and vines here. My mother's family have owned vineyards for three generations and my father's family owned cattle, but his first love has always been horses. They met through some friends and eventually brought the two together."

"It seems to work well," Cutter commented, while looking out the window.

"At first they weren't sure how it was going to work, but they built this place from the ground up and it's something they're both very proud of."

Cutter could tell that Raylee was also proud. She spoke very highly of her family's success, although he did feel it was getting a little bit shoved down his throat. Especially since he didn't ask.

They drove to the main house and it was picture magazine perfect. Quite modern with a rustic feel. Everything about the house was in proportion and it complemented the property in every way. As the car pulled around the roundabout, Cutter noticed the details. The mix of slate and glass and the way the gardens wrapped around the verandahs and pathways. He could tell that it had been architect designed and built, with even the trees in the yard looking like they had been placed there intentionally. There was no other word for it... It was grand.

Raylee unlocked and opened the oversized heavy timber front door. "We never lock the house, but with my parents away, I'm just being cautious.

You can take your boots off and leave them here," she instructed, as if she assumed he had no intention of removing them.

"Yes ma'am," he replied, and he stepped out of them, thinking that the only time he took his boots off at home was to either take a shower or go to bed. Yet he'd never walk into someone else's house without removing them first, contrary to what Raylee had presumed.

"It's a nice house," he commented, as he looked around.

"Thank you. I live here with my mom and dad," she explained. "They're overseas on business at the moment. My room's upstairs and you can have the guest room straight ahead." She led the way.

Cutter looked everywhere at once. While it was quite modern and spacious, he also felt that it was cold and sterile. Almost too perfect and not at all homely. The guest bedroom was oversized and over accommodating. It was filled up with lounge chairs, entertainment and a library, as well as a fireplace and a bed so big that Cutter thought that he might get lost in it.

Raylee opened a door and turned the light on. "Here's your bathroom. There's fresh towels and everything you'll need, and you can make tea and coffee over here." She walked to the other end of the room and pulled the curtains back to let the natural light in, showing him where everything was. From the moment they met, it seemed like Raylee Tremayne was in a hurry, and it almost bothered him.

"You know, I would've been happy to sleep in the barn," he said honestly.

"I'm sure you would." Raylee genuinely believed him. "But I'm not having the best horse trainer in the United States come all the way to Australia as my guest and have him sleep in the barn." She was sincere, and it seemed it was her way of giving him a friendly compliment. It was also her way of keeping control of him.

"I think I'll take a shower and then if you don't mind, I'd like to go back down to the colt," he requested.

"After you have something to eat," she said, then she closed the door behind her.

Cutter looked again around the room. While he'd never stayed at a five star hotel, he imagined that this is what it would look like. The linen on the bed was crisp and white, with tons of pillows and a throw rug across the bottom.

"What does anyone need one, two, three, four, five, six pillows for?" he said out loud to himself, while he was counting them with his fingers. The towels in the bathroom were hanging perfectly on the towel rail with the Tremayne emblem stitched on them, while four spare towels were folded neatly on a shelf. There were products of all kinds and he picked them up one at a time to read them. Mini bottles of organic shampoo, organic conditioner, oatmeal body scrub and wash, massage oil and luscious bubble bath. "Mmm, wonder what time the massage is?" He was amusing himself.

The shower was so good. It was hot and steamy, and he stood under it letting the water run over his head and down his back, temporarily taking away any cowboy aches and pains that take a lifetime to achieve. The towels were softer than he'd ever experienced and organic soapy aromas filled the bathroom. He wiped the steamed up mirror, looking closely at the lines on his face and decided that maybe he'd leave it a couple more days before he'd have a shave.

He picked up the jeans he'd been wearing and thought they were okay for another wear, then walked out into the bedroom and threw his bag up onto the bed. His hair was still wet and was dripping down his bare back. He pulled his jeans on, and was just about to button them up when Raylee knocked on the door and opened it before he could answer.

"Do you prefer tea or... coffee?" she asked, looking rather embarrassed. She let her confidence shine through and didn't turn away. "I'm sorry, I thought you'd be ready."

Cutter buttoned his jeans and pulled on a blue tee shirt. "That's okay. Ten seconds earlier and you'd have been more than sorry... Coffee please."

Raylee didn't know what to say in response. She left it at that and walked out, closing the door behind her again. Cutter smiled to himself. He knew he'd just got one over her and it made her feel uncomfortable, even though she tried to hide it.

When he opened the guest room door, the smell of the coffee brewing was warming and filled the house. Unlike that strong, bitter tasting plane coffee that he had on the way over. Raylee was fussing around in the kitchen and carried on as if nothing had happened.

"Our chef is cooking up a storm for tonight, but I can make you something now if you like," she offered.

"Thanks. That would be great... But what do you mean your chef?" Cutter asked.

"Well, my mom incorporates the vineyard with a restaurant, so we have a chef. He's here most of the week so he also cooks for us. It's great because he samples his new ideas on us all the time." She explained this as if it were normal for people to have a chef on hand. "Now, you've seen the property and heard about the Tremayne family, what about yours. What's the Jones ranch like? Is it like this?"

"Well..." Cutter began, then paused as he thought of how to say it politely. "It's a lot like this, except without all those vines."

Raylee didn't say anything, although her expression suggested she was impressed.

"And our house is a little smaller, with a view to die for," he said. "We've also got a chef. Her name's Marnie and she also does the cleaning."

"Wow. Our chef would never do the cleaning as well," she naively said. "What horse facilities do you have?"

"My barn is like my second home and I've also got an arena where I do all my training."

"Sounds perfect."

"Yes ma'am, it is," he confirmed. "I've spent most of my life at Double J Ranch and I wouldn't trade it for any other place, anywhere."

"Well maybe I might get to see it some time?" she suggested casually.

"You'd be welcome." Cutter was only being friendly, since he thought that she'd never have the need to visit. Yet he was as proud of his place as Raylee was of hers.

While everything about the Tremayne property was amazing, there also seemed to be an imbalance between it and Raylee. His first impression of her was mixed. She was young, beautiful, confident. He also found her to be bossy, hurried and superficial. He couldn't work her out and after the first hour or so, he wasn't sure if even after a month he'd be able to.

Together they ate their sandwiches and had their coffee, and now Cutter was anxious to get back to the colt. He hadn't discussed the issues with Raylee yet, while they were still getting through those awkward getting to know a person conversations.

"You want to go back to the stables?" she asked not a moment too soon.

"Ready when you are. I'll just grab my hat." He went back to the bedroom and returned with his hat on and his spurs in his hand.

He met Raylee at the front door and pulled his boots on. She was standing in front of the hall stand mirror applying her lip gloss and it didn't bother her that he was there. For a moment, Cutter thought that she may have been doing it on purpose.

As they drove back through the vineyard, Cutter noticed how well manicured everything was. The vines were still leafy although the season was nearly over. Each of the rows had perfect lawn between them and at the end of every fourth row was a pink rose bush. Raylee pointed out in the distance where the restaurant was, with a cluster of country cottages for weekend stays. Cutter imagined that this would be the kind of place two people would go for a romantic getaway. Not him. He was more interested in the other side. The complex.

Raylee parked the car just outside the main entrance, as if that park was reserved especially for her. When they walked into the stables, Cutter thought that it was the right time to discuss the colt. "So, when did you first start to notice a change?" he asked, wanting to know the details so he could assess the problem.

"When he first came here, he was everything you said he was. He was exactly as you described him. How he performed and how he moved. We kept with his same diet and training program and he was great. Then over time he seemed to get agitated and anxious, and it kept getting worse as the weeks passed. That's when I rang you the first time."

Cutter didn't reply straight away. He was just thinking and taking in what she had said. "And you say he's lost interest when he's working the cow?" he eventually asked.

"Yes," she agreed. "He went from being extremely cowy to being very uninterested. It didn't make any sense. It was like he didn't want to cut anymore."

Again, Cutter didn't comment straight away or offer any ideas. He was in deep thought. "Okay, let's get him out and go for a ride then."

"Sure. I'll just get Ryan over here to get him ready for you," she said, then she turned around and called out to him. "Ryan?"

Immediately Cutter stopped her. "No... You do it." He gave his head a slight shake at Ryan who was making his way over. "I want you to saddle this horse," he said firmly to her.

"Okay then," she reluctantly agreed. "But I don't know what difference that's going to make."

The colt was being arrogant while they stood there looking into his stall and Cutter knew that it was out of character for him. He opened the gate while Raylee waited outside, watching every move he made, and the colt instantly calmed when Cutter approached him.

She noticed how close Cutter got to him, and how he talked to him without her hearing what was said. He made it look so easy and it was clear to her that there was an unbreakable bond between this cowboy and his horse. Her horse.

"What's his daily routine?" he asked over his shoulder, without looking at her.

"He's exercised every day... He's in the arena on the mechanical cow or in front of cattle at least three, maybe four times a week... We followed everything you recommended."

"What's the vet say?"

"Perfect health."

"You know, if I'm gonna work with this horse, then I need you to give me some space," he suggested, although it was more or less expected that she would agree.

"Okay then," she said with a slight hesitation, knowing she had no other choice. After all, that's what he was there for. "So what do you have in mind?"

"Let's just take it one day at a time."

"Can you fix him?"

"Yes ma'am, I can fix him." He sounded very sure of his ability. Not in a convincing tone but rather in a factual one.

They saddled him up together, talking and laughing a little. When Cutter put his boot up on the rail to put his spurs on, Raylee led the colt towards the arena. He followed them down the breezeway and he couldn't help but notice that he liked what he saw. Her small frame made even smaller by the size of the horse. He just wasn't sure if he liked her yet.

She opened the gate and waited for Cutter and as soon as he got on, there was an instant connection. He was back in the saddle, on the horse he loved, and nothing could feel better to him than that.

He exercised him in circles one way then changed direction soon after. He dug his left spur in lightly, then released the pressure and changed to his right. The colt did nothing wrong. Raylee sat on the top rail of the arena and watched Cutter work. He was a natural and he made it look effortless, running him through a series of warm up moves and cutting techniques. The horse responded to his rider.

They trotted around the outside, staying close to the rails. He rode past Raylee although he never spoke to her. While she enjoyed the close up and the way he put the horse through this routine, she knew the quality of his trainer skills were not yet shown.

Cutter then broke out into another series of moves that were more complex and more accelerated than before. With more pressure applied the moves became sharper. He was building him up gradually and was preparing him ready to walk amongst the herd.

A dozen cows stood easily at the back of the pen, not bothered by anything going on around them. Cutter held the reins high with one hand and gripped the horn with the other, coming in along the fence line from the side. The four turn back riders were in position as the cattle shifted slowly out of the way when the colt glided through the middle, singling one cow out from the rest. The lone cow stood still and looked the horse in the eye while Cutter lowered his reins, placing his hand down as he anticipated the next move.

The pause was long...

Then it was electric. The cow moved quickly and the colt's instincts made him move at equal pace, keeping focused with his ears laid back. Suddenly, it all stopped. Bang. Like lightning the cow retreated across the pen with Cutter doing very little as the colt knew his job and kept it from returning back to the herd. Raylee was more than impressed. He'd only been on the horse for fifteen minutes and already had him moving at his best again.

Low to the ground the colt was shifting his weight slightly, anticipating the cow's next move, not taking his eyes off it and blocking every attempt to get past him. The focus was incredible and Raylee could see that this horse was cowy. The moves were edgy and the stops were severe, which at times caught Cutter off guard and made him almost lose his balance when the colt responded more sharply than he expected. He was smooth and accurate, powerful and dynamic, and Cutter couldn't help but think to himself that there was nothing wrong with this horse.

Towards the end of his run, the colt was beginning to slow down. Missing some easy turns and losing heart, he wasn't interested in keeping up the pace of the cow. Cutter didn't push him too hard, since he wanted to see what the colt would do naturally. It confused him how the colt had a perfect first and second cow, then how off pace the third cow was and he let it go.

He finished with a few tight circles in the middle of the arena followed by some warm down time. He was far from disappointed, and was more confused than anything else as he rode around in large circles while he was thinking.

Raylee called out. "So, what do you think?"

He didn't answer. Instead, he continued to go through a series of light exercises which was routine to both of them, before he made his way over to Raylee at the gate. "He's still got all the right moves," he said, sounding pleased.

"But what do you think's wrong with him?" she asked again, as if he didn't understand the question.

"I'm not sure. But it's only the first day. Tomorrow I'll try something different."

"So let's call it a day then. You must be tired."

Cutter could tell that she wasn't asking. He got off the horse while still on the sand and led him back to the stables. Together they unsaddled him and brushed him down. It was getting late into the afternoon and too cold to give him a wash. Instead, they threw a rug over him and gave him a feed back in his stall.

They drove back up to the house and as the sun was sinking towards the mountains, it cast long shadows over the vineyard. It was breathtaking. Cutter could see the appeal of this picturesque place and could understand why Raylee loved it so much. Looking over at her, although she was much younger than him and quite beautiful, Cutter didn't feel any instant connection to her at all. In fact, while he thought that she was nice, he also thought that she was a little stuck up and way too spoilt.

But he was there to do a job, and that job was his passion. He was there for one reason, and it had nothing to do with Raylee Tremayne.

Chapter Three

When Raylee opened the front door, the smell of something amazing instantly wafted through the house, lifting both their spirits.

"Mmmm, dinner has arrived," she said unsurprisingly.

"What. You've had it made already?" he asked, as he was stepping out of his boots and leaving them where he was instructed.

"Ordered, made and delivered. Wait 'til you try it. Our chef is a great cook." She walked over to the kitchen where two plates were sitting out on the kitchen counter and the table was already set for two. "Beer?" she asked casually.

"No thank you, ma'am," he replied, while he was looking at the table, noticing it was set up as if it were at a restaurant.

Raylee had her head in the fridge. "Do you prefer wine?"

"I'm not a drinker," he explained.

She immediately turned around and looked at him in disbelief. "Well that's a first. A cowboy who doesn't drink. You're full of surprises."

"Yes ma'am," he agreed. "But you go ahead." He took his hat off and ran his hands roughly through his hair. She grabbed two sodas, closed the fridge and handed one to Cutter. "Thanks."

She pulled several dishes from the oven and served two plates, then placed them on the table and they sat down opposite each other.

Cutter didn't feel very hungry until he began to eat. "Wow, this is really good," he complimented.

"I knew you'd like it," Raylee said with certainty. "Tell me something. It might be personal, but why'd you sell the colt? Why'd you let him go when he was so good?"

It was a fair question, and one that he had wondered himself at times. It was the moment when he could either brush it aside or be totally honest and open about it. There was music playing softly in the background which took that eerie awkward silence away while his thoughts went straight to Macca. His eyes began to water and he breathed deeply to gain control.

"You know, I raised that colt from a foal. My dad's horse was well bred but was getting old, and we crossed her with a stallion that we bought years ago... Macca always said he should've been gelded but now thankfully he wasn't." When Cutter talked about the past, Raylee could tell he was relaxed about it. It was almost as if he didn't speak or think of the past often enough and so it was refreshing for him to reminisce out loud. "Turned out he came from a good line of ropers too," he added.

Raylee was so intrigued. He had her full, undivided attention and she just listened.

"As a foal there was something special about him that I can't explain. I wasn't sure exactly what he would be capable of, and I didn't find out until I broke him in and started him on cattle. I put in endless hours and started to see some real potential as the weeks went on. He just got stronger and faster and smarter, and was like no other horse I'd ever trained."

Cutter stopped and took a drink. He looked at Raylee who was hanging on every word and he continued on. "I would've been happy if he turned out to be a decent cutting horse. I never expected that he'd turn out to be as good as he is."

"So, you have an average cutting horse mare. Cross her with a stallion of no real value that you knew of at the time, and you end up with a champion?" It was more of a statement than a question that Raylee asked.

"Pretty much. But there are some good genetics mixed in there somewhere. From both sides."

"And how much did you win on him? If you don't mind me asking."

"Enough that we could buy some more land." Cutter was not giving away exact details.

"So you haven't said. Why'd you let him go?" she asked again, not aware that she was prying into his private life.

"We figured after he'd won just about every competition he went into, that in a few more years we'd retire him to stud," he explained. "It was all going to plan and then my dad got sick. For the first two years he fought hard and we thought he'd beat it, then he had a relapse and it really got a hold of him."

While it was emotional for Cutter to talk about his father like that, he was too far in to stop, so he continued. "The doctors put us in touch with a specialist in Dallas who was experimenting with a new treatment, but it was gonna be a lot of money. Dad said we couldn't afford it..." His voice was starting to break up so he stopped to take another deep breath. "But I told him I'd find the money."

"And so you sold the colt." Raylee helped him to finish his sentence and he looked thankful.

"And my horse truck. And he never knew... He was too sick to go to the barn and we all agreed not to tell him."

She looked into Cutter's eyes and could tell that it was still fresh. He looked away momentarily, then added. "You know, I could've sold him back home for more money."

"So why sell him to me?" she asked with curiosity.

"Because in my mind it was a compromise... I didn't wanna sell him but I knew I had to. For Macca's sake. I didn't wanna see him again or see someone else ride him, so the best way was to send him to Australia."

"And then I call you."

"Yeah. About a dozen times... Look, the only reason I came here was because I hate to see this talented, amazing animal that you paid a hell of a lot of money for, go to waste. It wouldn't be fair on you or on him if I didn't come."

"Well I'm really grateful that you did." Raylee was sincere and it softened her.

While they sat opposite each other, he tried to figure her out. She was young. Possibly in her early twenties, although Cutter knew that it would be rude to ask. The time they spent over dinner was friendly enough and on the first night, Cutter knew that a month wasn't going to be as bad as he first thought.

He was getting tired now. The travel and the day had finally caught up with him and he was ready to turn in. He stood up. "Can I help you clean up?" he offered, hoping this was the one time that he would be excused.

"You look tired," she said, reading his mind. "Why don't you get some sleep. My room's upstairs above yours, so just call out if you need anything."

"Thanks. I'm sure I'll be fine... Goodnight." He grabbed his hat and walked towards the bedroom.

"Hey Cutter?" Raylee called out, and he turned around. "I meant what I said... I'm very thankful that you came over." Cutter appreciated her comments and he smiled in return and kept walking.

The night was cooling down quickly, so he added some more wood to the fireplace before going into the bathroom. The tiredness was beginning to be something that he couldn't control and all he could think about was removing five of those six pillows and climbing into bed. The fire burned gently and made a subtle flicker over the entire room. As he lay in the crisp white sheets, he closed his eyes and thought about the day. It was only yesterday that he left the ranch behind and today he was riding the colt again.

His thoughts swayed between the colt and Raylee, the vineyard and the house, and for the next few minutes his mind wandered in those circles, until he fell asleep.

Out in the kitchen, Raylee finished cleaning up. While it was still early, the house was now dead quiet. With her parents away and Cutter gone to bed, she decided to go upstairs for the rest of the night.

Her room was exactly as you'd expect. A big bed full of pillows and too much designer furniture. She went into the bathroom and ran herself a bath, lying in the warmth of the water with the bubbles filling the tub and just touching the back of her hairline. She wasn't tired enough to go to bed and the day kept running through her head, over and over. Not that anything out of this world had happened, but everything about it made her happy.

Cutter Jones was in Australia. She had the best horse trainer in the world at her property and he had ridden the colt in her arena. Everything was on replay in her mind.

After her long bath, Raylee threw her extra pillows to the floor and snuggled into the enormous bed. The night was still and the moon shone into her room through a partially open curtain. Although the lights were out, she stared at the ceiling unaware of the time. She knew it was late and yet she smiled, thinking about the day and knowing that Cutter lay in the bed directly below her.

Downstairs in the guest bedroom, Cutter woke up. He looked at the bedside clock and decided it was time to get up for an early start. It would be normal for him to rise every day before five a.m. and be out the door as soon as he was dressed, and today was no exception. The house was in complete darkness and when he snuck to the front door, he put his hat on and picked up his boots. He opened it slowly, looking around to see if he disturbed Raylee. He hadn't, so he closed it behind him and pulled his boots on outside.

The morning was quite chilly and the walk to the stables was a good way to warm up. He looked back at the house expecting to see a light on. It was still in darkness. Only smoke coming out of the chimney was a sign that someone was home. He could have taken a shortcut through the vineyard, only it was too dark and the grass was wet from the dew. He knew the way by road from the day before and there was enough light from what was left of the moon to see the edges of the road. He could just make out the shape of the stable roof in the distance and with every step closer, it came into focus. By the time he reached the car park, he was hot.

He slid the door open and closed it behind him. The lights were dim inside, although it was enough to see his way around, noticing that it wasn't completely full but still had an impressive amount of horses in there. He didn't take much notice of them as he walked through to the stallion alley and the colt's stall, yet they all saw him and stood to attention as if ready for their morning feed.

The colt responded immediately and Cutter didn't hesitate to go in. He talked quietly to him and rubbed him all over while he was taking his rug off, and he hung it on the rail. He grabbed a brush and began to brush his tail and mane while the colt stood still. It only seemed like yesterday that he was going through the same routine, only it was on his own ranch, in his own barn. After he put the halter on, they left the stall and went to the tack room looking for a saddle and bridle.

One of the riders had just turned up for work and was surprised to see Cutter there before daybreak. "Hey, morning. You're starting early."

"No time to waste," Cutter replied, and he threw the saddle on. "Randall, isn't it?"

"Sure is. You going for a ride?" Randall asked.

Cutter didn't need to comment since it was quite obvious.

"I'll turn the lights on for you then," Randall said, referring to the arena.

"No, that's okay. Thought I'd go out on one of those trails." Cutter pointed westward towards the surrounding mountains.

"Really? I don't think Raylee would like that very much."

"Why not?"

"That horse has never left the stables or the arena unless he's gone to a show. We work him, give him plenty of exercise, but he's always close by. And that's the way she likes it done," Randall said, summing up quickly the colt's routine.

Cutter thought about it for a moment while he finished adjusting the saddle. "Well then, tell her that you never saw me." With that, he got on and rode out the side door.

It was getting lighter now and Cutter rode up the driveway towards the front gate. He pressed the button and waited patiently for it to open, and rode through the middle out onto the main road. There were no cars in sight and he crossed over to where a no-through road led up to a sign that read 'National Park'.

He looked up. The mist was sitting high up on the mountain and Cutter knew that by the time he reached the top, the now rising sun would have burnt it away. He followed the wide trail up a slight incline. The further he went up, the narrower it became until it opened out into a clearing. It was only a walking track for hikers, with several picnic spots along the way. He exercised the colt, cantering at intervals and walking briskly to keep them both warm.

The track became steep and narrow again as he was nearing the peak. When he reached the top he immediately went to foot, leading the colt to a cleared grass area. It looked as though it was rarely visited and he walked over towards the edge. There was a sharp drop over the rock face which over-looked the vineyard and stables in the distance below, and as Cutter took in the breathtaking view of the valley, he let the colt pick at the grass. It was a beautiful sight and it made him think of home.

He knew that Johnny would be overseeing everything on the ranch and riding the filly most days. Marnie would be in the kitchen, cooking up a storm for Johnny and giving him a big breakfast before he headed home for the rest of the day, and the cattle would be getting nice and fat on the good body of spring feed. He didn't need to be there to see it. The only two things that were missing from the ranch now, were Cutter and the colt.

He looked over at him grazing. While the colt was very fit and strong from his regular exercise, Cutter knew that the steepness of the mountain had pushed him harder than any round yard would. He was used to all day riding back home. Over the ranch daily, checking the fence lines, rounding up cattle and tending to the general maintenance where it was needed. His job was not just to be a cutting horse, but to be Cutter's horse.

The sun was now fully beaming and was beginning to give out some warmth. It shone onto the rows of vines and cast long shadows over the landscape. He sat there on a rock for a while longer and rested, thinking of all the shows they'd been to and won at and he wished that he hadn't sold him. It was a big regret, and one that he couldn't change now.

It was still relatively early and yet it was time to head back down. He talked to the colt like a person. Like a best friend, and it didn't bother him to hear his own voice in the quiet subtle sounds of the bush. When he got back in the saddle, Cutter felt the relaxed mood of the colt. Like it was his first taste of freedom since he arrived at the property, making the ride back home easy and carefree. It was only his second day with the colt and already Cutter could feel a change in his stride, while he used his riding time to think.

As he neared the front entry, all he thought about was the last twenty-four hours. His main concern was for the horse and yet he also couldn't help but think of Raylee. He knew that she meant well and treated the colt with the best of care. He also knew that she was inexperienced and naive, and he had the feeling that no one dared to tell her.

Both Cutter and the colt were now hot and tired as they walked back casually to the complex, and both were equally satisfied. The riders would all be at work now, including Raylee, who was looking everywhere for him. She found the colt's stall empty. They weren't in the arena and she eventually found Randall in the feed room, unaware that he was trying to avoid her.

"Have you seen Cutter or the colt?" she asked.

"Not today... Must've been out early," he half lied.

As she walked around the complex, Cutter led the colt into the stables to his stall where he tied him to a rail.

"There you are... Missed you this morning," Raylee said as if they were great friends, not two people who had met just yesterday.

"Morning. I couldn't sleep any longer and I didn't think you were getting up," he explained, without offering anymore details and not looking at her.

Raylee pushed on with more questions. "So, where've you been?" she asked, noticing how hot they were. "You look like you've done the quarter mile."

"We've been out on some trail." His response was firm, without hesitation. "I think it was that National Park up there."

It was enough to fire her up. "What? You took the colt off the property?" she asked. She was instantly annoyed and the tone in her voice had changed. "Into the National Park?"

"Yes ma'am," he replied, keeping it short.

"Are you kidding me? That horse is not to leave this property."

"Well I did," he stated, overruling her.

"Hang on, what gives you the right to take that horse anywhere you want?"

He looked at her and found that her soft green eyes had darkened. "You asked me to fix the problem? Well, I'm fixing it. That's my right."

"You can't do that." Her voice was now rising. "You can't just take that horse and ride it up some mountain, especially without my permission." Cutter could tell that she was angry, yet he was annoyed at her lack of understanding about horses. "I paid a lot of money for that horse, and I say where it goes and where it doesn't."

The other riders were unsaddling their horses and were about to head to the wash bay. Once they heard the argument begin, they slipped out of sight to avoid the confrontation.

"Let me tell you something, Raylee." Cutter stood up straight and looked down into her face. "I've been riding my whole life. I live and breathe horses. It's all I know and I do it well. But you... You come down here in your shiny boots and your perfect clothes and you pretend to be a cowgirl. That's all you are. I mean, look at you. You dress up like one, but really, you've got no idea what goes on here inside this barn or out there in training. All you do is turn up at a practice or at a show and ride. Then you walk around looking like you know how to run this place."

"That's because I do run this place," she said in defense.

Cutter was getting more wound up and Raylee immediately backed down. He wasn't finished there and he kept up with the truthful insults. "Look at you... I bet you never even mucked out a stall or been on a roundup. And from what I've seen, you don't even saddle your own horse."

Now that part wasn't always true, Raylee thought. She could saddle her own horse. She just chose not to.

Cutter picked up her hand. It was soft and clean, and her gold bracelet slipped down her wrist. "If you wanna be a real cowgirl, then you need to get rid of those pretty pink nails and start shovelling some shit around here. Maybe then you'll start to understand the time that's needed and the hard work that goes into this place." He untied the colt and handed Raylee the reins. "He's all yours. Just like you said." Cutter turned around and began to walk away.

Her eyes filled up. "Where are you going?" she asked.

"The airport."

Raylee wiped her face and straightened up. "Cutter, wait," she called out in a less demanding voice, but he kept walking. "Cutter Jones?"

He stopped still. He didn't turn around although he did turn his head to hear what she had to say.

"I'm sorry... Please. I want you to stay." She walked over to him, still holding the colt with one hand while she wiped her face dry with the other. "Please, I need you to stay... You only just got here and I need you to help us."

Cutter took a deep breath and turned around to look at her. He looked into her eyes and immediately felt sorry for what he'd said. He was never one to throw insults at anyone and he really didn't know where it came from, except perhaps the recent grief of losing a horse and a father. He knew he couldn't take it back so while he had the upper hand he decided to lay down his demands.

"If I stay, then we do this my way. No questions asked," he said with authority, and Raylee could only nod her head to accept his deal. "And you're gonna be there every step of the way. No excuses."

"No excuses," she repeated back to him.

He took her hat off slowly and hung it on the horn on the saddle. The only way he could make it right now, was to reach down and give her a friendly kiss on the cheek. "I'm sorry," he apologized. "I didn't mean to make you cry." He put his hand around the back of her neck and they walked to the wash bay. "Now, let's get this saddle off," he instructed, breaking the gloomy silence.

Together they unsaddled the colt and hosed him down with warm water. They shampoo him all over and they had suds everywhere. They stood on opposite sides of the horse, not saying too much, rubbing him and giving him a good wash. Cutter knew that he'd upset Raylee and believed that none of the other riders had ever told her the truth before. He could tell that she was still sulking as she worked quietly and avoided looking at him.

He called out to her. "Raylee?"

She looked up and he splashed her with a light spray of water. She gave a girly squeal and retaliated with more than a spray and Cutter blocked the water with his arm. They began to flick water and suds at each other and as they played this game, it brought a smile to them both as well as a bit of harmony.

After the colt was dried and rugged they took him back to his stall where he enjoyed his morning feed. They stood together and watched him.

"Wow I love that horse," Raylee exclaimed, and Cutter could tell that she meant it.

"Not as much as me," he added, and he closed the gate.

She turned to look at him and tried to read his mind. "Hey, you must be hungry too?" she asked.

Cutter couldn't agree more. "Yes ma'am... I'd love some breakfast," he said, giving her a warm smile.

Chapter Four

"When did you say your parents would be back?" Cutter was standing in the kitchen making the coffee while Raylee finished the cleanup after a late breakfast one morning.

"A few more weeks yet," she replied easily. "They're on a business trip abroad. The only way Mom can get Dad away for a holiday is to say it's business. So, they've gone to France for some wine growers' convention. But really, she's gone for the sun and the shopping."

"Smart woman."

"Yes she is," Raylee agreed. "Hopefully they'll be back to meet you before you leave."

Cutter took a seat at the breakfast bar and sipped his hot coffee while Raylee stood behind it, leaning on her elbows. "So what ties your dad down that he doesn't like to take any breaks?" he asked.

"My dad grew up on a cattle station. His family owned a lot of cattle country around here, but as the mines expanded, they made an offer they couldn't refuse. Now he's gone into property development and consulting, so he's always busy."

"So deep down he's a real cowboy just like me?" Cutter asked with a hint of humor.

"He's nothing like you. Trust me. He's more into business now than ranching. But he still loves his horses."

The phone interrupted their friendly talk and Raylee excused herself to answer it in the other room. Cutter stood up and wandered around. He had been there for a few days now and was feeling more comfortable about being in the house. He found some framed photos that were sitting on a side table, noticing more of Raylee's family.

"Sorry about that," she apologized, when she walked back into the room.

"You've got brothers?" He placed the photo back down where he found it.

"Two. Both married and have two kids each. They're both tied down with work and their families now, so they hardly have time to come out to the property anymore."

"What about you, you date anyone?"

"One of my brothers is a lawyer in the city, so he's always trying to fix me up on dates with guys from the office," she explained without interest. "But I always tell him, I've got a weakness for boys in boots, not boys in suits." She looked at Cutter and he was staring at her. Neither of them spoke. He wasn't sure exactly what she was implying and she wasn't sure if he took her comments the wrong way.

"What you got there?" Cutter asked, breaking the silence and changing the subject when he noticed some promotional material for a rodeo.

She handed him an advertising flyer, thankful for the diversion. "It's an event that's coming up in a couple of weeks and we're the main sponsor."

"Wow, that's great. So you're into rodeos too?" he asked, reading it over.

"Some of the guys that work here are good riders, and some aren't so good. But we support them all and in return it's good for our business."

"Are we going?"

"You bet we are," she assured him. "Have you ever been into rodeos?"

"Yes ma'am. Growing up I was. But eventually I had to choose between bulls and horses."

"And let me guess. The horses won." Raylee liked completing his sentence for him.

"Hands down. My mom always said, *'You can love both but you can only choose one. Make it the one that takes you further.'* And she was right."

"She must be proud of you?"

There was a short silence. It was the first time that he had mentioned his mom in conversation with her and it was awkward. "She would be. She died before I turned pro." His voice remained controlled while he explained even though he was broken inside.

"Oh. I'm sorry. I had no idea."

"Well you can't change the past."

"No you can't," Raylee agreed.

"But rodeo stays in your blood. I still have my card to ride. I can't give it up even though I don't need it anymore," he explained, and Raylee could tell that he still loved it. "Anyway, rodeo and cutting don't mix that well."

"Yeah, well don't tell that to the guys here," she said, making him laugh. "Hey, do you want to go to town? I could show you around." She was diverting him away from the thoughts of his mom and was keeping it light.

"Sure. But how about we ride there?"

Raylee's reaction was instant and abrupt. "Are you kidding me?"

"It's not that far. I saw it from that trail the other day... No excuses remember?"

She thought about it for a while before she agreed. "Alright then."

While at first it sounded like a crazy idea, for Raylee, spending time together wasn't so crazy. In fact, she liked to think that it was a kind of date, but after the way Cutter had cut her down, she didn't think he'd look at it the same way. Still, they were getting to know each other better every time they talked and she would just be happy if they turned out to be good friends.

When they arrived at the complex, Cutter suggested that the colt be let out into a yard for the rest of the day and Raylee agreed. Instead of asking one of the boys to do it, she grabbed a halter and led him out through the breezeway, heading towards a lane that branched off into four reasonably sized yards. Cutter was impressed. He didn't say anything to her and continued to get two stock horses ready for a ride.

They made their way out the front gate, talking and laughing about nothing in particular. Riding along the roadside, they cantered where there were wide open spaces, only slowing down for gullies and difficult crossings. Raylee had never thought about riding to town, thinking it was too far and never having a reason to. Cutter was very easy about it and the time spent with him was all the reasoning she needed.

"You come to town often?" Cutter asked when he slowed down, letting Raylee catch up.

"Not by horse," she replied. "But who knows... You might have me onto something here."

"Hey look," he said, and he pulled the horse up quickly.

Raylee did the same, thinking there was something wrong. "What is it?"

"Over there," he pointed out.

Raylee looked into the fenced yard on the side of the road where a small group of kangaroos were grazing. "They're only kangaroos," she said, as if it were no big deal. Cutter seemed to be taken in by them and was happy just to sit for a while and watch.

"You know, if my brother were here, he'd wish he'd brought his rifle," she teased.

"What, and shoot them?"

"Yeah. Roo steaks are his favorite. Great on the barbie."

"Shut up... Really?" Cutter wasn't sure if she was serious or not, although the look on her face suggested that she wasn't.

"Come on, we're nearly there," Raylee said, and she led the way.

When they reached the edge of town, they stopped for the horses to pick at the grass. The fullness of the trees and the small town country charm reminded Cutter of home. They followed the river bank around. Riding through the park areas, neither horse was bothered by the cyclists and skateboarders sharing the footpaths, and although it was quiet at that time of day, the traffic was picking up as they neared the bridge that divided the town in half.

Raylee was having so much fun being with Cutter, although she wasn't enjoying all the attention from everyone, especially when they had to cross the bridge. While holding up the traffic, Cutter couldn't have cared less. He didn't know anyone there so was quite casual about it all.

He looked at Raylee. "You hungry?" he asked.

"Maybe... What did you have in mind?" She was unsure of what he was going to suggest, until he pointed towards a burger sign at the end of the street. When they rode up to the driveway, Raylee hesitated to follow him into the car park with the horse.

"Come on. They don't do roadside service," he joked.

She was quite uncomfortable about it and reluctantly followed him in. He then rode the horse up to the car drive-through where an illuminated menu sign and speaker box were mounted in the garden and he began to order.

"You've got to be joking. You can't do that," she said, laughing at him. "You're crazy."

While he was ordering, he waved for her to catch up. "...and my friend will have the same," he added into the speaker box.

The little voice repeated the order. "That will be fourteen dollars. Drive through please," she said, as if it were rehearsed.

"I'm sure my parents will hear about this before they get back," Raylee said in all seriousness.

"Well, you can blame me. Just tell them I was hungry."

"I'll tell them you're insane."

They followed the car in front around to the next window and waited in line. The two horses stood patiently side by side, not understanding what all the fuss was about. Cutter pulled out a twenty dollar note ready and made his way in line to the window. The young girl stared at them in shock and asked for the money, not knowing what else to say. She handed him the change and a brown food bag.

"Thanks. Have a nice day," Cutter said to her in his very noticeable American accent, and they followed the driveway back out to the road with the young girl hanging out the window, watching them until they were out of sight.

They tied the horses up to a tree in the park and sat down opposite each other at a vacant picnic table. Cutter unpacked the food, handing Raylee her burger.

"How do you get away with it?" she questioned him, as she opened the packaging and took a bite.

"Get away with what?" he asked just to clarify her question.

"I don't know... With being so charming, and funny...and daring."

"Well, if there's one thing I've learnt, it's that you only live once. So make the most of every day and every situation. And don't take a second for granted 'cause you can't get it back when it's gone." He was now being genuinely honest and Raylee wondered how such a young cowboy could have so much wisdom. "And live life with no regrets."

"Is that what you do, live life with no regrets?" she asked.

"Yes ma'am. Except selling you my colt." While Cutter was only teasing her, it left Raylee wondering if he was serious or not. His eyes locked onto her across the table from underneath his hat, and when she caught him staring, he looked away. It was too late. It only took a second for her to see that look in his eye.

The ride home was slow and steady and they talked non stop. Cutting horses and breeding was their common ground, and occasionally they'd share family stories that normally were kept private. It was easy, and the mood they were in broke down those barriers.

Raylee was slightly trailing behind, enjoying the view in front of her. "Is that your real name?" she asked, and she spurred the horse to level with him.

Why did she have to ask that, he wondered. He looked at her. "Is it my real name? Yes, of course it is. But not the one I was born with."

Now Raylee was confused but intrigued. "Why'd you change it?"

They had shared some deep personal details already, so it was bound to come up sooner or later. It always did. Cutter was hoping that it would have been later. Much later.

"I was only three when my mom and I came to the ranch. My real dad was an alcoholic but thankfully I don't remember too much of him... My mom got the courage to leave the city and decided to make a fresh start in a small town away from all the bad memories. She picked up a job at the local diner and that's where she met Macca. He'd drop by regularly and they became good friends, and it wasn't long before he invited us to the ranch... permanently."

This blew Raylee away. The way Cutter had talked about Macca, she had never thought that he wasn't his real dad. "Wow. Did they get married?" she asked, like it was some kind of fairytale.

"Yes ma'am, after a few months. But Macca said that if I was gonna take on his name as well, then my mom should change my first name too. And she agreed."

"Was it that bad?" she asked, expecting his name to be quite lame.

He laughed. "No, not at all. Macca didn't like that I was named by my father. And besides, Jake and Jones together was a real twister, so my mom let him give me a new name. He rode cutting horses before he met my mom and he just liked the name."

"It sounds to me like Macca had your future cut out for you," she said and Cutter laughed again, totally agreeing with her. "That's awesome. Your life is so much more interesting than mine. Nothing ever happened in our family like yours."

"Yeah well, it's not always been great. We've been through some really tough times too."

Raylee enjoyed every bit of the afternoon together, yet it was now gone and they were back at the complex. The lights were on in the arena and the music was playing in the background. All the boys were there making a ruckus, calling out to one another.

Back in the stables, the colt was in his stall for the night. Cutter and Raylee unsaddled the horses and brushed them down, going through the usual routine of stabling them ready for a feed while Cutter was distracted by the noise. "What's going on out there?" he asked after he was done.

"They're just practicing for the rodeo. They do it every night leading up to an event."

Without hesitating, Cutter went over to the arena to watch and stood on the middle rail opposite the chutes. The bull chute was loaded. Ryan was lowering himself down onto the bull while the others stood around him on the rails, with tense anticipation. There was a nod, then a count to three before Tyler pulled the chute open. The bull bucked and twisted and bucked some more, while the rider was clearly not in control. It was a shameful three second ride with Ryan face-planting the dirt. There was a roar of laughter from the boys while he scrambled as fast as he could to the side and leapt up onto the fence.

Once Ryan was clear of the bull, Cutter and Raylee also laughed as it was a display of a totally screwed up ride. Ryan copped a mouthful of sand and a heap of shit from the other boys as he walked back to the gate shaking his head and spitting out the dirt.

"Like I said, some of them are not so good… Hey, you should have a go," Raylee suggested, as if it was a good idea.

"I would. But I made my decision years ago."

"Well why don't you go over there and give them some help. They look like they need it."

"Well that's not a lie." Cutter threw his leg over the fence and landed in the sand.

"Hey," she called out, and he looked up at her as she spoke, their eyes locking onto one another. "Just so that you know, all these guys think that you're a legend."

"Oh yeah, and what do you think?" he asked.

Raylee's heart began to race. "I think that I'm beginning to know the *real* Cutter Jones."

Every morning was an unusual early start for Raylee, but not for Cutter. Back home he was always up before daybreak, preparing the horses for a day of training. When he was younger he'd have done two, sometimes three hours of horse work before he went to school. It was set in his body clock. No alarm, no one to wake him, and every morning he would be the first one up and out the door. He always said that mornings were the best part of the day and if you missed seeing the sun rise, then there was no need to get out of bed.

For Raylee, it was painful. She wasn't an early riser, but the no excuses deal she made with Cutter was one she intended on keeping, no matter how much she wanted to stay in bed.

It had only been just over a week since Cutter arrived at the property and yet Raylee had spent more time in the stables and riding than she would have done in a whole month. Her presence was felt among the workers too and they noticed her contribution. They were now including her in even the smallest of decisions, valuing her opinions and pleased that she was taking an interest in what they did.

They all knew that it came from Cutter's influence. While in the first few days they gave him some space to work with the colt, they now began to involve him in their riding and training programs, asking him questions and including him in practice. He had more experience with cattle than all of the riders there put together, which meant he was good at reading the cow in the cutting pen as well as the rodeo arena. He tried to pass on some valuable tips to them, sometimes successfully and other times with a disastrous outcome. But they all listened and observed, taking in every word he said.

It was noticeably making a change in Raylee too. Not only the time she was spending with the colt and in the stables, but she was turning up in her three day old jeans and dusty boots. No longer did they have that shine. Some days she traded her black cowboy hat for a baseball cap instead. Her hair was pulled back roughly, as if she didn't have time in the morning to make the effort, and was lucky to make it out the door wearing sunscreen instead of her usual full makeover.

Her riding had improved also, from spending hours in the saddle. While Cutter was giving tips from the corners, everybody including Raylee was absorbed in his teachings. They all knew he was only there for a short time, so were making the most of every bit of advice he was giving.

While the colt had not been in the cutting pen since the first day, Cutter and Raylee would instead take him out on different trail rides exploring new tracks up in the National Park, most of which she had never been on before. Of an afternoon, he'd graze in a big open yard and was free to run, kick and roll in the grass as much as he wanted. Standing by the gate, both Cutter and Raylee thought it was like watching a child let loose in the playground. He clearly loved it.

With only a week out from the rodeo, all the riders spent the evenings under the lights in the arena, practicing from the bull chutes and roping calves. Some of them rode broncs and others steer wrestled. It made the days quite long, as Cutter and Raylee would go back down for an hour or more each evening after a quick dinner.

Cutter had tried just about every rodeo event there was. Roping calves and steer wrestling was something that he'd learnt early working on the ranch. His experience in the rodeo arena came from some of the real life situations he'd found himself in while working in the open pastures and yards. Though it was his knowledge of cattle and his love of horses that steered him towards cutting, just like his dad.

The more practice, the more all the riders were improving, with some levels of ability more noticeable than others. Cutter could see that they all loved what they did. It was like one big happy family, and he couldn't help but think how lucky these boys were to have found a job like the one they had.

Sitting on the sofa one night after dinner, Raylee mentioned that she had something planned for the next day. "Tomorrow morning I'd like you to give me some time after breakfast. If that's okay?" she asked.

"Sure," he was quick to agree. "What is it?"

"I'll tell you in the morning. Right now, I'm dead. I think that I'm sleep deprived."

Cutter looked at her. She looked tired and run-down. Not the Raylee he met a couple of weeks ago. The stuck up spoilt little girl who'd bought his horse was now looking grubby but natural. Spending time together softened her too. He had come to know her in a way that most people wouldn't, as they were sharing personal stories about family and life. All her bossy controlling ways had gone and for the first time she was part of the team, instead of being the leader of it. He was beginning to find her more attractive this way. Her beauty was starting to shine through from the inside out.

He was tired too, although he did like their talk time and wouldn't have minded if she wanted to sit a while longer. Her yawn decided otherwise.

"You'd better get some sleep. I think I'll catch an early night and give practice a miss too," he said and they exchanged their goodnights, both going their separate ways.

While Cutter lay in bed and stared at the ceiling, he thought about home. He hadn't called Marnie yet to see if everything was okay. He figured if there was a problem, then she would contact him. The ranch ran for three years without Macca, and Cutter only part time, so he was sure that nothing would drastically change in a month. Besides, he had Johnny there to keep an eye on things which eased his mind.

The time was going by fast. It wouldn't be long now and he would be going home. It didn't bother him so much, as he needed to get back to working the filly and tending to some chores on the ranch that had recently fallen so far behind.

He was pleased with the colt too. He thought that by the end of the next week he'd have him back in the cutting pen, although it was disappointing to think that he would soon be saying goodbye to him all over again.

And then there was Raylee... Raylee Tremayne... and he drifted into a deep sleep.

During their morning trail ride, Cutter didn't think about asking Raylee what it was she had planned for him. He presumed it was going to be some trivial job, like change a light bulb, so he didn't question it. He did notice, however, that she was in a clean pair of jeans and she had her black hat back on. Her hair was washed and styled, and her face was glowing slightly from the little bit of makeup she had put on. It was the old Raylee back, but keeping the new attitude.

After breakfast they wandered down to the round yard, where six horses were all saddled and tied up around the rails.

"What's this all about?" he asked curiously.

"This is the time you promised me yesterday," she said, as if his agreement last night was as important as the no excuses deal she made with him. She glanced at her watch. "They should be here soon," she said, taking a long look up the driveway.

"Who?"

"My students... They should be here by now." She caught sight of the mini bus turning in. "Oh, here they come."

"Is this a riding school?"

"Yes... I've got twelve of the most impressive young riders you'll ever meet," she said proudly.

"And you taught them how to ride?" he asked with a doubtful voice, but not meaning it.

"Yes," Raylee confirmed. "They're still quite young and there's some real talent among them. Wait 'til you see them ride."

Cutter stood back and watched the mini bus pull up on the grass just outside the round yard. Thinking that he could be spending valuable time with the colt, he wondered how long he had to be there for. While he didn't say it out loud, it ran through his mind that this girl would make money from anything and anyone.

The doors opened on the mini bus and a lady and man stepped out. Raylee greeted them both with a kiss as she was quite familiar with them. Then, the side door of the bus automatically slid back and a group of young children both boys and girls eagerly jumped down, landing on the grass. Cutter kept back and read the sign on the side of the bus. *Challenges - Bringing children and community together.* Immediately, he understood what Raylee's riding school was all about.

A few of the children needed help down off the bus. When they were all ready, they stood in a crooked line and their excitement was clear to see. Cutter felt instantly regretful for having those thoughts about Raylee. She called him over.

"Now, I want you to meet a very special friend of mine. He's come here all the way from Texas in the United States of America, and he's going to help you ride today." She spoke to them like a teacher would speak to a young child, making it very clear and simple for them to understand. They showed their excitement to her even though they had no idea where Texas or America was.

Cutter walked over to the start of the line. He figured the children were from six to ten years old and he immediately felt emotional at their obvious disabilities, although he did well to hide it.

He shook the hand of the first little boy. "My name's Cutter. What's your name?" he asked.

The little boy looked up into his face. "Alex," he said, speaking slowly and very clearly. "Are you a real cowboy?"

"Yes sir, I am. Is that what you wanna be when you grow up?" Cutter asked.

The boy just nodded his head and Cutter touched his hair affectionally then moved on to the next child.

"And what's your name?" he asked the little girl, when he knelt in front of her.

"Sophie," she said very quietly. "Are you Miss Raylee's boyfriend?"

Cutter laughed out loud. He didn't mean to, but he wasn't prepared for a question like that and it totally caught him by surprise. Not to disappoint the children, he looked back at Raylee who was beaming. "Well... I guess I am today," he said, and the little girl smiled with satisfaction, her arms swinging from side to side.

Cutter walked the entire line and met all the children one at a time. The class then broke into two groups of six, each child putting a helmet on. They all had a turn of riding the horses. They were led in circles and were taught how to control the horse with the reins. The children kicked the horses along and pulled them up when they were told to stop, the adults never letting go of the lead rope.

Their smiles were incredibly big. Although not as big as the smile that Raylee saw on Cutter's face when he explained to a little girl how to pull on the reins to turn left and she finally got it after half a dozen attempts. Her attention was divided between the children in her group and the interaction Cutter was having with his. She could tell that he was totally involved in it all.

At the end of the lesson the children took their helmets off and stood around giving Raylee high fives and hugs while Cutter stood back and watched silently. She adored them and it was clear that they loved her too. He could see that her heart was unconditionally in the right place.

"What about a hug for Cutter?" she called out.

The children that were able, all screamed and ran for him. He unexpectedly threw his hat back at Raylee and she caught it, as they hit him with a playful force and he fell backwards into the sand, laughing. The children were all happy. Boys and girls were squealing and giggling, stacking themselves on top of each other while Cutter underneath them all was having the time of his life.

One by one the children boarded the bus and settled into their seats. Cutter walked up to Raylee and stood near her, almost touching. She liked the closeness in the open space they were standing, giving her the sense that a close friendship had been founded.

"Bye," they both called out after the bus as it drove away.

The children's faces were at the windows, waving until they turned the corner and went out of sight. Raylee was content and she could tell that Cutter was humbled by the experience. It was time well spent together and they untied a couple of the horses and led them back to the stables.

"You are one hell of a woman, Raylee Tremayne. I can't wait to see what you do next." It was as close to flirting as a compliment could get.

"Well stick around, *boyfriend*. You might be surprised."

Chapter Five

The day of the rodeo came around fast. The daily routine at the complex was shortened so that everybody could get away early. Cars, trucks and horse floats filled the car park. Saddles and hay were coming out of the tack and feed rooms, filling the front of the floats, while the horses were being loaded up ready for the drive. It was busy and everyone knew their role in getting on the road.

Cutter and Raylee went back to the house to get changed. She would turn in her dirty work clothes for her more polished look again. Cutter thought that it was appropriate this time, since Tremayne Industries was the main sponsor for the event. She met him in the entry where he was waiting and he secretly admired how she looked.

"You ready?" she asked.

"Yes ma'am, but you're not."

"I've got everything... I think." She was looking around checking her bag, keys and phone. She couldn't find anything missing.

Cutter walked up to her slowly and very carefully took her hat off, and she didn't know why. What was he doing? Was he going to kiss her, she thought, and it gave her a fluttery feeling in her tummy. He looked at her hat and shaped the front of it, pinching the corners so it was sharp.

"That's better," he said, and he placed it back on her head. "Now you're ready to go."

In the days since the riding school, Cutter's feelings towards Raylee had changed. He found her to be soft and compassionate, and he liked these characteristics about her. Her self absorbed world was all for show. She really was caring and helpful to others who needed her, and deep down Cutter couldn't help but think that her privileged life was more of a burden to her than a benefit. That she had a role or an expectation to fill from her parents, rather than letting her be herself.

"Maybe I'll let you drive," she suggested when she unlocked the car, as if it were a date and he should be the one to take the lead.

"What, on the wrong side of the road? You're brave."

"Most of the roads are open, so I'm sure you'll be fine," she assured him. "Besides, it's you who drives on the wrong side of the road, not us," she added.

For the two and a half hour drive, they passed the time by talking about the kids' riding school. Raylee could tell that Cutter had loved every minute of it. Probably more than the children themselves. He learned some more about the property and how her parents came together in the first place. Cutter had no idea about vineyards since he didn't drink, and he'd never been to one, so a brief outline of the operation there filled in some drive time.

"What're your mom and dad like?" he asked, as the weeks were running out and he didn't think he'd get to meet them.

"Well, my mom's a good worker. She put her heart and soul into our place and she loves it. My dad's a bit of a control freak, but he does have a soft side. You just need to know how to find it sometimes."

"So what are they like together? They sound like they're a good team."

"Sometimes they are. It just depends if they're working on the same page or not. They've been married for nearly thirty years and sometimes I think they shouldn't be married at all. But you know, all relationships have their good times and their bad. I guess my mom and dad don't show us all their troubles, but we know they're there. I know they love each other, they just don't show it to us very often."

"So they have everything they want in the world, but it sounds like they're still not happy."

"You know what they say. Money doesn't buy happiness."

Cutter already knew this from his childhood. His parents weren't flash with money, yet they were so happy together and had everything they needed. "So what buys your happiness?" he asked randomly, and she wasn't expecting it.

She was very careful not to overdo it, so she tried to keep it simple. "I guess I'm no different to anyone else. I just want to love and be loved."

Good answer, he thought, even though he knew she wasn't giving too much of her personal thoughts away at this time. She was protecting her heart.

The scenery was changing the further they drove west and the sun was sinking slowly towards the top of the mountain ranges. Autumn leaves had fallen, leaving the ground covered in yellow and orange, and the temperature was dropping.

"What're your long term plans for the colt?" he asked.

"Well, my idea was to bring a stud into the country that would be in high demand for breeding. So I bought the best colt available."

"Yes you did," he confirmed. "Always got a business plan in there somewhere."

"My business plan was working out well until we pulled him out after a few shows. We said he had an injury. But he had everyone talking about him, that's for sure."

"So what do you think's wrong with him?" Cutter was only testing her.

"Nothing when he's around you," she said, in an honest and complimentary way.

"So what you gonna do about that?"

She smiled and looked over at him while he kept his eye on the road. "Keep you here," she said, making them both laugh even though Raylee thought it sounded like a good idea.

Cutter began to slow down when he drove over the last hill and could see the outline of what looked like the equine center. Raylee didn't need to tell him. As they came closer, the trucks and floats in the parking area were an obvious give away. Horses were tied up to fences and standing in make shift stable areas around the camp ground. The sand yards were full of riders exercising their horses, while others stood around chatting and waiting their turn. It looked like cowboy hat city.

This week long event of cutting and camp drafting was finishing with a few finals in the afternoon and the rodeo in the evening. Cutter began to feel nervous. Although he wasn't riding, he hadn't been to an event in years, which added to this immediate sick feeling in his gut. He remained silent as they drove through the gate and into the competitor area, parking in the first available spot.

They both got out of the car and put their passes around their necks and their hats on. Raylee walked around to the driver side while Cutter stood on the spot, leaning against the door. "Come on," she said.

"Do people know me here?" he asked, so that he knew what to expect.

"They might know you by name, but I'm not really sure," she answered, then noticed his hesitation. "Hey, are you okay?"

"Yeah. I'm fine."

"Well if you didn't want to be noticed, then you might have thought twice about wearing that shirt," she pointed out, and Cutter looked down at his bright, lime green shirt. "I'll try not to introduce you to anyone then," she added jokingly to lighten his mood.

They walked up the footpath to keep clear of the riders and horses, then up the steep steps of the center and showed their passes at the door. It was quite impressive inside. The sand arena was down on ground level with seating built up all around, all covered in under a large dome roof. There were shops and food stalls, and cowboys and cowgirls everywhere. Cutter could tell that this wasn't some small weekend show as it was packed with a good crowd.

They grabbed a couple of coffees and sat in the VIP area, overlooking the settling of the next herd. Music was playing in the background, just like it did back at Raylee's arena, and people were taking the time to catch up during the interval.

The VIP area was full of other sponsors, event organizers and anyone who was officially invited to the show. Raylee seemed to be quite well known among them all.

She went to introduce Cutter to some people behind them. "This is..." she started to say, before he gave her a look to tell her that it was a bad idea. "... my friend Jake from the U.S."

"Pleased to meet you, Jake," one of the men said, shaking his hand. "Do you cut?"

"I've seen it done a few times," Cutter replied over his shoulder, trying to play it down.

"Take it from me. It's harder than it looks. Takes years of practice and a lot of luck." The man was just being friendly, although Cutter didn't feel the need to respond. "But don't let that stop you from giving it a go."

Cutter was not deliberately trying to be rude even though he was totally uninterested in engaging with this man, for fear of getting himself into a conversation that he couldn't get out of. "Maybe I will. One day," he replied, then he turned back around.

He looked at Raylee. She was staring at him with an enormous smile then turned away also. "Liar," she said to him under her breath so that only the two of them could hear.

Cutter was still quite serious, even though he knew she meant it to be light hearted. "I'm just not ready to explain my situation to anyone," he said. "So I'd rather not open up that door."

Raylee thought that his response was justified. She also knew that he needed to overcome this anxious feeling he was having. "Do you not want to be here?" she asked, giving him an out.

"Of course I wanna be here," he said quickly. "But I haven't been to an event in years. I thought I'd be okay going straight back into competition, but just being here in the stands makes me realize that I'm not as ready as I thought I was."

In a way Raylee was pleased to hear this, although not because of what he was saying. They had only known each other for a little over three weeks and although he'd shared parts of his family's life with her, he was now going deep and very personal, making her feel like he trusted her more and more.

She wanted desperately to help him, while she had to be careful of what to say. "Your first event is always going to be the toughest," she said, easing her way in.

"I know I can train a horse to win, and I know I can give it everything at a show. But I left competition on top and everyone will be expecting me to come back on top. What if I screw it up?"

Raylee didn't look at it the same way. "Then you screw it up. So what?"

"So what? It's my reputation, that's what. My life's work."

"Are you sure it's not your pride?"

"It's everything. And that's the problem."

"You know the best way to deal with this?" she asked. While Cutter didn't reply, he looked directly at her for the answer. "Do your first show here."

It made perfect sense to Raylee, though Cutter wasn't immediately convinced like she'd hoped. "I don't know. People here would still know who I am," he pointed out.

"But they don't know Jake Jones, do they?" she said smartly. "I know some people high up in the Association through our family's support, and I think they could do me a small favor."

He liked that she was helping him and that she would pull a few strings to make it happen. Except that it wasn't the Cutter Jones way. He was one who tackled his problems head on, not hide behind a distraction. It was something that he had to deal with and figure out for himself and no one would be able to fix it for him, even if they wanted to.

The music changed suddenly to an upbeat song and the volume filled the arena. It was the lead in to the cutting final. The announcer's voice came over the speakers while people began scattering back to their seats. Cutter shifted in his seat to get comfortable. He had been in this position many times before, except he was now sitting in the stands, not on the horse.

"...over the last week and we've narrowed the list down to our top ten. Our competitors now leave their go-round scores behind and will start from scratch. They've only got one shot and two and a half minutes." The announcer's voice was quite entertaining, stretching his words and twisting his sounds as he came across the loud speaker.

Cutter switched the announcer's voice to background noise as he was more focused on the mare that had just walked across the timeline. The bell rang and the electronic clock on the back wall started the count down. Raylee could tell that Cutter was tense for the rider, although nothing she could have said would change it, so they just watched in silence.

The cowboy looked young and it reminded Cutter of himself quite a few years ago. He wondered what was going through his mind. Was he fearless or a wreck inside? Either way, he looked composed and Cutter couldn't tell.

He walked towards the mob at the back of the pen and immediately his team began pointing out potential cows to bring to the forefront. He was smooth and steady and was taking his time.

It never really bothered Cutter where he was in the draw, except to him, first out never resulted in his best score, so he'd always preferred any other position. But this wasn't his ride.

The rider had singled out one cow and at the same time he put his hand down, Cutter's heart nearly beat through his chest. Thump. With every stop, his heart rushed. With every turn, he was pumped. He was unaware that he was gripping his chair and hanging on, as if he were experiencing the ride.

The mare was accurately blocking every move. She had cow sense and was even turning out of the tight spots with speed and style. The rider was looking good and in control as together they set the cow up in the middle of the pen. Her snappy accelerated moves were only enhanced by the abruptness of the cow trying to get past, and they went head to head in a show stopping performance that would strike an unbeatable score from the judges. It was near perfect.

The crowd applauded and whistled when the rider pulled up the reins, turning back to the mob for another cow.

Cutter remained silent through the second cut, but the third cow was rank and with only ten seconds left on the clock, he unintentionally said what he was thinking. "No... No... He's gonna lose it..." His feet were now getting restless. "Keep it straight..." Buzzzz. Time's up. "Wow that was close."

"Thought you were riding the horse there for a minute," Raylee commented.

"Did you see how that last cow was getting him out of shape? One more turn and he'd of lost it."

Just then the man behind Cutter touched him on the shoulder. "Like I said... It's harder than it looks."

There was a pause while the announcer was waiting on the three judges to combine their scores. "A two thirteen," he called out. Cutter disagreed. He saw it more as a two sixteen, though he knew, from his experience, never to argue with the judges' score.

As each rider was taking their two and a half minutes, Cutter was feeling more relaxed. He saw some real talent and was taking mental notes on the breeding of the horses, many of which were sired from the U.S, and he was beginning to understand why Raylee had brought the colt over for an intended breeding program.

Together they discussed in detail each rider's style and their cuts, looking at their best moves and finding faults with their worst. As for Raylee, she had the best teacher in the world sitting right beside her, and she knew that it was a privilege as he wouldn't be sharing his knowledge and experience with just anyone.

She didn't mention that he seemed more at ease now, as she tactfully distracted his attention from himself to the other competitors. She was asking lots of questions about individual moves, and he was asking her about different horses and their breeding.

Together they were into it.

The way he looked at Raylee now had changed so much since they first met and he wondered if he had judged her harshly in the beginning or if she was just misunderstood. Her attractiveness was shining through, although it had been there the whole time. Cutter just wasn't ready to see it, until now.

The scores came in and the leader board was final. Cutter thought the results were justified and all round it was a good end to the cutting. There was to be a lengthy break between the cutting and the rodeo while the officials prepared the arena for the change. The stewards were busy moving panels and the judges' stand, while others were preparing the bull chutes. Tractors made circles in the sand and harrows dug in to turn the sand over. It would be an hour before the rodeo would start, giving Cutter and Raylee time to walk around to stretch their legs and grab a bite to eat.

She could tell that he was more comfortable now that the cutting was over, and was more at ease just walking around looking at the shops, even though they didn't buy anything. Raylee knew every other person there, and they all looked at her curiously but seemed more interested in her new friend.

"Hey Raylee," they'd say.

"Hey," she'd reply in passing, and Cutter thought he'd heard more *heys* in the last fifty yards than there was hay in the barn back home.

"Why is everyone looking at me?" he asked.

She was amused. "Because it's a small community of cutters and everyone knows everyone... But they don't know you."

"What, you never dated anyone here before?"

"Nope."

"Well why not? I thought you'd be the most eligible bachelorette in cutting." He was trying to be funny to cover up his curiosity.

"I probably am if truth be known, and that's why they're all looking at you... Trying to figure out who you are and where I got you from," she said. "And if only they knew," she added seriously.

"I'll tell you what. I'll leave them without a doubt." He picked up her hand. "This will really get them talking."

Was he sending her mixed signals? She wasn't sure. But while ever they walked around holding hands, whether it was heartfelt or not, Raylee was enjoying every minute of it.

They walked and talked and shopped, then stopped by the cafeteria for a light dinner, taking a table in the corner. "That was a good final," he commented. "I never expected to see the quality of some of those horses."

"So you're impressed then?" she asked.

"Sure am. Some of them would make the grade of our best back home."

"And what do you think of our trainers? How do they compare?" She was full of questions.

"There's some really good talent here. Some have got some shit hot moves," he said.

"Yeah they do. But not as shit hot as you." Raylee had let it slip out and couldn't retract it. "Moves I mean," she added quickly, to cover up what she had been thinking for quite some time.

They found it easy to talk to each other. Raylee danced around with the idea of asking about the issues Cutter had earlier. She wasn't sure how to approach it, then figured to tackle it head on. "Hey. You said to me before that you didn't want to screw up?"

"Does anybody?"

"Well no. But it doesn't mean that you have to be afraid of screwing up."

"Except people have high expectations. I've been labelled the best and clients expect you'll deliver," he explained. "There's a lot riding on it at that level. You can lose sponsors, clients, breeding prospects. It's all income. So if you screw it up, then you lose everything and I can't afford for that to happen."

She understood the problem he was facing.

"I was at the top of this game for years and it was my choice to let it slip away to take care of Macca." He spoke without the sense of regret. "But now, I don't know how or if I'll find my way back."

"Cutter. Have you ever thought that there was more to life than that?" she asked.

"Yes ma'am. But it's all I know and I do it well."

"But what about family?" She was diving into territory that he was totally unprepared for. "You've lost both your parents, and I can't even begin to imagine what that's like. But it sounds to me like your mom and Macca worked so hard and have left you a special place. Your ranch. Now who are you going to work hard for?"

It was not something he'd thought too much about. He was so consumed with cutting and competition that he didn't stop to think about life and how it was passing him by. "Just don't get too caught up on being the best that you forget to live a life," she added.

Cutter was thinking about what Raylee had said. He couldn't dispute it, as he knew she was right. Was he obsessing too much on being the best, and at what time in his life would he stop to think about settling down? Would he be able to have both?

Raylee thought that time went quickly when she was spending it with Cutter. She couldn't believe he'd been there for three weeks already. Their lunches and dinners, their trail rides and car trips all flew by. She knew that it wouldn't be long and he'd be going back home for good. That wasn't about to change. He had responsibilities he had to take care of and a career he had to pick up on. More importantly, he had a life he needed to start living and Raylee knew that she wasn't going to be in any part of it.

The bright lights in the arena went out and the music changed. People filled every spare seat in the stands and that familiar voice came over the loud speakers again, welcoming any newcomers to a night of rodeo. The colored spotlights shone in all directions and girls in sparkly outfits, holding flags, circled the arena floor on horseback.

As they stood outside the cafeteria, Cutter leaned down to Raylee's ear so that she could hear over the noise of the applause and music. "I'll think about what you said."

She turned it around and made light of it. "You'd better. Because I'd hate to think I was wasting my breath."

He picked up her hand and kissed it, then let it go and left. She watched him walk away into the crowd, knowing that his display of affection was not intended to be romantic, as it was more like the gesture of a thankful friend. She went the other way back to her seat and sat in the crowd among the other spectators, instantly hating the idea of being alone without him. Though she was happy for the Tremayne riders, that he was going to help them in the rodeo.

The noise of the crowd settled when the announcer introduced Jesse as the first rider out in the saddle bronc. He was standing on the rails within the chute and Raylee could see that lime green shirt with him and knew that Cutter was there coaching him all the way. The announcer rolled out Jesse's list of achievements before the music went up to the next level. There was an instant buzz amongst the crowd, anticipating the first ride of the night and Raylee felt sick from nerves.

Jesse lowered himself into the saddle and put his boots into the stirrups all the way to the heel. He squeezed his knees in firmly, keeping his spurs clear of the horse. Holding tight, he looked up into Cutter's face. They were silent, having a clear understanding between them. Cutter knew exactly what was going through Jesse's mind and he gave him a nod and when Jesse returned it, the chute was pulled open.

Jesse cleared the chute well and the crowd gave a deafening roar, showing their approval. The horse leapt forward and bucked when Jesse spurred him on, gripping tight and finding a rhythm with the horse. He maintained his form and was covering good ground around the pen, keeping in sync and showing more balance and skill than at practice back home.

As the horse fiercely tried to offload its rider, Jesse was lifted out of the saddle with every buck. Losing his hat but holding on for the full eight seconds. He let go of his grip and threw himself at one of the pickup men, while the other released the flank strap and directed the horse back to the gate.

Jesse was pumped. He retrieved his hat out of the dirt and waved it to the noisy crowd.

Raylee's nerves had settled now that the first ride was out of the way. She was proud of Jesse and knew that Cutter had a big part to play in his confidence, knowing he had the best standing in his corner. That advantage was clear to see. While the other riders were all equally talented and experienced, Jesse out-performed them and scored extra points for spurring his horse more aggressively, and riding out the full eight seconds.

Besides the bull ride, Raylee's favorite event of the rodeo was the steer wrestling. She had two of her boys in the event, Jesse, who would try his talent at anything rodeo, and Tyler, who was relatively new to it. They'd practiced at home into the late hours of the night and had seen their best times shortened by up to two seconds since Cutter had arrived.

It was rough and cowboy tough, throwing themselves off a fast paced horse onto a steer and pulling it to the ground while Randall would double up as their wingman to keep the steer straight. It was exciting to the crowd and when Tyler threw himself at the steer and wrestled it in the dirt, his fearless attempt earned him a close third place in the event. Unlike Jesse, who had encountered a near miss and a hard ass steer that wouldn't lay down.

His never give up wrestle, and 13.6 seconds later, earned him the biggest cheer from the crowd for his persistence. Raylee couldn't have been more pleased for her boys as their spirit was nothing to be disappointed in.

All the Tremayne team had a run in the calf roping with good results. Jesse, wanting to make up for his bad miss in the steer wrestling, managed an impressive and near perfect performance. He held the leader board for most of the event, until new boy Tyler knocked him off top position, beating his score by half a second.

Tyler's horse left the box at incredible speed and chased the calf, while he had the rope swinging above his head. He released it and looped the calf around its neck. He launched himself off the horse just as it pulled tight and ran towards it while the horse held the tension on the rope. Tyler flipped the calf over and used the piggin' string he had between his teeth, and tied the calf's legs together. It was fast and spectacular to watch. He threw his hands in the air to stop the timer then mounted his horse while he waited for the result to become official.

It couldn't have been any closer between the boys and for the first time, Raylee would have liked to have seen Cutter give all these cowboys a run for their money.

Although the events were rolling on, Raylee kept looking at her watch. For the first time in three weeks, time was dragging. She kept looking for that lime green shirt, just to catch a glimpse of him, and she almost wished the night over so they could be back in the car together again.

She was agitated, and went to buy a coffee before the ladies' barrel race began. She sat back down and enjoyed watching every ride, knowing many of the girls from her early days at the local pony club. As they grew up and came of age, they all went on to different events. Camp drafting, barrel racing and for Raylee, it was cutting. They'd always catch up at the bar after competing at the bigger shows and they'd all remained good friends over the years, often crossing friendships and business, which worked out quite well for Raylee.

She wondered what they'd all think, if they knew that Cutter Jones was with her at the rodeo. She suddenly imagined that if she had chosen drafting or barrels, then she would never have bought the colt and may never have met him.

The end was now in sight and Raylee was pleased with the scores her boys were achieving. It was one of the best all round results she'd seen from them in one night of rodeo and she automatically credited it to Cutter's presence among them and their long nights of practice that had paid off.

The bull ride would be the final event of the evening and the crowd were now ready for it, half tanked and the noise level rising from their rowdy antics with the music thumping in Raylee's ears. It was deafening, quite exciting, and again she felt that nervous feeling for her boys who were about to ride.

There were only eight in the line up, with two of them belonging to the Tremayne team. One by one they entered the arena. Their names blasting over the loud speakers with an introduction that made them sound world class, even though they were far from it. Still, they were gutsy and determined, and they waved with some lifting their hats at the wild crowd who were wanting to be fired up and entertained.

The chutes were being prepared with the bull locked in position while the arena floor was cleared of everyone, leaving only two colorful and very well padded-up bullfighters running amok and providing the fill in entertainment.

As the first cowboy entered the arena, he raised his hat, looking for an immediate rev-up from the crowd. They gave it to him and he climbed into the chute and lowered himself onto the bull. The sound of kicking against the metal panel put a shiver up Raylee's spine, and the rider quickly pulled himself up to let the bull settle again. His team were on the rails with him and they wait for the right moment... He gave the nod and the chute was pulled open.

The cowboy, fastened to the rope and digging his spurs in, leaned back and threw his arm high in the air behind him for balance. The bull came down at full thrust and the cowboy was nearly thrown over the front. He held on, even though the motion of the buck and twist was fierce. His experience was shown by his control and talent, as he skillfully rode out the time - eight exhilarating seconds. The buzzer rang and he celebrated as he hit the ground on two feet, showing the crowd just how happy he was.

As the official reset the clock, Randall came to the chute. He was Tremayne's most experienced rider and had always performed well. The crowd had seen him ride many times before and he'd been known to be the best all-round cowboy on the circuit a time or two.

Raylee could see Cutter on the rails. She couldn't take her eyes off him and although the chute opened and Randall did an impressive eight second ride also, it was Cutter who Raylee was intent on watching. Randall released the rope and landed on his knees. He got up quickly and ran to the fence with the bull in chase, as the bullfighters were now on the job, dramatically drawing the bull away from him. When the arena floor was all clear, he walked back towards the chutes, punching his hat in the air and doing his famous victory dance.

It was a competitive night of bull riding and the crowd were loving it. Raylee was pleased, especially that it was nearly over. With Ryan taking the eighth and last bull of the night, she'd soon be going home with Cutter.

It was a disappointing ride for Ryan, just like at practice. The bull didn't clear the chute well and he had no balance from the jump. Four erratic seconds later and he was having a close-up confrontation with the dirt.

Raylee immediately stood up as soon as it was over. She applauded her boys for a good night of rodeo along with the rest of the crowd, when the announcer came back on with his spectacular voice telling everyone that it wasn't over just yet.

"...and as the official results are yet to come in, we have a very special guest rider here tonight..." Raylee picked up her bag ready to leave and looked down at the chute. "He's a two time Futurity cutting horse champion and has an impressive list of achievements that's earned him the title of the best horse trainer in the world. He's from Texas, all the way from the United States of America. Please make welcome to the chutes, Cutterrrrr Jonessss..." The announcer dragged his name out so far that it was ringing in Raylee's ears.

"Noooo," she screamed so loud in her head that she thought everyone could hear it. "What are you doing?"

There was nothing she could do. Cutter was in the chute while Randall, Jesse, Tyler and Ryan were on the rails with him. She could only imagine what was going on over there and it seemed to take forever. The crowd were applauding to the beat of the music and the whistles were screeching through the entire building, echoing off the walls.

Raylee felt as if her heart had stopped, while she held her breath in anticipation. Randall gave Cutter the nod and a few seconds later when he was sure he was ready, Cutter returned it. This was it.

The chute was pulled open. The bull cleared it well and bucked higher than any other all night as it thrust Cutter more aggressively. His balance and skill even amazed Raylee, who was tense and watching with desperation in her eyes, hoping that he would safely ride this out. She knew that he rode bulls, but that was many years ago and it seemed as though he hadn't lost his touch.

Four seconds in and the bull was becoming angrier. Spinning and kicking with all his strength, the bull was desperate and determined to spit him off. Cutter was holding on, his rhythm was in perfect sync with the bull. He spurred him on even more, gripping tight, leaning back with his arm held high. He rode like a pro and when the eight second buzzer went off, he threw himself off the bull, clearing it safely.

He got a standing ovation from a very drunk and happy crowd, and Raylee didn't think that the noise level could get any higher. He'd rocked it. She let out a big sigh of relief. He'd done it. He had competed in front of a big crowd, albeit not on a cutting horse. But would it be enough to give him the courage to go back into the cutting arena?

As he landed on his hands and chest, his face hit the dirt. He immediately raised his head and looked around to see where the bull was and to determine his situation. He saw him out of the corner of his eye. He spat into the dirt and shook his head to get his bearings and began to raise himself up on his hands and knees. There the bull was, staring him in the eyes. The pause was long and drawn out and when the bull made him his target, Cutter went to foot and ran for the nearest fence.

Raylee's relief was short lived as she watched, putting both her hands to her face. She was panicked and couldn't believe what was happening. "Run," she shouted so the whole arena could hear. Her voice not making a sound over the rest of the crowd all yelling the same words.

The bull was faster than Cutter and was running him down. He leapt onto the fence but at the same time the bull side swiped him and slammed his body hard against the metal panels. His head hit with a force and as the bull ran off after the bullfighters, Cutter fell to the ground and lay motionless in the dirt.

Chapter Six

Raylee knelt next to Cutter in the dirt. The lights were shining into his face, highlighting the graze on his cheekbone while his eyes remained closed from the brightness. She leaned over him. "Cutter," she said quietly. "Cutter, it's me... Raylee."

He didn't move.

"He's already come to," the medical officer informed her. "He wasn't out for long, but we'll still have to take him in for a thorough check."

"Okay," she agreed, visibly upset. She stood up and watched them lift him carefully onto a stretcher.

"He'll be alright," Ryan said to comfort her. "Hey, that was one hell of a good ride."

It was clear the boys were all impressed with Cutter's eight second spectacular ride, although Raylee would have preferred a good explanation. She would now leave that for another day. They lifted the stretcher carefully into the back of the ambulance and the flashing lights were turned on, without the siren, as it drove out.

"Hey Raylee, we've gotta get the horses home. Do you want one of us to stay with you?" Randall asked.

She didn't. "No. That's okay. I'll go to the hospital and you guys go home. I'll give you an update later," she said, not knowing if she would even make it home that night.

When Raylee pulled up in the car park at the hospital, she felt sick. The ambulance from the rodeo was packing up and leaving, meaning that Cutter was already inside. She ran in and spoke to the woman on the front desk.

"My friend's just been brought in. In that ambulance. Where can I find him?" she asked quickly and was panting, trying to catch her breath.

"I'm sorry. You can't go in there just yet until the doctor has had a look at him," the woman said firmly. "Why don't you fill out this form so that we have his details. The more information the doctor has, the more it will help." She handed Raylee a pen and clipboard with one page to fill in. She didn't argue. Instead, she thought that the more helpful and cooperative she was, the sooner they'd let her see him.

I don't know any of these details, she was thinking, as she took a seat in the waiting room and started at the top of the page.

Name? Cutter Jones. Date of birth? She never thought to ask, and she wasn't exactly sure how old he was. Address? Texas. Phone number? She copied it out of her phone. Medical conditions? No idea. The more personal the questions, the more Raylee realized that she really didn't know him.

She could tell the receptionist that he had the most amazing deep blue eyes and a gorgeous smile. He was funny, witty and extremely hot. A champion cutting horse trainer who talks with a twang and has good old fashioned southern manners that makes your heart melt every time he speaks, yet there was nowhere on the page that she could put any of these things that she knew about him.

She took the form back to the woman and explained. "Look, this is a friend of mine who I only just met three weeks ago and is staying with me at the moment, but that's all the details I know."

The woman took the form and could see the concern in Raylee's eyes. "That's okay. At least we know what to call him... Is that his real name?" she asked curiously as she read from the top, and Raylee confirmed that it was. She was quite matronly. "Why don't you take a seat and I'll let the doctor know that you're here."

Raylee sat back down again and looked around the room, hoping that it wouldn't be long. There were only a few people there, reading magazines and flicking through their phones to pass the time. She looked at her watch. It was just after eleven and she sat back, thinking that it could be a long night.

An hour had gone past and the waiting room hadn't changed. She sent a few text messages, kept checking her watch for the time, picked up the newspaper but put it down out of boredom and rubbed her eyes from tiredness.

The main doors opened and she looked up. Randall and Jesse walked in and seeing her in the waiting room, they went straight to her. "Have you seen him yet?" Jesse asked as she stood up, handing her Cutter's phone, wallet and hat.

"Not yet," she said anxiously, and they both hugged her for comfort. "I'm hoping it won't be too much longer."

When she glanced over at the receptionist, the woman deliberately made no eye contact.

"We can't stay. We've got the horses loaded and we're on our way home," Randall explained. "We just thought we'd see how you were both doing."

"Thanks," she replied, pleased for the company. "But you'd better get on the road and hopefully I won't be too far behind you."

"You call us if you need anything," Jesse added.

Raylee agreed that she would and they turned around and walked towards the exit.

"Hey," she called out after them. "Good ride tonight."

Without words, they both gave her a cowboy nod of appreciation.

While she was up, she walked over to the receptionist. "Do you think I'd be able to see him now?"

The woman politely told her that she'd find out what was going on, and a few minutes later she came back in. "You can go through now. Turn left here, then right and go to the next desk," she directed Raylee with her hands.

"Thank you," was all she could say, and she rushed through the double swinging doors, not looking back.

The room was divided by curtains into small consultation rooms. Some open and others closed. The lights were bright and Raylee was looking around to see if she could find him. She didn't make it to the next desk when a curtain flew open and the doctor called her in.

"You must be Raylee?" the doctor said very softly and professionally.

"Yes," she replied, not taking her eyes off Cutter. "How is he?"

He was lying back resting on the bed with his glassy eyes struggling to stay open from the brightness of the overhead lighting. The bruising and cuts to his face were the evidence he'd been in an accident, and his left sleeve was rolled up high revealing the strapping on his wrist and arm. He was favoring his left side, holding it for support with his other arm. Raylee assumed it was a good sign though, that he was fully dressed still with his boots on.

"Your boyfriend's taken a fair knock to the head, so we've been monitoring him for any further head trauma. Concussion is serious no matter how long you've been knocked unconscious, and they tell me he was out up to twenty seconds." The doctor continued filling in paperwork while he was talking. "He's lucky the only damage was a broken arm... and a bit of his pride....

We're satisfied with our observation, so the good news is he can go home as soon as he's had his arm plastered."

It was what Raylee wanted to hear, though the doctor added more instructions. "But for the next forty-eight hours, I want you to monitor him closely. Any dizzy spells, headaches or vomiting, you need to get him back to the nearest hospital immediately."

"I will," she said, agreeing to everything the doctor was telling her. They discussed medication and the sling Cutter would need for his arm when he got home, although Raylee knew that would be a big ask. His ribs would need re-taping in a couple of days and the cuts on his face needed to be kept clean.

After he'd been taken to the plaster room, the doctor signed Cutter's release form and they were able to finally leave. Raylee went to the car and drove it around to the front entrance while one of the hospital staff brought Cutter out in a wheelchair, holding his hat in his lap.

They helped him out of the chair and into the front seat of the car. Raylee laid his seat back so that he was more comfortable and they left the hospital. Little was said on the way home. Cutter tried to sleep while Raylee drove into the early hours of the morning. She kept looking over to see if he was alright, but mostly she drove in silence, not even listening to the radio.

The moon shone brightly onto the vineyard and as Raylee crept the car down the driveway, she could see the trucks and floats at the complex and knew the boys were all home. Although she couldn't see anyone, the lights were on inside the stables and the side door was open wide. She knew they would be inside having a quiet drink, so she kept on driving to the house.

She pulled up close to the path, parking on an angle that would make it easier when she got him out of the car. He was still sleeping soundly when she opened his door, touching him on the leg and calling his name. The pain killers had hit him hard and it was difficult for Raylee to wake him. Finding the seat controls, she slowly brought his seat to an upright position, making him come to.

"Are we home?" he asked in a groggy voice, finding it difficult to open his eyes.

"Yes, and it's cold out here, so I've got to get you inside," she said in a quiet and direct tone. He twisted in the seat so that Raylee could get under his arm to help him stand up.

"Where's my hat?" he asked, as if it were important.

"Don't worry. I've got everything," she assured him.

They walked up the path, taking it slowly and with each movement Cutter gave an agonized moan. Her small frame supported him with each step while he held his broken arm tight to his body.

Once inside the house, Raylee pushed the door behind her, unaware that it didn't close. They walked side by side towards the bedroom, with Cutter limping from what seemed to be a sore leg that he had hidden well from the doctor. The house was deathly quiet until they stumbled into a pot plant, knocking it off its stand and onto the floor, smashing the ceramic on the tiles. It startled them both, but they kept struggling on to the bedroom anyway, ignoring the mess left behind them.

All Cutter wanted to do was lie down and go to sleep. Raylee sat him on the side of the bed while she turned the lamp on and removed some of the pillows. He was careful, spreading out across the bed, making noises of discomfort while she turned the sheets down as far as she could. They hadn't spoken much since that friendly kiss outside the cafeteria and it didn't look like there was going to be much said now.

Even though the remains of the fire were still warm, the room was cooling down. Raylee decided to ignite it again with a few pieces of kindling that were left over from the afternoon. She pulled off his right boot and sock, gently lowering his leg down. Then his left leg, as she was careful not to take his boot off too quickly, using his responses as a guide. She left them in the middle of the floor then climbed up onto the bed and looked down at him. He was looking back at her with glassy, half closed eyes full of pain and tiredness.

"I'm going to take your shirt off now. Is that alright?" she decided to ask first.

"Yeah. Just watch this side," he said, indicating his sore ribs which Raylee already knew about.

She unbuttoned his shirt from the top down. Raylee had already seen him bare chested on the first day, something that she always thought was worthy of another look. She just didn't envisage that it would be this way. The bruising on his ribs was hidden by the tape they had wrapped around one side of him for support.

"It'll be easier if you sit up," she suggested and without waiting for a response, she wrapped his good arm around her neck to help him sit upright. She took his sleeve off, then pulled his shirt behind his back and down over his plastered arm as she knelt on the floor in front of him. "Are you still okay?" she asked, already knowing the answer.

"I'm good," he lied, managing to give her half a grin.

"You know you can't go to bed in those dirty jeans, don't you?" she said, looking up into his face, as she was only trying to take good care of him.

"You've been trying to get my jeans off since the day I arrived. Now here's your chance."

She laughed quietly with him but wasn't about to engage in any comeback, since she wasn't sure if he was being his witty self, or if he was flirting, or if it was because he was under the influence of some heavy medication.

Cutter was still wearing his buckle. It reflected with the flicker of the firelight and since she was kneeling on the floor in front of him, she now got a good look at it. It was his Futurity Champion pride and joy, and Raylee knew that it was the colt that had won him that buckle. She undid it while he leaned on his good arm and stretched backward as much as he could. If Raylee wasn't nervous before, then it suddenly hit her when she had to unbutton and unzip his jeans, and get him to lie down on the pillow so that she could wriggle them off him. In her mind it was happening in slow motion, even though they came off easily and she threw them to the floor, next to his shirt.

He lay back, closing his eyes when Raylee covered him up. She went to the bathroom and a short time later came out with a bowl of warm water and a clean towel. The lamp was shining onto his face and she turned his cheek towards the light so that she could see the graze that had to be kept clean. With his eyes closed, she dabbed it to wipe the blood away.

There was a darkness around the outside of his eye and the graze on his cheekbone was weeping. He opened his eyes and looked at her closely, feeling very guilty. "I'm sorry, Raylee," he apologized, while she kept cleaning his wounds. "I'm sorry for riding that bull."

"We can talk about it tomorrow." She looked at the time. It would be daybreak in only a couple of hours. "Or later in the morning," she added, knowing he was in no fit state to be having that conversation.

He closed his eyes again when she took a clean wet towel to wipe around his neck and down his arms and chest. He was drowsy, although she could tell that he was fighting to stay awake and she kept cleaning his face and body until she was certain he'd fallen asleep.

Upstairs in her room, Raylee went for a quick shower and came back down in her long white robe. After throwing some bigger pieces of wood into the fire, she looked at Cutter sleeping peacefully in the bed. She couldn't leave him in the room alone, since the doctor wanted him monitored, so she propped up a pillow next to him and lay down.

She was beyond tired. It had been a long day and an even longer night, and while she stared at his side profile, as instantly as she closed her eyes, she fell asleep.

It was one of the first sunrises that Cutter had missed and he had no concept of the time after suffering the effects of being drugged. Daylight was faintly lighting the room from the perimeter of the curtains and the fire had now settled into a warm glow.

Raylee woke slowly, temporarily forgetting the night before, until she looked around the room and realized where she was. What was she doing in Cutter's bed? And more importantly, where was he? She sat upright. He was gone. She looked around the empty room. "Cutter," she called out. "Cutter, where are you?"

He opened the bathroom door and turned the light out behind him. "I'm here." He wandered back over to the bed, holding his ribs and walking like a wounded soldier.

"You frightened me," she said when he sat back down, still favoring his left side.

He lay back on the pillow and relaxed again. Raylee could tell that while he was still in pain, the drugs had subsided and the high he was on last night was now gone. He was normal again.

"I can't believe it's past noon. Did you stay here all night?" he asked.

"I couldn't leave you. The Doctor wanted me to keep an eye on you," she said, and she began inspecting the graze on his face closely.

"Did he now?" Cutter was feeling embarrassed and wanted desperately to make it right. "Raylee, I'm really sorry for what happened last night."

Before she would engage in that conversation, she took the bowl of cold water and the bloodied wash cloth. "Hold that thought," she said, and she went to the bathroom and closed the door.

While running the tap warm, she looked into the mirror then cleaned herself up. Raylee always prided herself on looking her best for any situation, and this was one of those times that she wanted to, but clearly couldn't. There was little remaining of her make up, her hair was messy, and she thought to herself that she couldn't look any worse if she tried.

The connection they were starting to make last night before the accident was a long way from where they were three weeks ago. Cutter had been sharing his personal thoughts and feelings, and Raylee had taken in every word. Making herself look as good as she could, she went back out with a fresh bowl of warm water and sat on the bed next to him.

"You know, Cutter, the more we'd been talking, the more I was understanding everything that's weighing on your mind. I totally get what you're feeling at the moment about starting your career again… But riding that bull. I mean, what on earth were you thinking?"

She didn't come across as being angry, although Cutter wasn't sure yet how she felt about it. His eye was darker today than it was last night and more swollen. Though it didn't make his face look ugly. Instead, it gave him that sexy hero look, as if Raylee needed any more persuasion that she was already attracted to him. She took the wash cloth and dipped it in the warm water, then began wiping the graze on his cheek. She loved playing nurse and while she disliked him being hurt, he was hurt, and she was going to make it her job to take good care of him.

"The problem was, I was thinking too much. About everything you said to me earlier. The ranch, my parents, my career." He stopped and looked directly into her eyes and reached into them. "About starting my own family and doing all this for them."

"I know you think that I'm disappointed in you, but I'm actually very proud of you," she reinforced as a comfort, and she stared back at him, catching that look in his eye again and feeling that a connection had been made.

"Why would you be proud of me?"

"For taking a chance to overcome your fear. For seeing an opportunity and taking the bull by the horns..." The intensity of their stare was interrupted when they began to laugh. Cutter held his ribs for extra support. "Oh, that was so lame, wasn't it? I didn't mean to say that. Can I take that back?" she asked, still laughing at her own stupid comments when she was trying to be serious.

"No. I loved that," he said. The laughing was short lived and there was silence again. Raylee thought there was so much more to say about last night. She wanted to open up everything that had replayed in her mind about the rodeo, when he fast tracked past all that and surprised her instead. "And I'd love to kiss you..."

He was asking her permission to kiss her. While it was everything she wanted to hear, she didn't have the voice to say yes. She couldn't speak the words, while her heart was pounding so hard that she thought he may have heard it. He touched her face and leaned up to her, giving a slight inclination that the movement gave him a sharp pain in his side. When he pulled her face into his, she closed her eyes and felt the soft sensation of his lips touching hers. Raylee had been kissed before, but it had never made her feel like this.

Given that he had a deep cut on his lower lip, she took it slowly so as not to cause any reason for him to stop. Their time together, their growing friendship and all their flirting had led them to this kiss, and Raylee wasn't about to let any of it go. She kissed him back and let him know that she wanted this as much as he did.

But he did stop. He pulled back slightly so that he could look at her. "You are seriously driving me crazy," he whispered, and Raylee could see the want in his eyes. Hearing this and feeling his hand touch her leg made her heart race faster, and still lost for words, she leaned in and kissed him again.

The most incredible thoughts were running wild through her mind, as she had already imagined what this moment would be like and now she was experiencing it. It was perfect. She didn't stop kissing him while she repositioned herself on his lap and faced him. What she really wanted now, was for the next move to be his.

He touched behind her neck and ran his fingers down her shoulder, feeling the softness of her skin and making the sleeve of her robe fall down easily. He pulled it open to look at her, taking his time and wanting to slow it down, being totally absorbed in her. She helped him take it off, throwing it to the floor next to his boots, then picked up his hands and placed them carefully on her waist. They didn't speak. For Cutter, her skimpy black pajama set was the only thing between them.

Cutter wasn't about to push Raylee into doing anything that she didn't want to do, but as she leaned into him again, their kiss intensified, and when he pulled her in close, she could feel that he wanted her. Leaning over, she turned out the bedside lamp then rolled in under the covers of the bed and pulled him over with her.

Passion in the Tremayne house was alive.

Outside in the quietness of the driveway, a car pulled in behind Raylee's. A man and woman both got out and looked through her car window as they walked past.

Raylee had left her handbag in the middle console with her phone still attached to the cable. This unusual sight and the angle the car was parked raised an eyebrow.

They walked down the footpath to the front door. It was left ajar, adding to the man's suspicions. He put his finger to his lips and signaled to the woman to keep quiet, and they went inside and looked around. Nothing inside the house looked out of place, except the pot plant knocked to the ground with dirt and broken ceramic spread across the floor and dirty footprints left on the tiles. He then put his hand to his ear, miming to the woman to make a phone call, and he went to the cupboard under the stairs and returned with a rifle.

"Stay here," he said quietly to the woman.

Stepping over the mess on the floor, he followed the footprints into the hallway where they stopped at the closed guest bedroom door. He kept calm, totally confident with his rifle in hand. Whoever was in there was going to see his full rage... if they were still inside.

His heartbeat began to rise.

The man listened before opening the door very slowly and he crept inside, adjusting his eyes to the darkness of the room. The softness of the firelight allowed him to see the clothes that were scattered everywhere across the floor and the bed that gave the impression of an eventful undressing. Two people were in the bed and neither of them were aware they had company.

He stood at the end of the bed and watched momentarily, before he took a step back and cocked his rifle. The noise startled them both. Cutter and Raylee looked wide eyed at each other and the moment was broken. They scrambled. Cutter turned around, protecting Raylee behind him and raising his good arm up at the man like a shield.

Raylee was hiding behind his back. Her legs were still wrapped either side of him with the covers pulled up far enough to hide their sin, though their vulnerabilities were evident.

"Hey, who are you? Put the gun down," Cutter said, in an attempt to reason with the man, but Raylee's father only raised it higher. "You shouldn't be here. If you want money, my wallet's..." He scanned the room and pointed to where Raylee had left his wallet and phone next to his hat on a side table near the door. "... over there. Take everything, but just leave."

Without lowering his weapon, her father walked backwards to the door where he flicked the light switch on. The brightness blinded them both. He reached for the wallet, not taking his eyes off the strangers in his guest room as they were now sitting directly under the spotlight. He opened it up. There was a load of cash, although he wasn't interested in the money.

"Take anything you want. Take everything, but just leave us alone," Cutter pleaded, trying to convince the man.

He walked back slowly to the bed while he went through a few cards and papers, tossing them onto the floor until he found exactly what he was looking for. The identity of who had broken into his house and was fooling around in his guest bedroom. He held it up while he looked at him, then read the name out loud.

"Cutter Jones..."

Raylee was still keeping her head low. When she heard his voice, her eyes opened even wider and taking the courage, she looked over Cutter's shoulder.

"Dad," she said, already knowing what was coming next.

"Raylee?" her father asked, unsure if he'd heard right. "Is that you?"

"Dad?" Cutter repeated, as if he couldn't believe what he had just heard, and he pulled the sheets up higher to make sure they were both well covered.

"Dad, what're you doing here?"

"What am I doing here? What are you doing here... with him?" He raised the rifle towards Cutter who could tell that Raylee's father was immediately more annoyed by the tone of his voice and the direction he was pointing his gun.

"Dad, put the gun down," she demanded of her angry father.

"Would you like to explain to me what's going on here, Raylee?" Her father was now raising his voice, showing his disapproval.

"What do you think's going on here? Now can you put the gun down please," Raylee begged.

Raylee's mother heard the confrontation and hurried into the room. "Raylee?" she asked, then took a step back from the scene and put her hand over her mouth.

"Mom. What the hell are you doing back? And tell him to put that stupid gun down before someone gets hurt."

Cutter was keeping quiet, letting the family dispute unfold when Randall and Jesse ran into the room. "Ohhh crap!" Randall exclaimed to himself when he realized that the phone call from Raylee's mom about a break in, was instead a private moment between his two friends. The four of them now stood close together at the end of the bed.

"Hey, Cutter," Randall said almost too politely, while Jesse stood next to him in silence and couldn't resist a grin.

"Hey," Cutter replied casually.

"This is ridiculous. Will everyone get OUT." Raylee was angry now and she let everyone know it. "And someone take that rifle so that no one does anything they'll regret."

Raylee's father wasn't listening. He was fixed on Cutter and was eyeballing him, his finger firmly on the trigger and the rifle still aimed at his target.

Jesse went to take the rifle out of her old man's hands when it moved and went off, firing a shot into the ceiling. Everyone felt the deafening blast and ducked for cover while white powder fell like dust to the floor, taking time to settle. It left a hole in the ceiling and a ringing in everyone's ears.

Cutter couldn't help but voice his anger at the near miss. "Are you crazy?" he yelled.

It had shocked her father that he had pulled the trigger and he immediately handed the rifle to Jesse before he stormed out of the room, followed by Raylee's mom. Randall and Jesse left also, shaken by the gunshot but entertained by the family commotion. They were pleased there was no break in or thieves to apprehend.

Cutter's body immediately relaxed and all his weight fell back onto Raylee. Her arms were wrapped around him for comfort and relief and she could feel how fast his heart was beating. The seconds ticked by in complete silence.

"I can't believe I just met your parents," he eventually said, then he closed his eyes and rubbed his face in total disbelief.

A shower had never felt so good. Cutter had washed the dirt from his hair, letting the water run over his face, stinging his cuts but soothing his aching body. He held his plastered arm up high against the tiles, keeping it out of the water while not even considering the strapping on his side. He wanted to stay in there all day and hide from Raylee's parents out of embarrassment. Except that he was desperate to see her, and he knew he had to go out and face them sooner or later.

What would he say to Raylee's parents? Should he shake her father's hand and greet her mom with a hug? Would they apologize for rudely interrupting the most special intimate moment he was sharing with their daughter for the first time? Or maybe there would be a car waiting outside to take him back to the airport.

Cutter looked into the mirror and wiped the steam so he could look at his reflection. Taking his razor, he shaved his face, thinking that a clean cut would be more impressive than the rough look he'd been wearing of late. He was comparing the lines around his eyes to a few weeks ago. They were still the same. Really, he was wasting time and delaying coming face to face with the man who nearly shot him. Raylee's angry father.

He was totally consumed with Raylee. Every thought was of her and he was starting to question all these stirred up feelings he had of lust and love, mixed with friendship and sex appeal. He still couldn't believe they had just crossed the line from friends to lovers. This was different from any other girl he'd ever been with and she took his mind to another place, away from Macca, the ranch and the colt.

The colt... That's what he was there for. Not to fall in love with some little Aussie rich girl, who would have no intention of moving away from her privileged life here to some old run-down working ranch a million miles away.

He was driving himself crazy with all these thoughts at once.

Very carefully he pulled on a clean pair of jeans and a white v-neck tee that was more for comfort and convenience rather than for appearance. He didn't want to go out into the kitchen, as he really liked it better when it was just the two of them in the house alone. He listened first, then pulled the handle to see if he was walking into another firing line.

While rooted to the spot, Cutter took a deep breath and puffed out his chest to give the impression that he was confident. Immediately he had to exhale and release the pressure from his ribs, and hunched slightly to his left side to ease the pain. The truth was, he was shit scared.

He walked out to the kitchen and there was no one in sight. He looked into the next room and into the office. It was empty. Out on the front verandah, overlooking the pool and the vines, there was no one to be seen. Where was everyone, he wondered.

He took a glass and held it under the cold water dispenser at the fridge and drank it. The car was gone, but where did they all go? Was Raylee alright? Of course she was alright, she was with her parents. He was now desperate to find her, to see her and talk about what had just happened.

Was it a mistake or was he in love with her? He didn't know what to think, so he went back to his room and lay down on the bed where they had just been together. He could smell her perfume faintly on the pillow and he closed his eyes to try and settle his feelings, eventually drifting into another zone.

Avoiding his cut, Raylee kissed Cutter gently on the side of his mouth and he woke up suddenly. "Where have you been?" he asked.

"Down at the stables with the colt," Raylee explained.

"Why, is he alright?" he asked in a panic.

"He's fine. I just wanted to take him out for a while and I thought you needed the rest."

Cutter was impressed. "What about your parents? What did they say and where'd they go?" he asked all at once.

She knew that her father was seriously angry though she tried not to worry him. "They've gone for a drive... to cool off."

He couldn't stop looking at her. "I can't believe that just happened," he stated.

Raylee kissed him again. "Me neither." She ran her hand over his sore ribs, feeling the tape under his shirt. "Are you sure you're feeling okay?"

"Apart from nearly getting killed by a bull last night and shot by your dad today, I'm doing great," he said with a witty smile, then touched her face. "Raylee?"

"Yes?"

"Do you have any regrets?" he asked.

"Yes. That I didn't lock the door," she said, giving him a fun smile in return.

"I mean about us. Do you have any regrets about us?"

"No, not one. Do you?" she asked for reassurance.

"To be honest, I can't stop thinking about you. About us. And I'm starting to think that I've fallen for you."

They were the words that Raylee longed to hear and although Cutter didn't say the L word, he still said how he felt and her heart boomed from excitement.

Chapter Seven

The complex was much slower the day after the rodeo. The horses had been fed early and some were let out to graze for the day, while it was an afternoon off for the boys. It was quiet when Raylee led Cutter up the stairs to the loft. She had his bag over her shoulder and she threw it onto the end of the bed.

"Well, you said you were happy to sleep in the barn... Now here you are," she said with a touch of humor, feeling on top of the world.

"You know I'm still under forty-eight hour surveillance?" he hinted.

"Oh, I have no intention of going back on my word with that doctor," she said, and she reached up to kiss him again.

The room was cosy. Nothing like the guest room at the house. But for Cutter, it felt more like home. The ceiling was low under the pitch of the stable roof and the timber lining covered all four walls. He looked around at the simple decor and thought how perfect it was.

He also thought that Raylee was perfect, even though she had done very little to impress him three weeks ago. After spending every minute of every day with her, he'd come to know her in a way that he didn't expect. Every ride together, every private detail they shared and their love for the colt, was adding to the intensity that was growing so steadily that he hadn't even noticed it. The way he was feeling about her now was very new to him.

He'd never been short of girls lining up to throw themselves at him and he had the occasional fling after the shows. As for a serious relationship, that wasn't something he had the time or the need for. Just like Raylee had said, he was so busy working and training that relationships didn't fit into his schedule. It was easier to use and be used with no strings attached, then go back home to his life as a trainer and cattleman.

The one thing that Cutter always admired about his father was the way he loved his mom. He adored her and he let the world know it. Cutter never heard them argue once, and they only ever spoke words of love and kindness. His softness towards her made him the strongest man Cutter ever knew and because of that, he never wanted to be with anyone unless he felt that same way.

Was he looking the same way towards Raylee, how Macca looked at his mom? Forgetting Raylee's beautiful smile and soft green eyes, just the touch and smell of her was now driving him crazy.

"I'm lucky your dad didn't drive me to the airport himself," Cutter remarked, thankful that he hadn't.

"So, when do you think you might want to meet them?"

"Never would be too soon," he said, although Cutter knew he was going to have to be a bigger man than that. If there was one thing that his father had taught him, it was to stand tall and be accountable for your actions, no matter what the consequences might be. However, this could well have been the one time he'd rather have got on that plane and gone home. If it weren't for these strong feelings for Raylee, then he might have opted out.

How was he going to explain himself to her father? What could he possibly say that made it alright to freely walk into this man's house and take his only daughter to his bed? The more he thought about it, the more it was making his head spin.

It was now getting late into the afternoon and they decided to take the colt out for a walk, and they both needed some fresh air. Cutter stood outside the stall and watched Raylee throw the colt's rug over the rail and put his halter on. How much had changed since the first day he arrived, he thought, and they walked out the side door, taking the first road around to the vineyard.

The sun seemed to hang still for the longest time and the shadows stretched out lazily on the ground. Cutter held Raylee's hand while she held onto the colt, and the three of them walked through the vineyard and over the cobblestone bridge.

When they heard a car coming up behind them, they left the road and moved onto the grass. It would be one of the boys coming to the complex for the night feed. As it rounded the corner and came into view, they could see it was her father's black BMW. It slowed down and they looked in through the front windscreen, her father giving Cutter the death stare and her mom not looking in their direction at all.

Cutter would barely raise his broken arm to acknowledge them in passing as he held Raylee's hand tight. All he could lip read from her father were the words *"son of a bitch"* and to his relief they kept on driving, speeding up after they passed.

The last thing Cutter wanted right there and then was another confrontation. He still wasn't sure how he was going to explain his way out of this one and it kept playing on his mind. Without telling Raylee, he decided that tomorrow he would make things right.

Cutter wasn't well enough to get back on the colt. He had ridden with a broken arm twice before, both times when he was young. Now it would be his aching ribs that were going to slow him down. He desperately wanted to ride him before he left Australia, only a few more days away. In the meantime, it meant spending more time with Raylee and trying to mend any damages he'd caused within the family.

He rolled over in bed and looked at her. It was another sunrise he'd missed, except this time he didn't care. He watched her sleeping peacefully. Some very early mornings as well as the last three weeks were catching up with her and he knew it. Very carefully folding back the quilt, he slipped out without her knowing and he pulled his jeans on. He would get ready, since he'd already made up his mind that today was the day and the time was going to be now or never.

Her keys were on the bedside table. Picking them up quietly so that they didn't jingle, he managed to sneak downstairs unnoticed. He would drive to the house and face whatever he had to deal with head on. It went through his mind what he was going to say, over and over again, although whichever way he tried to justify it, it didn't make the reasoning any better.

He sat in the car outside the house and stared at it. Inside was a very angry father and he wasn't sure if it was courage or fear that made him walk up the path to the front door. He knocked and stood back, just to be out of arms reach while he waited for someone to answer.

The wait was long and it was almost a relief to think that no one was home. Just as Cutter was about to turn around and walk away, he heard footsteps coming towards the entry. The door swung open and Raylee's father stood there, taken aback that Cutter was standing there facing him.

"Mr Tremayne. I'm Cutter Jones," he introduced himself, and he held his hand out expecting him to shake it.

"I know who you are. Now what do you want?" His reply was harsh and straight to the point, and he had no intention of greeting him as a man does.

"Do you mind if I come in? I'd like to talk to you."

"I doubt that there's much to say." Raylee's father gave no sign of allowing Cutter a chance.

Cutter was running out of begging options. "Please. I'm going home in a few days and I think there's plenty that needs to be said."

Reluctantly, Mr Tremayne stood aside to allow him in and he closed the door hard behind him. They walked to the sitting room in silence, and it reminded Cutter of the one and only time he had to walk to the principal's office to explain why he had cut school. A mare foaling out was not a good enough reason for skipping class, but since he was honest about it, the principal gave him a warning and it never happened again. Cutter was hoping for the same response from Raylee's father today.

It seemed very official. In the time spent at the house, Cutter had never seen her father's private sitting room and he figured it must have been used for formal business meetings. It was decked out with big leather chairs, a whiskey bar, photos of a young Mr Tremayne on his cattle property riding horses and a lifetime of achievements which decorated the walls.

He looked around after he took a seat and thought that this was her father's way of intimidating him even more than he already was.

"Mr Tremayne. I need to apologize for what happened yesterday. I'm sorry for..."

"I'll tell you what I think," he interrupted. "I think you're sorry you got caught."

Well that was true.

"I know what you saw must be every father's worst nightmare, but..."

"Allan. Who are you talking to?" Raylee's mom walked into the room and was surprised to see Cutter there.

"It's alright, Evelyn. We're nearly done here," her husband said, without taking his eyes off Cutter.

Cutter stood up a bit too fast and his ribs caught his breath. "Mrs Tremayne... 'Morning." He didn't know what else to say yet he knew it was polite to greet her on his feet. She didn't answer, although the corners of her mouth turned upward into a forced smile that was her way of saying hello, even though Cutter knew it wasn't a sign of her approval.

Allan Tremayne stood up too. He was a bigger man. Strong looking, and he was much younger than Cutter's own father was. He dressed like a business man too, standing opposite Cutter in his jeans and boots... Oh Shit, he thought. He had forgotten to take his dirty boots off... that he could see why Allan Tremayne wouldn't want his daughter with a cowboy like him.

"If you think that anything good can come of this, then you're sadly mistaken, son. My daughter belongs here on this property and has been raised the decent way, and I don't see you fitting into her life here or anywhere else for that matter." He spoke like a business man. While not raising his voice, he was speaking with an authority that Cutter knew most people wouldn't challenge.

Evelyn was keeping quiet. It was obvious to Cutter that either she agreed with her husband, or she was not one to challenge him. He looked into her face and saw an older Raylee.

He wasn't sure what he could possibly say to make it right as it seemed Allan Tremayne had made up his mind and would close all doors. "And if you weren't so banged up and all, you'd have been gone from here yesterday," he said, referring to his injuries.

Cutter knew that he'd lost this battle and no explanation would change that. He thought about telling them that he loved their daughter, but even that was so new to him that he didn't want to come across like a love sick teenager. He stood tall. "Thank you for your time Mr Tremayne... I'll see myself out." He walked past Evelyn Tremayne and left the room.

Cutter walked up the stairs to the loft and looked into the room. Raylee was still in bed, lying there awake. She had a feeling he'd gone to the house and she was sick from worry.

"I would have gone with you," she said when she sat up.

"No." He sat on the edge of the bed next to her. "I had to deal with your parents myself. I wasn't about to hide behind you to get me out of this."

"So what did they say?"

"Put it this way. I think your father will be happy when I've gone home this week. He wants to see the back of me."

"I'll talk to him."

"It won't do you any good. Your father has other plans for your life and he made it quite clear that I didn't make the grade." Cutter didn't sound dejected, though was more realistic. "Raylee, I'm going home in a few days and I want you to come with me," he said, ignoring her father's expectations. The invitation brightened her up immediately, giving her the reassurance that he was wanting to take their relationship further. "You know I can't stay here. I've gotta get home," he added.

"I know you have."

"When I picked up that phone and called you, I had no intention of coming here. My life had been put on hold long enough. But I came here to do a job and now I need to get back... I just wasn't expecting us..."

She understood this was always going to be the case. She was never disillusioned to think that he'd just pack up and leave the only life he knew for her life in Australia. Still, she too had responsibilities to take care of and she was confused about how it could possibly work.

"I can't go with you," she began to say, and Cutter felt his heart sink. "But when I get a few things sorted out around here, I'll come and visit."

It was good enough, since he understood her situation. He touched her face and reached over and kissed her. Neither of them knew what they could do to make it work, but for the next couple of days they had to put it aside, only focusing on the colt and their time together.

Cutter was still too sore to ride, leaving Raylee to take the colt on the trail rides up in the National Park. She explored different trails and while she hated being on the ride alone, it gave her the time to revisit the events of the last month. When she looked back to when Cutter first came to the property, she could see the change in herself. Raylee had no idea that things would turn out the way they did, and Cutter had changed her in ways that even he would never know.

When she reached an open plateau half way up the mountain, she looked out over the property. It was only because of Cutter that she had discovered her home from this angle and it made her love it even more.

The complex stood out in the center, surrounded by black rail fences that were divided into small yards. Horses grazed and cattle stood idle, ready to be worked in the arena. On the other side, she could see the house. Her mom had the fire burning to keep warm, and she knew the house would be empty without her. She was very close to her parents and they had been looking forward to seeing her when they arrived home from overseas.

She took it all in, the vineyard adding that romance to an already spectacular setting. There was no other place in the valley that would compare to what she had in front of her, and she wondered if Cutter's ranch had the same appeal.

As she rode on, the colt felt strong underneath her and she wanted to see what he could do. Tomorrow would be the day they'd all find out. It would also be the last day that she would have with Cutter. Her heart was heavy. By tomorrow afternoon, she would be driving into the city to the airport.

Why did things have to be so complicated? Wasn't love supposed to be easy? She rode home, taking the time to clear her head and wanting to stretch the last two days out as far as possible.

The stables were quiet and when she rode back to the complex, she could see all the boys were in the arena. They had several horses saddled up and tied to the rails, taking one at a time into the mob of cattle. Cutter was sitting in one of the corners on a horse, slightly slumped over and protecting his side. He wasn't looking world class, even though everyone there knew that he was. He not only had their respect as the best horse trainer in the world, they now labelled his bull ride as one of the best they had ever seen.

Raylee sat on the colt and watched.

If the boys weren't handling and breaking in young horses, then they were exercising and keeping the others in good shape ready for sale or breeding. Randall had also trained a few successful and competitive roping horses and would teach the younger boys how it was done. Everything worked like clockwork.

They all knew their roles and had their strengths. There was a lot of upkeep on the property and there wasn't any spare time when there was nothing to do. Since Cutter had arrived, Raylee had allowed them to practice more often in the arena than usual, making the most of his talent and benefiting the future of the business.

With so much time spent with the horses this last month, it meant less time in the vineyard. After Cutter left, she knew everyone would be hands on catching up, especially now her mom was home. She considered whether she would be missed there. Raylee knew deep down that if she stepped away, everything would continue as usual. Her job of overseeing everything within the four boundary fences could be done away with, or she'd be easily replaced by someone else.

She rode over to Cutter. He was focusing on Jesse's ride and was giving him instructions from the corner. She pulled the colt up next to him and without looking at her, he reached over and touched her butt without breaking his concentration.

When Jesse turned away from the cow and walked back into the mob, Cutter gave Raylee a warm smile and he leaned over as best as he could and kissed her smack on the lips. He didn't care that the boys were all there. Besides, they'd seen them in bed together anyway, and now Cutter was going to take every opportunity he could with only two days left, just the way Macca was with his mom.

"You just missed your dad," he said.

Raylee was surprised. "What, he came down here?"

"He was just looking from the fence."

"What did he want?"

"Don't know. He only stayed a few minutes and then left."

Raylee hoped more than anything, that her father had second thoughts and had come down to apologize before Cutter left the following day. She hadn't seen her parents since she'd moved into the loft and while Cutter thought it was a better idea if she stayed at the house, Raylee felt that her father was treating her like a child and that he needed to recognize her as an adult. Cutter could see that there was going to be a standoff, and that only time and his flying back home were going to fix it.

"Are you going back to the house after I leave tomorrow?" he asked, implying that it was a good idea.

She was not committing. "That depends."

"On what?"

"On how well they take it when I tell them that I'm going over to see you and stay a while."

"Which nothing would make me more happy if you did. But you really need to sort this out with them first, before you come over."

"Then I might not ever see you again..."

Jesse was coming out with half the herd in front of him, and Raylee went back to the stables leaving Cutter in the corner to push them back.

Chapter Eight

The horses were all fed and settled into their yards and stalls for the night. The stables had quietened down and the lights were dimmed. Raylee felt emotional, knowing that this was going to be the last night she had with Cutter, at least for a while. She decided that they should do something away from the complex.

While Cutter took a shower downstairs, Raylee slipped home unnoticed to get ready. Her parents were in the house and she had no other way in except through the front door and directly past them both.

Her father was sitting on the couch, reading the newspaper. "Has your boyfriend gone home?" he asked with hopeful sarcasm.

"Tomorrow," she answered abruptly.

"And when do you think you'll be home?"

"When you start treating me like an adult and not like a child."

"I'll treat you like an adult, Raylee, when you start acting like one," he said, firing up again.

Her mother was standing in the kitchen. "Your father's only got your best interests at heart, Raylee. Can't you see that? We both have," she pleaded.

"If you had my best interests at heart, then you'd be happy for me." Raylee was annoyed and stood her ground.

"What, happy that some cowboy from Texas has swept you off your feet and into his bed? I'm sorry, Raylee, but I find nothing happy about that," her father said sternly.

She was not winning any part of the argument and it was wasting the precious time that she had left with Cutter. "I can't do this right now." She rushed up the stairs to her room. "You're both impossible," she yelled out, and she slammed the door behind her.

"Allan. I don't believe we're wrong here. But she doesn't need us telling her that she is." Evelyn spoke quietly and with control.

"What do you want me to do, Evelyn? Let her think that it's okay to bring his kind into our house and take advantage of her like that?"

"No, of course not. But she's not seeing it through your eyes, is she? As a father."

"The son of a bitch... I should've shot him when I had the chance," he said.

"And we'd be having a whole different discussion right now, wouldn't we?"

Upstairs in her bedroom, Raylee was going through her wardrobe looking for something to wear. She took items of clothing off the rack, holding each one up against her while looking into the mirror, screwing her nose up at everything and tossing it aside, until she pulled out a short skirt that she hadn't worn for a while.

This is the one. Finding a matching top and a pair of heeled boots, she went for a shower so as not to waste any more time.

She did, however, take the time to apply her makeup and do her hair. Every day for the last month she had worn a hat, so she decided to style her hair and curl the ends to make it softer and fuller around her face. With a spray of her favorite perfume, she took one last parade in front of the mirror and was confident that she was going to knock Cutter's socks off.

She went back downstairs, uninterested in another debate with her parents. When she walked past them, she avoided looking in their direction and could hear her father grumble under his breath.

"Don't say a word, Allan. Just let her go," her mother insisted.

She drove back to the complex, knowing that Cutter would be waiting for her. He was sitting on a chair in the corner of the room with his boot crossed over his knee, reading under the lamp. Raylee stood in the doorway, the softness of the light only magnifying her sexy new look. He didn't speak. He put the magazine down and walked over to her. She looked stunning and it took his breath away.

"Are you ready to go?" she asked.

He picked up her hands and stared down into her eyes. The grazes on his face were the evidence of his bull ride and his blackened eye was still looking fresh. He reached down and kissed her.

"You look amazing," he stated, and Raylee knew from his kiss that he was blown away.

"Thank you," she said, playing it down. "So, are we ready?"

"We could just stay here all night, if you like," he suggested, and he began to walk backwards into the room still holding onto both her hands.

Raylee pulled him away from the bed. "That's a promise. After you take me out on a date."

He couldn't take his eyes or his hands off her, but he would take her out on a date on the last night before going home. "I can't believe I'm going home tomorrow," he said.

"Let's not talk about it. I don't even want to think about tomorrow."

They grabbed their jackets and went downstairs, Cutter never letting go of his girl and Raylee feeling protected. They drove to the restaurant. After three short minutes, they pulled up in the car park.

"Why are we going here?" he asked.

"Why not? I wanted you to see it before you left and I know you like the food."

Cutter hadn't met the chef before but was impressed with every meal he'd had since he arrived at the property. The restaurant was small and had the Tremayne stamp all over it. The signage, the presentation and the bottles of wine. It was intimidating to say the least, although Cutter didn't show it. From the outside, it looked like an old farm house. On the inside, it opened up with small intimate tables set in front of a grand open fireplace. The timber beams held old tack and the walls were lined with framed photos and charm from yesteryear. The crisp white linen reminded him of the guest bedroom. Everything was placed perfectly and was of the very best Tremayne quality.

"Miss Raylee, your table is ready," the waiter said and he led them to a table set for two, to the left side of the fireplace. He was very professional and quite proper, handing them both a menu and placing their napkins over their laps. At first, Cutter thought that the restaurant was well suited to him, until he looked at the menu and couldn't read a word on it.

"You know, if I had of known we were coming here, I would have gone out and bought myself a suit," he said, being his witty self again.

"You look great just the way you are. You know, Cutter, I wouldn't change anything about you," she complimented, giving him the reassurance that she loved him exactly the way he was.

But would she love the ranch? Cutter knew that he didn't belong in Raylee's world. The property, the complex, the vineyard, and reading the menu only reinforced to him that he would never fit in there.

"Where's the steak and fries?" he asked, still reading the menu. He put it down and looked at her. "Well, you said you wouldn't change anything about me."

The waiter came back over when he noticed they were ready, with pen and paper in hand. "We'll have two steaks and fries please," Raylee ordered. "And two waters."

He didn't question Raylee. He didn't repeat it and he didn't even write it down. The look on his face said it all and they laughed when he left.

The restaurant was starting to fill up, mostly with couples and small groups with enough space between them to keep it private. A candle flickered in the center of the table and a woman sang while she played a guitar in the far corner of the room.

They kept it simple, not discussing tomorrow and not mentioning Raylee's parents. Over dinner they shared their passions. Cutter talked about resuming his career and how they ran their cattle program back home. Raylee talked about the complex and her business plans for the colt. He gave her some ideas to consider and she knew they'd make one good business team, except that geographically, she also knew that this would be impossible.

After they finished dinner, Cutter wanted to take Raylee back to the loft. He had looked at her across the table all night and was now wanting to complete the evening with the perfect ending to a perfect month.

They walked out to the car. It was a clear night and they stopped to look at the spectacular starry sky. "How on earth did this happen?" he asked, holding her close and keeping her warm.

"How did what happen?"

"When I needed to be at home picking up the pieces of my life and my career, you managed to get in between all of that and get me here. Now look at us."

She was pleased that she was in the middle of everything that was going on in his life, and she knew there was only one way she'd manage to stay there.

"I can't believe it either... Do you really want me to visit you back home?"

"I want you to come on the plane with me tomorrow." Cutter knew that wasn't going to be an option, although it pleased Raylee to hear him say it anyway.

She kissed him. "We'd better go. You're going to be so tired in the morning," she said, sounding very concerned for him.

"Why?" he asked.

Her playful giggle was teasing. "Because I'm planning on keeping you up all night."

Cutter woke up the next morning before Raylee. Their sleep time was short, just like she promised. She was still snuggled into him, with his broken arm stretched out on the bed and his good arm wrapped around her. Listening, he could hear her breathing and was torn between wanting to go home to the ranch, and wanting to stay with her.

Four weeks ago, Cutter had imagined that it would be the colt that he'd have trouble saying goodbye to. He never expected it would be a girl who would have such a hold over him. His connection with the colt was still as strong as ever, but now it was Raylee who was consuming his every thought.

Even though he had little sleep, he was awake and fired up to go for a ride. He needed Raylee to take the colt out first, then he would take over once in the arena. In the stillness of the room, she could feel him tickle her arm and she opened her eyes, still living in the moment from the night before. Her head was resting between his shoulder and chest, and she'd have preferred to stay there feeling his touch and listening to every heartbeat. Conscious of the hours they had left, Raylee knew that Cutter needed to finish what he came there to do, and that was, ride the colt.

Before they went downstairs, Raylee took the strapping off Cutter's ribs. The bruising looked painful and she could see the line from the metal panel of the fence on his skin. He had hit it hard and she couldn't understand how he'd got away without any breaks. All she could do now was reapply the tape, making sure it was firm.

They had missed another sunrise, yet it was still quite early when Cutter went down to the colt while Raylee was getting dressed. The boys had been turning up one at a time and the stables once again became a hive of activity. Ryan and Jesse took the horses out to bring the cattle in, while Randall and Tyler were preparing the sand in the arena.

When Raylee arrived downstairs, Cutter, with some help, already had the colt saddled up for her to ride. She kissed him, then rode out the side door, deciding that a ride through the vineyard was exactly what she needed. Wanting to take it all in, she rode through the rows of vines and around the dry creek bed, admiring everything around her. It was her home and she loved it. As much as she wanted to be with Cutter, she wondered how anyone could lure her away from the beauty of the property. But he was. He was wanting her to go to Texas to be with him, and she would have to give it all up if she were to follow him home. In her mind, she'd already made her decision.

When the colt was warm, she rode back to the complex. Cutter adjusted the length of the stirrups and took to the saddle.

"Do you feel alright?" she asked, referring to his newly strapped ribs.

"Let's find out."

He rode around the outside of the arena close to the rails, putting the colt through his series of exercises. Raylee joined the boys in the corners, all sitting on horses, watching and taking in any last minute tips they could see. They knew this wasn't where the magic happened. Nevertheless, they still watched every move he made.

Raylee could tell that Cutter was in pain. She also knew that he wanted to see this job through to the end and would endure whatever pain he was in. He rode the colt in a tight sequence, testing his responses. His short bursts of speed and sudden stops were a mere routine that the colt seemed to know as well as Cutter.

He hit the right spots and when he felt the colt was ready, he gave a nod to the boys.

He tried to sit tall in the saddle, which was not easily done, and rode down the side of the arena close to the rail. The herd were settled and he took a deep cut from the back wall, nudging his way through slowly and moving them aside one at a time. Jesse and Tyler pushed onto the cattle, helping him make a clear cut with one cow, and when it turned to look for the mob, it looked the horse in the eyes.

Cutter put his hand down, full of anticipation. The horse lowered himself into position, his ears twitching, ready to make a move. Like lightning, the cow ran across the pen trying to return to the mob and the colt responded with precision. He blocked it at the turn and retreated with it back across the pen towards the middle.

Raylee was holding her breath, not only for the colt, but for every sharp sudden stop that Cutter was feeling. While she was anxious for him, she was also confident that he'd do the job. Nose to nose with the cow down at eye level, both were excited and equally fast. They were having a good ride.

The colt was all over it, making every maneuver look effortless, swooping low and showing off, with Cutter pushing his buttons and the cow testing his abilities. When the cow stopped suddenly and looked away, Cutter pulled up the reins and went back into the herd for his second cut.

Out the corner of her eye, Raylee saw her father. He was standing on the rail near the stables, watching from a distance. She wasn't sure how long he'd been there and her nerves had just deepened to a sickly feeling.

For Cutter, he was amidst the cattle, focusing on his next cow and eliminating the ones he didn't want. He picked a light red cow and positioned it to be among the last three out front. The boys came in from the corners and only one ran back to the herd. Cutter made the jump and spooked both cows that were left and they separated, leaving the red cow standing alone. He put his hand down and gripped tight.

The cow made short runs and the colt was quick to keep up. He kept his head down and faced him square on. With every run, Cutter had the colt do exactly as he was trained, his fast sharp turns were mirror imaged to perfection. He was kicking ass, while the colt had some big stops that even Raylee had never seen him do before. Cutter pulled him up and went back into the herd for his third and final cut, taking a cow from the top.

Raylee was keeping one eye on her father and the other eye on Cutter. She was impressed with his ride and was sure that her father would be too, and by the end of his run, Raylee let out a sigh of relief. Her tense body released and she began to relax. She looked over towards the stables to see that her father had gone. Without giving him another thought, she was more interested in talking to Cutter and reliving the last two and a half minutes.

"He was awesome," Raylee said with a rush of excitement.

"Wow, that felt amazing," he exclaimed, showing every bit of how pleased he was. "He never put a foot wrong."

"See what happens when you put the best trainer on the best horse... You totally smashed it."

With the fresh cattle still in the arena, the boys continued riding while Raylee and Cutter took the colt back to the stables and unsaddled him.

Once he had cooled down they gave him a wash, just like they did together a month ago.

"Before we put him in his stall, I'd like to take him for a walk," Cutter requested.

"Sure. Let's do it now," she replied enthusiastically.

"I mean, just me. If you don't mind." Cutter gave Raylee a look that told her that he needed to say his goodbye in private.

She understood. "I'll be here when you get back."

He led the colt out through the breezeway, while Raylee stood outside the tack room and watched them go. It was heartbreaking for her, watching a man and his beloved horse spend their last minutes together.

It made her emotional to think what Cutter had been through in the last three years. To have said goodbye to the colt, then to his father and now he'd be saying goodbye to her in a couple of hours, and she wondered how this broken cowboy was so strong.

The trip back to Sydney was nothing like the day he arrived. All those unsure feelings Cutter had a month ago seemed so far in the distant past, that he could barely remember them.

The mood in the car was flat. They talked about the colt and what last minute suggestions Cutter had for Raylee to follow. He explained how he'd ridden him every day, not only in the pen but also on the ranch, checking cattle and repairing fences. He was a cutting horse first, as well as his work horse. There wouldn't have been too many times he'd have left him behind in the barn, especially on a roundup.

Raylee could see that he needed to be out and ridden. She had wrapped him up in cotton wool and done everything she could to protect her investment, when really, all he wanted was to be out and free. To be a horse.

It was tempting for Raylee to turn the car around and take Cutter back home to the property, as she was very conscious of the minutes ticking away. They drove into the airport and had already decided before they arrived that Raylee would pull up in the drop zone to make the final goodbye quick and easy. She left the car running and they both went around to the back to get his bag. Standing on the edge of the sidewalk, Raylee leaned on the car with a tear starting to build. Cutter looked at her and dropped his bag, then hugged her tight. He felt the same way. He couldn't find the words that would make their separation any easier and the silence said everything they already knew.

"I love you," he said.

It made the tear swell and fall onto her cheek. She wanted Cutter to say it first and he did. "And I'm so in love with you," she said, giving him the reassurance that he really didn't need.

He held her face and kissed her passionately, only breaking away to pick up his bag and walk through the automatic doors. But not before he promised to call as soon as he arrived home.

He was gone.

Chapter Nine

The taxi pulled up outside the house. Cutter had sat in the back seat from the airport, not wanting to engage in any conversation with the driver. His head was constantly full with thoughts of Raylee and he closed his eyes and kept silent, for fear of blurting out the events of the past month to a total stranger.

He still wasn't sure if he would even tell Marnie just yet. Wanting to keep these feelings he had deep inside, he knew that when the timing was right he'd be able to share her with everyone.

Cutter closed the door of the car while the driver put his bag on the porch then drove away, leaving him to look over at the barn and the horse yards. Taking in the view of everything he loved, he took a deep breath. He was home.

As he looked around he noticed there was so much to do. Everything was exactly how he'd left it, except that the air was warmer and spring was well underway.

He hoped to get the filly back into her training program as soon as possible and trusted that Johnny had taken her for rides when he was there checking the cattle. But it was her hours in the cutting pen that he needed to pick up on, if he wanted to stay on track for this year's Futurity comeback.

When he walked up the steps to the front door, for the first time he took his boots off, leaving them neatly to one side. Cooper looked up at him and he greeted her with a rub around her ears. The sounds in the kitchen were familiar, and there was Marnie, standing over the stove, stirring a pot and reading her recipe book.

"Smells good," he complimented, then dropped his bag onto the floor.

"Good Lord. You're home." She turned the stove down and rushed over to hug him. Marnie didn't show affection to him very often, though this was one time that she couldn't contain herself and Cutter needed it too.

"Ahh," he gasped, when she squeezed him a little too tight.

"What is it?" she asked with concern, then noticed the plaster. "Have you broken your arm?"

"Yes ma'am... And bruised my ribs."

"Sit down here," Marnie insisted, and she pulled a chair out from the kitchen table. "Did you fall off the colt?" she asked, while closely inspecting the graze on his face.

"Actually, it was a bull."

"What? What were you doing riding a bull?"

"It's a long story, Marnie, and I promise I'll tell you later. Right now I'd love any leftovers you've got in the fridge. That plane food sucks."

She immediately went to the fridge and pulled out a dish. Marnie never said no to whatever Cutter requested, not even as a little boy. She popped it in the microwave and prepared him a plate and a glass.

"So tell me... how's the colt?" she asked, as she leaned on the kitchen counter.

"He's great. Wow that horse is smart and fast," Cutter said, thinking back to his last ride yesterday.

"Did that girl have any idea what she was doing with him?"

"She was doing what she thought was right." Cutter was half defending her.

"Yeah, well it sounds to me like she had no idea. More money than sense, I'd say."

Cutter didn't respond. It wasn't the right time for him to explain his feelings to anyone and he let Marnie continue. "No one would ever take care of that horse the way you did."

"Actually, Marnie, she was taking better care of him and that was the problem."

She looked at him totally confused, although she didn't press it any further. "It's so good to have you home. The house was too quiet without you here."

Cutter could tell that Marnie had genuinely missed him. "I needed to get back... I need to pick up on the last three years and start over again."

Marnie turned around and picked up an envelope that was hidden among her recipe books, then pulled out a chair next to Cutter and handed it to him. It had his name written on the front. "I was cleaning out your father's room while you were gone... I found this for you." She touched his arm. "You should take your time. Don't read it until you're ready."

Cutter's heart felt heavy again, as if it hadn't been weighing enough already. He didn't expect this at all. With the time he had left with his dad, he thought they had said everything they needed to say. Now Macca would have the last word.

"Thanks Marnie," he said quietly, and he stared down at Macca's handwriting. It looked shaky.

She looked at him holding the envelope. "Your parents would be so proud of you, Cutter. You were the apple of your mom's eye and the man that Macca wanted you to be." It was something that only an elderly woman would say and it meant so much to him. Marnie was the only person that knew his parents as well as he did, and that would always bond them together.

"What would Macca do right now?" he asked for her thoughts.

She didn't hesitate. "Well, I'd say he would be out on a horse and checking the heifers out the back. We've got a few calves on the ground this last week," she announced.

This lifted his spirits. The thought of new life on the ranch was always the highlight of spring. "I think I'll unpack later and go to the barn... See what I've been missing," he said, eager to see the filly again.

The timer on the microwave went ding. "Not before you have something decent to eat," Marnie insisted, and she went to serve him a plate.

Cutter stood on the porch and pulled his boots on, having had full intentions of going to the barn. He crouched down beside Cooper, giving her a rub around the ears and her droopy eyes closed from his gentle touch. The porch held good memories for him, as his mom had been there to greet him many times throughout the day. Her favorite place was without a doubt the swing, and Cutter felt close to her every time he sat on it. He could waste time lost in his own thoughts and he took the time now to sit on it and he began to sway.

He missed his mom. Not ever having the chance to say goodbye to her was what ate him up the most. She would stay beautiful and forever young in his memory. It was so long ago now and it was Macca who remained fresh in his mind.

He pulled the envelope out of his back pocket and opened it. He rubbed his face with his good hand, to help prepare himself for what he was about to read. While Macca always had a nice hand, Cutter could tell that it was written later in his illness as he had clearly lost that neat hand.

Cutter,

When you first came to the ranch, you were quiet and shy, just like your mom. But that smile said more to me than any words ever could. At your first riding lesson, you held onto me for dear life and from that moment on, I felt like I was your father.

You grew up into a great kid, with the talent that sure surpassed any of my ability, and I knew early on that you had the makings of being better than the best.

I never knew anyone who had the drive and determination that you did, and you lived every day to be with those horses. Your mom and I were so proud of your achievements. If only she could see how far you've come now.

I can't begin to tell you how thankful I am that you were there for me when I needed you the most. I know you sacrificed your career for me, and it showed me just what a special son you are. Lessons of love, loss and sacrifice, are the lessons that make us who we are. Take them on and they'll make you a stronger man.

This ranch meant everything to me, as it does to you, and your mom gave me every reason to wake up and go to work each day. She was my reason for living, and I want you to know that I loved her more than life itself.

Cutter, what ever you do in your life, at the heart of everything, be a good man. Time will pass you by, so take every opportunity you have been given and make the most of every day.

Take good care of the ranch. Find your Mary-Ann. And love well.

I love you son,

Your dad, Macca

Cutter leant forward, putting his head in his hands and sobbed. It was the first time he'd let go of his grief and he needed to get it out. It was everything he needed to hear from the one person who he owed everything to, and he couldn't control the sadness that he'd held in for so long. He folded the letter and put it back into the envelope and leaned back on the swing, finding a rhythm that finally soothed his heartache.

Thoughts ran through his mind of his mom, of Macca and of Raylee. He felt the need to call her as he promised he would when he arrived home. With his grief too overpowering, he sent her a message instead.

Hey Raylee. Just got home. Everything here is ok. I miss you and love you. Call you soon. Cutter x

He needed to hear her voice. But with the weight of the world resting heavily on his shoulders and the need for some head space first, he would wait to call her a while longer.

Instead of going to the barn, he went upstairs and walked past his parents' room. He looked in. It was where Macca had passed away. The last place he saw him. Cutter had sat on the bed holding his father's hand when he took his last breath, and he stood in the doorway and relived that final moment.

Marnie had cleaned it up and it looked exactly how it always did, with his mother's handmade quilt and both their personal items still in place. It gave him some comfort and he wasn't sure if he'd ever change it. He went next door to his room.

It had changed over the years. From a toddler bed with cowboy pictures on the walls and toys everywhere, through his teenage years with colorful ribbons that he had won at shows, to the room it was today. He threw his bag onto the bed and started to unpack. The walls were now lined with a few photos of the ranch and a couple from his early days of competing. In the corner was a saddle sitting on a wooden stand. It was a prize he'd won at his second Futurity as a professional trainer when he took the honors for a client. He walked over to it and felt the smooth leather. It had never been on a horse.

His favorite item in the room was a handcrafted display box that Macca had made for his buckles. Of all the spaces, he only had one more buckle to win and it would be full. Except for his favorite, which he'd won on the colt and wore every day since. He wondered if he'd ever be able to win another buckle or if those days were now behind him. Cutting had been his life, although there was one buckle that he'd won from a bull ride many years ago and it made him think of that crazy decision to get back on.

He looked around the room. It was a far cry from the guest room that he'd been staying in at the Tremayne house, the room where Raylee shared his bed for the very first time. To Cutter, this was his space, full of his comforts, and it was everything that he knew. He changed into his work jeans and went back downstairs where Marnie was cleaning up.

"Hey Marnie. Next time you go to town, do you think you could buy some more pillows?" he asked.

"Why, something wrong with the ones you've got?"

"No. I just want a few more," he said, without offering a reason.

She didn't question him after that and he went out to the porch. It was getting late but he needed to go to the barn to check on the filly. It was the only investment he had in the cutting horse world until the new foals were on the ground and the older foals were broken in. Every other horse was either too old or was used solely for cattle work.

He walked into the barn. It smelt like home. Everything about this place was perfect. Not in a Tremayne kind of way but in a Jones kind of way, and it was exactly how he'd left it. The smell of the barn and of the hay was ingrained in him, and Cutter always felt that this ranch and this barn defined who he was.

The filly was standing in her stall. He walked in and unbuckled her rug, then ran his hand over her while he talked quietly. She stood still and wasn't bothered by his presence, unlike the colt who knew Cutter by sight, sound and touch.

She was in good shape and was shiny and clean. He leaned over with a hint of pain and ran his hand down her legs. He picked up each hoof, then looked her all over. He gave her a brush, although she didn't need it, just to give himself something to do. He was grateful that Johnny had looked after her so well and tomorrow he'd take her out for a ride. Right now, he couldn't sit in the house all alone and drive himself crazy.

He found little jobs to do, just to fill in the time. He sat on a bale of hay and cleaned his saddle. It hadn't been done for so long and it was in desperate need of attention. Never had he felt lonely on the ranch, even when he was in the barn on his own. Now for the first time, he had the sense that he needed company. While his mind was a million miles away, he rearranged the tack room and refilled the feed bins, keeping busy until it was late.

That night he lay in bed, tired from the trip and from the events of the last month. He tried to stay up as late as he could, to adjust to the time he'd lost in travel. Drowning himself in thoughts of Raylee, he drifted off, content that he was home.

Before sunrise, Cutter was again at the barn, admiring how his saddle looked. There was nothing to do, as he had done everything the night before. He took the filly out of her stall and saddled her up. All his hopes were riding on her and he didn't want to waste any more time in getting back into a regular training program.

It felt good being home. As impressive as the Tremayne complex was, it wasn't his. His barn was special to him and held many memories that could never be replaced. He sat in the saddle and rode out, feeling the coolness of the early morning breeze around his face.

Riding out through the first gate was like being free again. Nothing compared to how he felt when he looked back down towards the house. He would do this every time he went for a ride, just to reassure himself of his love for the ranch. It had a ruggedness about it that only a true cowboy could appreciate.

Everything on the ranch was now regenerated and there was no shortage of feed and water. When Cutter slowed the cattle program down last season to take better care of Macca, it was to give himself more time with his dad. Now he needed to re-invest into more stock. But things were so tight that he had to be careful not to overextend the rising debts, and add more pressure to the ranch that he didn't need.

Riding along the fence lines and checking the dams for their water levels, he made mental notes of trees that had fallen and of fences that needed straining, before riding to the larger pasture of young steers. They were in good shape and had been sheltered well during the winter, and were fattening nicely now on the spring feed. He did a quick head count.

Riding further out the back, the filly was feeling strong. More cattle grazed, unfazed by his presence, even when he rode in amongst them. The filly was quite interested when he brushed her close by, weaving her in and out of the mob. It was tempting for him to pull one out and give her a run, yet he would test her patience a little while longer.

Finally, he made it to the back of the ranch, diverting away from the field of flowers and the resting place. He wasn't ready to go there just yet, knowing that it would dampen his mood. Marnie was right. The heifers were calving out and he counted at least sixteen on the ground. Tiny calves were staying close to their moms, suckling from fright when they saw Cutter riding towards them. It warmed his heart. He loved this sight, almost as much as watching a mare with a new foal, but not quite.

He sat on the filly silently and watched. The calves stayed close, but with a little time, they ventured away playfully running, losing interest in Cutter and his horse. He checked the heifers that were still to calve and counted them as best as he could. Another forty-six. Still a long way to go.

Leaving them to play and lazily lie in the warm morning sun, he rode back home the other side along the boundary fence that joined his ranch to Johnny's, still noting the jobs that needed attention over the next few weeks and looking at which mobs he would bring to the yard for his next cut.

It felt like he had been away for an eternity, and being home made him feel that his ranch life was just beginning all over again. As the long days stretched out into nights and back into days again, Cutter kept busy tending to the running of the ranch as well as catching up on some general maintenance, and preparing the filly for her last stint of intense training. He had talked to Raylee on the phone twice since he arrived home, and both times only reinforced his love for her. She was still consuming his thoughts, even though he had a job to do with the responsibilities resting solely on him now.

It was late in the afternoon when Cutter came into the house for lunch, although it was more like an early supper. Marnie always had something prepared, for his schedule never had any kind of regular routine to it. Though he didn't look tired, he was possibly feeling emotionally run-down more than anything else and Marnie could tell that he was low.

Looking at the table, he noticed that she had it set with two plates. Cutter never thought about Marnie being lonely. She'd never eaten with the family before but since it was just the two of them now, he agreed that she should start.

He went to the fridge. "You feeling a bit lonely, Marnie?" he asked, referring to the table.

"Me? No, I think it's you who's lonely. I've been on my own since before you were born. It's you who I thought could do with some company."

He took a soda and stood at the kitchen counter, flicking through the mountains of mail that he still hadn't opened.

"A package arrived for you today," Marnie said, noticing him picking out the envelopes he wanted to open first. "I think it was from overseas."

His eyes lit up. "Was it from Raylee?" he asked. Marnie now had his full attention.

"I think so... Funny you never mentioned anything about her when you got home."

Cutter was looking around the room. "Well, where is it?"

"I put it in the other room, out of the way." Marnie was very casual about it, giving him the impression that it was nothing to get over excited about.

Nevertheless, Cutter was excited. He had no idea what Raylee would be sending him. She hadn't mentioned it the last time they spoke, which was only two days ago.

"It's only small, but you can't miss it," she called out, as he wandered down the hall to the sitting room.

He stood in the doorway and looked over at the table that sat in the corner of the room and couldn't see any package. It wasn't big enough to have it sit on the floor, and it wasn't on either armchair that sat in front of the fireplace. He was about to call out to Marnie, to ask where exactly she had left it, when he walked further into the room and looked over the back of the couch. Someone was curled up on the couch. He froze. Not from shock, but from the mental process that was taking place.

Raylee Tremayne was in Texas, in his sitting room, asleep on his couch. He was overwhelmed, and didn't realize that he'd been holding his breath for so long until his heart began knocking loudly on his chest to let it out.

The room was quiet and the late afternoon sun was streaming in through the window. He walked around to her while she was calmly sleeping. He crouched down and watched her. She was a sight for sore eyes. Beautiful.

More stunning than ever. Cutter reached out and pushed her hair away from her eyes, making her stir.

"Raylee?" He was almost whispering as he touched her cheek.

"Hey," she said quietly when she opened her eyes, then broke out into a smile.

"You came... I wasn't expecting you so soon," he said, and he held her hand and pulled her up.

"I hope it was okay for me to just turn up like this?" she asked.

"Absolutely." He gave her a kiss and she threw her arms around his neck.

"The last week was torture... I've got so much to tell you."

"I'll bet you have." He wanted to hear all about it. First, he wanted to introduce Raylee to Marnie, even though he knew that they had already met. It was still important for him to do things the proper way.

He led her by the hand out to the kitchen, yet Marnie was nowhere to be seen. He looked at the two plates on the table and he knew that she hadn't set it for herself at all. Marnie always had a knack for being around when you needed her, and disappearing when you didn't. This was one of those times when she was nowhere to be found.

They went out onto the porch. The sun was sinking low, highlighting the ranch in a way that you could only really appreciate from the house. Leaning against the rail, Cutter couldn't let her go. He was holding her and touching her everywhere he could, just to be close. She just stared out towards the barn and was quiet. The ranch couldn't look any better than it did right then and there with an orange sunset. If Raylee didn't like it now, she would never like it, and this worried him.

"So what do you think?" he asked. "Honestly."

She continued to gaze at the sight before her. "I love it. It's so peaceful here. So beautiful... It's so you."

"But what about you?" he wanted to know.

She let the tears roll down her face and Cutter was worried for the first time that Raylee didn't like the ranch as much as he hoped.

"What is it? Don't you like it here?" His voice was showing his concern.

She put her head down and cried, only for him to lift her chin up and look into her face.

"It's my parents... They're getting a divorce."

There. She let it out and for a moment Cutter was relieved, until he saw the pain that Raylee was dealing with.

Divorce was something that he'd never experienced before, just as Raylee hadn't dealt with losing a parent. He wasn't sure exactly what to say. He was too young to remember the details of his mom leaving his dad, so he just held her and she let it go.

They moved over to the swing. Cutter put his arm around her to give her a sense of comfort and support. "How's your arm now?" she asked, touching his plaster.

"I'm over it... Thought I might take it off myself."

"You can't do that," she said firmly. "You've got to keep it on for at least another month."

"Don't worry about my arm. Tell me about your parents. What happened?"

She was sad again when she spoke. "After you left, I drove back to the loft and I stayed there the night. I didn't want to go home, I just wanted to be by myself," she explained, and she started to get teary again. "The next morning my mom called and asked me to come back to the house to talk to them. I was expecting another argument... about you. But it had nothing to do with us and everything to do with them."

Cutter just listened. He still couldn't believe what she was telling him. "They told me that they had talked about it before their trip to Europe, but they went anyway to make that final decision and to keep it amicable. They spent a few weeks at the convention, but mostly they talked about their set-tlement, money and us kids."

"So when they got home, they were going to tell you... and then they walk in on us?" Cutter was piecing it together.

"Yes. And because of that, they couldn't tell me straight away and it made the whole ordeal even more complicated."

Cutter felt sorry for her. He couldn't say that he disliked her father because he didn't know him. Still, from his own confrontation with Allan Tremayne and Allan's unwillingness to listen to anything he had to say, it made it difficult for Cutter not to think that Raylee's mom might be better off.

"And to make things worse, they froze my trust fund," she added.

"What does that mean?"

"It means that I can't get access to any of my money, indefinitely."

Cutter was starting to see how everything had unfolded in the last week. While he was at home consumed with his own grief and a list of problems he had to deal with, Raylee was on the other side of the world dealing with hers. Neither of them had been aware of the other's situation.

"Why would they do that?" he asked.

"Oh, I think that part had everything to do with you," she said as she looked up at him. "My dad was furious. And he still is."

Cutter was beginning to feel that her father would pull out all the stops to end their relationship. Even the lowest of acts.

"Well you don't have to worry about anything here. We're self sufficient. And besides, I'll take care of you." He was trying to give her some reassurance, although deep down he had no idea how he was going to achieve this. With less cattle, the ranch was barely breaking even and with no cutting clients, there was very little left in the kitty and the bills were still coming in.

"What about the colt? What will happen to him?" he asked with justified concern.

"He's mine. I bought him with my own money, out of my trust fund. He's owned and registered to me. There's nothing they can do about that."

That made Cutter breathe more easily. The colt was like money in the bank and he could be Raylee's backstop.

"Raylee, please tell me that your parents know that you're here."

"They've got no idea where I am. I had to borrow the money from Jesse to get here and I made him swear not to tell them."

"You have to let them know," he pleaded. "They'll be worried."

"Why should I? After everything they've done to me. They just cut me off, expecting me to fall back into line with them. Well they can go to hell. Who would do that to their kids?"

She was angry but she had a point. Cutter could never imagine doing that to his family let alone his own children, although he did think that it was probably just a desperate move by desperate parents.

"You know what you need?" he asked trying to cheer her up, and he got to his feet and pulled her up also.

"What?"

"Marnie's cooking... She makes the best apple pie, guaranteed to take your mind off everything, and I thought I could smell it baking earlier."

Cutter always knew the right thing to say at the right time. She didn't want to talk about it anymore, at least not for the rest of the night, and she was feeling quite hungry.

Marnie had taken Raylee's bags upstairs earlier. She wanted to take a shower after the long flight and Cutter lay on the bed, watching her sort through her entire wardrobe looking for something to wear.

"Looks like you left in a hurry," he noted, seeing how disorganized her bags were.

"I did," she admitted. "And I didn't know what to pack, so I filled them up until I couldn't get any more in."

"By the looks of that, you could stay a whole year."

"Would that bother you?"

"Raylee, you can stay as long as you want. Actually, I'm hoping that you never have the need to leave."

She threw her clean pair of knickers and pink shirt back into the bag then carefully jumped on him and they wrestled on the bed. Laughing. Happy to be together again.

"Did you mean that?" she asked, when he had her pinned down.

"Every word," he said, then he kissed her, as though he couldn't get enough of her.

Chapter Ten

They didn't make it back downstairs that night. The following morning after Raylee showered and dressed, she met Cutter in the kitchen where he was sitting with Marnie at the table. He immediately stood up and held her hand before introducing them.

"I know you've already met, but this is Marnie, our long time friend. Actually, she's more like family than anything else," Cutter explained, then looked directly at Marnie. "In fact, Marnie's the only family I've got left... And Marnie, this is Raylee Tremayne. My girlfriend."

Raylee felt a rush of excitement when she heard that the girlfriend status had just become official. They sat down for a quick bite to eat before they headed out the door to the barn.

Marnie stood at the window and watched them walk out hand in hand. She was the Allan Tremayne in Cutter's life. The one person who you had to get past and gain approval from. However, Marnie was so pleased for Cutter and could see the light shining in his eyes again and because of that, her approval was instant, unlike the disapproval Cutter had received from Raylee's father.

Everywhere he took Raylee, the house, his bedroom, the undercover sand yard and the barn, he watched her reaction with interest. Her expressions said everything and he believed her when she said that she loved it all.

In the barn, Cutter went into the tack room and found Raylee a small saddle that he had when he was younger. "You can use this one," he said, giving it to her to saddle the gelding, who proved to be a better horse for roping than cutting. While he could have done it for her, he didn't want to undo all the progress she'd made when he was in Australia. "You know you're a good rider. But I'll make you better." It was the trainer, not the boyfriend, that was coming out in him now.

"How?" she asked.

"Before you can be a great cutter, you need to be a good cattleman... Or in your case, a cattlewoman. And you've got everything here on this ranch that you need for your training."

"Including the best teacher?"

He smiled at her. "Including a good rancher."

Together they rode out the gate and Cutter stopped for his usual last glance back at the house. Raylee could see the beauty beyond the ruggedness and she was happy. He didn't need to explain anything to her as it was plain to see. He was feeling on top of the world. He had his girl with him and he put all his tragedies and losses behind him. At least for now.

They rode side by side through every pasture. They stopped and looked at each herd while Cutter explained the breed, how old they were, guessed their weight and filled her in on what stage they were at.

"Don't worry if you don't get it all at once. Every day you'll learn a little bit more and you'll see their progress over time," he explained.

"You just know it, don't you?" she said with admiration.

"Like the back of my hand."

"I can see now why you became the best."

He was slightly embarrassed by Raylee's compliment so he squashed it. "Well I'm not the best anymore. I'm not anything right now."

"But you can be again."

"It's a long way back to where I was. I don't know if I can ever get back there again."

"What about the filly? Will she be ready?"

"She's on track. But the other trainers will have a dozen or more horses to ride across all the events. I'm going with just one. What if she doesn't score the points?"

"Cutter. You can only be the best if you've experienced the worst, and you've certainly done that. Everyone has their off day and it wouldn't make you a failure if you did."

"I just wanna make the final and do well. That's all. If I can do that, then I'll be happy."

In the back pasture the heifers were grazing. Raylee spotted a calf. "Look," she said with excitement. "Look at them. Oh, they're so young. How old do you think they are?" she asked, as she got off the gelding and walked over for a closer look.

"Not very old. Some a week or a bit more. Others just overnight."

There were a few more than yesterday's count and it would still be a couple of weeks before they were all on the ground. Cutter noticed a heifer lying under a tree that had started the calving process, and he rode over to check on her.

"Raylee?" he called out. "Come here."

She led the horse over. "What is it?"

"This heifer's down and we need to help her get up, or we could lose her and her calf."

Raylee could hear the seriousness in his voice. Lost cattle meant lost money. She was smart enough to know that. She took both horses and tied them up.

"What do you want me to do?"

"She needs to get on her feet. Come around this side," he instructed her.

Raylee crouched down next to him behind the heifer, and together they put their hands under her to motion for her to stand up. They pushed, but she was heavy. Cutter was using all his strength and she wasn't moving. They struggled to make any difference and were getting tired out. One last try, and the heifer remained down.

"What do we do now?" Raylee asked sounding helpless. "What's wrong with her?"

"She can't get up. It sometimes happens, and it means that we'll probably lose her... But we've gotta get this calf out." He stood up and looked for the feet of the calf. He could see them, which was good news as far as Raylee was concerned. "She's gonna have trouble. It must be a big calf."

"Can you get it out?" she wanted to know.

Cutter ignored her question and was not committing to anything positive. "Pass me that rope off my saddle."

Raylee ran over to the filly and grabbed the rope that was tied to Cutter's saddle. She immediately ran back, kneeling next to him and handed him the rope. She watched him put his hand inside the heifer. It was slippery. He looped the rope around the calf's feet and pulled it tight, but the rope slipped off and he fell backwards. He was working fast. His broken arm not even a consideration over the wellbeing of both the heifer and the calf. He tried again, this time deeper inside her and he looped the rope higher up the calf's legs. The heifer was uncomfortable and was breathing heavily.

Raylee didn't know if she was panicked or intrigued, but she was happy when he pulled on the rope and it tightened.

"Get behind me," he said, holding the tension on the rope. "My arm's hurting, so you're gonna have to help me pull it out."

"Okay... Just tell me when."

Cutter was sitting on his butt with his boots against the heifer. "Ready?... NOW."

They pulled on the rope and while it didn't seem to move much, it did move enough to clear the feet and the tip of its nose was exposed.

"Ready?... PULL," he called out.

Raylee had her hands behind Cutter's and they were pulling with every bit of strength they had in them. Her hands were burning from slipping on the rope. With every pull they were tiring, until they could see the head and it gave them another short burst of adrenalin.

"Here's the head," Raylee exclaimed with excitement, not realizing that it wasn't out of danger yet.

"Keep the rope tight... If we don't get it out soon, we could lose it." He was now making the urgency of the situation very clear. "Sit here Raylee, in front."

She sat in his position and also put her feet on the heifer. Cutter sat behind with his legs wrapped around either side of her, both holding the rope firm, his arm now aching.

"Pull now," he instructed, and they pulled hard. The head was now fully clear. "Let's keep going." They kept straining as hard as they could. The shoulders cleared and with one last pull the calf slipped out, falling into Raylee's lap, the bloodied sack still partially covering the calf and now covering her. She sat there stunned.

"You did it," Cutter said proudly, though there was no time for celebrating and he immediately stood up and tended to the calf.

"Is it dead?" she asked, letting go of the rope and looking at her messed up jeans and shirt.

"I've gotta get it breathing," he explained, without having the time to tell her how.

She stood back out of the way and watched as he cleaned the remains of the sack away from the calf's face and cleared its throat. He held up its limp body, but it still wouldn't take a breath, and with his broken arm, it was becoming heavy.

"Help me get it over to that log," he said, referring to a dead tree limb that had fallen nearby. Together they managed to carry the calf and placed it over the log with its front and back legs on either side.

Cutter rubbed it all over. Under its chin, down its sides and on its back. The plaster on his arm was now covered in animal fluid, yet it didn't bother him at all. He was more worried about getting that calf to start breathing.

With Cutter rubbing it all over, the calf spluttered and opened its eyes. He had brought life into a lifeless body and he was ecstatic, while Raylee all of a sudden became emotional. He laughed at her, for her first calf delivery was traumatic and it showed just how strong she was, until it was over and then she fell to pieces.

"Look at you," he said, impressed by her efforts.

Raylee looked at herself, then looked at Cutter. "Look at you," she repeated. He was covered in the same amount of fluid as she was. "What will happen to the heifer?"

Cutter looked over at her. "Let's try to get her up again."

They left the calf to try and save its mom. She had delivered the afterbirth which turned Raylee's stomach, although she did well not to show it.

Again they tried to help her to her feet. Not that they could ever have lifted her, and were only trying to provoke her to move herself. It was no use. She didn't even look close to getting up. Cutter knew what the outcome was going to be and he walked over to the filly and came back with his rifle.

Raylee grabbed him by the arm. "What are you doing?"

"She won't make it, Raylee. No matter how long she lies there, she won't get up. I can't let her suffer... Go over there and sit with the calf."

Raylee could tell that he wasn't happy about it, but it was part of the life cycle on the ranch. She didn't argue and she crouched down with the calf, not watching Cutter line up his shot.

The echo went through her and sent shivers down her spine. It was quick and final. She knew that he'd done the right thing, even though it was still hard to have played such a hands on role delivering that calf, only to have lost its mother.

When Cutter put the rifle away and walked back over to Raylee, he squeezed her shoulder. He could tell that it had upset her, yet she was trying to be strong about it. They cleaned the calf up some more and put it across the front of the filly, riding home slowly, taking their time.

In the barn they had raised many calves who had lost their moms. It was Mary-Ann who took care of them, doing her motherly thing. Then later on it was Macca who raised them. They needed daily care and the powdered milk and bottles were never too far away.

Together Cutter and Raylee unsaddled the horses and put everything away. They watched the calf for a while, lying in a stall on a warm bed of straw.

"Not bad for your first day as a Texan cattlewoman," he complimented, and he put his hand on the back of her neck and gave her a squeeze.

"Do you think it will make it?"

"Well, it survived the hardest part. Only the next few days will tell." He didn't want to sound too positive and build up her hopes. The reality was, that life on the ranch didn't always have happy endings, as Raylee found out on her first day.

"Cutter," she said. "I'm sorry, but you smell."

"I smell? Like you smell beautiful." He grabbed her from behind. Raylee thought that he was going to cuddle her, instead, he wiped the front of his bloodied smelly shirt all over her back. She screamed and wriggled out of his grip, and he chased her around the barn.

When Cutter caught her, he let her know that he was proud of her. It wasn't an easy morning. Life and loss in one experience was always overwhelming and he knew that she would toughen up over time. It would be Raylee's first lesson in what was going to make her a great cutter.

"Hey, I need you to do something for me," he said.

"Sure. What is it?"

He went into a room off the side of the barn and came back with a tool. He plugged it in and gave it to her.

"What do you want me to do with that?" she asked, unsure about what it was and what she had to do with it.

"I need you to cut this plaster off."

His plaster was covered in the remains of the calf delivery and it needed to come off. He showed her how to hold it and how deep the blade should cut. Her hand was shaking for fear of cutting his arm, with the vibration and noise making her uneasy. She took her time and made a neat cut down the middle of his forearm, then another cut on the side so that he could slip his arm out of the cast. He gave it a rub. The bruise was still purple and blue.

"I'm going to strap that when we get back to the house," she told him in no uncertain terms, and he knew better than to argue.

Raylee missed the sunrise and woke up to find herself alone, although she knew exactly where Cutter would be. After she dressed, she went downstairs to the kitchen. Marnie wasn't busy and had just made a pot of tea.

"Good morning... Can I get you a cup?" Marnie asked.

"Thank you, yes," she said, and she took a seat at the kitchen table.

"You missed your boy this morning."

Raylee finished her yawn. "I think I'm still jet lagged. Where is he?"

"He's not far away... Only at the barn. Working that filly I'd say."

Marnie sat the teapot in the middle of the table and placed two cups with saucers in front of them. The floral pattern was out of character for the ranch, and Raylee immediately presumed that it must have been from Marnie's own personal collection. Something she saved only for special occasions. Not that Raylee thought this was a special occasion, but that it could open up a quiet intimate talk. She really wanted to get to know Marnie, as she seemed to know everything about the ranch and the family.

"Did you sleep well?" Marnie asked, breaking into the conversation easily and pouring the tea out.

"I don't remember anything after my head hit the pillow. All that riding and fresh air yesterday, I think it wore me out. Cutter's one hard person to keep up with."

Marnie agreed. "Yes ma'am, he sure is... Hasn't been any different since he was a little boy."

Raylee decided to dive right in and ask early. "What was he like when he was younger?"

She paused and took a long sip of her hot tea. "Why, he was the sweetest little boy when he came to the ranch. Very quiet, but had the biggest blue eyes and a cheeky smile that would melt your heart."

Raylee could see that not much had changed.

"He melted Macca's heart too. Won him over straight away. He loved that boy and wanted him to be his own... After he married Mary-Ann, Macca became Cutter's father in every way and he taught him everything he knows."

"Macca must have been a great man?"

"Yes ma'am. Sure was. You wouldn't meet a stronger, more honest and caring man than Macca... Except maybe his son," she added.

It made Raylee smile. It made her feel lucky to think that she had met a man like Cutter Jones.

"Marnie... Cutter's never said much about his mom." She knew she was walking on tender ground, yet she was desperate to know more.

"Mary-Ann... She certainly turned this place around. We all thought that Macca would never find anyone, until he met Mary-Ann. She was running away from a life of misery when she met Macca, and he made her feel secure and worthy. It was something she'd not felt for a long time."

It brought tears to Marnie's eyes when she spoke of Mary-Ann. Their closeness was evident in her recollections of her friend. She took a breather and topped up her teacup.

"How did she change it?" Raylee asked.

"Double J Ranch had been passed down through the generations from father to son, and without a family to pass it on to, it was beginning to look like Macca was going to be the last rancher of the Jones family. But when Mary-Ann arrived with Cutter, she turned this house back into a home and the future of the ranch was looking promising again." Marnie could have gone into deep detail, instead, she summed it up the simplest way she could. "After Mary-Ann arrived, she became the center of the family and the business. Mary-Ann completed Macca's life and this ranch."

Raylee could see that Mary-Ann's son had those same qualities. She wanted to know more about the events surrounding her death, but was reluctant to ask. Marnie knew that she would be curious and without asking, she decided that it was better coming from her and not from Cutter.

Her voice deepened when she explained. "Mary-Ann went to town to pick up a few supplies and run a few errands. She rarely went there alone, but everyone was busy on the ranch that day. On the way home, she ran off the road and hit a tree."

Raylee had no idea. Cutter had never mentioned the how, the when or the why, so this was a shock to her.

Marnie continued on. "They said it was instant. No other cars involved. No brake marks left on the road and no witnesses. We can only assume that there was an animal on the road and she swerved to miss it. But we'll never really know." She took another sip of her tea and wiped her eyes. "It was the darkest day this ranch has ever seen."

Marnie looked at Raylee. She was teary also. Even though she'd never met the woman, she felt the connection through her son.

She skipped the next details, although Raylee could imagine the police turning up and telling the family. It would have been a life changing, shattering moment, and it made her own family troubles seem so insignificant.

"Cutter didn't leave the house for over a week. He barely left his room... Then one day, he went back to the barn and made it his world. He channelled every bit of grief, and anger and talent, and he gave it to those horses... and he became the best."

Raylee was starting to see what made Cutter tick.

They had started to clean up the dishes. "Thank you Marnie," she said, just as Cutter walked through the door. They both turned to look at him with a smile, still wiping their eyes.

"Did you two have a fight or something?" he asked suspiciously, and Raylee walked over to him and gave him a huge hug. He wasn't sure what was going on, though he suggested that he needed Raylee's help outside and she walked past him to the porch.

"Marnie, can you pack us up a lunch?" he requested, and Marnie didn't have to ask him why.

"What are we doing?" Raylee asked, as she pulled her boots on.

"We're unloading that hay," he said, pointing to the truck parked at the barn.

They walked to the barn while the driver was unstrapping the load. Raylee stood on top of the hay inside the barn, while Cutter threw the bales to her from the truck. She stacked them neatly the way that he had shown her. It was hot and dusty and the bales were gaining in weight, yet she didn't complain.

She lost count after fifty and was feeling the load. "Did you buy the whole truckload?" she asked, looking at possibly another two hundred bales.

"No... Only a few more," he replied, noticing that she was slowing down. His arm and ribs were aching too, as the new strapping was not supportive enough for a job like this. Nevertheless, he continued until the job was done.

Cutter signed the paperwork and took a copy, then slipped it into his back pocket. When the truck left, they climbed the bales and sat for a rest. He took his hat off and laid his head in her lap. She ran her hands over his ribs and she could still feel the tape under his shirt.

"You did great," he praised her, knowing it was a heavy task.

"Is every day like this?"

"Yes ma'am. Pretty much... You never know what you're gonna be dealing with each day, and that's what makes this place like nothing else."

"I can see why you love it."

"I love everything about this ranch. There's nothing I'd change. But what I love the most is you being here." When Cutter spoke words of affirmation, it made Raylee feel more comfortable about being there and more in love with him.

He sat up and put his hat back on, then grabbed her by the hand. "Come on, let's go. I've got somewhere I wanna take you."

Every time they left the house or the barn there was something new to see or do, and Raylee had no idea what more surprises he had in mind.

He went to the stall and led the filly out, taking her with them for a walk.

"Aren't you going to need a saddle?" she asked.

"Not this time."

They went back to the house. Marnie had left a picnic basket on the porch and Cutter jumped the steps two at a time while holding his side and grabbed it.

"Where're we going?" she asked.

"You'll see," he said, not giving any details away.

They walked around to the backyard of the house and headed towards the gate. Raylee could hear the stream running. She hadn't noticed it before and was now intrigued to see it. He opened the small garden gate and they were careful walking the filly through.

The grass was overgrown and they had to high step as they walked. Hidden beyond the brush was the stream. The trees shaded it well as it trickled peacefully over the rocks. It was shallow enough to get across stepping from rock to rock, until it fell away to a deeper pool and ran a constant flow downstream.

Raylee could tell that it hadn't been visited for a long time, and she had the feeling that it held a special place in Cutter's heart. Maybe it was where he took all his girlfriends, she thought. This bothered her, but she didn't want to dampen the mood so she put it to the back of her mind.

They spread a blanket out on the grass and sat down. Cutter lay back on his good arm and watched Raylee dive into the basket for something to eat. "I'm starved," she said, when she remembered that she hadn't had any breakfast.

"Well Marnie would have packed everything out of the fridge. I doubt if there's anything left at the house."

She opened up a dish of cold fried chicken and they shared it. "Wow, she's a good cook," she said with a mouthful.

"She's the best."

The filly was picking at the grass around them and Raylee admired how the horses were part of Cutter's everyday activities. Unlike her horses at home, who were confined to the arena and the stables, never leaving the complex unless it was to go to a show.

"I can see why you have the best cutting horses," she said.

He turned it around. "Actually, it's you who's got the best cutting horse."

"Yeah, but you trained him."

"And now you own him. If I had him here now, I'd take him to the show in Dallas and he'd be my ticket in a final. I know he would. That's how good he is."

Raylee thought about this for a moment. She knew that she was the link between Cutter and the colt. "You've still got a couple of months to get the filly ready," she said, getting him to refocus.

"And are you ready?"

"Me? What do I need to be ready for?"

"You're gonna be in my corner at the show. I need people I can trust and I want you to be on my team."

This excited her. She also felt it was a huge responsibility and she didn't want to let him down. For the time being, she was just happy that he wanted her there.

"Is this place special to you?" she asked, referring to their picnic spot.

"It's where my mom would bring me and my dad once a week for our family time. It didn't matter what was going on with the ranch, it was her time with us."

Raylee could see the significance about it now, and she imagined Mary-Ann and Macca setting up their picnic lunch with a young Cutter and his horse in tow.

"So... you've never brought anyone else here?" she asked cautiously, testing her position.

He knew exactly what she was getting at, and he assured her. "Raylee, I've never brought anyone home to the ranch before, let alone here." He immediately put her mind at rest and she was pleased that he wanted to share this special place with her.

They ate and lazed in the shade, catching only short streams of sunshine through the trees. Raylee could see why Mary-Ann would want her family to come to the stream, and how it would hold special memories for Cutter now that his mom was gone.

"Do you think your mom would like me?" she asked, lying on her side, resting her head in her hand.

"My mom would love you. I know she would." Cutter was sincere and reached out to touch her cheek. "Not like your father. He hates me."

"He doesn't know you."

"And he never will unless he gives me a chance."

"Then it will be his loss."

"After what happened, I don't suppose I'm every father's dream son," Cutter stated, as if he almost agreed with Allan Tremayne.

"Look, they just thought that I'd end up with someone from their own world. They never thought that I'd fall for a cowboy from Texas. Their expectations was that I'd find Mr Right, wait until I was engaged and do everything in the right order."

Raylee's explanation made Cutter think. He was taking in what she had said and was doing his best to read between the lines. He sat up on his elbow and faced her, processing what she had just told him while Raylee was waiting for a response. This sexy cowgirl Cutter had in front of him all of a sudden started to look different in his eyes.

"Wait a minute," he said. "Do you mean to say, that you've never been with anyone else before me?" he asked, to clarify her explanation.

Her answer was simple. "Yes."

"Why didn't you say something? You could've told me... Not that I would've changed anything, but it's supposed to be special."

"It was special," Raylee confirmed. "It's something I'll never forget... And I don't think my father will forget it in a hurry either," she added.

Cutter was in shock. Raylee had waited for the right person and the right time, and somehow, she chose the day after the rodeo for him to be her first love. He immediately understood so much more. "Now I know why your father's so pissed with me," he said with certainty.

"You asked me if I had any regrets. I said I didn't, and I meant it. You're my first and I'm hoping you'll be my last too."

He was happy to hear this. "Well that will depend, won't it?"

"On what?"

"On you," he said, making it clear that she was in his plans for the long road.

They spent the time lazing around in the shade. The warmth of the sun was a sign of the hot summer yet to come. After they packed up the blanket, they took the filly back to the house and tied her up. Cutter could see a truck parked near the yards. It looked like Doug's, except there were no cattle coming in or going out so he wondered what he would be doing there.

As they walked up the front steps, they could hear laughing from inside the house.

"Who's Doug?" Raylee asked, before they went in.

"He's been delivering cattle here for years, but we're not getting any today," he answered suspiciously. "And Doug never comes to the house," he added to himself as an after thought.

Together they walked into the kitchen where Marnie and Doug were sitting at the table enjoying a cup of tea. Raylee noticed Marnie's special floral teacups and it struck her then that perhaps they weren't meant for her after all.

"Cutter," Doug said quickly, as he got to his feet.

"Hey Doug. What're you doing here?" Cutter blurted out, before he thought about how it sounded. He looked at Marnie. Doug and Marnie were both around the same age but it had never occurred to Cutter before that they could be friends.

"I was just delivering a load in the area, and I called in to see how everything was going here," Doug explained. "I didn't know you were back," he added, which made it clear to Cutter that Doug wasn't there to see him.

"Uhum..." Marnie interrupted, and she discreetly pointed towards Raylee.

When Cutter turned and looked to Raylee, he quickly tried to change the course of his thoughts. "Oh sorry. Doug, this is Raylee... Raylee, Doug," Cutter said, giving a speedy introduction while he was still trying to figure out the situation, and everyone could see that he was slightly awkward.

"Pleased to meet you," Doug said, nodding his head to her.

"Thank you. And you," Raylee agreed politely.

"Can I get you two a cup?" Marnie asked, inviting them to pull up a seat.

Cutter and Raylee looked at each other and were thinking the same thing. "Thanks Marnie," Cutter said. "But we'll take the filly back to the barn." He wasn't sure if they needed the privacy or not, but he'd learnt from Marnie's disappearing acts at different times, to know how and when to make a good exit.

They untied the filly and began to walk away clear of the house, before Cutter looked back with a blank look still on his face. "Do you think there's something going on there, or was it just me?" he asked, then kept walking.

"How long have they known each other?" Raylee asked. "You wouldn't make a good matchmaker, would you?"

"Well I didn't see that one coming."

"Well maybe you should," she pointed out.

"I didn't even see us coming, let alone seeing anyone else," Cutter said, explaining his naiveness.

"Well why not? They look so good together."

"Like we look good together?" he asked.

Raylee disagreed. "No. Like we look great together."

Chapter Eleven

Life for Raylee in Texas was steady, unlike the pace that she was used to back home. She had always been so busy with her work and social commitments that there never seemed enough hours in a day, and by the time she reached the end of the week, she seemed to have run out of days too.

The days on the ranch were slow and long. The early starts meant that she'd already cleaned the barn and fed the calf before breakfast. The rest of the day was spent repairing fences, checking the cattle and working with the horses in the sand yard.

Raylee had been there for over a week and still hadn't called her parents.

"If you don't call them and let them know where you are, then I will." Cutter felt strongly about it even though Allan and Evelyn Tremayne were the last people he wanted to talk to.

"Why should I?" she asked, while she was sitting on the swing looking over at the barn, feeling quite defiant.

"Because they've called you a hundred times and they must be worried."

"I sent my mom a message to tell them I was okay," she said. "And to leave me alone."

Cutter didn't agree. "But you need to let them know that you're here. With me. It might even help them to see that nothing they do will stop that."

Raylee could see his point. She had pondered over the thought of calling them and explaining herself, but she also liked the idea of letting them agonize about it for a time.

"It might not be as bad as you think," he said. "Use the phone in my office. I'll wait here." Cutter was prompting her gently to make the call, and it worked.

"Okay. But if you hear yelling, then you know it's not going down too well."

She left the porch and went inside the house, the screen door squeaking when it shut. Cutter stopped the motion of the swing and leaned down to pat Cooper. She was only a pup when he found her dumped on the side of the road near the school bus stop one afternoon. He hid her at the back of the barn and presented her to his mom a week later on her birthday. Her surprised reaction was quite convincing.

Cooper was getting old now. Her black and white hair had shades of grey through it and her teeth had yellowed from age. The arthritis in her legs would give her trouble in the winter months and this spring, she hadn't looked like she was going to bounce back. Yet she was loyal, and she sat at the front door expecting attention every time Cutter went in and out.

Raylee was taking a while and he couldn't hear any yelling, so he presumed it was going smoothly. He wished that things had turned out better with Raylee's parents, especially their introduction. Every time he replayed that day in his mind, now that a bit of time had passed, he felt like he'd failed her family's values and that disappointed him.

He couldn't change it. It seemed that all his successes and achievements in life were born from the hard knocks and tragedies that were all out of his control. If Raylee were to be his greatest success story, then it was off the back of losing the colt and Macca. Over analyzing was not something he did often, except that his head was now spinning fast and he needed a diversion. The filly. He needed to be pushing that horse along now, furthering her training and ability.

What could be taking so long, he wondered. It got the better of him and he left Cooper under the swing and went inside to the office, where he found Raylee sitting in his chair with papers in her hand. She wasn't on the phone. Instead, she was holding the opened mail and had been reading it.

"Did you talk to your parents?" he asked, before noticing that she was holding a handful of bills.

"Yes. I told my dad where I was and he totally flipped out. My mom got on the phone and asked me to come home, but she wouldn't listen to anything I had to say and so I thought it was better that I hang up. What are all these?" she asked, holding the bills in the air towards him, as if they were more important than speaking to her mom and dad.

"They're the bills that came in while I was away, and now I need to find the money to pay for them."

"Why didn't you say something earlier?" she asked.

"It's not your problem. It's something that I need to deal with."

"Let me help you." She looked at him and for the first time she could see the stress in his face. "You said you want me in your corner at the show, well why don't you want me on your team now? I can help you work this out."

Raylee did have a good business mind, which she must have inherited from both her mom and her dad. Then again, it's always going to be easy running a business when you have unlimited funds behind you.

"I don't know, Raylee. You've got a lot to deal with right now," he said, not wanting to put any more pressure on her.

"Cutter, you don't have to do this on your own. What have you got to lose?"

"Only everything."

"So let me help you. Two heads are better than one, aren't they?"

Cutter didn't want Raylee to know his situation. After three bad years on the ranch during Macca's illness, he needed the time to turn it all around again. He just needed more than a week.

He went behind the desk and Raylee stood up to let him sit down, then she perched herself on his lap. They went through the statements together and itemized the bills into date order. The bills that were priority were put aside and together they organized a filing system.

The truth was, it wasn't Cutter's strongest point. He knew how to train horses and how to run the ranch, leaving the paperwork side to Mary-Ann and Macca, with the last three years disorganized to say the least. In no time at all, Raylee had changed the system so that it made it easier to follow, giving Cutter a clear understanding of what the bottom line was.

"Can you borrow against the ranch?" she asked as an option.

"When the land behind us came up for sale, we decided to buy it, but had to take out another loan. Everything I won through cutting we paid off the mortgage until I wasn't competing anymore. I used the leftover money from the colt to pay more of it down but there's still a heavy amount owing. Now without a client list and a good turnover, the bank wont look at us... At me."

Raylee wasn't sure about the lending terms in the U.S, and she could see the predicament he was in. "Then we need to get you some clients again."

"Not this close to the show," he said with certainty. "Maybe if I do well in Dallas, then I'll have them lining up at the front gate. But if I don't score the points, then no one will want me to train for them again."

He threw his head back into the chair and closed his eyes while he rubbed his face. He was totally frustrated. Only now, he had someone to share his frustrations with.

"Don't worry. We'll figure it out," she reassured him, then she got up and pulled him by the hand around the desk towards the door.

"Where're we going?" he asked.

"To the barn." Raylee was taking full control, leaving him curious.

"What for?"

She flashed her seductive eyes at him. "Nothing a little roll around in the hay won't fix."

It was her flirtation that always took his mind off things, and whether she meant it or not, just the thought of it sounded like a good idea.

Later that morning in the corner of the pen, Raylee sat on the gelding and helped keep the cattle together. The filly was looking good. Raylee had seen a huge improvement since the first day she arrived and could clearly see that Cutter was doing an amazing job with her.

She wondered how the colt was going. She imagined him being foaled here in the barn, then broken and trained in this very pen. As she turned back the clock she saw a younger Cutter Jones making him into a champion. Now he was riding the filly, trying his best to replicate that same magic.

With her powerful execution of every turn and her commanding control over the cow, the filly had the same star quality as the colt. Raylee was too inexperienced in that area to know if it was good genetics or good training. Either way, she thought that it was downright impressive to watch, and she admired the way Cutter and the filly were so connected.

Besides a few misses that he corrected immediately and some habits that he was still working on, the filly was cowy, just like the colt.

When Cutter finished his run, they walked through the cattle just talking. He was explaining some of the fundamentals that she needed to know while being on his team. Raylee had never been in the corner at a show before, only in practice at home, and she was worried that she wouldn't be ready for him in time.

It was without a doubt that Cutter was a great trainer as well as a good teacher, and since Raylee arrived at the ranch, her riding skills had improved beyond anything she'd learnt in her own controlled environment. The working side of the ranch was giving her the experience that she never had before.

Her knowledge of the cattle was growing too, and she even put forward some suggestions that Cutter took onboard to consider. However, the show would be a whole different responsibility and she needed to step up her understanding of what he expected of her.

In the pen it would be her job to look at the herd and take notice of which cows had already been cut by the other riders. She was to look for a cow that would be responsive. She had to recognize it by its characteristics amongst the rest of the herd and point it out to Cutter when he walked into the mob. Together they worked on these areas to build up her knowledge and confidence.

After lunch, Raylee was in the kitchen with Marnie while Cutter was catching up on some maintenance around the yard. She was dirty from the morning ride, although it was nothing that Marnie wasn't used to. Marnie made a cup of tea and they sat at the table.

"Do you cook?" Marnie asked out of interest.

"Cook?" Raylee repeated, as if it was a foreign word that she had never heard before. "No. We've always had a chef."

"Clean?" Marnie asked.

"Ah, no. We have someone who does that for us too."

Marnie was beginning to see what sort of life Raylee had come from. "What about wash and iron your own clothes?" she asked, even though she already knew the answer.

"I've been spoilt, haven't I?" Raylee admitted, sounding embarrassed.

"You know, I won't always be here." Was Marnie delivering some bad news?

"Well where are you going?" Raylee asked with caution.

Marnie laughed. "Nowhere yet... I hope. But I won't always be around, will I? Now, if I'm not here for some reason, who's going to look after you two?" It was only giving Raylee something to think about, as neither of them would be prepared if it did happen.

It was quiet that night when they lay in bed, and they could hear the stream trickling in the background. Raylee had never been to bed so early in her life. Working on the ranch really took it out of her, and soon after dark each night she'd turn in totally exhausted. The last couple of weeks had been filled with experiences that she had only heard about or seen in movies back home. It was like being part of a Hollywood film. To Cutter though, it was reality, and it could just be the beginning of her world too.

"I can't believe you're lying here with me. In my bed. In Texas," Cutter stated, while he was holding her close, both looking at the ceiling.

"There's nowhere else I want to be," she said, and she sat up on her elbow to look down on him.

She rubbed her hand over his ribs. He had removed the tape and they were feeling good now, although he was still aware of any sudden movements that would strike a pain. The graze on his face had healed and there were barely any reminders from the night of his bull ride, except for the light strapping he still had on his arm.

"I've got a surprise for you," she teased.

"What is it?" he asked, suspicious of her tone.

"I'm not telling you just yet. But you will love it."

"You can't do that. Tell me, then not tell me."

Raylee laughed playfully. "Yes I can. Because I want you to know how excited I am."

"Are you sure it's not for you then?" he asked, spinning it around.

"I'm sure... And you'll find out soon enough."

He loved having her there with him. She was fulfilling everything that he ever needed in a woman. A soft touch, a good friend and a great lover. Of course, there was so much more that he admired and he knew that he needed her for all her good qualities. She was a great support when he needed it the most. More than anything, they were becoming a good team.

"Do you think it will always be like this?" she asked.

"It can if you want it to be. And I'm gonna do everything I can to keep you here."

He didn't elaborate on what he meant, but it pleased her to think that this could be her life now.

While Cutter was out of bed before sunrise each morning, Raylee would wait another hour before she'd go to the barn to feed the calf and clean the stalls before breakfast. After lunch they would go on their daily ride over the ranch. She was also spending any available time with Marnie in the kitchen. Marnie was showing her some simple ideas for cooking and preparing meals at a basic level. It was time well spent together, as they laughed and shared personal stories about their families, although their favorite topic was Cutter. They were forming a close friendship built on trust and their love of the same cowboy.

The calf was getting stronger each day, as Raylee had made it her mission to see that it survived without its mom. When Cutter was training, she would let the calf out of the stall and it would follow her everywhere she went. Her daily routine in the barn consisted of cleaning tack, mucking the stalls and preparing the feed, while the calf would only be two paces behind her.

"I think I'll call her Lucky," Raylee said one day, when the calf was following her around the barn and was nibbling at her fingers.

"You are not giving it a name," Cutter said abruptly.

"Why not? I've got to call her something."

"No names, Raylee."

"But she thinks I'm her mom," she pleaded.

"Yeah, but you're not, and it's not your child. It's a cow."

"Don't you listen to him, Lucky," she said to the calf with a sooky face, while she was rubbing its head. "Look, you're making her feel sad," she said, looking back at Cutter.

Cutter threw his hands in the air. "One day, you'll figure it out," he said, although he was far from annoyed. Her compassion for the animals was difficult to squash.

All the other heifers had survived their calving, although they'd had to pull out another three over the last couple of weeks, each one as difficult as the last but all with a good end result. Much to the relief of Cutter, who didn't want a barn full of orphan calves with silly names.

To see them running around with their moms was something Raylee never tired of. While sitting in the back pasture each day, she'd watch their playful games. Cutter gave her the time as he could see that she clearly loved it.

Halfway home in the middle run, the steers were still a few weeks away from a sale. They had been gaining weight on the spring feed and were doing well. Cutter had used them in the pen a number of times since they'd arrived and for that part, they were done.

"I know they're not exactly ready yet, but if we move them out now, we can get some money in to pay the overdue bills," Raylee suggested, while they were making their way home. She was looking for ways to get on top of everything, just to take the stress away and let Cutter do his training without the worry.

"I'll think about it," he half agreed, as if he had more options. He now had show entry fees to pay as well as the general running costs mounting up, and an overdue mortgage payment to make. He was running out of ideas. An early sale meant less money, but he was under pressure to do something, and fast.

"I'm going to call my dad. Ask him to release my trust fund," Raylee said in a matter of fact way as they were riding through the last gate.

Cutter was forceful. "No you're not."

"Why not? It's my money. I should be able to do what I want with it."

"It might be your money. But I'm not having your father think that I'm not capable of looking after you."

"But..." she started to say, before Cutter cut her off.

"No Raylee. Absolutely no way. I'd rather lose the ranch than let you do that."

She could tell that he was too proud. The situation that he was in was not of his own doing. He'd been dealt a bad card and he needed the time to get himself and the ranch back on track.

"You know, you could always enter in the next rodeo," she said jokingly.

He looked at her. "Very funny... I'll tell you what else is funny."

"What?"

"When you're the last one home and you have to do the night feed."

Cutter hooked his spurs in and the filly took off, leaving Raylee and the gelding behind. She immediately gave chase and they raced towards the barn.

"That's so unfair," she puffed out, when she pulled up behind him and launched herself off the horse to challenge him. "You cheated."

"Cheated?" He chased her down and picked her up, throwing her over his shoulder. She only managed a squeal, followed by fits of laughter. She lost her hat and her hair was swinging around her face, making her lose her bearings.

"Tell me I'm not a cheat," he insisted, while he was threatening to drop her in the large water trough outside the barn.

"No. Cutter, stop it."

"What am I?" he asked.

She couldn't stop laughing. "You're the best trainer... The best rancher, *and* the best cowboy."

"That's better. And what else?"

"You're the best at everything."

He put her down and they carried on laughing. Raylee could tell that while there was a lot of pressure on Cutter, he was far from his breaking point, still taking the time to make each day as much fun as he possibly could. She put her hands behind his neck and kissed him, before he threw them both into the trough, water splashing everywhere and completely drenching them.

"Don't forget about Johnny and Emma," Marnie reminded Cutter when they walked in the door.

"What about them?" Raylee asked, still shivering from the soaking.

"Damn it, I forgot. We've been invited to Johnny's tonight," he informed her. "He said I've hidden you away long enough and he wanted you to meet Emma." Cutter was holding each end of a towel that was wrapped around the back of his neck.

"And you'd better get ready. You don't want to be late," Marnie added, and she hurried them along.

They went upstairs for a hot shower. Raylee couldn't wait to get her wet clothes off and warm up. The ranch had consumed all their time since she'd arrived so that they hadn't even had any time for socializing. They were so busy working and training, and were spending all their time together. Every spare minute they did have, they were giving it to each other behind closed doors.

"What should I wear?" she asked, holding up a pair of jeans in one hand and a short skirt in the other while he was buttoning up his shirt.

"Mmm... Skirt," he opted, as it reminded him of how good she looked when she wore it to the restaurant.

She pulled on the skirt and a pair of long cowgirl boots. She would leave her trademark black hat behind, so that she could style her hair nicely for the first time since she'd arrived. Cutter always liked it better when she was dressed down, and when the timing was right, he loved that flirtatious look that made him proud to have her by his side. Tonight she looked hot and it always turned him on, leaving him secretly wanting to stay in for the rest of the night.

The sun was now so low that it was sinking out of sight, as they drove the old Ford truck out the front gate and onto the main road. Although they were neighbors, their ranches were of such considerable size that it still took a good ten minutes before they pulled up outside Johnny and Emma's house.

The porch lights were on and it gave Raylee that welcome feeling. The house was only a few years old and as it turned out, they had it built when they were married to have their own space away from Emma's new in-laws, even though she loved them dearly.

The welcoming was just as warm. Raylee took a dish of hot food that Marnie had prepared for them and she handed it to Emma when they were introduced. She immediately put it down on the kitchen counter and gave Raylee a big Texas hug, making her feel like this family thing the three of them had going on was now extended to include her.

There was no awkwardness, no apprehension, and no noticeable age differences that suggested they were more adult than her. Instead, they were fascinated by her home life, where she grew up and her family's business activities. Her involvement in the vineyard and the complex were what made Raylee mature beyond her years.

They sat down at the dining room table. Raylee admired every room of the house and the way Emma had decorated, having her own unique style. While the house was oversized for only two people, they had plans to start their family as soon as it was paid down some more. Raylee could imagine a house full of children running around everywhere and she looked at Cutter, and wondered if starting a family would be on his agenda one day.

Johnny explained to Raylee briefly how he and Emma had met at school. Really, he was more interested in hearing about the details of what happened in Australia to make his best friend come home with a girlfriend.

"I knew he'd come home with someone," Johnny stated, as if he was happy he was proven right.

"What was it... a sheila?" Cutter asked. "I had no idea what that even was," he admitted, before he laughed at himself.

"But it didn't take you long to figure it out, did it?" Johnny added, but not to embarrass Raylee.

Cutter looked at her. "Well we didn't hit it off from the beginning, did we?" he asked.

Raylee was quick to tease him back. "Speak for yourself," she said.

"Well, we just had to sort out a few problems first," Cutter said. "After that, she worked out that I was hard to catch."

Raylee laughed and she gave him a soft punch on the arm.

"And that's when she started chasing me." Cutter was really starting to play with her now.

"That's so not how it happened," she defended, although she understood that he was only taunting her in their company and it was good to see him relax and forget about the ranch for one night.

"And I made a really good first impression with her parents. Just ask her," Cutter stated, as if he actually had. Both Johnny and Emma looked to Raylee for the significance behind his comments.

"Did you say good impression or lasting impression?" Raylee giggled. "You know, if you had kept your jeans on, then maybe my father wouldn't have needed to use his rifle."

"Rifle?" Johnny asked looking at Cutter, not wanting to miss anything. "What rifle?"

Cutter ignored his question. "But it was you who took my jeans off," Cutter replied with a sneaky comment back to Raylee that would only bait Johnny some more.

"Wait... I'm lost. You took his jeans off... and then your father tried to shoot him? Am I missing something here?" Johnny asked Raylee, trying to fill in the missing pieces.

"Nah. That's about how it happened, wasn't it Raylee?" Cutter intercepted the question, deciding that he'd given Johnny enough information for one night.

"Yeah. It was something like that," Raylee agreed, putting a sudden end to the topic and leaving Johnny with a lot of unanswered questions that would keep for another time.

"So, when are you going home?" Emma asked, when the fun had died down.

Raylee instantly came down off a high. "I don't really know. When my visa runs out. Maybe."

Hearing this made Cutter think about their time together. He stared at her intently and he wished that she never had to leave. He knew that eventually it had to come to an end, unless he could somehow make it permanent.

Emma started to clear the table. "Well, I'm sure that while ever you're here, you'll be making the most of every day," she said.

They still had the start of summer to look forward to. Raylee wanted more than anything to be in Cutter's corner at the show and to see him do well. Everything after that would be dealt with then. There was no need to focus on her going home just yet, with six more weeks left in her passport.

Cutter and Johnny went out to the porch while Raylee helped Emma do the dishes.

"He's really taken with you," Emma confided to Raylee, as they stood at the kitchen sink.

"How do you know that?" she asked.

Emma spoke honestly. "Because Cutter could have any girl he wanted. Yet no one has ever come close to where you are now... We've never seen him like this before."

"What, never?"

"No ma'am. Many have tried. But you're the first one who's got a hold on him."

It pleased Raylee to hear this, and it gave her a sense of comfort that Emma confirmed he was settled now. Although he had assured her so many times already, it was still nice to hear it from someone else that knew him well. After they cleaned up, the girls put the kettle on and talked some more. Raylee shared the details of her parents' divorce, and Emma expressed her desire to start a family sooner, rather than later.

In the quietness of the front porch, the boys were also confiding as best buddies would do. They hadn't spent much time together while Cutter was taking care of Macca, and since Raylee had arrived in Texas, Johnny hadn't seen him at all.

"She's really something," Johnny said, giving Cutter his sincere approval.

He totally agreed. "She's great... Actually, she's perfect."

"I'm really happy for you bro. And I think your mom and Macca would be happy for you too."

"You know, I'm starting to think she might be the one... But I can't do that to her unless I can make a comfortable life for her here." He had obviously given it some heartfelt thought. "She's come from a special place to this, and I need to make sure that I can give her everything she needs. Everything she's used to."

"You will. You've just gotta give it some time," Johnny said.

"But time's something I haven't got a lot of."

The porch door opened and the girls walked out holding their coffee cups and handed one each to the boys. They sat on the porch listening to the night noises, looking out at the starry sky. Raylee felt Cutter's hand gently touch the bare skin on her leg. There was something about the warmth of his touch that was almost suggestive, and it made her feel so wanted.

She was missing home, but not enough to make her want to leave Texas and go there. The thought of seeing her parents separating and breaking up their estate only made her heart break. She didn't want to be there in the middle of their divorce, seeing everything they'd worked so hard for being pulled apart.

Cutter and Johnny distracted her thoughts of home by reliving the memories from their childhood. They shared their young adventures, rounding up cattle when they were out of sight from Macca, pretending to be big time ranchers. It was serious business, until they were caught out when two herds accidentally got mixed together.

The girls laughed at their honesty and lack of embarrassment. Raylee could imagine a young Cutter wanting to be all grown up and be a cowboy, just like his dad.

"Macca had a meltdown when he found them, and made me clean every bit of tack he could find... Took me two and a half weeks every day after school." Cutter could only laugh at the situation now that he had grown up.

"And I didn't come around for a whole month," Johnny said. "Thinking I was off the hook, I turned up one day and Macca gave me every stall to clean," he added, to let everyone know he took some of the heat as well.

"Bet you never did that again?" Raylee asked with certainty.

Both boys looked at each other and laughed some more. "Well, not that he found out about anyway," Cutter joked, and the girls laughed along with them.

Raylee was having the best time. She could see why Cutter and Johnny were great friends, and she really liked Emma too. She would be someone that Raylee could really bond with, especially if she had any future there on the ranch.

On the drive back home, Raylee sat in the middle seat and rested her head on Cutter's shoulder while he put his arm around her, holding her tight. She was in Texas, living the life of a rancher with her cowboy, and there was nowhere else she'd rather be.

Chapter Twelve

It was time to move out the steers, although not because they were ready. They needed to turn them over quickly now to cover the overdue mortgage payment and bills. Cutter had conceded that Raylee was right, even though a few more weeks would have finished them more to his liking. He arranged for Doug to make the pick up late the following evening.

After Cutter had done a training session with the filly and Raylee had fed Lucky, they rode out the gate to the steers and brought them back to the closest yard. Raylee practiced walking through them, brushing past them slowly then at times suddenly, as if she were settling the herd.

They discussed the obvious characteristics of each one, and Raylee could clearly see everything that Cutter was explaining. But some things were not so obvious, especially in such a large mob. How would she know if a cow was going to be responsive or not? The more time she had around them, the better she was getting at reading each one.

"You know, it won't be long and Lucky will be going off to the sale too," he said, looking for a rise from her.

He got it. "What? Lucky's not going to any sale. She's very comfortable in the barn, thank you."

"I'm sure she is. But Lucky's about to get unlucky and get put out where she belongs. She can't live in the barn forever."

"That's so cruel."

"That's ranch life."

"I'll buy her from you then."

"What? You'd pay me money for that unlucky little beast?"

"She's not unlucky. She's Lucky. And yes, how much do you want for her?"

Cutter thought about it for a moment. "I'll tell you what... If you love her that much, I'll trade you Lucky for the colt."

"Yeah right."

"Fair deal I thought."

"And what if I said yes?" Raylee asked curiously.

"Then I'd think I was lucky and you were crazy."

They rode back to the barn. Cutter looked at Lucky in the stall and shook his head, but really, he loved that Raylee was taking good care of her.

"Let's go to town. I need to pick up a few things," Raylee suggested. Secretly, she was looking for a diversion so she could fulfill the surprise she'd spent weeks organizing.

"Can't we go there tomorrow? I've got so much to do here today."

"Then you can do it tomorrow, and you can take me out to lunch today."

Cutter looked at her. She'd done so much work on the ranch without any complaining, and she'd not asked once to go to town for anything else other than picking up essential supplies. In fact, they avoided town as much as they could so they didn't spend money unnecessarily.

"Alright. I'll turn the horses out and you go see if Marnie needs anything picked up. I'll bring the truck to the house," he said.

It pleased Raylee to think that her planned surprise for Cutter was now so close. She felt fluttery, in a good way.

The few times they drove to town, Raylee wondered where Mary-Ann had the accident. She looked for any kind of sign or memorial that suggested this was the place. There was nothing that was obvious to her. She even looked at Cutter to see if he changed his mood or if he looked at a certain place on the roadside. He gave nothing away.

When they sat in the diner for lunch, a waitress came up to their table to take their order. She was an older woman who seemed to know Cutter well.

"Hello Cutter. Haven't seen you in town for a while," the waitress said warmly.

"Hey Josie. I've been busy at the ranch. Just trying to catch up on everything." He kept it simple and was quite friendly.

"I heard you went to Australia after the funeral?" Josie asked, to confirm the town talk.

"I just needed to get away for a while."

"It was a lovely service. Can't believe Macca and Mary-Ann are back together again."

"Me neither," he agreed, while he was just being polite, then he changed the subject quickly. "This is Raylee. My girlfriend."

"Girlfriend? Wow, it's so nice to meet you." Josie was genuine when she spoke.

"Likewise," Raylee said, unsure of what the connection was between them.

"Now, what can I get you kids to eat?" she asked, with her pen and paper ready.

They ordered their lunch and were left sitting in the corner far enough away from the other customers. "Do you know everyone here?" Raylee asked looking around the diner, but also referring to the entire town.

"Of course I know everyone," he stated, as if she shouldn't be surprised. The town was very small. Much smaller than where Raylee came from, so why wouldn't he know everyone? "This is the diner that my mom worked at when she first came to town. Josie gave her the job, and they stayed friends even after she moved to the ranch."

It was all starting to make sense now. Fitting the names, faces and places together was like a puzzle, and it wasn't so difficult to see the picture unfolding. Raylee felt that Cutter didn't mind sharing these details about his mom with her, except for the accident.

Over lunch, Raylee taunted him some more. "You know that surprise I've got for you?"

"Yes. But I thought you'd forgotten about it," he said, since she'd mentioned it a few weeks ago now.

"How could I forget? Well, I might give it to you today."

"Is that what we're in town for?" he asked.

"You could say that."

"Did I forget to tell you that I don't like surprises?"

"Well you're going to love this one," she said with total confidence. "And if you don't, then I'll take it back or keep it for myself."

He didn't answer. He had no idea what the surprise was. Looking at Raylee across the table, he liked to think that one day he could do the same for her. For the moment, he was struggling just to take her out for lunch.

They picked up a few supplies for Marnie and the few things that Raylee had come to town for. She instructed Cutter to go back to the truck while she went into the last shop to pick him up something special that she had ordered the last time she was in town. She placed the box on the backseat of the truck behind Cutter and told him that he wasn't allowed to look.

Raylee was feeling on top of the world, wanting the surprise to be one that Cutter wasn't expecting or would ever forget. They dropped off Marnie's order at the house, then drove back to the barn where she took the box off the backseat and made him wait until she took it inside.

"Okay. You can come in now," she called out after a few minutes.

He walked into the barn to where she was sitting on a bale of hay next to the box. He knew that box, since he'd had many before this.

"It's a hat," he said, sizing up the box.

"It's not just a hat. It's a hat that you're going to wear at the show," she said, then she opened the lid of the box and took out the jet black hat and gave it to him.

"Wow. It's nice." He took his old hat off and put the new one on. "How's it look?"

"Perfect."

"Hang on... Are you supposed to be joining my team or am I joining yours?" he teased.

"It looks great. If nothing else, you're going to look really good riding the colt," she said.

"You mean the filly?"

"No... I mean the colt."

What? His head hadn't caught up with what Raylee had said or what he was looking at. Standing in his stall, was the colt. Cutter was speechless when he looked at Raylee who couldn't contain her enormous smile.

"What the..." he said, and he rushed over to him. He was stunned. In total shock. Then he looked at Raylee and felt a rush of emotion that hit him like a ton of bricks.

She went over to them both. It was choking her up too, to see this cowboy that she loved and his horse back together again. It was something that she wanted to do for him and she had managed to do it, without raising the slightest suspicion.

Cutter hugged her so tight and it was only his excitement for the colt that made him let her go. "I can't believe it... How'd you pull this off?" he asked, amazed that he didn't have any idea.

"You wouldn't believe the lengths I had to go to so you wouldn't find out. All the sneaky phone calls. All the emails, and everyone knew except you." Raylee was well pleased with herself. "It took a lot of people and a lot of running around to get him here without you knowing."

Cutter couldn't stop smiling. He led the colt out of the stall and walked past the calf. "Looks like she's all yours now," he said, referring to Lucky who was lazing on her bed of straw.

They tied the colt up to a rail and spent the next hour brushing him down and looking him all over. Cutter was ecstatic. He couldn't help but show his love to Raylee and to the colt. While they talked about him non stop, Cutter came to realize that there was one key problem that he didn't understand yet.

"Wait a minute... If you had all your money frozen, then how'd you get him here? How'd you pay for it?" Cutter asked with justified suspicion, since he knew it was expensive.

Raylee took a deep breath. She knew that he'd wonder that sooner or later. "Don't get mad," she warned him in advance.

"What did you do?"

"What difference does it make?"

"Raylee?"

"Okay... I may have used my dad's credit card," she said hesitantly.

"What? Are you kidding me?" He looked up and closed his eyes to digest what she was saying, and was imagining what the ramifications would be.

"And there's something else," she added while she was on a roll.

He looked at her as if she was about to deliver another blow. "What else have you done?"

"Well... I kind of used it to pay for your entry fees too."

Cutter couldn't believe it. He sat down on a bale of hay and pushed his hat back to rub his face. He was lost in crazy thoughts. He didn't speak, and Raylee felt that all the happiness they'd shared for the last hour was suddenly gone, until Cutter began to laugh.

"What's so funny?" she asked.

"You. I can't believe you did that... for me."

"Well, I figured that dirty tactics from my dad deserved the same thing back... But don't worry. I have every intention of paying it back to him when they release my trust fund. I don't want this hanging over my head forever."

"When do you think that will be?"

"Who knows when they'll come to their senses. But when I turn twenty-five, they lose their control over me and I know I can get it back then whether they like it or not."

Cutter knew that it could take twelve months or more to turn the ranch around so that it was profitable again. Another three years for Raylee living without her independence would see her needing him more and more, and in a way, he liked that.

"You said if you had the colt back here, he'd be your ticket in a final," she said, repeating his exact words.

"He sure is... Let's take him out for a ride now."

Raylee led the filly into the barn and together they threw their saddles on.

"How'd you do it?" he asked, while he was making his final adjustments.

"Do what?"

"How'd you get him here without me knowing?"

"I had Randall and Jesse arrange everything at home and he arrived at Johnny's yesterday... You first," Raylee offered.

"It's your horse," he said, offering him back.

"Cutter... I kind of think he's our horse now."

He took the reins, leaned over and kissed her. "You are amazing... Thank you," he said, and he got on with the biggest smile to match Raylee's.

They rode out through the gate on the colt and the filly, retracing their daily ride. Even though they had checked the cattle earlier that morning, they still made it their business to oversee everything as they rode past.

It was Raylee's opinion that Cutter looked good when he sat on a horse, but it was nothing compared to how he looked when he rode the colt. Together they were one. Every movement and every stride they were fully united, and the time spent apart was unnoticeable in their instant reconnection to each other.

When they followed the fence line as far as it would go, they took their usual diversion towards the back of the ranch where the heifers were finished calving out. Raylee often wondered if the gate they always avoided was the boundary fence.

"What's through there?" she asked, when they slowed down to a light walking pace.

Cutter was too happy to brush it aside. The timing had never been right before but he was now ready to take Raylee to the resting place. "You wanna take a look?" he asked.

"Why, what is it?" she wanted to know first, not committing.

"Come and see."

Cutter swung the gate open and they went into the field of flowers. It was a sea of color and was full of spring bloom. He got off the colt and wandered through them with Raylee following suit. With the flowers reaching her knees, she bent down slightly and brushed them with her hand as she walked through. She wasn't sure of the reason he'd never taken her there, until he explained the significance of the flowers to his mom.

When Cutter was leaning down and picking a bunch, Raylee couldn't help but feel the sadness of a once happy place. There was a history there and it would be a constant reminder of their connection. A mother and a son, and the unbreakable love that would never die.

"Let's take them to her," Cutter said without explanation, and Raylee just went along with it.

Riding through the field of flowers towards the next gate, the resting place was beyond the trees, sitting out in the open surrounded by the wrought iron fence and overgrown pasture. At first glance, it looked like it hadn't been visited by anyone since the day they laid Macca to rest there nearly three months ago.

Raylee kept silent. She tied up the filly and followed Cutter into the yard and placed her hand on his shoulder when he knelt in front of his mother's grave. He laid the flowers at the bottom of her headstone where he would always place them, then touched Raylee's hand while he stared at the grave.

He looked over to Macca's grave. Someone had been there, as the new headstone was now in place.

Raylee was giving Cutter all the time that he needed. She didn't want to rush the afternoon away. Instead, she just touched him for reassurance to let him know that he had someone to lean on and talk to if he wanted.

He broke the quietness. "You're so lucky, Raylee."

"Me, why?"

"Because you still have your parents... No matter if they're together or divorced, you still have them in your life. You need to make things right with them."

She didn't defend her position or justify the reason for cutting them off. Instead, she just squeezed his shoulders to tell him that she understood. "I'll call them tonight," she promised. They left the yard, closing the gate behind them.

Cutter immediately picked up his mood again when he got back on the colt, and they rode home the long way, back to the barn. She was pleased that he'd taken her to the resting place and had shared the experience with her. It would help her to understand more of his life and the ranch that he loved.

Lucky could hear them when they rode into the barn and she let Raylee know that she was hungry. As they began to unsaddle, Cutter tried to sound irritated. "I'll deal with the horses. You go and shut that thing up." Although he was too happy to be at all serious.

Raylee fed the calf while watching Cutter prepare the horses for a wash. She knew that she owed it to him to call her parents, just as she had promised. He was right. She had both her parents and Cutter didn't like being the wedge that was driven between them and for that, he was feeling guilty.

She knew he would give everything he had to have his mom and dad back, and she believed that Macca and Mary-Ann would do the same for him. It was a close family bond, unlike her own.

When the filly was back in her stall and the colt was put into his yard near the barn, they went to the house. Marnie had left a note on the kitchen counter to explain that she had gone out for the night and had left their supper in the oven.

"She's never gone out before," Cutter said, after he read the note. He put it down and looked in the oven.

"What, never?" Raylee asked, as if that couldn't have been true.

"Not that I can remember."

"She might be out on a date. Starting to have a life of her own."

"Where do you think she's gone? Did she say anything to you? You two have become close lately."

"No. Nothing. She never said a word."

Cutter was feeling quite hungry. "Well let's not waste this," he said, and he pulled the dish from the oven, not giving it any more thought.

They sat down together and ate. Cutter couldn't imagine going back to the way things were before he met Raylee. Sitting at the kitchen table on his own was something that he'd never wish for now. He was pleased that he'd returned that phone call from Raylee and went to Australia, and even more pleased that she'd followed him home.

After supper, Raylee went to the office to make the dreaded phone call to her parents while Cutter went outside and sat on the swing. The porch light attracted hundreds of tiny bugs and was casting a soft light over the rail. Cooper was in her basket sleeping. She gave a slight whimper, which suggested to Cutter that she was dreaming. Only a minute or two later, Raylee joined him on the swing.

"No one home?" he asked.

"I talked to my dad," she said very shortly.

"Not for long."

"No... He didn't have much to say except that he got his credit card statement."

Cutter didn't need to comment. He could imagine that their discussion probably came to an abrupt end with Raylee hanging up in his ear as soon as her father raised his voice.

"I don't know, Cutter... It's going from bad to worse. Not better."

"Give it some time. I'm sure when they come out the other side of their divorce, they'll see what they're missing. In the meantime, I'm here for you."

The quiet of the night was making Raylee feel lazy. They swayed on the swing just lapping up the time. At the top of the driveway, headlights turned in and began to make their way towards the house. It was a car that Cutter didn't recognize. A visitor at that time of night was unusual, so he got up and stood at the top of the steps, leaning on the post with his arms crossed.

The lights shone at the house and Cutter stood his ground.

It was Marnie and Doug. They leaned on the side of the car for a minute saying their goodbyes before Doug gave a wave to Cutter and drove off. Marnie walked up the steps. She was dressed up like the day of the funeral, with a touch more color.

"Hello you two," she said very cheerfully. "Did you find your supper?"

"You're late," Cutter said with authority, in one of those rare playful moments that they sometimes shared.

"It's only nine o'clock," she defended.

"You were supposed to be home an hour ago," he called out over his shoulder, when she walked past him to go inside the house.

Raylee sat on the swing amused. She liked to watch the game the two of them had going on. Why couldn't her family life back home be as simple as this, she often wondered.

Cutter and Raylee followed her into the kitchen where she put the kettle on and loaded the sink with the dirty dishes.

"So, where'd he take you?" Raylee asked with interest, and she grabbed three cups down from the cupboard and placed them on the kitchen counter.

"We went to a nice little place just out of town," Marnie replied, with limited detail.

"And did he pay?" Cutter asked, with both of them giving him the look. "What? I'm just making sure he's looking after you."

"Sure you are," Raylee added.

"I'm protecting my own. If Doug thinks he's gonna come in and sweep Marnie off her feet and take her away from here, then he'll have me to answer to," Cutter said strongly.

"Oh, just like you swept Raylee off her feet and moved her here with you?" Marnie threw back quickly, although she was only teasing.

"Exactly," he agreed, then realized that he had done the same thing to Allan Tremayne's daughter.

Marnie walked around the kitchen counter to Cutter and patted his face. "I'm not leaving here, but we did have a nice time," she assured him, then she sat down at the table. Cutter was only making fun of the situation. It was his way of letting Marnie know that he needed her. "And he said he'll see you around six tomorrow night," Marnie added.

Raylee loved the time they spent all together, as the three of them sat around the table enjoying the quietness of the night. Marnie wasn't an intrusion into their lives. Instead, she was a comfort and support, and Raylee couldn't imagine the ranch without her.

Cutter was more at ease now. The sale of the steers would take away any immediate financial problems that were weighing heavy on him. He went to bed that night putting the ranch far behind him, and giving all his attention to Raylee.

It was a damp morning. Cutter wouldn't let the drizzle interfere with his training program and true to his five a.m. start time, he was out the door and gone. He now had two horses to work, so it doubled the load until Raylee would turn up after going through her morning ritual of feeding the calf and mucking the stalls while the horses were out.

She rode the filly in circles, while Cutter worked the colt on the mechanical cow. He'd run him through a series of moves and the colt knew the program well. His training days were long behind him, although Cutter would keep him sharp for the show.

They swapped horses, Raylee having to shorten the stirrups on the colt and Cutter having to let them down on the filly. She walked the colt for a while before taking him into the barn and unsaddling him. In the wash bay, he enjoyed the coolness of the water and Raylee made sure he scrubbed up like new. His coat was shiny and his mane and tail were thick and long. She threw a summer rug over him and would keep him in the barn until the weather passed.

After a later than usual breakfast, Marnie went to town, leaving the house to themselves. It was tempting to go back to bed on such a miserable morning, although it wouldn't be to catch up on sleep. Instead, as Raylee was looking out the sitting room window, she wondered about the garage.

"What's in there?" she asked curiously, when she pulled the curtain back.

He walked over and leaned into her, stretching his arm out to lean against the window frame. "That's Macca's garage," he answered, knowing exactly what was in there but not giving it too much thought.

"Well what's in it?" she asked again.

"You wanna take a look?" He grabbed her by the waist and pulled her away from the window.

They put their boots and hats back on and grabbed their jackets, then made a quick dash out into the rain and over to the garage.

"You wait here," Cutter said, leaving Raylee standing underneath the front awning. He went in through a side access door and pulled the garage door up, revealing a truck covered in dusty sheets. "It's Macca's truck," he announced.

Raylee was surprised. She didn't comment straight away and helped Cutter pull the sheets off, throwing them aside. The metallic deep blue paint hadn't lost its shine, although it was in need of a light buff to get rid of the dust and bring it back to showroom condition. They opened the doors and climbed in. The smell of leather faintly filled the cab and as Raylee ran her hand over everything, Cutter could see that she loved it.

"It's like new," she commented.

"Only a few years old. When Macca got sick, he parked it in here and it's hardly come out since."

"Well, why didn't you drive it?" she asked, as if it were an obvious question.

"Because it was Macca's... I needed him to have some things to keep living for. I always thought he'd beat it. Then go back to working this ranch, riding his horses, and driving his truck. I wasn't about to take that away from him."

Raylee understood.

The keys were sitting on the floor and Cutter put them in the ignition, then pulled the hood. "What're you doing?" she asked.

"Slide over here... I've just gotta reconnect the battery." He went to the front of the truck and lifted the hood. Raylee could hear him tinkering around with the battery terminals.

"Now try it," he instructed, looking around the side of the hood at her. Raylee turned the key and the truck tried to turn over. "Try again," he said hopeful.

Again she turned the key and the truck wound up and wound up, and wound up, before it finally turned over. It hummed.

"Yes..." Raylee could hear Cutter saying to himself. He put the hood down and climbed back in with Raylee sliding over to the passenger side. "Now, where do you wanna go?" he asked.

They drove out into the rain. Splashes of mud were thrown up the sides, although they weren't bothered by the mess or the tracks it was leaving on the driveway. Once they hit the road they drove with no real direction. Cutter showed Raylee the countryside, driving further away from town. It was too wet to stop and look around, but with the radio playing and time to waste, they drove for a couple of hours just enjoying being away from the ranch. All their worries were left behind there.

The sound of rain hitting the tin roof was comforting and the house was warm, while Marnie stood at the sink, peeling the vegetables. Raylee made the most of the wet afternoon and let Cutter go to the barn to clean up, while she helped prepare the dinner.

"He seems more content now," Marnie noted, referring to Cutter's high spirits.

"I think when the cattle go out tonight, it will really take the pressure off him for a while," Raylee said confidently.

"How'd you convince him to get that truck out? It hasn't moved in months."

"I don't know. He didn't hesitate when I asked him about it."

"Well that boy needs to move on. Not hold on to the past and start making this place his own."

Things were starting to look up.

When everything was taken care of in the kitchen, Raylee went to the barn to help Cutter get the cattle into the yards ready for the truck to arrive. They brought them in slowly and filled them three parts full, making sure the troughs had water and throwing some hay in for the couple of hours they had to stand there.

The clouds were gaining weight and the rain was coming in heavier. Thunder was rolling in the distance and both Cutter and Raylee were wet and cold. They decided to go back to the house for a shower while they waited for Doug to arrive.

When they walked into the kitchen, Marnie had the table set for four. "Are we having company?" Cutter asked Marnie.

"It was Raylee's idea," she said, passing the blame.

He looked at Raylee. "Was it now?"

"Yes... And you will be on your best behavior tonight," she insisted.

She went upstairs to get out of her wet clothes and warm up so that she could help finalize the dinner, leaving Cutter and Marnie in the kitchen alone.

"She's a keeper, you know," Marnie advised, as if he didn't already know.

"Yes ma'am," he agreed, then he followed Raylee upstairs.

When dinner was nearly ready, Marnie and Raylee were busy in the kitchen doing the last minute finishing touches. Cutter heard the truck reverse up. He put his waterproof jacket on and his hat, and went out into the rain to help Doug load the cattle.

Raylee was thankful that she was able to stay inside the house and keep dry. She wanted to make the evening nice for Marnie, so she dressed the table beyond anything the ranch had seen before.

When Cutter and Doug came back to the house, they were soaked. They took their wet jackets off and hung up their hats, leaving their muddy boots out on the porch. Cutter looked at the table. It had the Tremayne touch to it and it reminded him of the restaurant. He didn't comment, since he was on best behavior orders from Raylee.

During the night, both Cutter and Raylee were intent on watching the connection between Marnie and Doug. They were looking for signs showing just what sort of friendship they had, prompting the right questions and baiting them to slip in their conversations. However, Marnie and Doug both stayed composed throughout the entire dinner and kept their involvement with each other personal, leaving Cutter and Raylee second guessing.

The night flew by and everyone was having a good time. Since Doug had to get on the road, he had to cut the night short. The heavy rain had let up slightly and was only coming through in drizzly showers, with the half moon shining through in between breaks in the clouds.

He gave his thanks and said his goodbyes to everyone on the front porch. Pulling his jacket on, Doug then wandered back to his truck, leaving Cutter leaning on the rail and the girls going back into the kitchen to clean up.

Lightning was flashing nearby and lit up the sky in a spectacular display. Cutter could feel another storm coming through, as the rumbling sounds gained in depth and came in closer. A severe gush of wind picked up and he could feel the chill through his shirt.

Cooper lay in her basket near the swing and only woke up when she heard the truck start. Cutter watched as the truck lights came on and Doug pulled away from the loading chute. He drove up the muddy driveway. The sounds of the thunder drowned out the noise of the engine and Cutter looked to the sky as the flashes of lightning intensified.

The cattle were on their way. With a good price at the morning sale, Cutter could feel the weights being lifted already and it began to ease his mind. As another shower of rain came through and a clap of thunder that made him feel uneasy, he'd watch the truck reach the top of the driveway before he would go back inside to help with the dishes.

Just as Doug was indicating his left turn out onto the main road, he pulled the truck around more sharply than was needed, cutting the corner. The rear wheels fell away onto the grassy roadside.

Cutter stood up straight to attention. It didn't look right, and he watched in disbelief as the truck rolled over on its side and into the ditch.

Chapter Thirteen

"RAYLEE!" Cutter called out as loudly as he could.

She came running out through the screen door onto the porch. "What is it?"

Cutter was pulling his boots on. "Get the horses. Quick," he stressed, without giving an explanation.

Raylee looked towards the front gate. She could see the truck rolled with the headlights still on, shining into the surrounding trees. "Nooo," she exclaimed to herself, and she raced back inside to get their jackets and hats.

"And bring my rifle," Cutter added, and he flew down the steps two at a time.

He jumped in Macca's truck which was parked just outside the garage and made his way to the front gate. Raylee could only see the taillights as she ran quickly in the dark towards the barn, slipping over twice in the mud and feeling the sensation of wet feet when she ran through the puddles, the wind and rain lashing her face.

She grabbed two saddles from the tack room and threw them on as fast as she could. The gelding and the colt. Cutter needed the colt's experience, leaving the filly behind, as risking an injury to her was something they couldn't afford. She found his rifle and attached it to the back of his saddle.

The rain was coming down in heavy showers now, and she rode up the driveway in the dark, leading the colt behind her. When she reached the top of the driveway, the damage was clear.

The truck was completely on its side. The sound of cattle kicking the metal sides of the crate was sickening and their bellowing was quite distressing. On the road, dazed cattle were wandering around disorientated, while others were riled up and angry.

Cutter had parked Macca's truck so that the lights were shining into the back of the crate, trying to see what he could do to get them out if they were able.

"Cutter," Raylee called out when she came close.

"Stay on the horse, Raylee," he demanded, and he took the reins of the colt and quickly got on also. "You'll be safer if you stay on."

More headlights were coming up the driveway. It was Marnie in her car.

"Have you seen Doug?" Raylee asked, before Marnie arrived.

"He's alright," he answered. "But if we don't get these steers off the road, they could cause an accident." Cutter was stressing at the urgency.

A car had already come around the corner and confronted the scene. It stayed back with its hazard lights on to block the road, and the driver kept in the safety of his vehicle.

Marnie pulled up and wound down the window. "Where's Doug?" she asked.

"He's still in the cab. He'll be okay but you need to call an ambulance. Drive around the front, but don't get out of the car," Cutter instructed her. "He's not in any danger if he stays where he is."

She did, and she pointed her headlights towards the truck which now had the engine cut and was sitting in darkness. Doug was slumped over, leaning against the roof of the cab with a cut to his head. Blood had flowed down his face and was dripping onto his shirt. He was a mess and looked completely stunned, but at least he was moving.

The cattle were now freaked out, running aggressively all over the road and kicking at everything and nothing. They were completely rank.

"We've gotta get them back into the driveway," Cutter called out to Raylee, over the rumbling sounds of the thunder.

She already had the gate to the side of the cattle guard open and any steers that were close, she pushed them through to safety. Flashes of lightning lit up the sky and were helping her to see.

Cars were pulling up in each direction, although no one was prepared to help, with Cutter and the colt dealing with each steer single handedly while the rain had thankfully eased off. It was still quite slippery and as the steers were trying to get past him, the colt was blocking every move they made. His cutting training was helping to keep the steers from going further up the road as together they were pushing them back towards the front gate.

More steers were coming out of the crate. Their hooves were scraping on the metal sides. Each time Raylee heard it, she knew another one was coming out, bucking and running, Raylee was keeping clear of anything that was wild. She was blocking the front gate and was stopping them from coming back through onto the road again.

The colt worked his magic. Everything he did was perfect. He was strong and controlled the cattle as well as Cutter could. It was one unpredictable ride under the less than ideal conditions.

Cutter did a quick count. "How many you got?" he called out to Raylee.

She numbered them in her head. At least the ones she could see. "Twenty-six... I think."

Cutter could see another twelve, and he tried to round them up one at a time, pushing the closest ones first to Raylee who would then push them into the safety of the driveway. They were under pressure, Cutter not even feeling it yet from the adrenalin that was making him work through the chaotic situation.

The flashing lights of the ambulance arrived, going around the outside of the parked cars and pulling up at the front of the truck. Cutter had no time to help, and could only keep the steers away from them as the two officers smashed their way into the cab through the front windscreen.

One by one, Cutter was moving them on. The sounds in the crate were slowing down. The scraping noises were few, and when every steer that was on the road was now in the safety of the driveway, Raylee closed the gate.

They got off the horses and tied them to the fence out of the way. They were completely soaked.

"What do we do with these ones?" she asked, standing at the back of the crate with the headlights shining past them at the last of the steers.

"They don't look like they're in good condition," he commented. "Some are already gone."

"Can we get them out?" she asked, of the few that were still alive and responding.

"Not sure. Depends if they can get up or not." He walked cautiously into the crate. His closeness made the steers kick again, causing him to jump backwards out of the way. "Come in here," he said. Raylee knew that he wouldn't put her in danger so he must have been confident that they couldn't get up.

"What should we do?" she asked.

He rubbed his face while he was thinking. "There's only three here that are still alive but I'm gonna have to put them down. The others are dead anyway."

Raylee's heart sank. The cattle were suffering and Cutter had to do what any rancher would do. Though he didn't ask, she went to the colt and took out his rifle and gave it to him.

"Stand outside there," he ordered.

"Wait 'til I move the horses," Raylee requested, and while he was lining up the shot, she untied the horses and led them away.

He was shaking. His hands were trembling. Not because he hadn't done this hundreds of times before, but because he was one step closer to his breaking point. He closed his eyes hard, then refocused with his finger pressed on the trigger.

The first shot echoed off the metal of the crate, followed by the second and third shot. Silence fell. No more hooves scraping the metal. No more bellowing from inside. It was done.

An ambulance officer came running around the back of the truck only to see what Cutter had done. "How's Doug?" he asked the officer, while he stood amongst the dead cattle with his rifle lowered.

"He'll be fine. We're just taking him in now. Do you two need any attention before we leave?" he asked.

"No. We're both okay," Cutter replied, even though he didn't sound it, and the officer left in a hurry.

The sound of the siren rang in Cutter's ears and the flashing lights faded quickly as it sped away into the darkness. The cars began to move on, all taking a good look at the truck when they drove past slowly. One car wound down his window and called out to Cutter. "Hey... Good job," he said, before he drove off again.

Raylee met Cutter at the back of the crate. She hugged him tight and started to cry. She'd held it together while under the pressure of the events unfolding but as soon as it was over, she couldn't hold it in any longer. They looked at the dead steers. It was a loss. A huge loss that they couldn't afford, and now they were in a position that could really bring them down.

Marnie followed the ambulance to town, leaving Cutter and Raylee to deal with the clean up. But the night was only just beginning.

"Let's get these steers into a yard," Cutter said, and they untied the horses and pushed the steers steadily down the driveway.

The cattle had settled down somewhat, although they were still quite flighty when Cutter and Raylee applied pressure for them to move. It was slow going, only moving them at a pace that was safe. They didn't speak. There was nothing that could be said at that time that would make the situation any better. Instead, they worked as a team to get the steers into the first yard past the barn where they had been most of the afternoon.

Macca's truck was left up the top of the driveway for the time being, and Raylee unsaddled the horses while Cutter went to the house to make a phone call.

She met him in the office just as he put the phone down. "Who'd you call?" she asked.

"Johnny's coming over with his tractor... We'll pull the dead steers out tonight."

"Let me get changed and I'll come and help you."

Cutter got out of the chair and walked over to her. She was soaked through just as he was and she was shaking like a leaf. He touched her face. "You did so good out there tonight. I'm so proud of you," he said truthfully.

"It was you who did an amazing job," she returned the compliment.

"I'll get changed too, but I think you need to stay here and let us deal with it."

She wasn't sure if he needed to be alone or if he was protecting her, so she didn't argue to make the situation any worse than it already was. She knew that when he needed her, he would always ask. This time, he was asking her to stay out of the way and she would respect that.

When the headlights of the tractor came down the road, Cutter in his clean jeans and shirt pulled on a dry pair of boots and went outside.

"At least let me drive you back there," Raylee offered, and he allowed her to do that for him.

She dropped him off in the old Ford truck and went back to the house, even though she was desperate to be there helping them clean up the mess. The house was too quiet, so she sat on the porch in the darkness and watched the tractor lights work in and out of the crate. The sounds of the cattle in the yard were loud and traumatic, and a million things ran through her mind all at once.

How could this happen? Why did this happen? When all they needed the most was a lucky break...

It was late, really late when Cutter came to bed that night. He was physically exhausted and Raylee could tell that he was low.

"How many did we lose?" she asked quietly.

"Ten," he answered, without adding anymore.

She didn't know what else to say and felt that he needed to be silent. Instead, she snuggled in behind him and wrapped her arm underneath his. He pulled it in tight to his chest and Raylee felt content that through the disaster, he still needed her close.

It was the first morning that Raylee was out of bed before Cutter. She pulled her jeans and shirt on, then snuck downstairs quietly to let him sleep longer. The kitchen was still a mess from the night before and she began to clean it up, washing the dishes, wiping the counter and putting everything away.

Marnie's keys were on the side table so Raylee knew that she was home too, although there was no sign of her either. She made a cup of tea and went into the office. Pulling out everything she could find in the filing cabinet that had to do with insurance, Raylee flicked through all the documents that Macca had drawn up regarding the ranch.

It was now past nine o'clock and she made a phone call to the insurance company, eventually being put through to the man who had prepared all the policies and represented Macca on any claims over the years.

"Hello. David Chambers speaking," he said in a professional voice.

"Oh hi. My name's Raylee Tremayne and I'm calling on behalf of Bobby McKenzie Jones and the policies he has with your company."

"Yes, Miss Tremayne, how can I help you?"

She went through the details of what happened the previous night and they talked through the policy that was associated with that kind of incident. She explained about the passing of Macca, which Mr Chambers had not been advised of, although he knew that Macca had been sick for quite some time. He asked for the relevant paperwork to be emailed through and as she was winding up their twenty minute discussion, Cutter appeared at the door holding his morning coffee.

"Okay then, we'll see you on Wednesday. Thank you," Raylee said, then hung up the phone.

"Who was that?" Cutter asked.

"That was Mr David Chambers from the insurance company... I found the policy that your dad had on the ranch and I rang him to discuss what we could do."

Cutter looked thankful for the help. He hadn't even thought about calling the insurance company, since he was still reeling from the events that had unfolded last night.

"And what did he say?" he asked, hopeful of some good news.

"He said he'll look into it, and he's coming here at eleven on Wednesday."

"Okay then. Looks like you've got it covered."

"He didn't know that your dad had passed away either. So another reason he's coming is so that he can change the policies over to you."

"Okay, sounds good." Cutter wasn't bothered with the paperwork details. He'd have burned the whole lot if he could, so he was grateful that somebody was taking care of it for him and that he didn't have to.

"What time did you come to bed?" she asked.

"I don't know... Some time after three."

"You look tired."

"I'm shattered," he admitted. "And not just from the lack of sleep."

They walked back out to the kitchen where Marnie was now up and was jiggling her tea bag in her cup. She was staring at nothing.

"Morning," Raylee greeted her.

It startled her. "Oh... Morning... I didn't know anyone else was here."

"How's Doug, have you heard?" Cutter asked with genuine concern.

"Oh Cutter. He feels so terrible for what happened. He said he could barely see the road for the rain, and he didn't know he'd cut the corner so sharply," Marnie said. It was okay. They knew it was an accident that could happen to anyone.

"Did he stay at the hospital?" Raylee asked.

"Yes ma'am. But he can go home today. He has a deep cut to his forehead and a dislocated shoulder from when it went over," Marnie explained. "But the doctor said he was lucky. It could have been so much worse."

Cutter and Raylee could tell that Marnie was relieved.

The truck was still out the front lying in the ditch. The rain had stopped and the sun was shining through the clouds at times. Cutter had brought Macca's truck back last night and parked it at the side of the house. It was in desperate need of a wash now, with the metallic blue paint looking more like a dirty, muddy grey.

Cutter and Raylee went to the barn and took the horses out for a ride. They wanted to see if any of the steers needed to be vet checked. Riding through them in the slushy pasture, they saw several that could possibly be in need of a thorough examination. Cutter would use the colt, cutting the injured ones away from the herd one at a time, separating them and pushing them towards the gate.

There were at least half a dozen that he found with open wounds on their legs and still shaken from the experience. Together they walked them past the barn and placed them in the cattle yards before they called the vet.

There would be no training of horses. The colt had a big night and Cutter didn't feel like taking the filly into the cutting pen, keeping her in the smaller yards to graze freely.

They drove up to the front gate. The driveway was left with muddy tracks from Doug's truck and the tractor had left deep impressions on the grass. The cattle had turned everything into one huge muddy mess, while the sight that greeted them at the entrance was a complete shambles.

Local cars were coming out, pulling over onto the side of the road and looking at the wreckage of the night before. Cutter was devastated, and Raylee could tell that he was hitting an all time low. What should have been a good sale that morning, turned out to be their worst nightmare.

They went back to the house and hid away. There was little they could do until the vet arrived to check the steers in the yards. It would be a long few days while they had to wait for the ground to dry out and for Doug's truck to be taken away.

The vet left them with doses of penicillin that had to be administered daily. The only work they could continue with was to check over the cattle each day until the ranch dried out, and give the filly a good workout on the mechanical cow.

Cutter was feeling the heat. He had to answer phone calls now regarding the mortgage payment and overdue bills without knowing how he was going to pay for them. Raylee took some into her own hands and made the first contact, talking her way around it and buying some extra time. The cracks were starting to show and the stress levels were rising.

Cutter was close to losing it.

Chapter Fourteen

By Wednesday morning, Cutter was back in full training. He was up at his usual start time and had the filly worked by the time Raylee came to the barn to feed the calf. He was looking good, even though the load he was carrying was now a dead weight.

He was once again channelling all the catastrophes and tragedies into his training. He had done it before when he'd lost his mom and now he was at it again, giving that horse every bit of experience and talent that he had in him. He was focused on one thing now, and that was the show. If he let that slip away, then he'd risk losing the chance to pick up his career for good.

Raylee saddled the colt and she warmed him up by riding around in circles at the other end of the sand yard away from the filly. She watched Cutter with interest, giving him the support that he needed but also giving him the distance.

He cut the filly's training time short and rode over to her suggesting that they needed to check on the calves. Raylee didn't question it, and they made their way out the gate and up the first rolling hill.

Cutter pulled up and took a long look back down at the barn and house. Raylee thought that she was beginning to love the ranch as much as he did, and she thought about all the new memories they could make there together, even though their future there was starting to look doubtful.

"Will you still love me if I lose everything here?" he asked, staring out at the view.

"Cutter, I love you so much. What would make you think that this ranch is the only thing holding us together?"

"I've lost so much in my life... If I lose the ranch, and then lose you too, then I don't think..."

"Don't say it. I love you, ranch or no ranch. And I'm not going anywhere unless it's with you," she reassured him. "Come on. We've got a job to do," she said, giving him the distraction that he needed.

As they rode through each pasture, they looked over the cattle. The rain from the storm gave the ranch a much needed soaking and they could now go into the summer knowing that the feed would be plentiful.

The calves were growing. Playful and active to say the least. They were no longer afraid of them as they rode the horses between the cows. Raylee often got the calves to lick her fingers as she held out her hand.

"That's enough," Cutter said playfully. "I don't want them growing up to be babies and needing you to be their baby sitter... And don't even think about giving them all names."

They were doing well, and Cutter would move them out of the back pasture later in the summer to give it a spell before the next heifers were due to calve out next season.

Raylee was beginning to understand the way things worked around the ranch. She made it her job to take notice and understand everything that Cutter said and did. Raylee was confident that she could watch over the ranch on her own for a time if ever she was left in that position. She could even pull out a calf if she had to, or strain a fence to keep the cattle in.

As they rode towards home, Cutter stopped by the field of flowers and Raylee didn't need to ask him why. It had been the most trying of all the weeks since she'd arrived at the ranch and while she had only been to the resting place once, she felt like she needed to go there too.

They tied the horses up to the wrought iron fence and went through the squeaky gate to the grave site. Cutter crouched down, this time in front of Macca's headstone. He didn't speak at first, and Raylee stood directly behind him so that he could feel her near. He stared at it in deep thought. The silence was eerie on the sunny morning and the air was as clear after the rain as Raylee had ever felt it.

"What do I need to do?" he asked the headstone. "I need your help Macca... Tell me, what should I do?"

Raylee let him sit there. She wasn't sure if he was about to lose it, or was just needing a quiet moment. Either way, she gave him all the time that he needed before he stood up and put his arms around her. "How did things get this bad?" he asked.

"I don't know. But I do know that I would help you if I could. But with my trust fund in lockdown, I feel so helpless."

"You've helped me beyond anything I ever expected. And I love you for that. I couldn't ask you for any more than you've already done, even if you had your money."

"Can I ask you something?"

"Anything."

"What do you see happening with us?"

Cutter didn't rush into answering. Instead, he was interpreting her question. "I see that no matter where we end up, I wanna be there with you."

It was what she wanted to hear.

"Do you see us growing old together?" she asked.

"Yes ma'am... I'm planning on it."

It was so peaceful at the resting place. Cutter took her hat off and kissed her. It was like he had the three most important people in his life right there in that yard, and it gave him some temporary peace of mind.

He was more content as they rode home towards the barn. When they neared, they could see a white car out the front of the house and instead of taking the horses in to unsaddle them, they rode to the house and tied them up out the front.

When they slipped out of their boots on the porch, they could hear Marnie talking to a man. It wasn't Doug, as Cutter had first thought. It was David Chambers from the insurance company. Cutter looked at the clock on the wall. It was twenty minutes past eleven and he immediately shook David's hand and apologized for being late.

"Hey, I'm Cutter Jones, and this is Raylee who you spoke to on the phone," he said, introducing them both.

"Nice to meet you. Marnie's been taking good care of me and we were just having a talk," he said when they sat down, and he finished the last of his coffee.

His briefcase was already opened up on the table and he had a stack of documents grouped in piles. "I was really sorry to hear about Bobby... or Macca as I understand everyone called him. I didn't know him that well, but every time we met on business I could tell he was a man of great integrity," David said, making Cutter grateful to hear those words.

"Yes sir, he was," Marnie called out from within the kitchen.

"Now, Macca had a few policies with us, and what I want to do today is change the details over to your name. Everything will stay the same, but our paperwork will all be in order. That way, if you ever need to make a claim then it will be straight forward. You'll know exactly what you've got covered and for how much," David explained. He was going through the details as if it was a standard procedure.

Cutter tuned out to half of what David was saying, while Raylee was taking the time to understand each policy and what they were covered for. He had all the documents prepared for Cutter to sign and had the pen ready.

"I presume that is your real name?" he asked, before he handed Cutter the pen.

"Sure is. Why does everyone ask that?" he said, and he began reading each policy over quickly before he signed on the dotted line.

Once that part was out of the way, David filed the documents away in his briefcase. Cutter tossed the pen on the table as if he'd just signed his life away.

"Now, the claim for the cattle that you lost this week." David presented the document regarding the current claim. "You need to sign here... and here, to say you received the check." Which Cutter did without hesitation. David then handed him a copy of the policy and payout letter, with the check attached at the back.

Cutter looked at it. "You can't be serious?"

"What is it?" Raylee asked.

"It's only two thousand dollars," Cutter said disappointingly. "We lost ten head you know?"

"I know. But in insurance, covering stock is a bit of a grey area. There's no exact value. It's not like valuing a car or a truck. It's cattle, and there's no rule book to tell us what their value were, since they didn't make the sale yard to find out."

Cutter was pissed now. He looked at the check and slammed his fist hard on the table making everyone jump to attention. He stood up in a hurry and his chair slid back, hitting the wall while he leaned with both hands on the table.

"This is bullshit," Cutter yelled. "This check will hardly cover my vet bill for the rest of the steers that did make it," he stated, explaining his reaction.

"I'm sorry, Mr Jones. It's the cover that your dad took out," David said, justifying the amount.

"Well screw you and your check," Cutter threw back at him aggressively. He went over to the wall and hit it hard with his fist. Everyone was silent. "Damn it. Why is this happening to me?" His voice was becoming uncontrolled. Raylee could see that he had now reached his breaking point. He was angry and frustrated, and he was about to go into full blown meltdown. "Can't something go right?" he yelled, and he punched the wall again.

No one spoke a word.

He looked up at the photos on the wall. There was a photograph of him and Macca sitting on the front steps of the house, taken when he was a young teenager. His mom took it, and from that day on, it hung on the kitchen wall along with other everyday photos she'd taken over the years before her death.

It only distracted him for a moment when David broke the silence. "Mr Jones... I have one more document for you to sign, before I need to get to my next appointment."

Cutter wanted him out of his house and gone anyway, so the sooner he signed, the sooner he would leave. He turned around. Raylee was teary and he knew that his outburst had upset her. "What is it?" he asked in a manner that told David Chambers that he didn't like him very much.

"You might want to sit down for this one." David handed Cutter the pen then turned to the last page for him to sign.

"What's it for?" Cutter asked still standing, as he scribbled his name and handed the pen back without reading it.

David closed his briefcase and stood up to leave. He held out his hand and Cutter reluctantly shook it, knowing it was the only way to get him to go. He was handed a letter, attached to a copy of a policy.

"Your father was a good man, Mr Jones. He always looked out for you... Nice to meet you Raylee. Marnie, thanks for the coffee." David had stayed calm and was very polite, while he knew that he'd overstayed his welcome and he left.

"What was that all about?" Raylee asked him curiously.

Cutter sat down again in silence, reading the attached letter. "It's a life insurance policy," he said. "It's Macca's... He never told me he had life insurance." He turned the page and in between the letter and the policy was a check. "Bullshit," he blurted out loudly, then he began to laugh.

"What?" Marnie asked, barely holding onto her suspense.

"It's a check... for over a quarter of a million dollars." Cutter was shocked, and even when he said those words, it still didn't seem real.

"What? Are you kidding?" Raylee screamed louder. "I don't believe it." She got to her feet at the same time as Cutter threw his chair back and she grabbed the check out of his hand to read it for herself. $260,000.00 made out to Mr Cutter Jones.

She grabbed hold of him and she jumped around, then hugged and kissed him. Cutter was still taking it all in while Raylee was beside herself. Marnie stood there in the kitchen, laughing at them both.

"I can't believe it. I didn't even know he had a life insurance policy." Cutter was reading through the document for clues. "Here it is..."

"What?" Raylee and Marnie said together at the same time.

"Tell us, what is it?" Raylee added when he didn't reply.

"He took it out just after my mom died... He must have thought that if something ever happened to him, then I'd be taken care of."

"Wow, I can't believe he didn't tell you," Raylee stated.

He shook his head. "I never knew," he said, and Raylee could tell that he was genuinely surprised.

He turned and looked at the photo again on the wall. It drew him in. This man was a hero to him. Not just for taking care of every last detail that Cutter didn't even know about, but he was also a good man and everyone knew it.

"The first thing we're gonna do, is pay your dad back everything you racked up against him," Cutter said with authority.

"No," Raylee disagreed, and it shocked him to hear her say it. "If he wants everything back, then he needs to release my money. Then I'll give it to him."

"Raylee." His voice was deep. "I don't want that hanging over me."

"It's not. It's hanging over me. And besides, that little bit won't hurt him for a while." She was definite in her decision and he was too happy to debate it any further.

"Why don't you two go to town and bank that check. The sooner it goes in, the sooner you can pay the bills." Marnie's advice was spot on.

"We'll put the horses away, then I'm taking you out to lunch," Cutter said to Raylee.

Marnie stood at the door and watched Cutter and Raylee hold hands as they walked to the barn leading the horses. They looked good together and they were both happy again. It hadn't been an easy time since Macca had first felt sick and it was because of his illness that the events of the colt and Raylee Tremayne unfolded. Everything that had happened since then was the result of one man who ultimately brought them together.

She walked back into the kitchen and looked at the photos on the wall. She had a lonely tear in her eye. "Thank you, Macca... You've done more than you'll ever know," she said, then she went back to the sink to clean up.

Each day was warming up more than the last. It was lighter earlier and Cutter had less time in the morning darkness before daybreak as the weeks rolled on. His training sessions were intense, while Raylee was showing promising signs of being a good turn back rider. They'd spend hours in the pen and riding the ranch each day, keeping up with the cattle work, and only catching up with Johnny and Emma when they were finished early enough of an evening.

On their few trips to town, they found the time to go and see Doug at his home. He was improving every week with his shoulder and the cut to his face was now reduced to a pink scar. He was embarrassed by the accident and felt bad for Cutter, especially since he had no idea of the strain the ranch was already under.

"Don't worry, Doug. If you didn't have the accident, then we would never have made the claim to the insurance company and they wouldn't have known about Macca," Raylee explained. "We might never have known, or found out when it was all too late." She was trying to make him feel better and it was helping.

"So what will you do now?" Cutter asked Doug.

Doug ran his hand through his long mustache as if he was thinking. "Well, I've given it a lot of thought this last week, and perhaps it was time I retired... Take the payout on the truck and go on a long vacation," he answered openly.

"Marnie won't be too pleased to hear that," Cutter said, and they both looked at him with a sense of confusion. "Well, you won't be delivering cattle to the ranch anymore."

"Am I still allowed to visit?" he asked.

"Of course you are. We'd love to see you there," Cutter said. "And Marnie would too," he added, leaving it on a light note.

While in town they picked up their supplies and fueled up Macca's truck. It was sparkling again and it looked like new. Everything was changing and for the better.

The pressures were now gone and they had made plans with a distinctive direction for the ranch.

It was a countdown now to the show. With only a few days to go, Cutter was getting nervous, just like he was in Australia the night they went to the rodeo. Lying in bed one night, Raylee could tell that anxious feeling was building up in him again, especially when he wasn't busy.

"Now, you're not going to do something stupid again, like ride a bull are you?" she asked, resting on her elbow and looking down on him.

"You should be thankful I rode that bull," he said, as if she really should be.

"Why would I be thankful that you nearly killed yourself?"

"Because you got to take care of me, and because of that you got yourself into my bed."

"Are you saying that if you hadn't ridden that bull, then we might not have happened?" she asked with a curious smile.

"I'm saying that you were hell bent on getting me there. I just made it easy for you. You got me at a very vulnerable time you know."

She took a playful swing at him, then sat over him pinning his arms down. "You make it sound like it was all me. Like I threw myself at you, and you were too weak to resist." Raylee was having fun, just messing around.

He used his strength to roll her over and pinned her arms back onto the bed. "From memory, which is still a bit unclear since I had a major knockout, that sounds exactly how it happened." He was really teasing her now.

"Well let's see if you can resist me now?"

Releasing his grip, Cutter leaned in to kiss her and she kissed him back. She ran her hands through his hair while their legs became tangled together. He unbuttoned her shirt and pulled it down over her shoulder along with her lacy bra strap, then ran his hand from her back to her front, teasing her with the softness of his touch, making her skin tingle all over. His hand wandered and touched her all over while he buried his kisses into her neck. Raylee was feeling in the mood. She loved that he wanted her so much.

"Nah... I'm feeling a bit tired now," he said, and he fell back onto his pillow.

She took her pillow and swung it at him, hitting him in the face. They wrestled on the bed, laughing and swinging the pillows at each other. Raylee was no match for Cutter's strength, but he let her play and be competitive anyway.

When the fun had died down, Raylee brought out what was weighing on her mind. "You know after the show, I've got to go home." It was more of a statement than a question, and not wanting to suggest anything, she was looking for an answer.

Cutter knew this. He'd thought about it every day since she'd arrived at the ranch, that she wouldn't be able to stay any longer than her visa allowed. The time had passed by quickly and while he thought of all the events that had happened since that first week, he couldn't believe that she would be going home soon.

"I know. But maybe you need to go home and sort things out with your parents. Talking on the phone's not doing any good. Maybe you need to see them."

"Can't you come with me?" she asked.

"I'd try talking to your father again, if I thought it was gonna change anything. But the way he was when I left, and then you taking that money from his credit card, didn't do me any favors... I think I'm the last person he wants to see."

"Can you at least think about it?"

"I'll think about it. But you know I just can't leave the ranch again, especially now that I've got on top of things."

"I know... But..."

"Raylee. This ranch isn't going anywhere now and neither am I. You don't need to worry. I'll be here waiting for you when you get back."

He reached over and turned out the light, and made it quite clear that he really couldn't resist her after all.

The insurance check came at exactly the right time. Every bill they had owing was paid up to date. All their insurances were changed over now and their policies were restructured to suit the best needs of the ranch. Cutter had to swallow his pride and he gave David Chambers an apology that was worthy of being heard. It had been a time of learning for Cutter, and he couldn't have done it without Raylee's help.

She too was that extra pair of hands that he needed on the ranch. It had always been Macca and Cutter, and they were the perfect team. With him gone now, Cutter couldn't do it all on his own. Raylee was a great support to him with the horses and she was learning all there was to know about the cattle operation.

He was finding it difficult to think of her not being there, and going back to a lonely house again was not what he wanted. But they'd been in this position before and everything worked out then, so he had faith that fate would intervene and sort it out again.

As the show was closing in, Raylee was in the tack room going through everything that they needed to take. She pulled out the bridles and ropes, saddle pads and buckets and any spare tack that she thought would be useful. She put the hay aside and set it all out in the corner of the barn ready to be loaded into the float. She wanted to be prepared. They still needed their saddles for the time being, but in two more days, they'd be packing them up too and going to the show.

She opened the cupboard at the back of the tack room and found all of Cutter's show shirts. She pulled them out and looked at them, recognizing some of them from the photos hanging on the office wall. They hadn't been worn in years, and while they were still in good condition, she thought they were a little dusty and a bit outdated.

At the back of the cupboard, she pulled out his chaps and she looked them all over. They were dark brown with shiny conchos and she ran her hand over them, looking at the detail. They were worn and they had a history. A history of winning. She took them out of the tack room and placed them with everything else they had to pack.

When Cutter walked into the barn with the filly, he looked at everything piling up in the corner. "You going somewhere?" he asked.

"We're going somewhere... I'm just trying to organize you." Raylee stood there looking at everything, then wondered how it was all going to fit into the float with two horses.

"What makes you think I need organizing?"

She held up his outdated shirts that were in desperate need of another clean. "This is why you need organizing."

"They just need a wash."

"You need some new ones."

"Now Raylee, there's nothing wrong with those shirts," he said, and he picked them up and looked through them all. "Just take them up to Marnie and she'll wash them for you."

"I've got a better idea. Why don't we go to town and buy you some new shirts," she said, giving him a convincingly cute smile. "And some jeans... You could do with an update for the show."

"But these are my favorites," he protested, and she gave him that look. He knew that she meant well, so he quickly gave in and compromised. "Alright then. But I'm keeping my lucky shirt, and don't try to talk me out of it," he said. Then he picked up his chaps. "And I'm not getting new chaps, so don't even think about that."

"Actually, I like your chaps. And maybe later tonight you might put them on for me?" she flirted.

He threw them back down. "Leave them here. I'll bring them home for you later."

After a quick lunch, they made a special trip to town to go to the only shop that sold the right shirts for the show, the same shop where Raylee had bought Cutter's new black hat. She picked out a dozen for him to try on.

"That's enough. How many do you think I need?" he asked with a touch of frustration.

"Just try them on and behave yourself."

She waited outside the change room on a chair while Cutter tried everything on. He came out after each change and together they decided on a yea or a nay, and they settled on half of them and four pairs of jeans.

They walked up the street carrying their shopping bags and holding hands. The town's people knew Cutter well and gave him their best wishes for the show. They had heard about his Australian girlfriend, of the ranch worries and the loss of cattle. They'd even heard of Macca's life insurance policy. There was nothing in that town that wouldn't be public knowledge by the end of each day. Cutter was their boy who had put the town on the map, and they were as proud of his achievements as he was.

During the afternoon back at the ranch, Cutter was preparing the night feeds while Raylee was in the office paying any bills that were due while they were away at the show. They would be away for the week, with Johnny and Emma only a phone call away if Marnie needed them.

She was opening the mail and sorting through its priority, when she came across a letter from the Cutting Horse and Riders' Association. A receipt, and Raylee put it aside to ask Cutter about it later.

"What's this all about?" she asked, when he finally finished at the barn that evening.

He smiled, as if he'd been caught out. "It's a present... for you," he stated.

"For me? Well what is it?" she asked again.

"I bought you a slot."

"What for?"

"So you can ride the colt at the show."

She was stunned. She looked at the receipt and looked back at Cutter, then back at the receipt again. "I don't understand?"

"I bought you a late entry... You're entered to ride him in the Open Non Pro."

"Oh crap. What'd you do that for? I'm not ready for that," she insisted.

He laughed. "Yes you are. You've been riding here every day for nearly three months. Every day you've been around cattle and I think you're ready. Otherwise I wouldn't have wasted my money."

"But Cutter..."

"Don't worry. The colt will do most of the work for you. And besides, we could do with the publicity."

"But what if it's bad publicity? I don't want to let you down."

"You won't... I'll be in your corner, just like you'll be in mine. Now come upstairs and I'll show you what a real cowboy looks like." He swung his chaps over his shoulder and pulled his hat down low over his eyes, tempting her away from the office.

Chapter Fifteen

The road trip to Dallas was easy. When they entered the city, there were signs everywhere advertising the Summer All Stars Cutting Futurity. It was plastered on every lamp post, shopfront and billboard. It was a huge event for the city, where riders from all over the country came together to compete for the biggest prizes on the cutting horse calendar.

For Cutter, it wasn't about the money. It was more about the title. He'd been there before and he knew what winning that title meant. He was on a mission to get back to the top of his game, needing a successful week to launch his career again.

Earlier that morning, Cutter packed the float with everything that Raylee had prepared. Marnie sent with them baskets of food and Raylee packed their bags for the week they would be away. All his new shirts were hanging in the back of Macca's truck, neatly washed and ironed. Something that Raylee was all of a sudden proud to have done. She'd learned a lot from Marnie since she arrived in Texas, and was growing in her strengths in all aspects of the ranch as well as home life. The last thing to go on the backseat of the truck was Cutter's new show hat, still in the box.

With the horses on, they went to the house to say their goodbyes to Marnie. "You just have a good time," she said to Raylee, giving her a hug before she climbed into the truck.

Cutter was leaning against the truck with his hands in his pockets and one leg crossed over the other. There was something about Cutter and Marnie so that, at times, no words were needed. This was one of those times. She just looked into his face and he knew exactly what she was thinking. She gave him a hug also, which was another one of those rare moments, then he got in the truck and started it up.

"I'll see you at the finals," Marnie called out confidently as the truck pulled away, leaving her waving after them.

In Dallas, it was hot. It was still early in the summer and yet it felt like it was on the brink of a heatwave. It was nothing that Raylee wasn't used to from growing up with the long summers back home. Only when it got to boiling point, she'd make her way to the coast and hang out at the beach with friends. But the beach was miles away from where they were now and her home was even further, leaving them to set their sights on the show.

"Wow, there's so many people here already," she commented, looking around at the horse trucks and floats everywhere as they drove into the parking area.

"It's been going for the past week. There were too many entries across all the events so they've been running all the preliminary rounds just to qualify for this week coming," he explained.

"And you didn't have to qualify?"

"Nah. Not everyone had to qualify. And under the circumstances, they gave me a break."

"I can't begin to tell you how nervous I am right now."

Cutter laughed. "I know exactly what you mean."

They pulled the truck up in front of the D block stable area and sat there going through their paperwork and passes. "Well, this is it," Cutter said, and he put his pass on his wrist and handed Raylee hers.

"Yes it is… And no matter what happens here this week, you're still the best trainer and the best cowboy and the best at everything."

"That's enough," he insisted. "Now don't you go around saying that to everyone here."

He leaned over and kissed her, before they climbed out of the truck and went to the float to unload the horses. They worked well together, finding their stalls and unpacking the hay and tack. Raylee didn't know any of the other riders, so she was intimidated by everyone around her, as the oversized floats and goosenecks suggested that there were some big time, successful trainers there.

She looked back at their small three angle float and all of a sudden felt insignificant. When Cutter sold the colt and his horse truck to pay for Macca's treatments, all he was left with was the very basics to start over again. He wasn't bothered by it all. He knew all of the riders there personally and wasn't intimidated by the size of their trucks or how many horses they had. He'd sort that out in the arena. For Raylee, it was all impressive. She hadn't seen anything like it back home and was looking everywhere at once, taking it all in.

As soon as the horses were in their stalls and settled, Raylee wanted to take a look around to find her bearings so that she wouldn't get lost. Cutter, on the other hand, had been there many times before. It was where he'd won on the colt and the arena held many successful memories for him. He knew his way around the grounds just as well as he knew the ranch.

They sat down in the cafeteria for a coffee and studied the program. "Where's the go-rounds?" she asked, flicking through each page referring to her slot.

"There are none. Just a straight out final," Cutter surprised her.

"What? Why?"

"It's just an extra event that's been added to the program. Anyone can enter if they're eligible. But they only took the top thirty."

"What makes me eligible?" Raylee asked curiously.

He laughed. "Not you. The colt... His lifetime earnings guaranteed him a place."

"Oh great. So I'm out there with the top thirty horses in the country, with no go-rounds, and everyone watching me next Saturday for the final?"

"Yes ma'am. Pretty much."

"Okay, now I think I want to throw up."

Cutter laughed again. "Remember what you told me the night of the rodeo?"

"I told you lots of things that night," she teased. His wittiness was starting to rub off, but Cutter just looked at her. "No, remind me."

"You said that it's okay to screw up, as long as you're not afraid of screwing up."

"I'm afraid. I take it back."

Cutter held her hand across the table. "You can't take it back because it's true. Look, I'm shit scared of what's gonna happen here this week, but with you in my corner, I'm gonna give it everything I've got." He squeezed her hand and gave her a reassuring smile. "Or... you could always take the bull by the horns," he added, which made her laugh and eased her anxiety. "Let's go and check in at the hotel," he suggested as a diversion, and they left the cafeteria to head back to the truck.

They drove over to the hotel and checked in, taking a room on the third floor overlooking the complex. From their balcony, they could see their stable block and had a good view of the arena. As for Raylee, standing out on that balcony, she wished they were away on a break. For Cutter, it was all work and it was about to begin.

Raylee had the start of the week to get Cutter and the filly through the go-rounds, with the first round that morning. They were out of bed before sunrise and walked across the road to the grounds, leaving the truck back at the hotel.

He looked good in his new jeans and shirt, and he carried his chaps over his shoulder and showed their passes at the gate. It was his new hat that gave him a look that told everyone they were a team, and his professional attitude said he meant business.

The stables were still under lights as teams were turning up and going through the morning routine of feeding, brushing, saddling and riding. Young girls and boys were there doing their job, preparing the horses for their trainers. They were the support crew that kept the show going and they lived and breathed cutting, working hard behind the scenes. Starting early in total darkness, coordinating the dozens of horses throughout the day ready for their trainers to enter the arena, and leaving late at night after the horses were washed, stabled and fed.

With only two horses to ride over the entire week, Cutter and Raylee could easily manage their programmed rides with plenty of spare time in between. As they arrived, the sun was just breaking over the stable block which highlighted the dust in the sand yards. The smell of coffee brewing and the music on the overhead speakers was a sign that the show would soon kickoff.

Together they saddled the horses. Cutter would take the colt for some light exercise while Raylee loped the filly in circles alongside the other riders. While she had no idea who she was riding next to, she had the feeling that they all knew her. It was the talk of the show that Cutter Jones was making his comeback and he'd turned up with an Australian girlfriend. While they tried to ignore it, the announcer had voiced his comeback several dozen times over the speakers that morning, which only increased the attention and expectations even more.

When it was time, Cutter entered the loping area at the back of the arena on the colt. He unintentionally drew attention from everyone, while he sat there and watched Raylee ride in circles. When she saw him, she went over and they both went to foot. He was dressed in his chaps ready to ride and he looked like the world class horse trainer that he was. They changed the length of the stirrups and changed horses.

"You okay?" Raylee asked.

"I'm good," he lied. "How many to go?"

"You're up in two more," she said. "Everyone's looking at us."

"Don't worry about them. Just remember why we're here."

He rode away and started working the filly just like he'd done many times back home, giving her a tune up and making her respond to every bit of pressure he applied. He gave her some quick sharp runs and some sudden stops, while Raylee watched from the saddle. She kept one eye on Cutter and one eye on the other riders who were taking their two and a half minutes very competitively.

They had both been studying the cattle, and together they had them numbered. The riders from the first half of the herd had scored quite level. The horses were well trained and the cattle were controllable, unlike yesterday's herds, which saw some disastrous results from some great riders with only a few outstanding scores. That only added to Cutter's confidence today, although he knew better than to be complacent. No matter what happened yesterday, he knew that anything could happen in the pen on his ride today.

Raylee was feeling tense. She'd trained for this moment for months on the ranch and she'd been in the cutting pen hundreds of times before. Never had she felt that one ride could take them so far, or bring it all down. She rode out to the corner of the pen, while the other three turn back riders who were old friends were happy to help out. There would be no shortage of volunteers, though Cutter would be selective.

It was still early and the stands were scattered with people all around the tiered seating. The announcer gave Cutter a huge introduction and a welcome like no other rider had received, and people came from everywhere to watch his run, taking up the available seats. "...if you stop to watch any rider throughout this week of competition, then make sure you stop to watch this cowboy," the announcer added.

When Cutter and the filly walked across the timeline, Raylee's heart was racing. He was looking calm and composed as he held onto the horn with one hand and the reins high with the other. When he came close, Raylee could see his grip was tight. They exchanged only a few words about the cattle, before Cutter made a divide straight through the middle.

Taking his time and steadily moving the herd forward, he had his eye cast on one. He applied the right amount of pressure to the mob when the turn back riders moved in. He glided through them slowly, pushing each one aside and singled it out to the front. Now he was in the middle of the pen with the cow, and when it turned to look for the herd, it found itself separated from them by Cutter and his horse.

Putting his hand down, he waited for it to move. It was steady to take off and when it did, it had Cutter and the filly go straight to full speed to block it. It stopped, panicked, and retreated across the pen with the filly not wanting to be outdone and eager to challenge its performance. This was what she was trained to do, and she kept level and worked that cow into a frenzy in the middle of the pen.

Just when Cutter thought it couldn't get any faster, the cow darted from left to right at full acceleration with the seconds on the clock ticking down and his heart going into overdrive. The filly was keeping on top of every turn and every stop. Her timing was perfect and her moves were accurate. She was on fire. When the cow stopped and turned away, Cutter pulled up the reins and made his way back to the herd with a massive applause from the crowd that drowned out his thoughts and concentration.

Pleased that the first cut was behind him, Cutter went to the back wall. He held the filly back somewhat, bringing the herd forward with him at his own stride.

Raylee was watching him closely. He was looking good. The cattle separated when the turn back riders added pressure, while Raylee pushed them together as they fled single file for the mob, leaving one cow in the middle of the pen.

Their game plan was to play it safe. Be correct, and score the points in the go-rounds that would safely see him into the final. When the cow took off at lightning speed, Cutter and the filly hightailed it across the pen and went for broke. The stop was severe and it sped back to the middle where the filly drew it in. Raylee was beside herself. What happened to playing it safe?

The cow wouldn't turn away and wouldn't let up, making quick tight turns in the middle and leaving the filly to dance to its rhythm. It was spectacular to watch. Sand flicking high off her hooves with every step, her electric charge came to a sudden stop as Cutter pulled up the reins when the cow finally gave in.

With little time left on the clock, Cutter took the first cow off the top of the herd and chased it out. His third cut was just as intense, as the connection the cow and the filly had going on showed her skills as a well trained horse. Low in the sand and eye to eye, she couldn't get enough of it and was hot for more.

Two and a half minutes of full adrenalin for Cutter and heart stopping fear for Raylee, as the buzzer went off. The crowd loved it and applauded to tell him so, giving Cutter that welcome back feeling.

"That was unbelievable. I don't know if I can take much more of that," Raylee said, as they rode back to the loping area at the rear of the arena, both relieved it was over.

"Hah. If you think that was something, wait 'til you see the colt," he exclaimed.

His confidence was back, his smile was broad, and the congratulations came in fast from other riders and officials. Raylee had seen him cut at home in her arena and had spent every day in training with him since she'd arrived in Texas, yet there was something special about watching Cutter ride in this competition that took him to a whole new level in her eyes.

Standing in the sand holding the horses, they waited on the score to come in. Raylee was telling Cutter every aspect of his ride from her vantage point. She was wanting to relive the last two and a half minutes, second by second, leaving Cutter to just laugh at her. He had done everything he could. Now his results were in the hands of the judges while they waited anxiously.

The announcer came over the loud speaker with a burst of excitement to interrupt Raylee's commentary. "A two twenty-three," he called out, and he went on about that ride well after the next competitor had crossed the timeline.

"Yes. That puts you up there," Raylee said, totally agreeing with the judges. "At least for the first go-round."

"But there's a full day and some good riders still to come, and anything can happen out there. So don't get too ahead of yourself."

Raylee was. "Are you kidding? I've got you in the final already."

After seeing that run with all the broken training the filly had, as well as the events of the last month they had to deal with at the ranch, she was suddenly full of confidence for both Cutter and the filly's ability.

"You take the colt back and I'll follow you in a while," Cutter said, wanting to go through his warm down routine.

One down and one to go. The final was looking good if he could just repeat that ride the next day. There was so much riding on it. Cutter watched Raylee and the colt until they were out of sight, and he knew that the four of them were the complete team. After an impressive run, he rode around in circles, feeling confident that the filly had what it takes.

When Cutter rode back to the stables, he could see Raylee talking to someone. He got out of the saddle and walked the filly in so that he could untack her before he'd take her to the wash bay. Raylee already had the colt away and was standing outside the stall with the brush still in her hand, as if she had been interrupted. He walked up to them.

The cowboy turned around. "Hey, Cutter. Good ride," he said.

"What do you want?" Cutter asked sharply to the cowboy, and he gave Raylee the reins so he could stand between them.

Raylee was shocked. She could tell straight away that Cutter and this cowboy had a history. They were of the same age and he had a roughness about him that Raylee disliked. It wasn't what he'd said, as much as it was the scar on his cheek and his muddy brown half closed eyes that made him look shady.

"Now that's no way to treat an old friend," he replied with a hint of sarcasm. "I was just introducing myself to your girlfriend here and was letting her know that she could come be my turn back rider anytime."

Cutter grabbed the cowboy by the shirt and slammed him against the stable, frightening Raylee. "I'm not your friend. And you can stay the hell away from her. You hear me? If I see you anywhere near her, we'll be going for round two."

Cutter was up in his face and the cowboy held his hands out as if he was backing down. Not from fear, but because he got the rise from Cutter that he was looking for.

"You alright there, Tommy?" a voice called out from the end of the breezeway.

"Yeah," Tommy said, while he was straightening out his shirt and fixing his hat. "I was just letting Cutter know that we were happy to see him back." He stared into Cutter's face and lowered the tone in his voice. "I'll see you around. Nice to meet you, Raylee." Tommy walked off, but not before he gave her a wink that totally pissed Cutter off.

"What was that all about?" Raylee asked, although Cutter was still fuming. "Well, who was it?" she asked, coming from a different angle.

Cutter started to unsaddle the filly. "That was Tommy. He's part of the rat-pack."

"The what?"

"The rat-pack," he repeated.

"Well that's original," she said. "More like the brat-pack if you ask me."

"It's what Macca used to call them. They're bad news, Raylee, and you need to stay away from them."

"Well how was I to know?"

He looked at her. It wasn't her fault. "I'm sorry," he apologized. "I should've told you about them, and I shouldn't have left you alone."

Raylee led the filly and they walked together down to the wash bay. "So who else is in the rat-pack?" she asked, trying to get him to open up some more.

"Only the top four trainers here this week," he explained.

"Well why didn't you mention it before?"

"A lot of bad blood and bad history. I was trying to forget about it."

After they washed the filly and put her back into her stall, they went for lunch upstairs in the cafeteria. Taking the first bite of his burger, Cutter was interrupted by a couple who were enquiring about his training schedule.

"We've got a colt that's been broken in and started on cattle, and we're looking for a trainer for next season," the man explained politely.

After discussing the breeding, they swapped phone numbers and exchanged cutting horse talk, before they were left to finish their now cold lunch.

Raylee was ecstatic. "It's starting," she said, and she saw the light shining in his eyes again. "Your career is starting all over again."

After lunch and a leisurely walk around the shops, they made their way down to the stables. By the time they made it back to the horses, they had exchanged phone numbers with two more potential clients.

It was a long afternoon, waiting until the last herd had finished before the final scores were in for the first go-round. They watched and waited for the judges to pass on the official results and when they flashed up on the big screen, Raylee jumped up and down while she squeezed Cutter's arm.

"Third place. Not bad for someone who's been to hell and back," she said proudly. "And only one full point between first and third."

"I've got you to thank for everything good that's happened to me lately," he confirmed.

Cutter was up there on the leader board along with the rat-pack. That totally got under his skin and that night when they went to bed, Raylee couldn't help but bring it up again, wanting to know more.

"That Tommy guy said you used to be friends?" she questioned him.

"Used to be," he confirmed, without offering his reasons.

"What happened? Were you fighting over a girl or something?" Raylee was only playing with him. "Is that why you didn't like him talking to me?"

"You could say that," he replied, lying on the pillow with his arm behind his head for support and his eyes closed.

She stopped the playfulness and found her serious voice again. "Really... You guys fell out over a girl?"

"It's a long story."

"I've got all night."

Cutter looked at her. She was wide awake, wanting to know all the details. He'd never get any sleep if he didn't give her an explanation and it would help her understand why she needed to stay clear of the lead rat and his pack.

"As teenagers, we were all good friends and came out of the youth cutting around the same time," he explained. "A few years later we all started to take on a few clients and went pro. I'd be in their corner and they were in mine. Then we started to get real competitive in and out of the cutting pen." He looked at Raylee who was taking in every word. "Tommy had a girlfriend at the time. Sarah. And one night after a show she got real drunk at the bar and started coming on to me... I took her back to her float and was gonna put her to bed, when one of the guys saw me and thought that I was... you know..."

"So what happened?" she asked.

"Nothing."

Raylee looked like she had missed a vital part of the story. "I'm not sure I understand."

"Nothing happened. Nobody said anything. But after that, every time they were in my corner they were all of a sudden having trouble keeping the cattle together. They'd let them slip out and were pushing them in the way instead of holding them back."

"So how'd you work it out?"

"It was happening too often. Then Macca sat in the stands one night and watched. It was at a big show in Vegas and I was only scraping through the go-rounds. He figured it out. As soon as I changed my team I was back on track."

"Did you confront Tommy about it?"

"Yeah. But it didn't end too good."

"Do I even want to know?"

"Put it this way. We both spent a couple of hours at the hospital waiting to get stitched up and were banned for three months from competition."

Raylee was beginning to see the depth of their rivalry and from what she had already seen, she knew that if it was up to Cutter, it would never be repaired.

She was trying to put it into perspective. "So Tommy talking to me was his way of getting back at you for helping his girlfriend?"

"He's a complete jackass. You don't need to be talking to him anyway, no matter what he was trying to do."

"And that scar on his face... Did that have anything to do with your fight?"

Cutter half grinned when he thought about it. "He has to look at that scar every day of his life and know it's a reminder of me."

Raylee had heard enough of Cutter's run-in with Tommy and his pack, so she changed her thoughts. "You were so great today. I can't believe you're up there. And by the way, what happened to playing it safe?"

"Nah. I was just trying to calm your nerves."

"Well hell. My nerves are going to be shot by the end of the week if you keep doing that."

After breakfast at the hotel, Cutter and Raylee wandered over to the stables. It was still early but had all the signs that it was going to be another hot day. More trucks and floats had arrived and the car park was filling up.

The filly wasn't out in the second go-round until mid afternoon, so they took both horses out for some exercise, riding around the available sand yards that surrounded the complex.

After they had lunch, it was time to get ready again. Raylee saddled the filly and took her into the loping area, while Cutter went to the stands and watched some of the runs.

Two of the rat-pack were in this herd and Cutter watched and studied their rides, mostly with criticism, finding every fault and justifying their low scores, both under two twenty. It satisfied him, and with another good run like yesterday, he'd pull further away from them up the leader board and leave them behind.

He was watching the cattle, even though he wasn't out until the next herd, keeping one eye on Raylee riding in circles at the back in the loping area. He took the time to take it all in. Looking around the arena, listening to the music playing and the announcer introducing each rider and horse, as well as its breeding. It was as if he was there on the arena floor only yesterday, winning the Futurity on the colt. Macca was standing there with him at the presentation and they were celebrating.

How much had changed in those years? Macca was gone and Raylee was there. He'd wish Macca back in a heartbeat, but knew it would be at the loss of ever meeting Raylee Tremayne.

Life had dealt Cutter the highs and the many lows, but he was feeling good that everything from this week on was looking up again. It was time now to focus. He made his way back to the stables while they changed the herd and he saddled the colt ready for Raylee to ride.

When the sudden change in music came back on, the announcer came over the loud speakers introducing the seventh herd for the day and the first rider past the timeline. Cutter rode back in, ready to go into the cutting pen. They swapped horses, and he took the filly away from the loping area and ran her through her routine.

Raylee was watching the herd. She was keeping count and was studying the cattle just like Cutter had taught her back at the ranch. Her nerves were building again and her stomach turned one too many times, making her feel light headed, until she rode out to the corner and waited for him to walk across the timeline.

His play it safe game plan was not on his mind when he cut that first cow, giving it as much back as it was giving him. Raylee couldn't take her eyes off him, and all she could think about was how Tommy got his so called revenge on Cutter by purposely pushing the cattle out, instead of holding them back.

His first cow was good. No misses and clean moves. The filly didn't put a foot wrong and she was strong and in control. The second cow which Raylee pointed out, turned out to be a real challenge. It ran from one side of the pen to the other, and while the filly kept up with the speed and its quick stops, it was untidy and Cutter felt relieved when it turned away. He went back into the herd for his third and final cow with just twelve seconds left on the clock.

They finished on a good note. The filly had performed well considering the cattle were unpredictable and as they walked back to the loping area, Raylee apologized three times for choosing the wrong cow.

"It's not your fault. That can happen to anyone. You never really know what they'll do 'til they're out in front of you," he said to ease her mind.

Raylee knew this. She'd been in that same situation before. With a horse and a cow in the same space, anything can happen. Still, she felt personally responsible when the score came in and it was only a two seventeen. She would have no idea where that would put Cutter on the score board and with more riders to come, they wouldn't find out until tomorrow night anyway.

Cutter was half pleased with the results. The cattle were tougher today and he wasn't the only one who was having trouble. Many of the top riders from the first day had now finished their go-rounds and were pulled right back on the leader board. Some had come to the conclusion that they were out of the running altogether, and would now set their sights on the Derby and Classic events. For Cutter, all his hopes were resting on the final and riding the colt in the Open.

When the horses were back in their stalls for the night, Cutter and Raylee walked around the arena to watch the last of the herds. People gave their congratulations to Cutter on a good, but difficult ride. Others expressed their sympathy for losing Macca, and some were feeling out his training schedule for next season.

A man's voice called out. "Jake." It didn't register to Cutter and he kept walking, until he called out again. "Jake Morgan."

Cutter froze on the spot. He hadn't been called that name since he was three years old, and nobody would ever know him by that name except for one person.

He turned around. The man was leaning against the railing with his hands in his pockets and with one leg crossed over the other, looking directly at him. Cutter was stunned. It wasn't a question of who it was, but rather, why was he there?

"What did you call me?" Cutter asked as he walked over to him, unaware that he'd left Raylee behind.

"Jake Morgan... That's your name isn't it? At least, that's the name I gave you when you were born," the man said.

"Who is this?" Raylee asked, when she caught up and heard the last of his claim.

Both Cutter and Raylee stared at him. He was an older man who was well dressed, although Raylee looked into his eyes and could tell that he'd been through some tough times. He stood up tall and was standing his ground. Cutter didn't know what to say, until Raylee touched him on the arm to break their stare and then reality caught up with his thoughts.

"Raylee, this is Pete Morgan... My father."

Chapter Sixteen

Raylee was stunned. If ever there was an awkward moment... this was it.

"What do you want?" Cutter demanded of Pete.

"I just wanted to see you," he said cautiously.

"Yeah, well I don't wanna see you," Cutter threw back at him severely, and he started to walk away.

Pete was not giving up that easily. "Jake?" he called out.

He turned to look at him. "It's Cutter."

"Okay then. Cutter... I heard that you were coming to Dallas. Your comeback's been all over the radio." He was now fumbling for conversation. "I was sorry to hear about Macca."

"You have no right to mention my father." Cutter was mad and he let Pete know it.

"I'm sorry. I'm not here to pick a fight," he defended.

"Well since you mentioned it, why are you here?"

Pete could never have thought this would be easy. "I wanted to tell you how sorry I am. I need you to give me a chance to explain everyth..."

Cutter cut him short. "Sorry... You're sorry? Were you sorry when you used to come home wasted and mess up my mom's face? Or take every last dollar we had so you could go get yourself drunk while she couldn't even buy us food? Or were you sorry that she left you for a better life?"

Raylee had never heard the details of Cutter's younger life, so these insights were a rare glimpse of the reasons Mary-Ann had left his father. She was standing behind his shoulder, looking into Pete's eyes. She felt sorry for him. Not because of what he'd done, but because they were standing in front of a man who'd missed out entirely on his son's life.

"I need you to know that I've been sober now for over twenty years," Pete said proudly. "And I've never forgiven myself for all the things I've said and done to you and your mom."

"And I can't forgive you either." Cutter turned to walk away for a second time.

"Jake?" Pete called out, then corrected himself. "Cutter?"

He turned back around to give Pete one final blast that would give him the message to never bother him again, before Pete cut him off. "Your sisters want to meet you. If you're interested?" he said, holding out a piece of paper. "Take it... It's my number. Think about it and give me a call if you wanna meet them."

Cutter was floored. Raylee was surprised and when she looked at Cutter, she could see the confusion in his face. They both stood there looking at Pete in total disbelief. He'd never thought about having brothers or sisters before. He was an only child, and it never occurred to him that his father had moved on and had another life after his mom.

He walked out anyway. It was too much to hear. Raylee had remained silent and just stood there not knowing what to do. She grabbed the piece of paper from Pete, giving him a smile then left to follow Cutter to the stables.

He was in a world of his own. Silent. Checking the horses and giving them their last feed before they'd go back to the hotel. Raylee didn't say anything about Pete. It wasn't the right time or place to have that sort of discussion, although she couldn't wait to get back to their room where she would bring it all out into the open.

"I don't wanna discuss it," Cutter said sternly, when they were back in the privacy of their room.

"Why not? Cutter, you've got a family." She was trying to put a positive spin on it but it didn't help like she intended.

"They're not my family," he snapped. "My mom and Macca are my family."

"I know that. Everybody knows that... But you've got sisters. Aren't you curious to meet them?"

He looked away and changed the subject. "I'm really tired."

Raylee felt for him. He did look tired. He was looking washed out from the long day so she let it be, at least for the time being.

The bathroom door closed harder than he intended, even though he wasn't angry at Raylee. Totally confused by the sudden twist of fate he'd been dealt, he took his hat off and looked into the mirror at those lines around his eyes. His head was spinning out of control. He had sisters. How many? How old? He'd walked away with a lot of questions unanswered and it was all of a sudden starting to bother him.

"I'm sorry," he apologized, after he had a shower and sat next to Raylee on the bed. He was in the bathroom for so long that she'd fallen asleep still in her jeans and shirt.

"It's a bit hard to take it all in, isn't it?" she said.

"I never thought about my dad much over the years... Macca was my dad, and Pete was just some drunk that my mom used to know. That's how I always dealt with it in my head."

"That's okay. You said that you didn't remember much about him, and Macca was the only father you ever knew. There's nothing wrong with that."

"But why is he here? Why now?"

"I don't know. Maybe you need to ask him," she suggested, even though she knew he wouldn't accept Pete's explanation.

"First Tommy. Now Pete... This wasn't the week I had planned," he stated.

"Do you want to know what I think?" Raylee asked, and before he could answer, she was explaining her thoughts. "I think he just wants your forgiveness."

"Well I don't know if I can give it to him."

"Well you can always listen to what he has to say before you decide that."

"Why should I?"

"Because everyone has a right to explain their story. Even you."

"Me? What do I need to explain?" he asked.

"When my father walked in on us, all you wanted to do was explain your side of the story and have his forgiveness. You wanted to make things right with him and it was important to you. You know what it's like to have that door closed in your face, how it makes you feel, and now you're doing the same thing to Pete."

Raylee was right. Allan Tremayne hadn't given Cutter the opportunity to apologize in the way he'd have liked, to clear up the events that had happened between him and Raylee after the rodeo. He felt hard done by and now he was closing that door between himself and Pete, with the possibility of never knowing another side to his family.

"Aren't you even curious?" Raylee asked.

It was starting to sink in. "It does make you wonder," he admitted.

"Well then, the way I see it, you've got nothing to lose and everything to gain."

"Stop it, Raylee."

"Stop what?"

"Stop trying to convince me that it's a good idea. I think it's you who's curious."

"Well maybe I am. But it's not every day you get given a new family."

"I told you. They're not my family," he said abruptly.

"Okay. But give it a couple of days and see how you feel about it then. If you don't want to meet them, then we'll go home after the show and won't discuss it again. But if you do want to, then I'll make the phone call."

Cutter was satisfied with that. He didn't want to go on and on about it. He was there at the show to do a job, and there was a lot of pressure riding on this week without ex friends turned rivals, and new family drama getting in the way.

When the official results came in after both go-rounds were complete, Cutter and Raylee were sitting in the stands as they'd just watched the last herd for the night. The announcer was winding up with the highlights of the last four days of cutting, and Raylee was sure that she heard Cutter's name mentioned at least half a dozen times.

It seemed that everyone was pleased to see him back. Everyone, except for the rat-pack. Tommy Parker, Brock Lee, Brad Carlton and Matt Hartley, were all up on top of the leader board. They'd all had several horses in the event and between them, they had eight of the twenty places in the final.

Cutter just scraped through on points and qualified in eighteenth position. But he was in it. The filly had done a good job and he felt that her best was still to come.

"Well, you said you'd be happy if you just made the final," Raylee pointed out, to make him see that he should be pleased with the result.

"I'll be happy when I wipe that smile off Tommy's face."

"So you're not happy then?" she questioned him.

He looked at her and touched her leg. "I'm happy... Happy to go back to the room and get you to try these on," he said, and he held up the shopping bag.

It wasn't until a few hours earlier that Cutter and Raylee realized that she didn't have any chaps to wear. It was such an afterthought for her to ride the colt and it could have been a huge oversight, if they hadn't seen a nice pair for sale at a saddlery stand in the shopping area of the complex. Cutter sized her up and bought them as a gift. She'd worked so hard for the past three months and he could have bought her anything at the show, but he liked the personal touch that her chaps were from him.

He took his boots off at the door and stretched out on the bed. It had been a more laid back day, only taking the horses out for a few rides and getting roped into helping out in the corners for a few competitors when they were short of turn back riders.

He wasn't competing though, and that gave Cutter a chance to get back into the cutting zone without the pressure, catching up with old friends and finding out about new bloodlines that were coming through. There was so much he'd missed out on in the last three years. He eased his way back into it and from the outside looking in, you couldn't tell he'd ever been away.

Raylee was taking her time in the bathroom. As soon as they got in the door, she went in to try her new chaps on, just to make sure they fitted well and didn't need adjusting before she needed them on Saturday.

"Are you okay in there?" Cutter called out after the time was dragging on.

"I think so," Raylee called back.

"Do you need some help?" he volunteered.

"Very funny... Do you want to see them on or off?" They were flirting through the closed door and Cutter loved that she was always willing to light that spark for him.

"I'm not really sure," Raylee said, sounding doubtful. "I don't know if they fit so well."

"So come out and show me. I can't see you through the door. If they're not right then we'll take them back tomorrow."

"Okay. But if you don't like them, just remember you picked them." Without a further response, Raylee opened the door and walked out into the room. Cutter was resting on his elbows with his legs crossed. When he opened his mouth to speak, no words came out, although his eyes were working perfectly.

Raylee stood in the dim light. Her jet black hat matched her lacy knickers and bra, and the dark brown chaps hugged her legs tight showing just how petite her figure was.

She spun around. "Well, what do you think? Do you think I can wear these?" she asked over her shoulder, with her hands on her hips.

Cutter still didn't answer. He couldn't. He sat up on the side of the bed, taking it all in. She turned back around and walked over to him. "What's the matter, don't you like them?" she teased. "I'll take them back if you don't like them."

"You are so not taking them back," Cutter stated. He reached out and pulled her by the hand and she sat over him. "You are too hot for words, Raylee Tremayne," he added, then he kissed her passionately.

Raylee gave every ounce of love that she had in her to her cowboy that night. She was totally in love with him and she let him feel it.

It was the well deserved break that both Cutter and Raylee needed. Away from the hard work that the ranch demanded and with the financial pressures gone, they now had time for each other, at least until Cutter was to ride the colt in the Open.

They would spend hours over at the arena. Riding, socializing, shopping and living life in the cutting world, rubbing shoulders with other trainers and some big time investors in horse breeding. It made for good business connections and Raylee's book was filling up fast with contacts and phone numbers. A good ride on the colt would certainly give Cutter back the status that he had left behind years ago, and give the colt an impressive boost to his list of breeding opportunities.

Tommy and his pack were never too far away. Cutter and Raylee avoided them wherever they could, though they had crossed paths several times where sly remarks only added to his hatred of his rival. Cutter was getting to the point that he didn't care where he finished in the final on the filly, as long as it was ahead of Tommy Parker.

For Raylee, every day was one day closer to Saturday's final and she was feeling it. They bought some passes to the practice pen where she took the colt for a run on the mechanical cow, with Cutter giving her instructions from the fence.

She had grown as a rider since they'd met almost four months ago and her connection with the colt was fast becoming obvious. She too was looking good when she rode him.

"I should have entered you in the Futurity as well," Cutter suggested when she left the practice pen. "You could've ridden the filly in the Non Pro."

"I'm sorry, and don't take this the wrong way, but not a chance in hell."

Cutter laughed. He could see that she lacked confidence, as they walked the colt back to the stables. "You'll be fine... Just don't over ride him." He was always giving her the best advice and she took on everything he said. "Your riding has come a long way since you've been working on the ranch, and he's got more talent than you know. Just let him work the cow, and you just hold on for the ride."

If only it were that simple. Cutter was trying to build up her confidence and Raylee let him. Deep down, she knew that she had to work the colt to get him to do that magic. Only, it was helping with those little butterflies that kept fluttering around inside her tummy.

Standing outside the stall, he watched her unsaddle the colt. He was always watching her from a distance, and would often wonder how on earth this girl had stolen his heart and consumed his thoughts. He replayed in his mind the events of the previous night. She'd provoked every desire he had in him, leaving nothing left to wonder.

He was beginning to understand that the way he loved Raylee, was the same way that Macca had loved his mom. It was something he could never create or find just because he wanted to. This was the real thing and he was sure of it.

"What are you looking at?" she asked, breaking his stare.

"I was just thinking how much I love you," he said sincerely.

It caught her by surprise. "It's the chaps, isn't it?" she asked with a cheeky smile, and she pulled on his buckle to draw him in close.

"Well, that might have a little bit to do with it," he agreed, not totally revealing his softer, truer side of his feelings for her. However he did kiss her, and he wasn't embarrassed to show her affection even though it was a main thoroughfare for other riders and their horses.

"While you're in a good mood, I was thinking that we should call Pete... I really think you should meet his family." Raylee was almost insisting.

"Well you know how to spoil a good moment, don't you?"

"You know, we'll be too busy here in a couple of days. Then we'll be going back to the ranch, and then I'll be going home and you won't want to..."

"Stop it. I told you I'd think about it, but stop pushing me." Cutter put his hands in the air. "I know you're full of good intentions, but I'm not convinced it's the best thing to do. And even if I did want to, I'm not sure that this week is the best timing."

"Well maybe it's not all about you," she said without harsh intent. "Maybe there are some girls out there that just might want to meet their big brother... None of this is their fault."

"You said you weren't gonna mention it. Now you just can't help yourself." His mood had turned on a dime and he was beginning to fire up. "And since you mentioned it... It is all about me. You weren't there. It wasn't your father who knocked your mom around and had to wear the scars every day. You weren't the three year old kid who had to hide under his bed every time your father came home drunk. You didn't live it, and my sisters didn't live it. But I did."

Raylee instantly regretted her comments. She thought she'd only be helping the situation, not thinking that she was pushing him into doing something that he really wasn't ready for.

"I'm going to get some air," Cutter said and he walked out of the stables, leaving Raylee to put the colt back in his stall.

She was upset that she had pushed the issue but she couldn't take it back now. It wasn't that she was picking a fight. She actually thought she was helping him to make the right decision. Even though Cutter didn't remember much of Pete as a little boy, he knew enough from his mother to know what sort of man he was.

Right now, he just needed some space.

He found a tap. The heat of the day was not wavering and he crouched down and ran his hands under it, then splashed his face to cool off. He needed time to think. He was in a dilemma. Cutter knew Raylee was right in one way. It wasn't his sisters' fault, but he just couldn't forgive Pete enough to be able to meet them yet either.

The show was his priority. Everything he'd worked for as a trainer was depending on this show and he'd already made an impressive comeback into the cutting world, yet he still had a long way to go.

He was not wanting to fight with Raylee either. He hadn't meant to raise his voice to her. He was more angry at Pete than anyone else. Cutter decided that he wasn't going to let Pete Morgan get in their way and he wandered around the other stables for a while, just to clear his head and get some focus back.

He took his time before walking back to D block, ready to make up. When he rounded the corner of the breezeway, he saw Tommy Parker talking to Raylee. His blood boiled. What was he doing talking to Raylee when he'd already warned him to leave her alone?

"Hey," he called out, making Tommy and Raylee both turn around.

"Hey, Cutter," Tommy said casually, as if they were great friends.

"I told you to leave Raylee alone," Cutter reminded him, and he walked up to them both.

"It's alright. I was just giving her some friendly advice," he taunted.

"Oh yeah, and what was that?"

"Just to keep an eye on you... That you like to go after other girls, just like you went after Sarah."

Cutter didn't comment. With all his anger, he grabbed a fistful of Tommy's shirt and threw him against the stable door. Tommy, thinking that he would only be letting off steam like the other day, didn't defend himself, until Cutter threw a punch that hit Tommy in the eye.

They both stumbled. Raylee stood back and yelled for them to stop, although neither boy heard her screams.

They fell to the ground and wrestled in the breezeway, throwing punches at each other. Tommy hit Cutter in the ribs and it took the wind out of him, slowing him down. It made him so angry that he gripped his fist hard and punched Tommy again in the face. Blood came from Tommy's nose. He returned a swing at Cutter and split him under the eye where it had only healed a couple of months ago from his altercation with the bull. It was years worth of hatred coming out of both boys and it was violent.

Everybody stood back keeping their horses locked up, with a crowd gathering at each end of the breezeway to see who was fighting.

Two security guards came running in. One of them called for backup on his radio while the other ran to pull them apart. The boys were so aggressive with each other that the security guard didn't stand a chance and was pushed aside, falling to the ground.

Cutter and Tommy didn't let up. Covered in cuts and blood, they punched each other senseless. Raylee was still crying out, screaming for them to stop.

She was too scared to go anywhere near them and pinned herself against the stable door to keep clear.

This was the round two that Cutter had warned Tommy about. They had never fully settled their issues before, and it was clear that this was not going to fix it now. The rat-pack stood around, letting the fight go on with neither cowboy giving in. Tommy feeling that Cutter's weak spot was his ribs, laid into him some more.

When the security backup arrived, it took four men to pull them apart. The barn official also ran into the breezeway and the crowds that had gathered at each end to watch the spectacle quickly dispersed.

Cutter was still kicking from adrenalin while he was trying to break loose. Tommy was roughed up but looking satisfied, with a smirk on his face and blood-stained teeth. This had been a long time coming. For Cutter, it was his grief, stress and hate all coming out against one person. Tommy Parker.

Raylee went to Cutter. The security guard still had him restrained, then slowly released his grip. The cuts on his face were far worse than the night of the rodeo, and he spat blood on the ground then wiped his mouth on the sleeve of his new white shirt.

Tommy smiled smugly when he saw the deep gash on Cutter's face below his eye. He had just evened the score.

The barn official had also called for backup, and the President of the Association arrived at the scene when it was all over. He could clearly see the evidence of what looked like a wild brawl. Buckets were overturned. Hay and tack were spread across the breezeway. He was abrupt, telling them to both be in his office in fifteen minutes or they'd be banned from the final and escorted from the grounds immediately. The last thing either of them wanted, was another three month ban.

Tommy and the rat-pack walked back to his truck. Cutter sat on a bale of hay while Raylee took a dry cloth and wiped the blood off his face. She was still shaking when she looked into his eyes. "I am so sorry," she said tearfully.

"It's not your fault. I told him not to talk to you again."

"I mean about Pete," she said. "If I didn't push it on you, then you wouldn't have left me to go for a walk and Tommy wouldn't have found me alone."

Cutter was only half listening. His heart was still racing and he was still reeling. His knuckles were covered with Tommy's blood and his new shirt was torn down the sleeve.

"You're going to need stitches," Raylee told him when she closely examined his face. He had one deep cut under his left eye that needed medical attention.

"Well it will have to wait... I've gotta be upstairs in the President's office in fifteen minutes."

Cutter found his black hat covered in dust and hay. He brushed it off and put it on, then pulled it down low over his eye and held the cloth tight against his cheek to soak up the blood. Together they walked up to the office. Cutter was holding his side, as he only felt the pain in his ribs again when he stood up and began to walk.

When they arrived at the office on time, Tommy was nowhere to be seen. Cutter knocked on the door and they were called in. The President of the Association was sitting behind a large desk that was set up purely for the show, with his name plaque the only introduction that Raylee received.

He was a big, strong man with tanned skin and a long mustache. His oversized Texan hat cast a dark shadow over his face that matched his voice. "Take a seat, Cutter," Mike offered. "You can wait outside there, miss," he said to Raylee, and Cutter agreed.

"You don't need to be in here. I won't be long," Cutter said, and she closed the door behind her.

Waiting in his office were two women from the medical team. One of them was already looking at Cutter's face when Tommy walked in a couple of minutes later. Cutter was sitting still as the woman had already begun stitching him up, while he held an ice pack on his ribs for comfort.

"Sit down, Tommy," Mike said firmly. Cutter wouldn't look at him.

The other medical officer then tended to Tommy and both boys sat in chairs that they had purposely pulled away from each other. Mike looked at them both. They were a mess. It was a sight he'd seen before in Vegas and it was getting too familiar for his liking.

"I'll get straight to the point," Mike said in his broad Texan accent. "I knew both your fathers well and I'd have to say they'd be disappointed in both of you here today."

"I'd doubt that," Tommy murmured under his breath, but since he was blocked by the medical officer, only Cutter heard his cunning remark.

As Cutter's stitches were going in and Tommy's nose was being assessed for the damage, they both kept very still, making Mike's job of addressing the incident much easier.

"What I should be doing, is giving you both a six month ban from competition, starting immediately," Mike said to them both, and Cutter's heart felt like it hit the floor. "But under the circumstances and you both qualifying for the final, I'm not gonna do that this time. I won't draw attention to your stupidity."

Cutter was instantly relieved. Neither of the boys moved and they sat in silence, while Mike was just getting wound up. "But you boys hear my words. If this shit happens again, anywhere in the country on site at a show, you will be banned. You've got my word on that. I've done it before and I'll do it again. Now, I don't know what the hell the problem is between you two, and I sure as hell don't wanna know. But there ain't no place for that kind of bullshit here. Do you hear me? This is not the time or place and your issues don't belong here. Now, I've given both you boys a second chance, don't let me regret it."

Mike was angry and he let them know it. His tirade was justified and after giving them a further five minutes of drilling over their inappropriate behavior, he was done. "You can go now, Tommy," Mike said in an unfriendly manner, and he more or less told him to leave his office. "Cutter, you can remain seated."

Cutter had known Mike for many years. He'd been the President of the Association for the past eight years while Macca was on the board of directors for three of those before he got sick.

"I was sorry to hear about Macca. Your dad will be greatly missed by everyone here. He was a good man." Mike had changed his tone once Tommy had left the room.

"Thanks, Mike."

"Look, I don't know what your problem with Tommy is, but something tells me there's more to what's going on here than just another run-in with Tommy Parker. And if I'm right and you've got something going on in your personal life, then I'm suggesting that you sort it out and soon."

Was it that obvious? Had word got around about Pete?

"I'll tell you one thing, Cutter. All the trainers were unhappy when they heard of your comeback. They've had three good years sharing the different titles and winnings, and you coming back this year has really pissed them off. The last thing you wanna do now is lose your focus and let Tommy keep you from getting back on top of your game. You're good for the sport, and it's good for you. Now you know what it takes, go out there and damn well do it."

Cutter had a lot of respect for Mike and he could see why Macca and he were good for the Association. "Thanks, Mike. I appreciate it," Cutter said, without explaining his personal life.

It seemed like Mike was on Cutter's side. He'd always liked him and was genuinely pleased to see him back. "Just don't let Tommy Parker or anyone else for that matter, be your downfall," he added, before Cutter stood up.

Cutter had only one problem with Tommy and it was a big one that would never be resolved. With the financial pressures of the ranch behind him now, the only thing that was hanging over his head, was Pete. Maybe he did have to face those demons from his past so that he was able to move on in his life one way or another.

Raylee had been sitting on a chair outside the office and had seen Tommy leave. He didn't look at her, but she could see the white tape that was spread across his nose as if it were possibly broken. She was panicked as to why Cutter was taking much longer. She wondered what sort of trouble he was in, since she knew he threw the first punch. Maybe his punishment was getting dealt with now. She regretted her comments about Pete and made a definite decision not to mention his name again.

Cutter went to the door to leave. "Good luck for the rest of the show," Mike said sincerely.

"I'll do my best," Cutter replied, with eight stitches intact and the ice pack pressed firmly against his eye.

When Cutter opened the door, Raylee jumped to her feet and looked at him. "What did he say?" she asked when they walked away. Cutter wanted to get out of there and go back to the hotel as soon as possible. The horses were both settled in their stalls and he had a pounding headache.

As soon as they were back in the privacy of their room, Cutter relaxed on the bed. Raylee went to the bathroom and ran a warm bowl of water. It was only three months ago that she was cleaning his face from the night of the rodeo. Now she was cleaning the mess that Tommy had made.

She turned the lamp on and sat next to him on the bed, pulling the ice pack away gently to look at his eye and the stitches. "You're lucky you didn't have to go to the hospital," she said, like the good nurse she was.

"How's it look?"

"Like you've been in a fight, and that you came off second best," she said. "Except that I saw Tommy's face and I think you might have just had it over him."

It pleased Cutter to think that Tommy looked worse.

"So, what happened? Are you getting another ban?" She was desperate to know what went on in that office behind closed doors.

"Not this time... But one more fight will see us both sit on the rails for six months."

"Then you need to stay away from him."

"I can handle Tommy. It's you he needs to stay away from."

"I can handle myself. He was shooting his mouth off and I was just explaining that he got it all wrong about you and his girlfriend."

"Oh yeah, and what did he say to that?" he asked, although Cutter already knew what Tommy's answer would be.

"He said that you were a good liar."

Cutter laughed. "He'll never change."

Raylee was wiping his face. "You know the only way to sort this out?" she said, ignoring Tommy's claim.

"How?"

"In the arena."

Again, like so many times before, Raylee was right. Neither cowboy was ever going to get over their hate for each other and settling it with their fists was only going to get them banned. The only way they would settle the score was in the cutting pen and on the score board. Except that at this show, Tommy was a long way ahead and Cutter was so far behind.

"There's one more thing I need you to do for me," Cutter said, and she stopped wiping his face and rested her hand gently on his ribs. "I need you to call Pete. I have to do this so that I can let it go and get back to cutting."

It surprised Raylee. It was the last thing she expected to hear and it pleased her to think that he needed it. "Okay then... I'll arrange something," she said casually, and she left it at that.

Chapter Seventeen

Cutter was torn. Torn between never wanting to see Pete again, and knowing that if he didn't, then he'd never be able to fully let it go. He was still curious about his sisters. They would be the only family he had left in the world and whether he liked it or not, they were blood.

Raylee had arranged to go to their house on Friday afternoon. While she didn't tell Cutter the details about the phone call, she heard a very happy Pete on the end of the line.

She had gone over to the stables to feed the horses and let Cutter sleep. He wasn't competing until the afternoon and when she arrived back at the room, she turned the side lamp on to wake him.

The swelling around his eye hadn't blown out too much overnight thanks to the icepack. The bruising around his stitches was coming through in shades of blue and purple, and his lip was cut again. He looked worse this morning than he did the previous night, although it would now be his aching ribs that were causing him the most discomfort, and he was feeling it.

There were no regrets. He was pleased that he'd messed up Tommy. It was worth every cut and every bit of pain he was feeling just to have had the chance to lay into him again.

"Where did I draw?" he asked about the Open.

"Middle herd. Eighth out." Raylee had looked it up while she was at the stables. "And I'll have to go back over soon to start getting him ready."

"I'm coming with you."

"I'll be okay. I don't think that Tommy will bother me again."

"I'm sure he won't, but I'm still coming over."

While at the arena, Raylee had picked up some tape from the medical team to strap Cutter's ribs for support, and she was getting good at it. He couldn't rest anymore, and it was time to put his cutting head on and fasten himself up for a good ride.

The Open had the same format as the Non Pro event. The top thirty horses in a straight out final. It was an important event that would draw a big crowd where he could showcase the colt, since he had been out of the spotlight and he needed to attract attention to him again.

Cutter was pleased with the draw too. As Raylee saddled the colt and took him into the loping area, Cutter went in to watch the rounds. Tommy was already sitting in the stands with his pack, so he avoided them by sitting on the other side, watching the cattle and the other riders. He would predict the scores and see where they lost points, playing judge and critic at the same time.

The last things on his mind now were Tommy and Pete. He would put that behind him and spend the next hour reflecting on the colt's last ride there. He thought of Macca and the hell he'd been through since. It weighed heavily on his mind, but it got him fired up again and when the time was near, he went back to the filly to saddle her up and put his chaps on.

Riding out through the breezeway, the warm air brushed past his face giving him a sting on the cheek where his stitches were. Although it was nothing compared to the sharp stab in his ribs that he felt with every step. He would have to bear the pain for the two and a half minute ride and show everyone what he and the colt were made of. There was no getting out of it, he would just have to cowboy up.

He met Raylee behind the cutting pen in the loping area. Again they exchanged horses and changed the length of the stirrups, but they didn't exchange words. There was very little to say and Raylee knew that Cutter was fully determined to just get on with the job.

"How many more?" he asked.

"You're up next," she replied, and that was all that was needed to be said.

He took the colt into the prep lane and gave him a quick workout. Finding those spots that made him respond. In the cutting pen was Brock Lee, with the rest of the pack in his corners, while Cutter watched with one eye.

The other scores were irrelevant to Cutter. He would go out there and give his run the best he could give, and no score from any other rider would make him perform any better. As the buzzer went off to end Brock's ride, the announcer would soon come over the loud speakers to give him a score of a two twenty-five, which put him in second place on the leader board.

As Raylee rode out to the corner, she passed Tommy who was on his way back in. "Let's see if your boyfriend can beat that," he said, just to wind her up.

Under the circumstances, she knew that it was a big ask, as they would have to both be exceptional in every way. However, she ignored Tommy's baiting tactics and felt tense for her cowboy, and the colt's first appearance back in the spotlight.

"...for die hard cutting fans, you won't wanna miss this ride. He's already been labelled the best trainer this country's ever seen, and is twice the National Futurity Champion. He's won countless Derby and Classic finals and has trained some of the best horses in the country. I have it on good authority that he's pretty damn good on a bull too. He's back here today after three years out of the cutting pen and has already made an impressive return to the arena floor this week. He's from Texas. Please make welcome, Cutter Jones riding Midnight Dynamite." The announcer couldn't have praised him anymore than he did and his voice filled the arena, attracting everyone's attention.

It was true there were other riders who had won more events over their life long careers, whereas Cutter had only been a pro rider for five years before he took that long break, and in that short time his record spoke for itself. He still hoped to have a long and successful career ahead of him.

Everyone flocked to see his ride. They weren't only interested in how Cutter would show, but the colt had a good reputation and one of the highest ever scores recorded in Futurity history. He was a real crowd pleaser.

As Cutter walked across the timeline, Raylee could see that his shoulders were sunken and he was sitting slightly to one side, protecting his ribs. When he came closer to her, his blackened eye became obvious and his cuts and bruises made him look like a true cowboy.

They briefly spoke about the cattle before he went in deep and walked the herd slowly towards the judges' stand. He took them out straight, selecting his cow early. Without any effort, the cattle rounded back to the herd with the added pressure from the turn back riders, where they huddled together on the back wall in a close mob. This was it. He lowered his reins when he was left with his chosen one and held on tight, bracing himself for the next two minutes rush of pain and suffering.

The colt responded to the cow and lowered himself into position, ready for the break. When the cow charged across the pen, the colt took off at full force and followed it with perfect attention. Every short burst, the colt reacted. Every sudden stop, he predicted. The more panicked the cow, the more excited the colt was, and with every stop and turn the colt was all over it, blocking every move and provoking it to fret more. He was smashing it.

The crowd were loving it too. They hadn't seen a ride like this since Cutter was last on the colt, and he didn't look like he'd had any time away at all. Every step and the timing was perfect. Every turn and the colt was in sync, and when the cow turned away, Cutter pulled up the reins and heard the whistles and applause from the excited crowd. He knew he'd had a good ride, he just needed to choose another cow like that and he was home free.

With over sixty seconds left on the clock, he needed to slow things down. The speed of the colt and his sharp stops were hard on Cutter's body, and he wasn't sure how he was going to get through another minute of it.

He went into the mob for another cow, making his way forward and giving himself valuable seconds to catch his breath. He needed to waste a bit of time, trying to look at ease when really, he was feeling the agony from the burning pain in his ribs. The cattle folded back to the herd effortlessly again, leaving him with no more time to relax and wonder if he'd be able to ride out the clock.

With one cow standing alone in the middle of the pen and forty-five seconds countdown, Cutter knew he had to pace himself. As soon as he put his hand down, the colt's instincts took over and he had to brace himself for another wild ride.

He slumped down even lower to give himself more comfort, but it was the quick edgy sideswipes from the colt that Cutter was having the most trouble with. While his spectacular moves were impressive, it was the rider who couldn't keep up and every explosive stop was adding to the severity of his pain like a twisted knife in his side. He had a few bad misses in the last thirty seconds that were out of his control and would ruin his run.

Struggling to restrain the colt's energy without pulling him up, Cutter couldn't get off the cow. It wouldn't turn away, leaving him no choice but to hold on and try to ride it out.

Tearing up the sand with those powerful turns, the colt was drawing the cow in with a force that he was famous for. What would be a dream run for any other rider, turned out to be a total nightmare for Cutter who could do nothing to match the colt's performance in the twenty second countdown.

Raylee was watching the timer, knowing the colt had performed well and had pleased the crowd, and that it was Cutter who had messed it up. With seven seconds left on the clock, Cutter did the unthinkable. He couldn't hold on any longer and he picked up the reins and pulled him up. His worst fears were realized when he saw how close to the end he was, as he wrapped his good arm around his sore ribs, leaning forward to give ease to the pain. Raylee was as shocked as the crowd were confused, as the sudden early end to his run was abrupt.

It was cowboy down.

Raylee could see he was in trouble and she rode over to him. "Are you okay?" she asked with justified concern.

"I'll be fine," he said, although she didn't believe him.

"Let's get you back to the stables."

They rode out of the arena towards D block as the zero score came in. It totally gutted him, adding humiliation and frustration to the pain he was already feeling. He knew that he'd lost points in the last thirty seconds where he had a few misses and was struggling to keep up to the colt's powerful pace, but he only had to hold on for a few more seconds to at least give him a score on the board.

He was now sitting at the bottom of the leader board in this elite group when he should have been on top. Even though the colt had performed that magic that he was well known for, it was the rider that let him down and he knew it.

Raylee held both the horses when they got back to the stables. "Do you want to see the medical team?" she asked.

"No," he said sharply, and he leaned forward for comfort.

She was only trying to help. "Why don't you go over to the room and let me deal with everything here," she suggested.

"Damn it. I can't believe I let him down like that."

"Hey. You were having a good ride and he was amazing... You just need to go and rest for a while and get yourself ready for the final on Sunday. There's nothing more you can do now."

It was over and done, and he couldn't change it. Cutter took the opportunity to go back to the hotel room and rest up while Raylee took the horses one at a time to the wash bay before feeding them. He wasn't wanting to see anyone after that screwed up performance. He'd rather spend the night behind closed doors and settle his anger with himself.

It was an hour or so later before she too got back to the room, and Cutter was stretched out on the bed sleeping. He had taken his boots and shirt off and turned the air conditioner on to cool down.

Raylee looked into his face. It was bruised and battered, and the combination of sweat and dust left dirty streaks across his neckline. He had removed the tape. Tommy had done a good job of hitting him where it hurt the most, and it looked painful. She let him sleep. He was physically exhausted and she knew he was mentally feeling it too.

Everything about the last four months would bond them together. She couldn't imagine going home next week and she didn't know how long it would be before she could return. The thought of seeing her parents again made her feel uneasy, although not because she didn't love them. They had made a conscious decision to tear everything apart and Raylee felt that there was no family to go home to.

They'd also have a difficult time understanding and accepting what she wanted out of her life now, still wanting to control her and have a say in everything she did.

She was tired too. Kicking her boots off, she lay on the bed next to him and rested her hand on his chest, feeling the rise and fall of every breath.

The following afternoon, Cutter was still down on himself about his ride. He knew that it was the guaranteed one shot that could've put him back on top and he'd missed it. Raylee could see that he was beginning to lose faith in the final also. Not from the filly's training and talent, but his fitness could be the one thing to bring them both down. At least he had two more days to rest before he had to ride again.

It was now Raylee who was feeling the pressure. The colt was in a league of his own and she had every bit of confidence in him. It was her own ability that she doubted. Still, she had the best team behind her and everything else would be out of her control, including a little bit of luck that wouldn't go astray.

With the show behind them for the night, the evening belonged to Pete. Never did he dream that his son would accept the offer to come to his house and meet his family, and he told Raylee on the phone just how much it meant to him and the girls.

The blue truck hadn't left the hotel since they'd arrived in Dallas. They followed the directions that Raylee had mapped out on a piece of paper and pulled up outside the pale green and white double story home, in a quiet outer suburban street. It was as neat as a picture and the picket fences that lined the sidewalk were straight out of a storybook scene.

"Are you sure we have the right address?" Cutter asked, and he took the map out of Raylee's hand and studied it.

"You look surprised?" she commented.

"It's not where I imagined Pete to live."

"Well what were you expecting?"

"I don't know," he admitted. "Maybe some run-down old shack, with a fallen down fence and a rusty old car out front."

"Well I hope you're not disappointed then." Raylee was trying to lift his spirits. "Are you sure about this?" she asked, as a last minute option to back out.

Cutter picked up her hand and kissed it. "I couldn't do this without you. Let's do it."

They walked through the arched gateway and up the garden path to the front door. Before they reached it, the door opened and they were greeted with a friendly smile from a woman. She extended her hand. "Hello Cutter... Raylee... I'm so pleased you came. My name's Beth. I'm Pete's wife."

This blew Cutter away. He never really thought about Pete having a wife. "Hi Beth. Nice to meet you," he said politely, holding in his surprise as he shook her hand. Raylee also exchanged pleasantries and they followed Beth inside.

"The girls are excited to meet you," Beth said, as they walked down the hall towards the kitchen. "They've got so many questions and so many years to catch up on, but I told them not to bombard you today with a life-time's worth."

Beth was so nice that both Cutter and Raylee liked her instantly. She was younger than Pete, and was dressed stylishly from head to toe in a way which Raylee likened to her own mother. Everything so far was perfect. Far from what Cutter was expecting.

The house detail was Beth all over. Every item, painting and piece of furniture had her signature on it. There was nothing out of place and not a thing that looked like it didn't belong, leaving Raylee quite impressed as she looked around at everything.

Through the glass kitchen doors, they could see Pete out on the deck standing at the barbecue. Raylee could feel Cutter's hand begin to sweat when he was gripping her tighter than he realized. She went out first to break their greeting.

They stood at a distance. Raylee let Cutter's hand go when Beth offered him a seat at the table and Raylee went over to the barbecue to say hello. Beth made Cutter feel comfortable. There was something about her that he was almost thankful for. She poured him a glass of iced soda and sat with him.

"You'll have to excuse the cuts to my face... I had some trouble at the show this week," he apologized.

"You look perfectly fine. Like a real cowboy." Beth made him feel that there was no need to be sorry. "The girls will be down soon. They're about as nervous as you are I'd say."

Beth was right. Cutter was suddenly feeling nervous about meeting his sisters. He still didn't know how many he had or how old they were, although he'd soon find out.

He looked over at Raylee and Pete. They seemed to be getting along fine and she was doing a good job of keeping them apart while Cutter settled in.

"So, how did you two meet?" Cutter asked out of curiosity. Really, he was wanting to know everything that had happened since he was three years old.

Beth took a sip of her soda before she began. "I was a social worker... When Pete made it through the program, I was assigned to be his case worker and get him from rehab back into normal life again. Finding a job and getting set up in a house. That sort of thing."

"So it was as easy as that?" Cutter asked.

"No. Not exactly," she slightly laughed. "When my job was done, I moved on to other clients. It wasn't for another two years that I did a routine followup. To check on his progress... He asked me out to dinner to say thank you for helping him. Let's just say he was a changed man. A good man."

Cutter found this hard to believe even though the evidence was there to see. A beautiful wife, a stylish home and children. He looked around. Everything seemed so... normal.

His thoughts were broken by the sounds of the girls coming through the kitchen. It was at this point that everyone looked to Cutter and he felt this was the one time in his life he hoped to make a good first impression. He stood up.

Coming through the doorway were his sisters. Cutter held it together when he felt a rush of emotion coming on. They stepped out onto the deck, all smiles and they seemed full of confidence. Without needing their parents' introduction, they walked up to Cutter and threw their arms around him one at a time.

Aimee, being the older at eighteen, gave him a gentle squeeze when she hugged him and he returned it. Her not much younger sister Cassie followed, and once they were all properly introduced, they sat around the table filling in the initial unanswered questions and details about everyone.

Both girls loved that Cutter was a cowboy. They didn't know what to expect, and were genuinely surprised when he turned up at their house in his boots and hat. His modesty told them very little, and it was Raylee who proudly shared his status as the best horse trainer in the entire country, which only enabled him to climb up the hero brother tree faster and higher.

Pete was still standing at the barbecue. He hadn't said one word to Cutter yet, as he wanted Cutter to make the first move. Today wasn't about himself. It was all about the girls and his son. When Beth went into the kitchen, it left Cutter, Raylee and the girls sitting at the table to talk.

"So how long have you known about me?" he asked, as if it were important.

"Maybe three months," Aimee said. "I overheard Dad telling Mom that you were making a comeback and that you would be in town for this big show. But I had no idea what they were even talking about. All I knew was that she was encouraging him to go and meet up with you."

Cassie immediately came in to begin where her sister had finished. "Aimee sat there and listened, and couldn't figure out who they were talking about. She thought that it must have been someone important, 'cause Mom was making a big deal out of it."

"Then Mom said that he should do it for us, and that they shouldn't keep it a secret any longer," Aimee explained. "That's when I burst into the room and asked who they were talking about and why they were keeping such a big secret from us."

"But they didn't spill straight away," Cassie added. "We worked on them for a couple of weeks. Then one night we had dinner and they announced that we had a big brother."

"Wow, that must have come as a shock?" Raylee weighed in.

"We didn't expect it," Cassie admitted.

"Then, when Dad said he couldn't do it, he was straight away out numbered. Three against one." Aimee was letting Cutter know just how desperate they were to meet him.

Cutter sat back in his chair, taking it all in. Yesterday he had no family in the world and today he had sisters. It was a surreal moment. He looked closely at them from across the table. While Cutter always thought that he looked like his mom, he could see a strong resemblance in them both. It was something about their eyes and noses. He'd looked into the mirror and stared at his own eyes long enough to know that theirs were of the same bloodline.

There was no question about it. They all had the same father.

When Beth came out of the kitchen with the salad, Pete turned off the barbecue and brought the meat over, placing it in the middle of the table. Pete sat down at one end of the table while Beth sat at the other. Cutter's view of Pete was blocked by Raylee when he leaned back in his chair and that was the way he liked it.

"So, how did you two meet?" Beth returned the question, as they began to fill their plates and eat.

"Oh, that's a long story," Raylee said. "But it is a good one, so I'll let Cutter tell it to you."

"Thanks Raylee," he said, looking at her like she had just left him out to dry. "Raylee bought my horse and shipped him back to Australia. Then rang me a hundred times to come over and take a look at him. Which I did."

"And?" Cassie asked, as if she knew that the long part of the story was still to come.

"And he fixed my horse, rode a bull and fell in love..." Raylee was briefly outlining the events of that first month in a teasing way that she knew would entertain the two girls.

"What, you rode a bull? Are you serious, what made you do that?" Aimee asked, although everyone was just as intrigued.

"Just some crazy wild idea that I thought was a good one at the time," Cutter defended.

"Why, what happened then?" Aimee wanted to know.

Cutter was more shy about what took place next. "Ask Raylee," he said, and everyone looked to her for the rest of the story.

"Well, he'd been away from competition for a few years and was having issues about going back, so instead, he rode a bull. The full eight seconds. It was the best ride I think I've ever seen. Then when he got to his feet, the bull chased him down and slammed him against the rails and knocked him out." Raylee was reliving the night of the rodeo again, as she had done so many times before. "I took him home from the hospital and had to look after him."

"She looked after me alright," Cutter said. "A bit too well." He laughed, and without going into the details, everyone could see how they came to be together and laughed with him.

"That sounds like Mom and Dad's story. She was the nurse and he was the patient, and the rest is history," Cassie said innocently, although it was enough to quieten the table suddenly.

Beth broke the awkward silence when she changed the subject. "When are you competing again?" she asked Cutter.

"The final's on Sunday. But Raylee rides tomorrow." Cutter squeezed her leg under the table to calm her nerves when he mentioned it.

"Can we go to the show, Mom, and watch the final?" Cassie asked. "Please…"

"I'm sure that will be okay, if it's alright with you both?" Beth asked, not wanting to intrude.

"It's open to everyone," Cutter said, and he left it at that.

They spent the time talking about how long they'd lived in the house, where the girls went to school, and what Aimee would do when she finished high school. It was easy, and Cutter really liked Pete's family. His new family. He still couldn't bring himself to connect with Pete on any level, and Beth and Raylee did all the fill in talk, which Cutter was thankful for.

Before Cutter had gone to Pete's house, he was sure that he would only want to meet his sisters then leave. After he'd arrived, he enjoyed the time they had getting to know each other and the night flew by. Everyone was having a great time, sharing stories, answering questions and most of all, laughing. Cutter would be more than happy to see them again at the show for the finals, but it was now time to head back to the stables to check on the horses before they returned to the hotel for the night.

When they walked to the door, Cutter and Raylee thanked Beth and hugged both the girls. For the first time that evening, Pete manned up and held out his hand to Cutter. "Thank you for coming. It means a lot to them."

Cutter was strong, looking Pete in the face but avoiding his eyes. He shook his hand. "Thanks for having us over."

It made Raylee and Beth feel like the effort was worth it, just to bring the two of them together.

When they climbed into the truck, they sat there looking at Pete and his family standing on the front porch, then gave them a wave as they drove off.

"Well that wasn't all that bad, was it?" Raylee asked, anxious to hear his thoughts.

"Okay, I'll admit, you were right," he agreed, then laughed at her.

"Yes I was. And now you can let go of everything and we can go cutting."

As Cutter lay in bed that night, he stared at the ceiling. He was content. Never did he imagine that Pete's life would turn out the way it had. He always had visions of a lonely old drunk man in a filthy dilapidated house with two cats and rubbish piled high to the fence line, something that had been pictured over and over in his mind as the years had gone by.

His wife Beth and their daughters changed Cutter's perception of the man he never wanted to meet. While there was no instant connection between him and Pete, he did admire how he'd picked up the pieces that were left of his broken life and had become a decent man.

One thing Cutter would be thankful for, was that through the rocky, turbulent marriage Pete had to Mary-Ann, it was what ultimately led him to Macca and the ranch. Fate had a way of sorting through the roughness of life and turning out the best outcomes.

Raylee had a sleepless night. She tossed and turned and was restless until daybreak. When Cutter woke up, she was already in the bathroom with the door closed, and he thought he could hear the sounds of her throwing up over the running water of the shower.

Chapter Eighteen

Never before had Raylee felt so much pressure about competing at an event. It was one thing to be going to a local show back home, where she knew everyone by name and was surrounded by the Tremayne team. That was there, and this was Dallas. In the cutting world, it didn't get any bigger than this and she was feeling it.

Cutter knew exactly what she was going through. He'd felt it the night of the rodeo, when he threw good sense and judgement aside in place of a spontaneous irrational act that made him question even his own sanity.

He sat on the edge of the bed and rubbed his ribs, still unsure if they were broken or not. They were feeling slightly better for having a restful day, although there was no possibility he'd be able to lope the colt for Raylee if he wanted to be fit for the final.

Finding his jeans over a chair, he pulled them on, then ran his hand roughly through his hair. The water of the shower was still running and there was nothing he could do for Raylee except wait for her to come out of the bathroom. He made himself a coffee and wandered around the room. Bare chested, he went and stood out on the balcony and watched the morning sun rise over the stables.

The coffee was warming. For the first time in years he felt like everything was coming together. Raylee had been instrumental in tying up the loose ends in his life that he'd never have been able to deal with on his own.

She was good for him, and he was thankful for her.

He thought about his sisters. All these years they had each other while he had nobody. Johnny was as close to a brother as it was possible to be and he couldn't imagine anyone else taking his place. Yet he often wondered why his mother and Macca didn't have children together and now he would never know.

Cutter took his time enjoying his coffee while watching the stables come alive for the final weekend of competition. He leaned on the rail and was taking it all in. This is what he did best. This is what he lived for. To be in that arena after working endless months preparing these horses for this moment. It was a passion and a feeling that he couldn't explain. It was his life.

Now he had someone to share it all with. The one person who understood everything about competing and was the great support he needed with his training. She would be the extra pair of hands on the ranch and would take care of the business side that he never had the time for. The partnership with Raylee completed him.

Today was all about her. She needed him more today than ever before and he went inside to see if she was okay. As he walked back in and slid the door closed, Raylee opened the bathroom door. She half smiled and looked pale.

"What's the matter with you?" he asked, trying to lighten the seriousness of her problem.

"I just want to lie down," she said, and she crashed back into the bed. "I feel so sick."

Cutter laughed. "Are you sure it's not just nerves?"

"I can't believe you signed me up for this."

He sat on the bed and rubbed her lower back. "You'll be fine... I promise."

"I'm so going to totally screw this up. I just know it," she stated, fully down on herself.

"Hey, what ever happened to not being afraid? I thought you got over that."

"I thought I did too, but look at me... I'm a mess."

Cutter looked at her. She definitely looked pale and washed out. "I'm going over to the stables to feed up and let you sleep for a while. When I get back, we'll have some breakfast... You need to go about everything today as normal. It's just another day and it's just another show," he said to ease her mind.

"I know. I'll be fine."

He kissed her on the cheek, pulled a shirt on and left Raylee to sleep for as long as she needed.

The stables were quieter today than earlier in the week. Many of the riders who hadn't qualified for the finals had already left to go home, and the last two days of competition saw empty stalls where they were once filled to capacity.

The car park was filling up however, as spectators were flocking to Dallas for the weekend of finals. The morning would be the start of some fierce and competitive cutting as it was now the end of the go-rounds. Finals meant focus and placings meant prize money. Both would be needed to kickstart a brand new season for Cutter if he wanted to be at the top of his training again.

Cutter saddled up the colt and took him out through the breezeway. He was reluctant to push him any faster than a brisk walk, until he felt how his ribs would hold up. There were different areas that he could take him for a bit of exercise and he found a quiet sand yard on the far side of the complex, though his pain was uncomfortable and he only walked him in circles until he was hot.

He wanted to get him right for Raylee before the final, giving him a very light workout and a few of his familiar pre-cutting moves to test his responses. He was now aching and couldn't do any more, deciding that the rest would be up to Raylee.

On his way back to the stables, Cutter went by the practice pen and pulled the colt up when he saw Tommy riding one of his client's finalists. He was having a few problems with the filly, keeping her focused and missing a few turns. Tommy was frustrated and was over riding her, letting his anger show. He pulled the filly up and walked out of the pen with a steel face.

Cutter gave him a whistle and when Tommy turned around, he saw Cutter sitting on the colt with a big smile on his face. "Hey Tommy," he called out. "The novice event was last week." Cutter rode away without waiting for a comeback. It made him feel good. He knew that Tommy wouldn't risk a six month ban especially with the final so close, so any dig now was a game to undermine each other.

He had just enough time to take the filly out for a walk and it wasn't long before he was really starting to feel the pain and was short of breath. He needed to get back to the room to see if Raylee was alright, so he cut her time shorter than he'd prefer and put her back in the stall.

The hotel room was in darkness. Cutter turned the side lamp on to wake her gently. He pushed her hair away from her face, and hoped that the smell of hot coffee and a fresh bagel would waken her.

"Cutter?" she said weakly.

"Hey, you had a good sleep... But it's time to get up now."

"I was hoping it was over."

He laughed. "It's not over. It hasn't even begun."

She rolled over and looked at him, trying to wake up fully. "What time is it?" she asked.

"Time for you to get dressed," he said, encouraging her to get up.

"Wouldn't you rather stay in bed with me for the rest of the day?" she tempted him.

"Yes ma'am, I would. But this is the one time that I will have to wait."

She dragged herself out of bed and pulled on a fresh pair of jeans and a checkered shirt. Taking her time, she did her hair and makeup, while downing her caffeine and basic breakfast. She had no appetite, so appreciated having something light to fill her tummy.

Cutter had already changed and was waiting. "Come on, Raylee. You're gonna be late."

"Alright. I'm ready," she replied when she opened the bathroom door.

Before they went over to the complex, Cutter took a minute that he wouldn't have found later. "You're gonna do great. I know it. Everything you've learnt at the ranch, everything that we've been through together, has got you to this day. I want you to know that I have every bit of faith in you."

She threw her arms around him. "I don't want to let you down," she said.

"You won't."

"Do you know how much I love you?" she asked, pulling back and looking at him closely.

"And I couldn't love you any more if I tried. But right now, you've got a job to do."

"Then let's do it," she said confidently, then kissed him before she put her hat on.

Once they left the room it was all cutting talk. The horses, the cattle and the final. Everything revolved around the stables and getting geared up. The saddles came out and they prepared the horses. Raylee took the colt and Cutter the filly.

"You ready for this?" he asked.

"No... But I'm starting to feel better. As long as you have faith in us both, then what will be, will be."

"Just remember, you have the best horse under you. You need to trust him."

She rode over to the loping area and left Cutter to ride around wasting time. Riding the colt gave her the time she needed to calm down. The more she rode, the better she was feeling. She passed the time and distracted herself by having flashbacks of the last four months. Cutter and the colt. The rodeo and her parents. The ranch and Marnie. The calf and the cattle truck. David Chambers and the insurance check. Pete and his family, and now, it was the final.

The last four months had been one hell of a ride and everything about it had prepared her for this day. She had wasted enough time and it was now getting close. She rode over to where Cutter was leisurely sitting on the filly at the fence, watching the cattle.

"Did you get my chaps?" she asked, as she got off the colt and landed in the sand.

Her chaps were hanging on the horn on his saddle. "Just remember how good you look in these," he said, and he passed them to her.

"Very funny."

"No, I'm serious. You score extra points for that."

While Raylee stood with the filly and put her chaps on, Cutter took the colt into the prep lane and tuned him up. He was already perfect.

"Are you sure you're ready for this?" he asked, when he handed the colt back over to her.

"I have complete faith in him... And I'm just in my arena back home with no one watching," Raylee said, trying to convince herself as she took to the saddle.

"That's a girl... Now go out there and kick some cow cuttin' butt," he pumped her up.

When the last rider finished his run, Cutter and the turn back team went into the corners, waiting for Raylee to get herself together.

"...and if you missed his run in the Open, then this is your last chance to see Midnight Dynamite ridden by Aussie girl, Raylee Tremayne." Her introduction by the announcer was thankfully played down somewhat, and she only caught some of the colt's spectacular achievements he was rolling out over the loud speakers.

"Come on, Raylee. You can do this," Cutter said out loud, to himself only.

As she walked across the timeline, the bell rang and started the countdown. Cutter had seen this done thousands of times before, and never had he wanted so much for another rider to shine as much as he wanted Raylee to. She looked good. Totally in control. Except her heart was pumping fast and when she met Cutter in the corner, she looked at the cattle and the blood drained from her face. He ignored it and pointed to some good cattle options.

"You look good," he encouraged her.

She didn't reply.

She had to hold back the colt's enthusiasm and bring the herd out more steadily than Cutter would. She had to get some control over him and not let him dominate the arena floor just yet. The turn back riders came in to pressure the cattle back to the mob, and when she was left with one cow in front, there was no pause. Immediately she put her hand down, anticipating that the next rush would be intense. It was on.

The colt intimidated the cow and captured its attention as they went nose to nose with every short burst of runs. Raylee was using her spurs cautiously, not to over-ride him, letting him do his job. His ears were laid back, his head was down low and his stance in the sand had everyone in the stands cheering for more.

He danced in the middle of the arena to the tune of the cow. Driving it to want to find a way back to the mob and cutting off every attempt. He was imitating the cow in a perfect performance, and the judges would have trouble finding any faults in this run. It was flawless.

Powerful and athletic, the colt's skills were impeccable. His eagerness to control the situation and his strength almost too much for Raylee, and when the cow looked away, she picked up the reins and turned to look at Cutter.

He was impressed. She was relieved.

"That was awesome... You've got just over a minute on the clock now, so take your time. Don't rush this," he instructed, and he pointed out another cow. "You can do this, Raylee. Come on."

The next cut into the herd was a little more messy. She managed to draw out a few and when the turn back riders did their job pushing them back, Raylee was left with the one cow she didn't expect. It wasn't noticeable, and she put her hand down for what would be the ride of her life.

The cow darted across the pen like an arrow and it tested the colt's speed and agility. But it couldn't outrun or outsmart this well trained horse and he kept level with it at every turn. Drawing it back to the center of the pen, he hustled the cow and anticipated every short sharp step it took, keeping constant eye contact. His nose only inches out of the sand.

Neither the cow nor the horse was giving in. He was in a league of his own and was totally full of himself. He had what it took to carry Raylee through to the end, if she had the endurance to keep up with him. Together they were putting on a thrilling ride. The seconds were counting down though not fast enough. His front legs fully extended and his tail flicking the sand aside.

Twelve seconds to go and Cutter was now tense, holding the horn on his saddle tight. He had one eye on the clock and the other on Raylee. She was holding on, unaware of the show she was putting on and letting the colt do his thing. Spurring him very little, only to keep him sharp as the seconds on the clock were coming down. With three, two, one, buzz. Time was up. Raylee pulled him up and for the first time she noticed the crowd who applauded her efforts and whistled in appreciation of a great ride. She'd nailed it.

Cutter rode over to her. "Now if that doesn't score big, then we're going home," he said with excitement, and he couldn't hold back his big smile.

"That felt so amazing," Raylee commented, returning the happiness. "He did so good." She rubbed the colt on the neck as they rode side by side out of the pen.

Back in the loping area, they got off the horses and tied them up to the rail. Raylee started to unbuckle her chaps while they were reliving the last two and a half minutes. Cutter was totally absorbed in her excitement and impressed more than he was letting on. The colt had lived up to his name. He was dynamite.

The score came in... It was the moment that could make or break your spirit and Raylee's heart was pumping fast in anticipation. It was the announcer's excited and raised voice when he called out a two twenty-three that totally stunned her.

"What?" Raylee screamed in complete shock.

"Wooo!" Cutter picked her up off the ground and swung her around, then had to put her down quickly when he felt the sharp stab in his side. "That puts you on top," he stated, more than pleased with the result.

"I can't believe it... I've never scored anything that high before."

"Well now you have."

"But there's still another herd to go."

"Don't you worry about that. You had a great ride and you've put yourself in a good position, and you did your best."

"I did better than my best... I don't really know where that came from."

Cutter knew exactly where it came from. She deserved the high score and every bit of praise that had come from all her hard work back at the ranch.

The excitement was too much for Raylee and she didn't want to go back to the stables. Instead, they rode around for a while and watched the next herd to see who would be a threat to her position on top of the leader board.

It was the longest hour of her life. Watching the other riders on their outstanding horses was tense. Of the top thirty horses that entered, Raylee couldn't see one of them who didn't live up to their status or didn't belong there. They were all well bred and talented beyond their scores, although none of them were pushing any higher than two twenty, and Raylee was feeling confident to say the least.

It would be the last rider of the herd that would crush her win and pip her score by a point. A two twenty-four pushed Raylee down to second place, and while it didn't wipe the smile off her face, she did feel robbed of the win. That was cutting, and the good sport that she was enabled her to congratulate the eventual winner on a fantastic ride.

With the herd pushed out of the pen and the sand being prepared for the presentation, Raylee and Cutter waited around, talking about her ride. She was on top of the world and he loved to see her there.

"What happened this morning?" he asked, bringing up what was a bad start to the day.

"I couldn't sleep. I was awake all night thinking about today, and the more I thought about it, the worse I was feeling."

"Well then, see. You had nothing to worry about, did you?"

She laughed. "What a turn around."

"You turned it around. You needed to stop doubting yourself."

Raylee rode out on the colt and sat at the back wall waiting, along with the other riders who'd finished in the top ten. She soaked up the moment. This moment that would stick in her mind for the rest of her life. When the announcer called out her name following the other finalists that had already been introduced in order, she came forward and was presented with her ribbon and prizes.

Cutter didn't tell Raylee that her prize consisted of one of the best trophies a cutter would ever earn. A buckle. She was the Reserve Champion in the Open Non Pro and she had won a silver and gold buckle to prove it.

A ribbon was wrapped around the colt's neck and cameras clicked, capturing the presentation of her winnings. Raylee accepted the buckle and looked at it, running her hand over the detail and inscription. She had been cutting for many years and had never come close to winning a prize like that. When she rode back to Cutter, she couldn't wait to show him.

"Nice," he said. "Your first one."

"And I couldn't have done it without you," she said, giving him most of the praise.

"Well maybe you can bring it back to the room and try it on for me tonight? Make sure it fits just right," he teased her.

"Shhh. Someone might hear you." Raylee looked around but they were alone. "Baby, you're never gonna see this thing off me," she teased him back in a flirtatious Texas twang that was near perfect.

"Now that's what I wanna hear." He lifted his hat slightly and gave her a congratulatory kiss.

Nothing could take the smile off Raylee's face. Not even when they passed Tommy and a couple of his rats who were working in one of the open sand yards.

"He'll be pissed at you," Cutter said, as he purposely rode close to the edge and flashed Raylee's new buckle at him.

"Why... and what was that all about?" Raylee asked, with a sense of knowing there was an underlying message that she was unaware of.

"Well, let's just say that you whipped his horse in the final and beat it by four points."

"Did I? Why didn't you tell me?"

"Because you were a wreck. And I didn't wanna make it any worse than it already was," he explained. "Besides, it didn't really matter who you were up against, you didn't know any of them anyway. You just had to worry about your ride and you did."

She could see his point. Knowing that Tommy's trained horse was in the same final would have only added to her anxiety, and she was pleased now that she had no idea.

They unsaddled the horses and took them to the wash bay. They stood in line waiting a while, talking to the other riders before one of the bays became available. Cutter watched Raylee in the wash bay with the colt. He was something special and she was even more. His horse and his girl. There was something about the timing that made him want to ask her right then and there.

His thoughts were broken by the next bay becoming available and he took the filly in, hosing her down in the cool water.

"How are you feeling about tomorrow?" Raylee asked, as they walked back to the stalls.

"Good," he confirmed. "You've inspired me in more ways than you'll ever know."

Together they fed up for the night and put everything away before they headed back to the hotel for the rest of the evening.

Chapter Nineteen

It was scaring Raylee to think that their separation was going to be for an unknown time. She would be back on a plane in a few days and it was making her feel like the high she was on was about to come crashing down around her.

She wouldn't say anything to Cutter just yet. She needed him to be focused on the final and he didn't need that sort of distraction. Instead, they had a quiet dinner downstairs in the hotel restaurant and talked about everything, except her going home.

They wondered if Marnie would turn up for the final, whether Pete, Beth and the girls would come to watch him ride, and where he would draw out of the two herds.

"I think the colt's ready to go home now," he said, knowing he'd been restricted to the stables long enough.

"He's done well, hasn't he?" Raylee was so proud of him. "But to be honest, I can't wait to go back to the ranch either."

"Me too. I need some of Marnie's home cooking, and there's nowhere on earth like the ranch."

Raylee could tell that Cutter's heart felt fulfilled when he was at home. "Wait 'til she sees you," she added.

"Why?"

"Look at you. The last time you came home you were all broken and knocked about. She'll think that every time we're away you do something crazy."

"Yeah, well roughin' up Tommy wasn't crazy, and Marnie would be the first to agree," Cutter stated, then had a laugh to himself.

"What?" Raylee asked, suspicious about what was so funny.

"I was just thinking. You've been cutting for years, and yet you come here to the biggest event on the national calendar and you walk away with a buckle."

The buckle had been sitting on the table during dinner and Raylee picked it up to look at it. She ran her hand over it again. "He really is the best horse, isn't he?" she questioned him, already knowing the answer.

"Yes ma'am, he sure is. There's not another that comes close," he said, and Raylee could tell that he was convinced of it.

"Not even the filly?"

"Maybe. But she's gotta prove herself first. But I know one thing for sure."

"What's that?"

"I've got the best girl."

Raylee laughed at his compliment. "And I've got the best cowboy." She looked into his bruised and stitched up face. "A bit rough around the edges... But still the best."

The bruising was worse today and she was hoping it would start to settle down soon. The stitches were neat and his lip still cut, though Raylee was more concerned about what she couldn't see. His ribs. There was nothing she could do for him except re-tape them tight before he rode.

"You look tired," she said, even though she was feeling the same.

"Let's get outta here," he suggested, and they left the restaurant to have an early night. It had been a long and exciting day, and it was beginning to catch up with them both.

Cutter had a shower and went to bed, watching an old movie in the darkness of the room, while Raylee soaked in the bath. The bubbles filled the tub and the warmth of the water soothed her aching body. She'd received a message from home.

Congrats Raylee. Saw your results, well done. Everyone here waiting for you to come home. Jesse.

It initially made her feel happy, until the thought of going home devastated her. She hadn't had any similar messages from her mom or dad, so was expecting that her welcome home would be strained. The only smile she could manage, was at the thought that she would see the kids again for their riding lesson.

When she went out into the room, Cutter was sound asleep. The movie was still playing and was throwing flashes of light onto the walls. She took the remote control from him and switched it off. She lay in the dark next to him and listened to him breathe.

There was a big division between her happiness with the cowboy she loved living in Texas, and her unhappy family drama back home in Australia. Raylee knew that this was where she wanted to be.

Cutter was pulling on his jeans when Raylee woke the next morning. The room was still in darkness and only the bathroom light allowed her to see that he had removed the tape from his ribs. He would need her to reapply the tape firmly to give him the best support, so she knew that he wasn't going anywhere just yet.

"Couldn't you sleep?" she asked, adjusting her eyes to the light.

"Are you kidding... I was exhausted."

It pleased her to think that he had a good night's sleep, unlike the night before she had to ride. He'd been in this position hundreds of times before and sleep was something that wouldn't suffer over the pressures of competing.

Refreshed and ready to go, Cutter sat around the room and waited on Raylee. She was quick to dress and came out from the bathroom looking perfect with her shiny new buckle in place. After she applied the tape, he pulled on a shirt. Raylee stood up close to him and started to button it up.

"What, no lucky shirt today?" she questioned him, noticing that he'd not worn it all week.

"Nah, I've got all the luck I need right here in front of me," he said, and he pulled on her buckle. "And I wouldn't wanna do this without you," he added. Suddenly she felt his sincere comments were becoming more serious. "You know, I had no time in my life for this and that one phone call to you changed everything. You were right when you said that I needed to do this for someone. To make it all worthwhile. And now, you're the one I'm riding for."

She loved to hear it and it made her want to hear more, but her heart was breaking at the same time. "I don't want to go home after the show," she blurted out and couldn't take it back. "I want to stay here with you." She had held it in for so long that it just spilled out.

"I know," he agreed. "But we can't deal with that right now... But I promise you Raylee, everything will be okay."

While Raylee didn't ask how, she believed him. He tucked his shirt in and did up his buckle. After packing their bags, they put their hats on and walked out of the room for the last time.

It was now all business. Horses, feed and tack. They worked like a team and without too much talking they knew exactly what each other was doing and needing to get ready. The draw was out and Raylee was keeping an eye on the time. Second herd, second last out, just ahead of Tommy Parker. For some reason, Cutter's position in the draw didn't seem to bother him and he didn't give Tommy another thought.

They rode around while the final from the Derby was about to start. They needed to exercise the filly and the colt needed to be out too, even though his work there was done. Cutter took the filly through her routine while Raylee just walked the colt around. Many people came up to her, who didn't know her before yesterday, to give their congratulations and contact details to pass on to Cutter.

Everyone was impressed with the colt and Raylee couldn't speak highly enough of him either. His performance and result spoke for themselves and he had everyone talking about him again.

The morning was moving on fast and since they had missed breakfast, they decided to grab a bite to eat before it was too late. Making their way to the far end of the arena towards the cafeteria, they stopped to watch the last rider in the Derby final before they went in. When Raylee's phone rang, she walked away to answer it.

"That was Beth," Raylee said when she returned.

"Are they here?" he asked, and Raylee could tell that he was keen to see them again.

"They've been here for a while. They're meeting us at the cafeteria now."

Beth and the girls were just ahead of them and had already found a table in the corner.

"Hey," everyone exchanged, and both the girls gave Cutter and Raylee the biggest of hugs and smiles.

"Where's Pete?" Raylee asked. She knew Cutter would be curious and wouldn't ask for himself.

"He's at work, although he should be here before the start of the final," Beth explained. "Now let me get you something to eat." She left the table to order, leaving the four of them to catch up.

The girls were in awe of everyone wearing hats. The place was crawling with hats and boots with spurs everywhere, and they were totally cowboy struck.

"You just keep your eyes off these cowboys here. They're no good for either of you," Cutter said, like a big brother would.

"What about Raylee? She got you, didn't she?" Aimee asked.

"Well yes... But I'm different," he defended.

The three girls laughed at him. "Different, how?" Cassie wanted to know.

He wasn't sure how he was going to explain his way out of this one, so he dismissed it. "You just have to trust me. I am, and they're not."

When Beth came back to the table with the coffees, sodas and sandwiches, everyone began to dig in. "This is great. Thank you," Raylee said, as she didn't realize just how hungry she was.

Cutter looked at his sisters. They had no cowgirl in them whatsoever. They dressed nicely and he could tell they were really well looked after. For that alone, Cutter was happy.

He gave them all a brief outline of cutting, explaining how the two and a half minutes worked, what the judges were looking for and how the turn back team played an important role for the rider. He went through the go-rounds, the ages of the horses and finished with the retelling of Raylee's outstanding ride yesterday which earned her that big shiny buckle she was proudly wearing.

It was another world for them, one they had never experienced or known about. Now they were at the biggest event in the country, with the best trainer who just happened to be their brother.

Raylee didn't want to leave, even though she had to go to the stables and get the filly ready. "I'll be down later," Cutter said, when she leaned down to kiss him goodbye.

"You'd better. 'Cause I'm not riding her in that final if you don't show up," she said, half joking and the other half serious. "I'll see everyone after the final."

"She's a nice girl, Cutter," Beth commented when Raylee had left.

"She's great," he simply replied, and he watched her until she was out of sight, and Beth could see that he was more than connected with her. "Beth, do you mind if I take the girls shopping for a while?" he asked, wanting her approval.

"Shopping?" Cassie repeated quickly, flashing her convincing eyes at her mom. "Can we, Mom, please?"

It was obvious that Aimee was old enough so that she didn't need her mom's permission, although Cutter would still ask. He didn't want to overstep the mark.

"I'm sure that will be fine. But they have their own money," Beth said, and the three of them stood up from the table.

"We won't be long," Cutter assured her, and they left Beth in the cafeteria to walk around the other side of the arena to the shops.

Cutter found himself in the middle of them. Cassie held onto his arm and Aimee just walked close. He had some curious looks from the people he passed in the walkway, and when everyone said hello to him, it helped the girls understand that their brother was well known and big time in this world that was foreign to them.

"Do you know everyone here?" Aimee asked.

"Not everyone. But everyone knows me," he said, not to brag, but to explain all the attention he was drawing.

They tried on hats. All shapes, sizes and colors. Laughing at the ridiculous and happy with the right ones, both settling on black, just to be part of the Cutter and Raylee team. In the changing room they tried some jeans and shirts on that were a far cry from their city wardrobe, and the heavy cowhide belts had so much bling on them, they sparkled and blinded everyone at the same time.

He finished them off with a pair of square toe, high topped cowgirl boots. When he stood back and looked at them both, he could see there might have been a couple of country girls in there somewhere.

"Mom's going to freak," Cassie stated, without believing her own words.

"Well, you can blame me," Cutter said and he handed over his card to pay, knowing that Beth wouldn't take their new outfits away from them. "At least when you come to the ranch, you'll look like you belong there."

"Really. Can we come to the ranch? When?" Aimee wanted to know all at once.

"When your mom and dad say you're allowed," he said, and it instantly sounded strange to mention Pete as the girls' and his own father in the same sentence even though it wasn't intended that way.

Back at the cafeteria, Beth was still sitting at the table reading a magazine. She almost didn't recognize them, except for the second look she gave when she saw Cutter walk in.

"Look at what Cutter bought us... What do you think?" Aimee asked her mom as she spun around on the spot.

Beth looked at him. "You weren't supposed to pay for them," she insisted. "But... I suppose you both look good. Different... But good."

Cutter put his hands on their shoulders and pulled them in. "They look great. But I have to start getting ready now. Why don't you take a seat in the stands and I'll see you after the final."

They gave their thanks and good lucks all at once and they watched him leave.

"He's so awesome, isn't he?" Cassie complimented him to her mom.

Beth couldn't agree more. "He's a good man," she replied. "Your dad missed out on having a good son."

Cutter went to the stables to get the colt ready and met Raylee back inside the arena. He carried his chaps over the horn on his saddle and looked at the board to see how long it would be. It was getting close. The first herd was done and the announcer was introducing the first rider out in the second herd. There were some variations between the scores, from a couple of low two hundreds to the leader on a two twenty-four.

One of Tommy's rides saw him out of contention with only a two sixteen, and Cutter knew that he'd be gutted. His other rats were higher up, although they'd all have another ride with a chance to show better this herd.

"I was beginning to think you weren't going to turn up," Raylee said, as she handed him the reins.

"I got distracted. But I'm here now. How is she?" he asked of the filly.

"She feels good. But you're the best trainer in the world. You tell me," she said with a smile, and she lengthened the stirrups for him.

He tied her up while he put his chaps on and Raylee lifted the stirrups up on the colt.

"Have you seen Marnie yet?" she asked, since Cutter had been upstairs for the last while.

"No ma'am. But I'm sure she'll be here somewhere," he assured her.

"I can't believe it's nearly over. That this is it."

"Now don't you fall apart on me now."

She took a deep breath. "I think I must be nervous enough for the both of us."

"You'll be fine... And I'll be fine, so don't you worry." Deep down Cutter was worried. He was just trying to settle Raylee so that she could go out and do a good job in the corner.

The loping area had only a handful of riders left in it, as the show was winding down and coming to a close. He took to the saddle and rode around in circles with everyone, while the riders were going into the pen one at a time, giving it their best shot. He wouldn't watch their rides, although he couldn't help but hear their scores at the end of their run, placing everyone on his own leader board in his head. One score that unexpectedly shook it up, was a two twenty-five, which pushed the chase out just that bit further.

Raylee sat on the colt and watched the cattle. It was a big herd and there were lots of colors and markings that were making it easier for her to differentiate. The crowd's cheers and whistles, as well as their ooh's and ah's, told the story of what was going on in the pen with each rider.

With one ride to go, Cutter took the filly out into the prep lane and gave her a tuning like never before. He knew her capabilities and he had complete faith in her. She was the first foal produced by the colt and had replaced him at the ranch when he was sent to Australia, so she had a good balance of cutting as well as ranch and cattle life. She had the right DNA. Now would be a good time to shine, if ever she was going to.

As the cowboy and his turn back team left the pen at the sound of the buzzer, the announcer delivered him a disappointing score. Raylee passed them, making her way to the corner, immediately looking at the cattle up close for the best options.

This was it. The one time when your performance was everything and luck was out of your control. Where breeding and good training exposed your talent, and points could be lost with one wrong cow. Raylee wished she could have closed her eyes and opened them again at the sound of the buzzer. She was a bundle of nerves although she would never let Cutter see it.

When he walked across the timeline, he briefly made eye contact with her. They shared comments about the cattle and he went to the back wall and took his time to position the steer with the white star on its face among the few that he would bring forward.

The filly was becoming eager. He restrained her a little, while the turn back riders moved in and pushed the cattle back to the herd, leaving Raylee to keep them together. The steer was singled out and when it stood alone, it was captured by the eyes of the horse. It was showtime.

Cutter put his hand down and in a split second, the steer bolted from fear. The filly, knowing her job, moved like lightning and blocked the steer in a freakish stop, triggering it to accelerate back to the center of the pen. The abruptness of the steer saw Cutter use his body, shifting his weight for comfort when the steer and the filly began to do that magic in the center of the pen, nose to nose. Her tail sweeping the sand and her legs shaking from anticipation, she was ready to pounce on every move it made. It was spectacular.

The filly had full domination over the steer. Stalking it to react. Pushing it to retaliate. Restricting it to return to the mob. She was all over it. The crowd couldn't be contained, as they were now on the edges of their seats, showering Cutter with an eruption of whistles and shouting, spurring him on even more.

The filly was showing heart. Thriving on a very fired up steer and matching every move it made. The intensity of their connection was going beyond her training, showing just how cowy she was.

She had the steer so mesmerized that Cutter couldn't get off it, as it was darting from side to side desperate to get back to the herd. He kept blocking off its every attempt to get past him, even though it was tiring him out. Raylee was gripping tight the horn on her saddle and feeling his pain with every big stop.

It was to the relief of both when the steer stopped numbly and turned away, leaving Cutter to pick up the reins and walk back to Raylee's corner where she had a look on her face that had mixed expressions. The crowd were in his corner too, wanting to see more of what this talented horse could do.

He took the time to relax, going in for a deep cut to find the steer that Raylee had pointed out. As he pushed it forward with the mob, he needed to waste some time to ease the pain in his side and catch his breath, with the first run taking longer than he'd have liked. The seconds had come off the clock and he wasn't sure if he'd have enough time for two more cuts, leaving this steer to make a lasting impression and get some good points on the board.

He would give it everything he had left in him. There was no place in this final to play it safe. It was all or nothing. When the turn back riders moved in, the steer was singled out on its own and it immediately responded when the filly fixed on it, drawing it in and commanding its full attention. The pressure was back on.

The filly's second steer was more thrilling than her first. She swooped low in the sand and executed every abrupt stop and every sharp turn with perfect timing. She was impulsive, and Cutter had to use his spurs with the right amount of pressure to keep her in position so that she didn't push onto the steer.

While the filly was taking on the steer head to head, Cutter was gripped to the saddle. Flaunting endless talent, her swift footwork showed her skills and entertained the crowd as the music was drowned out by their applause and filled the arena.

The steer was no match for the filly who was in full blown control and now showing her best. But with thirty seconds still left on the clock, every explosive stop was having an impact on Cutter's body while every acceler-ated turn thrust him to the point where he was now needing desperately to hear that buzzer. The last thing he wanted, was a repeat of his last ride where his endurance fell short of the timer. He had just passed his pain tolerance level and couldn't take much more, even though they were giving a heart-stopping performance.

The filly was tough and had fight in her, working hard and taking no bullshit from the steer. She was determined to keep it separated. Everything about this ride was outstanding.

The steer shot from one direction to another, making the filly excited to replicate its exact moves as she ripped up the sand with every stop. She had complete dominance over it, and provoked it to react. On edge, the steer was frantic to join the mob and was desperate to get around them, making the filly hungry for more.

It was finally over.

The buzzer sounded not a moment too soon and Cutter pulled her up. The filly had stolen the show. With plenty of working time as well as a superb performance, she was sure of a high score.

He was done. He leaned forward over the horn on the saddle and his hat touched the filly's mane. He put his hand down low and rubbed her neck, feeling the sweat and steam coming off her. She was hot. All he could think about was how unbelievably amazing that felt and that he was so thankful it was over. All he could hear was a crowd full of praise and appreciation, and when he sat back up, he held onto his side with his good arm, his face showing the pain he was in.

He turned around to look for Raylee. She was riding over to him beaming broadly, until she saw his discomfort. "Are you okay?" she asked.

"I'll be fine," he replied. When the pain had eased slightly, he showed her just how happy he was.

They rode back to the loping area behind the judges' stand and when they tied up the horses, Raylee couldn't contain herself. "That was ridiculous. I don't know how you did that or held on for so long."

"I'm not real sure either."

"Listen," Raylee said with her hand up, to silence everyone and everything around her.

After the longest pause, the announcer came over the speakers with an explosive voice that filled the arena. "Folks, looks like we got ourselves a new leader in the Open Futurity with a score of a... wait for it... a two twenty-seven, puts Cutter Jones and Midnight Dancer at the top of the leader board. Two points clear of second place and with only one rider left in this final to contest him for first prize."

Raylee jumped up and threw her arms around him. It was the most exciting time they'd had together so far and Cutter couldn't have been more pleased. He had done everything he could and already had other riders coming up to him to congratulate him on a great ride.

But there was still one rider that could take it all away... and that was Tommy Parker.

He'd already gone over the timeline for the second time this final and had half the herd out in front of him by the time Raylee and Cutter made it to the fence to watch. Although Cutter couldn't admit it, Tommy was a class act rider and when he put his hand down on the first steer, it began to worry Raylee. His colt was powerful and thrilling to watch, hotfooting from side to side in one intense ride that made this showdown a close contest. It was going to come down to the wire.

The crowd responded when he pulled up the reins and went into the herd for his second steer. Raylee couldn't believe that Tommy Parker could be the one rider who might take it all away from Cutter, and she was feeling the bitterness just as much as he was.

The rat pack were doing their job superbly, pushing the steers back to the rest of the herd and isolating one for Tommy to work. The steer was stirring the colt on in the center of the pen and he was strikingly sharp in his reactions. With his ears laid back and his muscular front legs spanned wide to gravitate the cow in, he was a big threat.

Together, both Tommy and his colt were dynamic. Delivering a powerful performance equally as impressive as Cutter's, Raylee had trouble separating them on points.

He was having a dream run and it was the ride that could turn the leader board over, when a steer came out from the herd and they teamed up. Now he had two steers running the pen and when the colt switched and followed the wrong steer, he pulled with the reins and the final was all but over for Tommy.

Cutter leaned forward, resting his hands on his legs and he put his head down and closed his eyes. He was taking in the moment and waited out the last seconds of Tommy's ride. He heard the buzzer and looked up to see Tommy leaving the pen with the pack, shaking his head and calling abuse at his boys.

Raylee grabbed Cutter and was beside herself, showing everyone just how happy she was. "You did it!" she exclaimed at an uncontrolled volume.

"We did it," Cutter said, to let her know they did it together. He put one arm around her while he was shaking hands with everyone that could get up close to him.

"It's been one of the most long anticipated returns to cutting, and Cutter Jones has given the performance of a lifetime." It was only a few words from the announcer that Raylee tuned into, and he was just as excited as everyone else in the stands and on the Jones team.

It was a feeling of relief for Cutter, as this had been one of the longest journeys of his life. He looked at Raylee. She was the reason he was able to ride his way back to the top of his game. Faced with every challenge that was thrown at him and struggling through the most stressful times of his life, he'd managed to dig deep and deliver his best because of her.

Then there was the filly. She was still warm. Cutter ran his hand over her while she stood there tied to the rail. She was the real winner. Exceptional in every way and Cutter knew that she was in a class of her own, just like the colt.

The cattle were pushed out through the gates and the officials prepared the arena floor for the presentation. It was only a short wait before all the finalists made their way to the back wall. For the first time, Cutter looked into the stands and scanned the crowd for his family. It didn't take long before he saw the two girls sitting with Beth and Pete. When they saw that he noticed them, the girls stood up and gave him a wave and he could see their happy faces from afar.

He looked around the stands further and there in her favorite seat, was Marnie. She always liked to sit in front of the timeline, a few rows back to get a better view. She wasn't there alone. Doug, Johnny and Emma were all there with her, and when Johnny stood up and yelled out "You're the man," it made Cutter laugh and hide under his hat from embarrassment.

He was soaking it up. Going through the presenting of prizes to all the finalists according to their points scored, Cutter sat on the filly with his arms crossed, until he applauded everyone's results when called out. Including Tommy's, which was easier done when he was sitting in the winning saddle. He wouldn't show anyone that he was pleased Tommy got what was a long time coming to him. While he didn't believe in revenge, he didn't feel sorry at all for Tommy Parker.

When the announcer called Cutter out to come forward and accept the first placing, the crowd erupted with a hysteria that nearly brought the roof down.

"This cowboy's had a dream comeback." The announcer wound up the crowd, as if they didn't already know.

Raylee met him in the center of the arena floor for the photos. The sponsors and officials presented Cutter with a brand new saddle and gold buckle, making it difficult for him to hold back just how happy he was. But it was the winner's check that would add to the relief of the ranch and give him a sense of confidence that he could take good care of Raylee now, in just the way that he wanted.

"I need to see Marnie," he said to Raylee, when they were back in the loping area. They tied the filly up before climbing the ladder to enter the stands, and walked through the crowd to the timeline. Everyone stood up and cleared a way for him to get through, giving him their congratulations as he went past.

It was one of those no words moments that made Marnie hug Cutter tight. She squeezed him a little too hard and he gasped. "Ahh," making Marnie stand back to look at him.

"What happened to you? Did you fall off the filly?" Marnie asked.

"Yeah bro, that looks like a serious cut you got yourself there," Johnny weighed in.

"I'm fine. I just had a run-in with Tommy... again," Cutter said, and he ran his hand over his stitches as if he had forgotten he had them.

Marnie and Johnny both looked shocked to think that Tommy had done so much damage to his face, until Raylee intervened. "If you think Cutter looks bad, Tommy looks worse. He really laid into him and broke his nose."

"Hey Cutter," Aimee called out. She was making her way through the levels of seating with the family, and everyone turned to look at her.

"Hey," Cutter called back, as he'd already started walking over to her. The girls threw their arms around him and he lifted them slightly off the ground when he hugged them.

Pete stood back and let them exchange words, before he reached over and grabbed his son on the shoulder in an unexpected show of affection.

"Congratulations Cutter," Pete said confidently. "That was a good ride."

Cutter was too happy not to accept the gesture. He looked into his father's face and this time he found his eyes. "Thanks, Pete... Thanks for coming," he said, and he held out his hand. Pete briefly looked at it, then grabbed it with feeling.

"Who's that?" Emma asked Raylee on behalf of Marnie, Doug and Johnny, who were all wondering the same thing.

"Oh, it's a long story, and we'll tell you all about it later. But that is Cutter's father, and those girls are his sisters," Raylee briefly explained.

"I can't wait to hear this one," Johnny said, not taking his eyes off them, although it was Marnie who looked shocked, surprised and horrified all at once.

"It's okay, Marnie. Cutter's good with it," Raylee added to settle her thoughts. "We'll have to get the horses loaded soon if we don't want to get back to the ranch too late. But I need to say goodbye to the girls first," she said, and she excused herself, then walked over to everyone.

"Hey, you girls look great," Raylee complimented, noticing their new look. "Nice hats."

"Thanks," Aimee said. "Cutter said we can visit you at the ranch."

Raylee looked at him. "Well, I've got to go home in a couple of days, but when I get back, I'd love to see you there."

Cutter squeezed her hand tight. It was something they needed to talk about now that the show was over. Nobody asked how long Raylee would be away, and she didn't know anyway, but now they had exchanged phone numbers, a visit could be arranged any time.

The horses were now restless. It had been a long week of being restrained to the stables and while they were out during the day being ridden and competing, Cutter could tell they were ready to go back to the ranch and get back to work. The colt had lived up to the belief that Cutter had in him. He was outstanding and had only gained in strength and show ability. But it was the filly that had impressed him. He'd ridden her beyond her limits and she'd given a performance that exceeded his expectations.

On the drive home they talked about the colt and the filly, the final and the bad luck Tommy had in his last ride, and the girls' visit to the ranch. They talked all the way home about everything that had happened that week. Everything, except Raylee having to go home in only a couple of days. She didn't want to bring a downer to their happiness and Cutter didn't want to discuss anything with her, until he got it right in his head first.

Chapter Twenty

By the time the filly was back in her stall and the colt was rugged and put out in his yard, it was the early hours of the morning. They would unpack the rest of the float in daylight, only taking to the house the bags that they needed for the night. Marnie had the porch light on and as they walked up the front steps, they could hear her messing around in the kitchen.

Cutter stepped out of his boots and crouched down, giving Cooper an affectionate rub before he went inside.

"It feels like I've been away for a month," he said to Marnie.

"I had the longest week," she agreed. "I'm so pleased you're both home. It's starting to get lonely here at times." She poured a hot cup of tea for herself and Raylee, and filled Cutter's favorite cup with the freshly brewed coffee.

"I don't know, Marnie. You didn't look too lonely tonight at the show," Cutter teased her.

"Leave them alone," Raylee said in Marnie's defense.

Cutter wouldn't let up. "He's probably been camped out on my front lawn all week while I've been gone."

"And you'll never know, will you?" Marnie teased him back to silence. "Actually... Doug's asked me if I'd like to go on a road trip with him," she added coyly when she sat down. "Just the two of us."

It surprised them both. They were sitting around the table as they had done many times before and were taking in Marnie's announcement.

"That's great," Raylee encouraged her, when Cutter didn't respond immediately.

"Yeah, that's just great. You're going home in a couple of days and Marnie's leaving me to go on some holiday honeymoon with Doug," he said dramatically, with a hint of actually meaning it.

"Well I didn't say that I was going," Marnie retracted, when she heard Cutter's reaction.

Raylee was more forceful and was firm about it. "Well you should go," she said. "In fact, we insist that you go. Don't we?" she added, and she gave him a nudge in his side.

"Hey. Whose side are you on?" Cutter asked, feeling totally alone on this one.

"To be perfectly honest, it would be nice to go on a vacation and I like spending time with Doug. He's a good man." Marnie was softening her position and Cutter listened fairly. "But... I will only go, if and when Raylee comes back to the ranch."

Cutter was quick to jump on her comments. "What do you mean if?" he asked. "She's coming back. I promise you, she'll be back."

"Then I'll wait until then," Marnie said in support of them both.

It didn't take long to finish their tea and coffee and they were all extremely tired. Marnie was desperate to hear all about the last week, including all the details about Pete Morgan and his family, as well as Cutter's run-in with Tommy Parker. She looked at the clock hanging on the wall and given the time, she decided that it could wait until morning and they all said their goodnights.

It was hot on the second floor of the house, even at two a.m. As they lay on the bed with the sheets pulled back, Cutter had his arm wrapped around Raylee holding her close, running his fingers up and down her arm.

"I did this for you," he told her of the show. "From now on, everything I work for on the ranch and everything I do in training, I wanna do it for you."

She sat up on her elbow and looked down into his face. She ran her hand over the stitches on his cheek and around his bruising, touching his lip where it was cut and down his chest to his ribs.

"I'm coming back," she assured him. "As soon as I can, I'm coming back."

"Of course you're coming back... You belong here with me and I need you." He reached up and touched her face.

"I need you too," she replied. Cutter looked at her intently and Raylee could tell he was holding out his thoughts. "What?" she asked, curious of that look in his eyes.

"I just wanna thank you," he said, without offering an explanation.

"What for?"

"For buying my colt." Raylee knew exactly what he meant. "You know, I wouldn't change anything that's happened," he added.

"Nothing?" Raylee asked.

Cutter didn't need to give it a second thought. "No, nothing. The good and the bad, I wouldn't change any of it."

Raylee leaned down and kissed him. "Me neither," she agreed.

It was a late start to the morning. Raylee woke up first and tiptoed downstairs so as not to wake the house. She put the kettle on and made a cup of tea, then went into the office to catch up on anything that needed tending to before she was to leave the next day. She wanted everything in order for Cutter, so that he didn't have to worry about the immediate paperwork for the ranch.

She opened the mail. There were new bills to pay as well as new entry forms and fees to mail out. She was on top of it, setting everything up and making it easy for Cutter until she could return.

"You know, I've missed more sunrises with you in the space of four months than I have in my entire lifetime," Cutter stated. He was standing in the doorway of the office holding a full cup of his morning coffee.

"Good morning... I didn't think you were getting up today," Raylee said, then emptied her cup.

He came into the room and sat on the edge of the desk. "What're you doing?" he asked.

"Well, I've just checked the answering machine. You have forty-one messages," she said with a smile. "Twelve from potential clients who want you to look at their horses for next season. Eighteen from mare owners who are very interested in breeding to the colt. Ten from some random people who I have no idea who they are, but wanted to congratulate you. And one call from two girls who are very excited to visit their big brother on the ranch as soon as they are invited. And... it's only Monday morning."

Cutter laughed. "I'll give them a call later," he said. He seemed more excited to hear from his sisters than any of the other potential business prospects. He was also ready to get back to work. "Let's get changed. I need to go for a ride. See how the ranch has held up," he said.

Raylee had started to pack her bags before they went to Dallas for the show. They were open in the corner of the bedroom and she had already begun piling her clothes into one of them. Cutter lay on the bed and watched her. It was depressing, and her mood was as flat as his.

She was aggravatingly throwing her clothes in with her back to him. "I'm going to miss this room... and this house... and Marnie... and the colt and the ranch and..." She was on a roll and wasn't slowing down.

"Wooo, hold up," Cutter said, and he walked over to her and held her from behind.

It was his touch that affected her and she began to cry. She couldn't hold it in any longer and she let it go. "...And you," she added.

"Hey, it's okay. I'm gonna miss you too," he said for reassurance.

She turned around and hugged him tight, burying her face into his shoulder and sobbed uncontrollably. Cutter wouldn't say anything, just letting her cry it out. She wiped her face and straightened herself up. "I'm sorry. I didn't know I was going to do that," she explained, as it had totally taken her by surprise.

"You have nothing to be sorry about," Cutter said, trying to be strong for the both of them.

"Let's go for a ride... I can pack later and I need to get some air."

Raylee changed into a clean pair of jeans and wandered down to the kitchen. Marnie had baked some savory muffins and they were sitting on the kitchen counter under a net, still warm. She was nowhere to be seen. Raylee was so hungry that she lifted the net and pinched one, then went for her hat and put it on while she waited.

"You ready?" Cutter asked. He was only a few seconds behind her and was lifting the net too. "I can't believe everyone's leaving me," he said quietly to himself, then he took a bite to satisfy his cravings.

Raylee unpacked their saddles from the float while Cutter brought the colt in. The routine was so familiar to them both and together they saddled up ready. This would be the last ride over the ranch that Raylee would have for a while, as tomorrow they would be going back to Dallas. Just the thought of it was enough to bring it out of Raylee again, so she put it to the back of her mind.

Outside the barn, she led the colt past the small day yards. "Hey, why is Lucky outside?" she asked.

Cutter took to the saddle. "She'll be fine. It's where cows live, you know," he said. "And don't worry... I'm gonna take real good care of her while you're gone."

As they rode out the gate, Raylee stopped on the peak of the first rolling hill and turned around, taking in the view of the homestead and barn so that it was fixed in her memory. For the first time, Cutter didn't look at it. He was too busy looking at her.

Following the fence lines and checking the water levels, the ranch was holding up to the hot weather. Cutter needed to keep an eye on the feed and water to maintain the cattle in good condition, and reinvest into more stock gradually over the next six months to build up the profitability of the ranch again.

The calves had grown over the week, playful and venturing further away from their moms. A quick head count confirmed they were all there, and Cutter nearly let it slip that they would move them to another pasture at the end of next week, before he remembered that he'd be doing the job on his own.

The ranch was looking good and was running just the way Cutter wanted. Now that the show was over and he was starting to get on top of everything, he was ready to look at a selection of horses that he would take on for clients.

They rode side by side looking at the progress of each herd, successfully distracting themselves away from the hours ticking by and talking about the week that had been.

On the way home, Cutter wanted to stop by the resting place. Riding through the field of flowers was uplifting for Raylee as it was still colorful, even though it had lost the volume due to the extreme hot weather. Still, she held the reins of the colt as she walked through them, picking a big bunch for the graves. Cutter leaned on the horn on his saddle, admiring the way she was taking on his tradition. It was as if she belonged there more and more every day.

When they arrived at the resting place, they tied the horses up to their usual place on the wrought iron fence. As they walked into the yard, they could feel the gentle breeze taking the sting out of the burning sun. The silence was peaceful and they both needed it, only the sounds of birds interrupted the quietness. They could tell that nobody had been there in the last week as the old flowers lay dry across the graves.

Cutter crouched down, pushing the old flowers aside while Raylee crouched down next to him and placed the new flowers in their place. He stared for a while lost in thought, a million things going through his mind all at once.

It was Raylee who broke the silence. "They would be so proud of you," she said quietly.

Cutter didn't respond straight away, just standing up while still staring at the graves. He took a deep and heartfelt breath. "Everything I am, I owe to them," he said.

Raylee felt the happiness of Cutter's win and the sadness at the same time, that his parents weren't there to share in another one of his greatest achievements. She stood up also.

"I have something to show you," he announced, after he pulled himself together. He reached into his jeans pocket and pulled out a ring. "It's my mom's. Macca gave it to her the day they were married."

"It's beautiful," she admired.

Cutter agreed. "It is. And you know, I still remember the day he gave it to her. Not real well, but I remember that I had to hold it for Macca while they were getting married."

It was a gold band with fine detail and three small diamonds, and it sparkled brightly in the sunlight. But it was the inscription on the inside that Macca had engraved that made Cutter hold it up to the light so he could read it to Raylee. "Mary-Ann. The love of my life. Macca."

"Wow, that makes me feel teary," Raylee said, welling up again on an already tearful day. "Is that why we're here? Are you going to leave it here with her?"

"Actually no. I'm gonna borrow it for a while," Cutter said. He picked up her hand and kissed it, then he unexpectedly pushed the ring onto her finger. "I'm reserving this place on your hand, until I can do everything I wanna do the right way. Starting with your father."

Raylee stared at her hand then looked at him. "I don't understand."

He straightened up and took both her hands in his. "Raylee Tremayne, I've decided that I can't live without you, and I know how much you wanna be here with me. Now I'm not asking you just yet, but I've decided that I'm going home with you tomorrow and if your father agrees, then I'm gonna buy you the biggest ring in Texas."

Her burst of excitement and shriek echoed through the open pastures and she threw her arms around his neck and kissed him.

"Are you asking me to...?"

"No," he cut her off quickly. "Like I said. I need to ask your father first."

She stood back to look at him. "And what if he says no?" she asked, fearful that this would be the case.

He squeezed her hands and stared into her beautiful eyes, and he felt hers searching his. She hung on intently waiting for him to answer while her heartbeat was racing away along with her thoughts. "Then I'd say... to hell with him, and I'll marry you before the end of summer anyway."

She jumped and danced around him, holding him close and not letting go.

"Now careful," he said, and he picked up her hand. "It's only on loan. You've gotta look after this."

She settled down when she admired how it looked on her hand and she imagined how Mary-Ann would have felt when Macca gave it to her. "Do you think your mom would approve?" she asked, still full of excitement.

"She'd approve of anything I did. Except bull riding."

"Well I can understand that," she agreed. "I'd like to think that your days of bull riding are behind you now."

"They are. And there's a whole new life ahead of me now, starting from today. And I wanna ride it with you."

He took off his hat and kissed her in that yard, in front of the two most influential people who had shaped his life. He was grateful, that the fateful journey he had been dealt had ultimately led him to this real cowgirl.

It was all work on the way home, checking the steers and walking the fence lines. It had to be a thorough check, as he was leaving again tomorrow to face his biggest challenge yet. But there was no fear in him. He would cowboy up and become the best man he could be for the girl he loved.

As they rode towards the last gate, Raylee looked at the house in the distance and knew that this would soon be her home. Their home together. When they pulled up outside the barn, it was back to business as usual, as they unsaddled the horses together and headed for the wash bay.

Acknowledgments

I've had the same dream for twenty-five years.

It took twenty-one years to find the courage.

The most humble, trustworthy, and kindest person I have ever known, happens to be my mom. For you to read my raw manuscript three times and offer edits and suggestions, showed your true belief in me and I am so lucky to have a mom like you.

Unbiased, I have never known two people who have put as much into their children as my mom and dad have. Love you both. xx

To Jessie. It took me six chapters before I let you look inside The Cutter, and I couldn't have asked for a better friend to support me through to the end. From cover to cover, you shine throughout this book in ways that you will never know. Thank you. x

To Anthony, thank you for taking the time to read a very early draft. I'm sure you will agree just how far The Cutter has come since that time. x

Just when I thought my manuscript was a masterpiece, I was recommended to Laurel Cohn for her professional editing services. My manuscript fell into the very capable and nurturing hands of Helen Williams, who helped shape The Cutter into the story it is today and has made me a better writer. Thank you to you both.

Who better to send a cutting horse story to, than a cutting horse family. Thanks Juliann for taking the time to look at my manuscript through the eyes of a cutter. Your honesty and support is greatly appreciated. x

While The Cutter has taken pride of place on my laptop for the past four years, it is thanks to Evan Shapiro from Cilento Publishing that it has been transformed into a book. Now I get to hold my work in my hand and share it with everyone. Also to Leone, I believed that I had nailed my writing, but your extra notes gave The Cutter the finishing touches that it needed. Thank you to you both.

To Greg, the biggest thank you of all...

No one will ever know where fiction crosses over into real life, except for you and me. Our story is hidden within the pages of this book, filtered through and buried deep among the love, the drama and the events that bind this story together. Your encouragement for me to write was surprising, as your belief in me was more than the belief I had in myself. The endless cups of coffee you made, the space I needed at the most inconvenient of times, and the days when nothing else got done except for a few paragraphs, you have been with me through the entire journey. You have introduced me to the world of cutting horses and the land, and you will always be my cowboy. xx

To our seven children. You are all amazing individuals and have aspirations and unlimited talent. Don't let fear stop you from living out your dreams. x

To the reader... I started to write The Cutter for the young women in the cutting horse industry who spend hours, days and even weeks at a competition, loping horses for your trainers. I know how much you love this sport and how much it is a part of your life. I wanted to create a story that you could escape into and become a part of, from either side of the world. As the story of The Cutter started to take shape, I felt that it was going to appeal to a wider audience, including tough cowboys, city moms, and anyone who likes a story with heart, soul, and good old fashioned country manners. I hope you enjoy reading The Cutter, as much as I have enjoyed writing it!

And finally, to all the cutters out there who make this sport their life, put your hand down and keep cutting...

Linda x

Book Two in The Cutter series coming soon

The Cowboy Code

By Linda Ellison

Chapter 1

His mind was racing away from him, so he breathed in deep to pull back his thoughts and gain some control. It was the day that he had never expected to happen; the day that had been playing on his mind for quite some time, and as he wandered around his bedroom, he began to feel anxious.

He walked over to the wall and looked closely at the handcrafted display box his father had made. With the buckle he'd won at the show in Dallas filling the last space, it was now complete. It took him back to the ride on the filly. The ride that gave him back his title as the best cutting horse trainer in the country, and it made him feel satisfied. Not only was his career back on track, but he had Double J Ranch restocked with cattle and it was profitable again.

It also made him think of Raylee, the girl who'd stolen his heart and had run away with it, leaving him constantly thinking of her. He knew that she was the reason for his latest success and he owed all of it to her.

It was their flirtation and their love for the same horse that had quickly turned their friendship into an intense love affair, and the events that followed resulted in his successful comeback in the cutting arena. She had helped him through the lowest and most difficult time of his life and Cutter knew that without a doubt, she completed him fully.

He had often wondered why he'd been dealt such a bad hand, constantly questioning what he had done to deserve it. To have lost his mom under tragic circumstances, then nursed his dying father to his long drawn out end, was something that most people would never recover from. To top it all off, when everything was said and done, he was left without his colt, without his career and with a ranch sinking deep in debt.

After meeting Raylee Tremayne, he'd never questioned again why these things had happened.

When Cutter returned home from Australia alone, he felt lost. He went to countless shows over the summer and into the autumn, with some outstanding results that only added to the filly's status as well as his prize money.

With his impressive win at the show, he bought a new horse truck to cater for the new clients that he now had onboard, as the three-angle horse float just wasn't going to cut it anymore. He had also picked up two new sponsors and everything from that show in Dallas was finally falling into place. What a remarkable restart to his career and he couldn't have asked for anything more, except maybe one thing.

As the months were rolling on, the outlook on his personal life was plunging down. A complete contrast to his work life on Double J Ranch and his career in the cutting pen.

He pulled on a fresh pair of jeans and a long sleeved black shirt, and he stood in front of the mirror while he did up his buckle. It was the buckle that he'd won on the colt many years ago. It was his favorite. He still wore it every day, not only as a reminder of his win, but the colt was also the connection he had to Raylee.

A closer inspection of the lines around his eyes revealed that nothing in his physical appearance had changed since he last saw her, even though he'd had a birthday just the other week.

He had celebrated it after a long day at work with his neighbors and best friends, Johnny and Emma, who'd invited him over for supper, knowing that he needed to be away from the ranch for a while. Emma had surprised him by baking a cake, and while they sat on the porch and shared it over their late night coffee, when Cutter looked out and stared at the sky, they could tell that he was still low.

So much had changed since then.

While still standing in front of the mirror, he traded in his old work hat for his black one, and when he pulled it into position and sharpened the front, he was ready to go. As he stood in the doorway, he took one long look around his room. It had changed since Raylee first came to visit there almost twelve months ago. She'd hardly recognize it now with a repaint, a new quilt and new curtains. But the bed was the same and he stared at it, remembering the last time they shared it together. He switched the light off, pulled the door closed and went downstairs to the kitchen.

The house was quiet without Marnie. She was gone and Cutter had been on his own for a couple of days now, hating every minute of it. Every room in the house felt empty. No Marnie and no Raylee. There were no delicious smells coming from the kitchen, where Marnie had baked and cooked every morning of his life since he could remember, and it wasn't the same. It was in darkness. He opened the fridge door and looked inside. Although it was full, there was an instant uneasy feeling in his gut, which made him close it again and he walked outside to the porch and pulled his boots back on.

It had been an early start and a long morning at the barn, and now he was back there again, taking the mare out of her stall and throwing a saddle on. He'd already worked seven horses and was now feeling it. The foals had been broken in and he'd started working with them soon after his return from Australia. He'd taken a look at another six prospects from clients he'd met during the show in Dallas, and agreed to train just two, while the filly was now in her Derby year.

He could have taken on more, except that he was without the help and he needed to focus on the ranch as much as his training. He wanted to be selective and give his clients a fair deal, taking on a limited number of horses. It was Raylee's idea. Take on less, charge them more. It was a win win situation between Cutter and his clients and although he was busy, he needed to be.

The barn was peaceful and the quietness echoed in his head as it had done every day since he was on his own. It had been driving him beyond crazy for quite some time.

"What're you looking at?" he asked the mare, just to break the silence, then he untied her and put the bridle on. With his boot in the stirrup, he grabbed the horn on the saddle and pulled himself up, throwing his leg over. He used his spurs ever so lightly as the mare was responsive to his pressure, and he rode out of the barn past the day yards towards the first pasture.

When he reached the gate, he took his usual long look back down at the barn and the house. Smoke was barely coming out of the chimney now as it had turned out to be an unexpectedly warm day and he was letting the fire burn out. With his need to keep busy, all the maintenance around the immediate house and yard was done and it looked like a picture, while the barn was looking fresh from a new coat of paint.

He took it all in. He loved it, and he knew that after today, it would never look this way again.

Riding over the first rolling hill, he was picking up the pace and the mare was feeling strong. She knew the ranch as well as Cutter did, and had only improved in her ability on the ranch in front of cattle, which was reflected in her talent in the cutting pen. With his training taking up all of the morning, this was his first ride over the ranch for the day. He now looked at everything as he rode past, checking the fences, the water levels, and doing his usual head count of stock as best as he could.

Even today would not stop him from going through his daily routine.

The calves that had been weaned were now in the middle pasture while the cows were back in calf, grazing freely out the back. The rest of the cattle were overindulging on the good body of feed and the cycle of the ranch was back to normal.

As he rode on, he had a flashback of his last trip to Australia. It was the one time in his life that he'd needed to cowboy up outside the cutting pen and rodeo arena, to face Allan Tremayne and convince him that he was the best man for his daughter.

But things didn't go as well as he planned...